EAST OF THE SUN

ENDORSEMENTS

In 1950, my father was among the numerous Korean pastors arrested by Kim Il Sung's corrupt regime at the beginning of the Korean War. As a POW, the outlook for my dad initially seemed bleak, but God was orchestrating a plan of redemption behind the scenes. If it were not for the US soldiers who opened a window of opportunity for my father's escape, he would never have been restored to freedom, later to become the first Korean Southern Baptist pastor in North America, and I would never have been born.

Often the stories of the "nameless and faceless" heroes resonate with us, regardless of the culture, nationality, or generation we were born into. In *East of the Sun*, Rebecca Price Janney gives us a glimpse of the everyday acts of courage that must have left an indelible print on individual lives and families during the Korean War. This book interweaves a compelling historical backdrop with vivid scenes, striking personalities, and most importantly, a God-honoring narrative.

—**Dr. Ché Ahn**, Senior Leader, Harvest Rock Church, Pasadena, CA, President, Harvest International Ministry, International Chancellor, Wagner University

Rebecca Price Janney has written a gem of a story with her new book, *East of the Sun*. This novel, set during the Korean War, is about a nurse, Shelby Kichline, a woman of great faith. She joins the army and is sent to MASH 8055, where she works furiously to save the young men brought in from the battlefield including a North Korean soldier. Filled with rich characters, scenes of the Korean countryside, and

the struggles of the medical teams, the story will engage you from the first page to the last.
—**Larry Diebert**, author of *Combat Boots Dainty Feet: Finding Love in Vietnam*

East of the Sun is a fantastic read about a lesser known but significant conflict, the Korean War. Rebecca Price Janney does an amazing job bringing a very human and relatable story to life, dressed in themes of faith, hope, and love.
—**Jane Hampton Cook**, author

Sometimes fiction can capture the anguish, valor, loneliness, and fear that accompanies war better than nonfiction, and *East of the Sun* does just that. Rebecca Price Janney is a wonderfully skilled writer and she brings her talent to this story about the relationship between a Korean-American and a MASH nurse during the grim Korean War. Janney's is an eye-opening and riveting account of people at war that sheds light on a long ago and faraway American conflict.
—**John Ferling**, author of *Winning Independence: The Decisive Years of the Revolutionary War*

Captivated early on by *East of the Sun*, I devoured this delicious read in one evening. The endearing main characters, Shelby and Parker, captured my heart as I followed their journeys that intersected in a MASH unit during the Korean War. Janney sweeps the reader into the world of the early 1950s, skillfully combining intrigue, Korean culture, and history as the backdrop for a tender love story that is truly "unforgettable."

—**Judy Gordon Morrow**, author of *The Listening Heart: Hearing God in Prayer*

What a delight to read Rebecca Price Janney's *East of the Sun*, a moving tale of love and sacrifice in the Korean war MASH camps and beyond. You will find yourself drawn into this warm, uplifting story in the midst of war as you root for characters you can't help but love. So, grab your coziest blanket, pour yourself a cup of tea, and embark on an adventure that is sure to stir your soul!
—**Marlo Schalesky**, award-winning author of *Women of the Bible Speak Out* and more

I so enjoyed the characters of Rebecca Price Janney's book. Each are very real and demonstrate the capabilities, willingness and intense dedication of our armed forces personnel as well as personal emotions of service, love and loss. The "forgotten war" is brought to the forefront in this work. As the oldest daughter of USAF Staff Sergeant Thomas R. Stauber, 51st FIW, 1951-1955, I highly recommend this historical novel.
—**Victoria J. Stauber-Pufall**, editor, 51st Fighter Interceptor Wing Association Newsletter, 2014-2022

EAST OF THE SUN

A Novel in the Heirs of Freedom Series

Rebecca Price Janney

A Christian Company

COPYRIGHT NOTICE

Cover and Interior Design: Kelly Artieri, Deb Haggerty
Editor(s): Cristel Phelps. Deb Haggerty

PUBLISHED BY: Elk Lake Publishing, Inc., 35 Dogwood Drive, Plymouth, MA 02360, 2025

Library Cataloging Data
Names: Janney, Rebecca Price (Rebecca Price Janney)
East of the Sun—A Novel in the Heirs of Freedom Series / Rebecca Price Janney

392p. 23cm × 15cm (9in × 6 in.)
ISBN-13: 9798891343283 (paperback) | 9798891343290 (trade paperback) | 9798891343306 (e-book)
Key Words: Christian historical romance Korean War MASH unit; Inspirational love story wartime godly sacrifice; Heartfelt historical fiction love Korean war; Religious clean and wholesome love historical; Military duty romance historical fiction Christian; Christian War historical inspirational romance God; Christian relationship frontlines MASH unit 1950s
Library of Congress Control Number: 2025933547 Fiction

ACKNOWLEDGMENTS

I never saw this book coming and am grateful beyond all measure for the gift of this story. Along the way I've enjoyed welcome encouragement and assistance from many places, including unexpected ones. I'd especially like to express my appreciation to the following people:

Mary Burchfield Bohan—cousin and sister of my heart.

Marlo Schalesky and Sandra Allen—encouragers and dream-sharers.

The late Dr. Samuel Hugh Moffett and Mrs. Eileen Moffett—lovers of the Korean people and Jesus Christ, for their friendship and guidance.

My Korean friends and students from Princeton and Biblical Seminaries.

Amy Soloway—college bff and immigration expert.

The late actor Soon-Tek Oh.

The actors and writers of M*A*S*H, especially Loretta Swit for her kindness and encouragement.

Dr. John Ferling for sharing his military expertise with me, again.

Dr. Richard Killblane, and Nolan A. Watson, Civilian US Army Medical Center of Excellence, who answered my endless questions about transportation during the Korean War.

Larry Deibert for information about the military discharge process. Thank you for your service!

Dr. Tom Little, cardiologist, for sharing his medical expertise.

Donald Rinker, whose Easton ancestors knew my Easton ancestors, and who provided photos and information about life there in the 1950s.

Sora Kim, for insights about Korean culture past and present.

The late Dr. Dennis Kinlaw, whose messages about marriage I have cherished and borrowed.

My editor Cristel Phelps and publisher Deb Ogle Haggerty for catching the vision for this book and the Heirs of Freedom series.

Dave Fessenden for his ever-present encouragement and the blessings of having my agent also be my dear brother in Christ.

Scott, the love of my life, my pearl of great price, and our beloved son, DJ, who listens carefully and cheers me on.

Finally, to all who served in the Korean War, including my family members Charles Perry Janney, Donald Huff, Cy Kurtz, and Adele Voell, I am grateful for their sacrificial service in the cause of freedom.

In Christ there is no east or west,
in him no south or north,
but one great fellowship of love
throughout the whole wide earth.
In Christ shall true hearts ev'rywhere
their high communion find.
His service is the golden cord
close binding humankind.

—John Oxenham

CHAPTER ONE

JUNE 1951

She hadn't been late for a single class and didn't intend to start now with a week left in the semester. In the early going, Shelby had skipped a few classes after staying out too late, a small-town girl dazzled by Philadelphia's beguiling night life. She learned early on, however, she couldn't party hard and make the grades her parents expected of her. She dashed across the quad and saw two other nursing students bringing up the rear. She recalled an old saying about spring turning a girl's fancies to love. In this case, distraction was the culprit, not romance—not since the breakup with Michael Hendry two years ago when he'd informed her with startling bluntness if she became a nurse, they would be finished.

"I have no time for a career woman. My wife is going to be a hundred percent about taking care of me, not some snot-nosed kid or a guy with hemorrhoids."

She returned his class ring on the spot and ordered him off her front porch. In her three years as a nursing student, he'd barely crossed her mind. Nor did she care if she ever saw him again once she returned to Easton and started working at the hospital. If Michael showed up needing a hemorrhoidectomy, she would treat him with cool professionalism, as if she'd never seen him before.

She laughed at the idea while rushing up the steps and into the classroom. Her lagging classmates followed closely behind, exchanging sheepish grins with her. With a minute to spare, Shelby's almost-flawless record at Temple-Episcopal Hospital School of Nursing was safe.

With fifteen minutes left in the class, a knock sounded on the door, and the professor stopped her lecture. "If you will excuse me, ladies, I think we have a visitor."

She welcomed a striking woman in an Army uniform whose presence filled the room. Shelby sat up straighter.

"Ladies, before we end for the day, I am delighted to introduce you to Colonel Gladys Stilby of the United States Army Nurse Corps. She's here to tell you about an opportunity that may be of interest as you graduate."

The woman stood at the exact center of the room as if she'd known instinctively where that would be. Shelby doubted the colonel wore perfume, but she exuded the scent of authority.

"I wish to thank Professor Greene for allowing me to address you ladies today. I realize most of you already have plans, but I'd like you to consider the possibility of a different course." She folded her hands in front of her trim waist. "The United States and twenty other nations are fighting to save Korea from communists in the north, who are aided and abetted by the Chinese and Russians. There's an urgent need for medical personnel, including nurses.

"Last year, the Army instituted an innovative concept of mobile treatment centers located ten-to-twenty miles from the front. They are called MASH units, short for Mobile Army Surgical Hospital. The purpose is to treat the wounded as quickly and efficiently as possible to enable the highest survival rate."

She paused, meeting Shelby's eyes.

"I will not kid you about the conditions—they're more rugged than any summer camp you've ever attended. Nurses aren't deliberately put in harm's way, but they aren't always out of danger either. Likewise, many of the casualties bear serious, heartbreaking wounds. Being a MASH nurse isn't for someone who'd rather be sending sick children home to their parents." She paced across the front of the room. "If, however, you are made of tougher stuff, and you want to serve your country, please consider being a MASH nurse. There are other opportunities in the Korean theater, and I will gladly discuss them with anyone who may be interested, but the greatest need is in those mobile hospitals." She paused. "Are there any questions?"

Shelby's neighbor raised her hand. "How long would we have to serve, Colonel Stilby?"

"Tours of duty are currently from twelve to fourteen months."

"Would that include basic training?"

"Yes. MASH nurses receive special training for twenty weeks at the US Army Medical Field Service School at Fort Sam Houston. Then, they go to Korea."

"Colonel Stilby?"

She pointed toward a student in the back. "Yes?"

"Where do the nurses live?"

"They reside in tents or Quonset huts on the MASH compounds."

Another young woman spoke up. "How big are MASH hospitals?"

"They are of varying sizes, depending on available medical personnel."

Shelby listened closely but didn't ask any questions. She knew whatever the answers might be, Easton Hospital was going to have to wait. She couldn't help but remember stories she'd heard from her youth about her illustrious ancestor Colonel Peter Kichline. He'd led a patriotic group of Northampton County farmers and tradesmen to New York where they engaged King George's finest and his fierce Hessian mercenaries. At the August 1776 Battle of Brooklyn, her five times great-grandfather had lost most of his men, been wounded, and was captured. He was a man tirelessly dedicated to God, his family, and his country. As far as she knew, Peter Kichline had never flinched in a time of need, no matter how messy or inconvenient. Subsequent generations of Kichlines had served in every other American war, and now she was being offered an opportunity to follow in their footsteps. A chill ran up her left calf.

Shelby sat on the window seat in the bedroom she shared with her younger sister Diane, who seemed unable to perch.

"When are you going to tell them?" She waved her arms. "Your graduation party is tomorrow, and everyone will be here thinking you'll be working at the hospital."

Shelby watched the boy across the street bang trash cans from the curb to the garage. "I'm waiting for the right moment."

Diane pointed to her wristwatch. "Yet the clock keeps ticking."

"I'm well aware of the clock, Sis. I'm praying about the timing."

"Well, I just hope God is paying attention." She flopped onto her twin bed. "I can't imagine what Mom and Dad are going to say."

"They might just be supportive, you know."

"Or they could blow a gasket."

Shelby tossed a throw pillow at her sister. "Thank you very much, Eeyore."

After dinner, the family gathered in the living room, John Kichline smoking his pipe and discussing his three sons' summer plans. His wife sat next to him on the couch, smelling like the onions and celery she'd been chopping for macaroni salad. Shelby dodged her sister's meaningful looks.

Her brother Neil tripped over their cocker spaniel and banged his leg on the sharp side of the coffee table, howling in pain.

Diane grabbed a geranium before it crashed to the floor. "Watch out, will you?"

Neil whimpered on the floor, rubbing his leg. "Man, that hurts! Shelby, will you look at my leg?" Chester hovered over the boy, panting.

Shelby examined the purpling wound. "You smacked it hard all right. You'll get a bruise, but some ice will reduce the swelling." She looked toward her youngest brother. "Paul, would you get a dish towel and wrap a handful of ice in it?"

"Sure, Sis." He shook his head on the way to the kitchen. "What a klutz."

"That isn't a nice thing to say about your brother," their dad said.

"It's true, though," Neil said without a trace of rancor. "I am a klutz."

"You're a lovable one, though." Shelby hugged him and rumpled his hair.

"Speaking of tending to the wounded, when does your new job start?" her dad asked.

She sucked in her breath. *Here we go! I hadn't pictured the entire family being in the room. Of course, if Mom and Dad get upset, they'll likely hold back in front of everyone.*

She gave a nervous laugh. "The job begins in two weeks."

He frowned. "I thought it was next week."

"I did too, Dad. Actually, I have something to tell all of you." She was surprised by how loud her voice was in the suddenly quiet room. Paul returned with the ice pack, and after Shelby positioned it on Neil's leg, she rose. "I'm postponing my work at Easton Hospital in favor of a short-term opportunity." She liked the way those words came out. *I don't know how to make the next ones go down as easily.*

"Whatever do you mean, Shelby?" her mom asked.

"Right before graduation a woman spoke to my class about an urgent need for nurses in Korea."

Her mom's face blanched. "Korea?"

"Korea!" her brothers whooped.

"Yes. Korea, where the war is."

The oldest son, Keith, spoke up. "I heard it's a police action, not a war."

Shelby didn't know if his remark would help or hurt her cause.

"I decided to sign up for a tour of duty with the Army Nurse Corps." She added as cheerfully as she could, "Then I'll be home again working at the hospital, and getting veteran's benefits." She hoped the last part would appeal to her practical father.

"Shelby's going to be an army soldier!" Paul cried.

"I won't be a soldier, silly. I'll be a nurse, helping soldiers who get wounded."

"Where will you be stationed?" her dad asked.

She relaxed a bit, wondering if he might have accepted her decision without a fuss.

"I'm not sure. The colonel said we'll be away from the fighting in mobile surgical hospitals. They're a new thing, called MASH units. The army hopes that by treating the wounded closer to the action, they'll have a higher chance at surviving."

Chester snuffled at her feet, and she reached down to pet him.

"You didn't ask us," her mother whispered.

Shelby met her hurt gaze. "No, I didn't."

"You've always asked our advice about big decisions."

"She's a grown woman now, Margaret," her dad said. "She knows her own mind."

Shelby reached for her mother's hand. "I didn't have any doubt about this being God's will for me, Mom. This has happened to me twice in my life. The first time was when I felt called to become a nurse. Sometimes, you just know when something's right."

The news of her enlistment into the Army Nurse Corps had gone well—only her Aunt June had required a whiff of smelling salts. Shelby's dad had revealed her plans at the graduation party as proudly as if he were announcing her engagement. Although Margaret Kichline had smiled dutifully, Shelby appreciated her mom's show of support. After the cake had been cut amidst a good deal of Brownie camera picture taking, her grandfather led her to a relatively quiet corner of the patio.

"I'd like a moment with my favorite granddaughter before she ships off to Korea."

"I'm going to miss you, Poppa."

He smiled. "And I shall miss you." He leaned back. "You know, I spent some time in Korea years ago."

"I've heard bits and pieces but not your whole story. When were you there?

In the background, her brothers and cousins played a noisy game of kickball.

"I went right after I graduated from Princeton Seminary."

"Were you a missionary before you were a minister?"

"Something like that. You see, I felt called to the ministry while I was in college. At Princeton, however, my faith came under fire in the debates about form criticism and evolution—modernism to be precise."

When she knitted her eyebrows, he said, "Those are fancy words for doubt. I became arrogant, believing my parents and home church were backward." He sniffed, closing his eyes. "I'd planned to take a church in the Lehigh Valley and marry my girl, but by the time I graduated, I'd lost her, and my sense of calling was in tatters."

"I had no idea." She leaned closer.

"Christianity was still in its infancy in Korea, and the Presbyterian mission board needed Bible translators. I was quite adept at Greek and Hebrew, and I went to Korea thinking getting away would be good for me. I thought I'd lead those backward people away from their superstitious beliefs." He clapped his hands onto his thighs and chuffed. "In the end, they changed me—or I should say, God changed me."

She leaned forward. "How, Poppa?"

The kick ball bounced between them, and she tossed it back to the kids.

"I was headquartered at the seminary in Pyongyang, in the northern part of the country. It was under the direction of a truly amazing man, Dr. Samuel A. Moffett, one of the first missionaries to Korea. A revival broke out, and so very many were saved. I encountered the living God in a way no high-falutin' theology book could dispute. I came to love the Korean people."

He reached out and held her right hand. "I'm so proud of you for going there, Shelby. You are also answering God's call. I'll pray for you every day." He reached into his jacket and pulled out a small, wrapped gift. "I want you to have this."

She undid the floral paper, her eyes filling with tears. "Your Bible?"

"The one I had with me in Korea."

Shelby hugged him tight. "Thank you, Poppa."

When she pulled back, he seemed to focus on something beyond her. "You will have hard days when you feel you can't go on. Don't succumb. The child of God is always safest while doing the will of God."

CHAPTER TWO

HOPEWELL, NJ—NOVEMBER 1951

Parker Tate juggled a handful of mail and his black bag, using his elbow to flip on the light switch. He plopped his items on a long table and removed his shoes as several envelopes cascaded to the floor. He would make a project out of sorting through the heap after dinner. Maybe his second set of car keys were there—or his cuff links, which he hadn't been able to find in three weeks.

He smiled to himself at the satisfaction of not having to answer a midnight summons. Since his brother John had completed his residency and joined the practice, Parker was shifting some of those duties. John was downstairs now with the last two patients, and Parker had promised to prepare the evening meal.

He lifted his eyes to the soft thunder of the little boy running in the third-floor apartment above him, no doubt with his mother in hot pursuit. Parker rather liked the toddler's joyful noise and having tenants helped pay the remaining mortgage on his combined business and residence. He took off his suit jacket and tie, choosing to ignore a cobweb swinging above one of his bedroom windows and laundry cluttering the floor. He would deal with them later as well. He pulled on a sweater and walked to the kitchen unable to recall when he and John had last visited the grocery store. They'd been eating out a lot, mostly at a nearby diner or the hospital cafeteria, but surely there'd be enough on hand for a simple stir fry of vegetables, eggs, and rice. Frozen meat would take too long to thaw.

He opened the cupboard to a half-full box of Uncle Ben's rice, something he would never have when his parents visited. Parker closed his eyes and swallowed hard, not knowing when they'd ever get to see each other again. They and his younger sister had been in the US for John's med school graduation in May a year ago, returning to Seoul right before all hell broke loose. If they had only known at the time what was coming. During their visit, his mother had run this place like the efficient Korean housewife she was. There'd been no piles, dust bunnies, or American convenience food, only the aromas of her kimchi, bibimbap, and manduguk.

Seized with longing, he wondered how his parents and younger sister were faring. The mails were slow, but at least he heard from them almost monthly now. During the tortured weeks of the Battle of Seoul, all the news he received was from newspapers and the radio. The last time he'd had a letter was in early October, and his family was still taking in refugees from the north. Parker and John often sent care packages with their own correspondence, squirreling cash into various hiding places.

Parker rummaged through the cupboard, finding two cans of condensed soup, corn flakes, rice noodles, and soy sauce. East meets west. Retrieving the box of rice, he opened the refrigerator door where he'd stored mushrooms and bok choy not long ago. What was this? The Chinese cabbage had congealed into a brown mush puddle and leaked onto three slimy carrots. The mushrooms had gone spotted and furry. Wrinkling his nose at the odor, he tossed them into the trash. Maybe he'd just fry a few eggs and open a can of soup. Inside the carton, however, Parker discovered two cracked eggs. The rest sent his stomach into recoil mode when he broke them open. Ah well, there was always kimchi to fall back on, but a quick sniff brought tears to his eyes. He'd never heard of kimchi going bad.

After bagging and taking the rotten food out to the garbage, he opened the windows to air out the apartment. Parker leaned against the kitchen counter, running his hand through his dark hair. Should he run to the store or get take-out—again? Nothing in his life had prepared him for the rigors of shopping, cleaning, and cooking—tasks his mother performed with precision, pride, and excellence. Maybe he should heed his receptionist's advice and hire a housekeeper.

He snatched his wallet and keys and headed past the hall table with its bloated contents. Maybe after he breathed in some fresh air and surveyed the grocer's fresh produce and meats, his own appetite would return.

After dinner, he sat in his lounge chair sorting through the mail, Sinatra crooning over the air waves.

John put the evening paper beside him on the couch. "I'm going to make some tea. Would you like a cup?"

"Yes, thank you."

A few moments later, he held out an airmail envelope with an unsteady hand. "I just found this."

Parker frowned. "I don't know how I missed seeing that."

"It was jammed under one of the table legs." John sat across from him. "This is Dad's handwriting."

They gaped at each other. Their mother did all the correspondence for the family. Their father claimed that as a minister, he favored spoken words over written ones.

"Since it's addressed to you, would you be okay sharing it with me?"

Parker detected a hint of woundedness in his brother's expression. "Yes, of course."

He reached out for the envelope then carefully slid open the top part with a letter opener. The crinkly airmail paper bore their father's bold Korean handwriting. Most of the time Parker conducted his life in English, which he'd learned as a boy, but now he switched to his native language. His father addressed him by his birth name, Tae-ho Park. In medical school, he'd adopted a more American version, Parker Tate.

> October 15, 1951
>
> Dear Tae-ho,
>
> I greet you in the name of our Savior, trusting this finds you and your brother in good health. Your mother and I are ever pleased you are working in a family practice together, now that John has completed his residency. You are pursuing an honorable profession bringing much good to the world. America is the land of opportunity, and nothing could be truer in these troubled times for Korea.
>
> Life continues to challenge us, but your sister's classes at the university have resumed. Conditions are more stable since the UN forces drove the communists out of Seoul last summer. We continue to minister to our church's families. Many have sustained heavy losses of life and possessions, and we do what we can to relieve suffering and bring hope.

He glanced at his brother, who was leaning forward, then resumed reading aloud.

> You are no doubt wondering why I am writing. It pains me to tell you that your mother has been confined to her bed for a few weeks. She has lost over ten pounds and has difficulty keeping food down.

Parker swallowed around a dry spot.

"That's not good." John rested his elbows on his knees.

> She has seen a doctor, but he cannot determine what is the matter. Most of our physicians have gone to assist the army, leaving us with older ones who are not up on the latest advances or are themselves impaired in their abilities.

The lump in his throat swelled to rock size. If only he could treat his mother, surely he could do something to help her. When John's eyes bored into his, Parker continued reading.

> There is something more to share with you and John. Your grandfather has been assisting refugees fleeing from the north, and he learned of a minister who was nearly caught by the PKA. Grandfather stationed himself with an army unit in the area Pastor Bahk was last seen and planned to find and bring him to Seoul under our army's protection. He was emboldened by the success he had last year in secreting your grandmother out of Pyongyang along with a dozen other families. We tried to talk him out of his errand, but he would have none of it. We do not know what has become of him. This has multiplied your mother's, and grandmother's, distress.

Parker's breath hitched as he read the last paragraph.

> Is there any way you can come to us, to assess your mother's condition and help us locate your grandfather?

> As you have petitioned to become a US citizen, perhaps you will have greater access to people and places than I do. John can look after your practice in your absence. Please write or wire me as soon as you can. Gladly, I will pay your travel expenses.
> Your devoted,
> Abeoji

He dropped the letter onto his lap, his brother whistled. The toddler upstairs began running laps again.

"Do they have any idea what they're asking?" John said.

"Does this bother you, his asking me to come?"

"Not at all. I'm rather honored he thinks me capable enough to run the practice."

Parker hadn't decided anything. He didn't even know if returning to Korea was possible.

John seemed to have read his thoughts. "How would you even get to Korea? You know how hard it is just to get our letters and packages through."

"These are formidable obstacles."

John lifted his hands. "This stinks."

Parker reached across the space and patted his brother's shoulder. "We must remember, when we are weak, God is strong."

Professor Cullen's cluttered office wreaked of books, dust, and pipe tobacco. Parker's jaw had been perpetually clenched after receiving his father's letter two days earlier, but now his tension eased. He was seeking the advice of his dearest American friend, a man who'd taught at the Pyongyang seminary, who knew and loved Parker's family.

Cullen puffed on his pipe, smoke rising to the ceiling before dissipating in a wispy mist. "I can't imagine what they're all going through—have been through. I'm grieved about your mother's illness. As for your grandfather, I'm not a bit surprised he would do such a thing."

Parker toyed with his hat, resting on his lap.

"What do you think you should do?"

"I am aware of my duty to my family and do not wish to disappoint them or God. On the one hand, I have no doubt I should go to them." He hung his head. "And then there is selfishness I must battle."

"What do you mean?" Cullen cocked his head.

He spoke as if confessing a sin, "Will John be able to run the practice efficiently? How long would I need to be away?" He paused and nearly whispered, "Will I endanger myself?"

"Don't beat yourself up, Parker. You're counting the cost, as our Lord urges us to do. We must always come to terms with ourselves."

He offered the professor a thin smile.

"There are other concerns, of course." He leaned back, biting on the pipe stem. "Even if you decide to go, you may not be able to. All transport is being devoted to carrying troops."

"I am aware of this."

"Your parents are reasonable people. You may, in fact, not have much choice in this matter."

His countenance fell as he stared out the window at the panoply of autumnal colors kindling the Princeton seminary campus. A gray squirrel scampered through the fallen bounty.

"Let's spend some time in prayer about this. We must remember what is impossible for us is child's play for the God we serve."

Parker sipped a cup of Korean tea after seeing five patients in a row. He hadn't been able to get past the pit-deep sorrow he'd fallen into the day after seeing the professor. The best the State Department could offer was the possibility of travel in a few months. He would write and tell his parents, asking them to describe as minutely as possible his mother's symptoms. Perhaps he could diagnose her ailment from a distance and send medicine. He had nothing else to offer besides his prayers. He didn't doubt their potency, but he wished he could do something hands-on. As for his grandfather ...

The phone buzzed, and he pushed the intercom button. "Yes, Mrs. Albano?"

"There's a call for you from Dr. Cullen. Shall I put him through?"

He clinked the cup in its saucer. "Yes, of course." A moment later he heard his friend and mentor's voice.

"Parker, do you have a moment?"

"Yes, Dr. Cullen, I am having a break just now."

"Are you able to meet me at four this afternoon? I may have some answers for you."

He consulted his watch—one-forty-five. He had a full afternoon, but if he ended his break early and John took charge, he could be in Princeton by four. "I will see you then."

He entered the professor's office in Stuart Hall two minutes late.

"Ah, there he is! Come in, Parker, come in! I want you to meet someone."

He took note of a balding man in an Army uniform in his thirties or early forties who carried a slight softness around his middle.

"Dr. Parker Tate, I'd like you to meet Captain Andrew Frank."

Parker shook hands with the man. "I am pleased to meet you."

"I'm glad you were able to come on such short notice. As I was sharing your dilemma with Captain Frank, he thought he might have a solution. Please, have a seat." He gestured toward the chairs across from his desk. "I do hope you don't mind that I told him about you, Parker, but my bumping into him last night seemed providential."

"I am happy you did so." Parker's stomach fluttered as he waited to be brought on board.

"Captain Frank is a chaplain in the Army reserves as well as the seminary's director of student housing. He's getting ready to ship off to Korea."

Parker's eyebrows raised.

"Dr. Cullen told me about your family, and I am truly sorry for your distress."

He bowed slightly. "Thank you."

"I spoke to my commanding officer about your situation, and he suggested you serve as an Army doctor in Korea ... they're in short supply."

Parker's ears rang. *Army doctor?* He willed himself to focus.

"... seemed possible."

He held up a finger. "If you will please excuse me, Captain, I missed the first part of what you were saying."

"Yes, of course. As I was saying, the Army has an offer for you. If you enlist as a doctor, you will get to Korea and serve at the Army's discretion. You'd most likely be stationed at the Seoul military hospital but possibly in a MASH unit, that's Mobile Army Surgical Hospital."

His heart swelled, then just as quickly, deflated. "I am most grateful for this opportunity. I wonder how long I would have to serve before getting back to my practice?"

Frank leaned closer, eye-to-eye with Parker. "You may not be aware of something called the Doctors Draft Act. I understand that you've applied for citizenship, and the Army needs doctors."

He swallowed. "What does this draft act mean?"

"It means all doctors under the age of fifty-one have to register for military service."

He got the point. Parker listened to the rest of the captain's proposal with a galloping heart. When Frank concluded, Dr. Cullen brought his hands down on his desktop with a grin. "I think the Lord has made a way when there seemed to be no way."

CHAPTER THREE

NOVEMBER 4, 1951
TROOPSHIP LT. RAYMOND O. BEAUDOIN (TAP 189)

Shelby savored her sister's letter for the third time, as well as the photo of Diane in her cheerleading uniform. Once she got to Korea, she wondered when she'd hear from her sister, or anyone else, again. At basic training in Texas, she'd received dozens of cards and letters and at night, limbs aching and a tad homesick, she'd answered each one. Shelby had never considered herself weak, but her time at basic had uncovered a softness she'd never imagined. Now, to borrow her grandmother's expression, Shelby was "fit as a fiddle," and ready for war. She grinned to herself as another childhood phrase rose within her; "ready or not, here I come." She knew Korea was ready for her nursing skills—she prayed she was ready for all that lay ahead.

She put Diane's letter in the discarded cigar box she'd found at Fort Sam Houston and tuned in to the engine's constant thrum. She'd been on the ship for two days of a three-week journey with enough time on her hands tonight to write back to her family. Her bunkmates were reading books and magazines, working puzzles, playing cards, and napping.

November 4, 1951

Dear Family,

How are all of you? I can imagine each of you going about your lives against the backdrop of golden leaves stubbornly clinging to trees. There wasn't much of autumn at Fort Sam Houston where summer never seemed to end or in San Francisco where we boarded the troop transport two days ago. Personally, I like the change of seasons and prefer cooler to warmer weather, something I've recently learned about myself.

Soon, Thanksgiving will be here—my first ever away from home. You'll gather after the Easton-P'burg game at the dining room table with all the leaves pulled out and Grandma's best tablecloth. I'll be cheering for our Red Rovers from Korea!

Congratulations to Paul for getting an A on his science project, to Neil on making the Pop Warner team, and to Keith for getting on the JV. Those Phillipsburg Stateliners don't know what they'll be dealing with when he makes varsity! I hope Neil stays engaged at school despite being several steps ahead of his classmates. I'm so proud of the way each of my siblings are using their God-given talents.

Mom, how did the church rummage sale go? Did you have enough baked goods? Those always go quickly, especially the shoofly pies. I can almost taste one now! I hope you didn't end up taking care of the leftover items by yourself, as has happened before. You do such a nice job with the sale, and those who are less fortunate in the community benefit greatly.

And Dad, how are your classes this year? Do you have any students who stand out in either direction?

I'm doing well, adjusting to all kinds of conditions, such as the intense heat and relentless training at Fort Sam

> Houston. My brothers should all be suitably impressed at how I learned to handle a rifle! I hadn't ever held, let alone used, one before, but even the nurses must be ready to defend themselves.

Shelby paused over the writing tablet, second-guessing herself over including that last statement. She didn't want to worry her mother, and if she were using a pencil, she would have erased the comment.

> I'm now on board a troop ship with some five hundred soldiers, nurses, and other Army personnel. I didn't know if I would get seasick, but after some mild queasiness the first day, I've been fine. I share a berth with a dozen other nurses. We each have a bunk bed and a small space for our belongings. Our trunks are in storage, so we're pretty bare bones with just our uniforms, a change of blouses, two of underthings, and a basic kit bag. Among my available personal items, I keep your letters, my Bible, and the copy of *A Man Called Peter* someone gave me for graduation.
>
> My roommate from basic, Vickie Egan, shares my compartment and will be in my unit in Korea. At first, I didn't know how to respond to her sassy New York style. She says whatever comes into her head, which can be hurtful at times, but I realize she doesn't mean half of what she blurts out. Let's just say she's growing on me. She's as deeply caring and true as they come. I think of the Bible verse about love covering a multitude of sins.
>
> When we arrive in Korea at the port of Pusan, we'll receive our assignments. There's been talk about our MASH being twenty miles from Seoul. In the meantime, life on board the ship is mostly pleasant. The food is geared to meat and potatoes-loving men and is tasty. We have lectures in the morning and afternoon, as our nursing training continues, but the rest of our time is free. I like to walk along the deck, breathing in the salt

air and lifting my face to the sea breezes. Still, I'm glad I didn't join the Navy—all that water sometimes feels overwhelming!

I'll close for now. As I count on your prayers, I lift you before our God and Father many times throughout each day. I love and miss all of you. Hug and pat Chester on the head for me.

Your loving daughter and sister,
Lt. Shelby Kichline

She put the letter in an envelope while jiggling her right foot, which had fallen asleep.

"What are you doing up there, Shelby?" Vickie called from her lower bunk.

"My foot fell asleep."

"Well, quit rocking my boat!"

She hopped onto the floor and shook her leg like a dog until the pins and needles dissipated. "I must've sat on my foot too long. I'm going to mail a letter to my family and take a walk. Do you want to come?"

"No, thanks. I don't do windy decks in the dark."

"I don't think the wind is that strong, and it's not completely dark yet."

"Says you."

"Okay, I'll be back in a bit." She grabbed her jacket and left.

She wondered whether she should've heeded Vickie's advice. The refreshing breeze she'd anticipated was more like a gale, and the ship had begun to pitch. Shelby didn't want to end her brief life in the lathering sea, so she gorilla gripped her way to the post office. With the sun setting and wind lashing her hair across her face, she couldn't see clearly. Vickie was right—coming out here had been a foolish idea.

"Excuse me, but perhaps you should not be out here tonight."

She nearly jumped out of her skin at the sound of a man's voice. "Oh, hello! I didn't see you there. I came up for some fresh air and to mail a letter. I wasn't expecting a hurricane."

He stood a few feet away with his legs astride, as if to keep himself from blowing away. His wind-tossed hair semi-obscured his face. "The weather is quite wild. I also have decided being inside is safest."

Shelby gazed at him in the semi-darkness, detecting a smile and—were those dimples? If she wasn't mistaken, he'd spoken in what sounded like an Oriental accent. Why she started to tingle, drawn to him as if she were delighted to bump into him again, she hadn't a clue. She'd never laid eyes on this man before. When he caught her staring, she drew back.

"Would you like my assistance getting to your quarters?"

"Oh, thank you, no. I'm fine. I mean, I need to mail a letter. To my family. It'll only take a minute, then I'll go back." She turned this way and that, disoriented, stumbling. Feeling his hand on her upper arm, adrenaline shot through her core. She stood so close to him she could feel the whisper of his breath. "Oh, how clumsy of me! Thank you for keeping me from falling."

"Are you all right now?" His hand remained on her arm.

"Yes, I am, but I ... uh ... can't seem to remember where the post office is."

He loosened his hold. "I do not recommend going there tonight. Perhaps your letter can wait until morning."

The cadence of his voice was almost musical and nimble with humor.

"Y-yes, I will ... um ... do that ... wait, I mean, until tomorrow." She started backing away, planning to retrace her steps. She was shivering.

"You are cold." He looked as if he were about to remove his coat.

"Oh, that won't be necessary. I can find my way back, thanks." She squeezed her eyes shut, mentally berating herself. *Why did I say that? I'd love to see his face in the light and find out who he is.* She clearly was attracted to him.

"As you wish, but do be careful."

A man called out. "Hey, Doc, are you out here? Oh, there you are." He seemed to size up the situation. "You're wanted in sick bay."

"Just give me a moment."

He's a doctor.

"I must go. Are you sure you can return safely?"

"Yes, thank you for your help and concern."

He bowed before turning away. "Perhaps we will meet again."

"Man, am I happy to see you," Vickie said. "You had us all going. As soon as you left, the bronco busting started."

"I'm fine."

"Then why are you quivering?"

"And your face is all lit up," the redheaded nurse from Vermont added.

Shelby ran a hand through her hair. "The wind is really bad."

"So why are you smiling?" Vickie's eyes narrowed.

She couldn't bring herself to respond.

"You look like you saw a guy."

The other nurse laughed. "And not just any guy, more like Clark Gable or Errol Flynn."

"I assure you, I did not see Clark Gable or Errol Flynn."

"But you did see a guy, right?"

Shelby wagged her finger at Vickie. "You're like my dog when he gets hold of a bone—you don't let go."

Her roommate grinned. "You got that right!"

The next day Shelby went about her business, wondering if she might bump into the intriguing doctor again. Their brief interaction on the blustery deck seized her imagination. Was he, perhaps, Korean? What features she could make out seemed Oriental, plus there were his accent and formal manner of speaking. When she ventured to the post office the first chance she had, Shelby regretted having Vickie tag along.

Shelby posted her letter and bent closer to the clerk, a pimply private. She didn't want Vickie to hear their conversation. "Excuse me, but do you know of a Korean doctor on board?"

She jumped when he answered much too loudly. "There's too many docs to keep up with them all, ma'am, and those Orientals all look alike to me."

She breathed easier when she noticed her roommate chatting with one of the soldiers. "Oh, okay. Well, thanks."

"Hey, wait a minute!" The clerk lifted his right index finger. "There is a Doctor Parker—or something like that."

When Vickie signaled to her, Shelby knew this would be the end of her fact-finding.

Three weeks later, on their drizzly day of disembarkation at Pusan, Shelby and the other nurses lined up, followed by male officers and noncoms. She wasn't exactly sad to leave their floating home, but she was grateful for the bonds she'd forged with the other nurses. Then there'd been that intriguing encounter on the second night out.

A Vickie-inflicted jab brought her to the present.

"Come out of that daydream, Shelb. Look out, Korea, here we come!"

Hitching her shoulder bag, she noticed a group of male officers—standing among them was her elusive doctor. At least she thought this must be him. There might have been other Oriental doctors on the enormous troopship, but the postal clerk had just mentioned the one. This man's face was the shade of kindness itself, and she sucked in her breath when their eyes met. If this was him, would he recognize her from their brief encounter in semi-darkness weeks ago?

"C'mon, Shelby, what're you waiting for, an invitation?"

When she glanced over her shoulder, his lips curved into a smile.

CHAPTER FOUR

Parker's emotions swelled like the waves that had borne him to Korea. His mother reclined on the sofa with a blanket draped around her shoulders, but when she saw him, her faded eyes lit up, and she hurried to greet her son. His father's jaw dropped. His sister and grandmother made way for the maternal hurricane, all of them teary-eyed.

"Tae-ho!"

He covered the distance in a heartbeat. "*Eomma*!" He wrapped her tiny frame in his arms and breathed in her floral scent in the place he still dreamed about as home.

After a lengthy embrace she pulled back, her eyes examining him head to toe. "How handsome you are, my son! How distinguished!"

He quickly assessed her condition. "And you are looking far better than I expected."

When she didn't respond, Parker guessed she wasn't ready to discuss her health just yet. He felt his sister's arms encircling him, and he greeted the beautiful young woman he barely recognized. Tall and straight, she looked like someone who'd been through an ordeal and survived.

"Yuna! You have grown so lovely."

She lifted her face. "My name is Anna now."

"Well, Anna, how happy I am to see you!" He smiled into her eyes, then turned to his grandmother. "*Halmeoni!*" He gathered her in his arms, feeling her trembling body.

"You have come home to us, Tae-ho."

"Yes, I have come."

Anna had sailed into the kitchen, and he heard the sounds of hospitality at work. His father urged him to have a seat after briefly introducing him to two refugees, a woman and a little boy. They retreated at once to the edge of the family reunion. Parker sniffed at familiar fragrances, guessing the women had been preparing food for his homecoming. He hadn't known what to expect, whether they would immediately get down to serious business or take time to reacquaint themselves. He tried to focus on what they were saying while immersing himself in the reality of being with them after so long.

His grandmother grinned at him. "You are very handsome in your American uniform."

His mother was back on the sofa, appearing spent, and insisting he perch next to her. "Yes, you are very handsome, indeed. Soonja will surely think so as well."

"How is Soonja?" he asked.

"She is a delight as always, full of beauty. She has been looking forward to your reunion." His mother's eyes twinkled. "When did you hear from her last?"

He couldn't recall. He didn't often respond to her letters. "She writes from time to time."

"She is a fine young woman." She squeezed his hand.

His shoulders stiffened. Apparently, his mother hadn't relinquished her long-term desire for the two of them.

"She will be paying you a visit."

He wasn't sure what to say, and when his father broke into the conversation, Parker's tension eased.

"For how long are you able to be with us?"

"I can stay for three days, if you have room." He glanced toward the refugees. "I must report to the US Army hospital each day, however. Then, I am to reside in the Army barracks at the hospital and go wherever they have need of me."

"We always have room for you," his father said.

His mother smiled. "I will ask Soonja to come tomorrow."

He didn't know how to honor his mother while conveying his disinterest in Soonja as a marriage partner. He would pray about this problem and, for now, deflect.

"I am interested in examining you and getting you back on the road to health."

When his grandmother closed her eyes, he knew he must address her pain as well.

"And you, *Halmeoni*, I will do all I can with God's help to find *Harabeoji*.

She patted his hand. "I know you will, Tae-ho. I have prayed for you to come, and God has brought you back to us. He will see us through."

He just hoped he didn't let her—or God—down.

Following a thorough examination and bloodwork, Parker diagnosed his mother with acute anemia. He also learned that between her last stateside visit and the commencement of the war, she'd had a hysterectomy with a difficult recovery. Fortunately, there was no indication of infection. He put her on a protocol of folic acid and vitamin B12, and believed with time, she would make a full recovery. He also urged her toward quieter acts of church service closer to home, employing her sewing machine and her prayer book. This was not time to be traipsing around Seoul ministering to war-impacted families. Although she responded with a tightened jaw, she agreed to follow her son's advice.

Soonja arrived on his second day in Seoul, her dark eyes widening at the sight of Parker in his American officer's uniform. She bowed in greeting.

"How nice to see you, Soonja," he said, rising from his own bow.

"I am happy to see you as well."

He noticed the familiar crooked front teeth which had always lent a winsomeness to her smile. She wore a western-style suit but her deferential mannerisms shouted *I am Korean!*

Parker's mother relinquished her usual seat in the living room to Soonja. His father was at the church, his sister, at school. Grandmother Oh sat in the background.

"Tae-ho is going to make me well again," his mother said.

"I am pleased to hear this."

"My son is very gifted." Her chest seemed to swell.

Parker squirmed, assuming as pleasant an air as he could manage. "How is your family?"

"They are much better since the liberation of our city."

"The siege was trying for all of you."

His mother spoke up. "Soonja helped take care of the women with babies, risking her safety so they had food and water and shelter. She is very good with babies."

Parker's ears pinked. Could she have been more obvious?

His mother dominated Soonja's hour-long visit, the subjects starting and stopping like an ailing Model T.

With his mother leading the charge, Parker found normal interaction impossible. When Soonja finally rose to leave, he restrained himself from rushing her out the door.

"You must come and join us for dinner tomorrow," his mother said. "Perhaps your parents will come too."

Parker stifled a desire to look up at the ceiling and shake his head in disbelief. His mother was a force to be reckoned with, and yet, she was physically vulnerable. He wished he could use an expression from an American cartoon—"back off"—but there was no way he'd be so disrespectful.

After Soonja left, his mother turned to him. "She will make you a good wife, Tae-ho."

He stroked her cheek with the back of his hand. "*Eomma*, you are pushing too hard. You must let such things take their own course."

"Sometimes they need a little help."

During his four weeks at the US Army Hospital, he rarely enjoyed a spare moment. When he wasn't catching up on sleep, he checked on his mother, pleased at her returning strength. Then, he would look at his grandmother, her eyes imploring him to do something about her missing husband. Just before Christmas, he held her tightly.

"You must have faith, as I do, that God will show us how we can help *Harabeoji*."

She smiled and nodded her head. "He is our ever-present help in time of trouble."

He had to report for duty on Christmas, but he attended his family church on Christmas Eve. Back in the States, he was a member of an English-speaking Presbyterian congregation he'd started attending as an undergraduate.

There would, however, always be a special place in his heart for this dear congregation. He smiled at the children reenacting the ancient nativity tableau with shining faces. The lights, beloved natal songs, and presence of his family filled him, and he wished John could be there too. He was grateful for his brother's capable stewardship over the Hopewell practice, which he wrote was running smoothly.

The one annoyance was his mother's choreography. She seated Soonja next to Parker in the family pew, a clear declaration to the congregation they were a couple. His sister had raised her eyebrows and snickered, seeming to understand the true nature of the situation. Soonja's face reflected the sanctuary's glowing candlelight. When more than one of the men shook Parker's hand a little too heartily at the end of the service, he decided to put a stop to the maneuverings. He just didn't know how or when.

Soonja and her family were invited to the Park home for the Christmas feast, without his prior knowledge. He couldn't do or say anything there, an action that would disgrace his family. Soonja presented him with a watercolor she'd painted of a tiger. He had nothing for her but a hastily produced box of chocolates from the Hopewell drugstore he'd tossed into his suitcase.

"*Appa*, before I return to the hospital, I must speak with you." He had already said his farewells to the rest of the family after Soonja and her folks had left. "Will you please come with me outside where we will not be heard?"

The pastor's brows knitted. "Of course, son."

In the brisk winter night under a moonlit sky, Parker explained his position. "I think Soonja is a fine woman, and she has always been a good friend, but Mother acts as if I am going to marry her."

His father took a step back. "And you are not?"

Parker exhaled, his breath steaming on the evening air. "I have never declared myself to Soonja. I have no romantic feelings for her. Mother is smothering me."

His father clucked his tongue. "She had me fooled. She does have a way of creating situations as she wishes them to be."

"I cannot dishonor her, and she is still physically vulnerable. But as you see, my reticence has led me down this rather unfortunate path."

"And you are certain this is not what you want."

"I have given little thought to taking a wife since I started my medical training. The war has further postponed any plans."

"Would you take Soonja if you were ready?"

"No. She is not the woman for me."

"How can I help you?"

"Would you please talk to Mother about this? Tell her I do not want Soonja for a wife, and I would like her to stop pushing us together."

"Yes, I will tell her. Should I also speak to Soonja?"

"I will. I do not wish to hurt her, but the truth must be told."

Parker knocked on his commanding officer's door, which stood ajar.

"Enter!"

He did as he was told, offering a salute to the cigar-smoking man. "Colonel Borsch, you wished to see me?"

"At ease, Tate. Have a seat." He signaled to a splintery-looking chair. "Care for a cigar?"

"No, thank you, sir." His spine prickled, alert to a coming change.

"Don't smoke, eh?"

"No, sir."

"Good for you! Well, then, I'll get right to the point. You're doing a fine job, but there's a MASH unit thirty miles from here in dire need of doctors. I see from your record you have some surgical training, but you're not a surgeon."

"This is correct, sir."

"Do you think you can handle assisting the surgeons?"

"I could certainly try, sir."

"That's good enough for me." He blew out a puff of smoke while shuffling through his file-splattered desk. "Pack up your things and be ready to head up there at 0700 hours tomorrow morning. Do you have any questions, Tate?"

"Yes, Colonel Borsch. I wonder how long I will be at this MASH unit. I would like to inform my family."

His gray eyes bored into Parker's, then brightened. "How's your mother doing?"

"Much better, thank you."

"I imagine seeing you has been good medicine."

"I like to think so, sir."

"I don't know how long you'll be there. I do want you back here, though, after this new assignment."

Apparently, this small reassurance would have to do.

CHAPTER FIVE

Shelby jolted awake, wondering where the football crowd had gone. An Easton Red Rover had just caught a crisp twenty-yard pass and scored the winning touchdown, but the frenzied fans were gone. She rubbed her eyes, taking in the shadowed nurses' quarters where her bunkmates slumbered and slept. This wasn't the first time she'd dreamed of domestic scenes since arriving in Korea. The MASH environment was all-consuming, leaving little room to consider even the existence of the idyllic homelife she'd left behind. Although they always left her temporarily befuddled, the dreams helped her hold on to that far more pleasant reality.

She reached for her watch with the glowing hands—4:45. Sighing, Shelby leaned back into her pillow, hoping to catch a few more zzz's before breakfast. When her need to use the latrine persisted, she dressed hastily, grabbed her jacket, and pulled on her boots. Whoever had set up the 8055th had done the nursing staff a great favor by locating the privies a stone's throw from their Quonset hut.

Like everything else at the MASH, Shelby had to adjust to the malodorous four-seater utterly devoid of privacy. She had tried to go only when no one else was in residence, but with a dozen nurses on the compound, she'd had to overcome her modesty in a hurry. The women followed an unspoken pledge to stay in their own thoughts. The semi-partitioned showers were another challenge. Shelby had never considered her bathroom at home luxurious ... until now. The veteran nurses said they were just grateful to have showers at all. The previous brutal summer, they'd been unable to bathe for a six-week stretch. Normal didn't seem to exist here.

After using the facility, she ended up in the mess tent for an early cup of coffee while the cooks began preparing breakfast. Being in the canvas cafeteria before dawn's early light gave her a rare opportunity to be alone, to start her day with the Bible and prayer. If there were time, she'd also write in the diary she'd begun on the troopship. She hadn't been able to make the first entry at the MASH unit until she'd been there a week. She and the other nurses had barely unpacked when helicopters and ambulances swooped into the compound bearing wounded. The major in charge of the nurses was just introducing herself to the newbies when she looked skyward.

"Here's your orientation! Stay close to me, and I'll assign jobs as we go. This is seat-of-the-pants time, girls. Let's get moving!"

To Shelby, the experience seemed to last for several days before anything resembling quiet occurred.

Shelby reflected on that experience from just three weeks ago. She'd swallowed bile more than once at gnarled limbs and shrapnel-filled intestines and lost one meal when a Marine came in with a shattered temple. She'd constantly kept her eyes on Major Nancy McKaig and Robert Danielson, the doctor assigned to Shelby, whose cool demeanor and genial brown eyes were blessedly reassuring.

"Good morning, Nurse Kichline."

She looked up from her Bible and beheld the curly-haired chaplain.

"Good morning, Father Stephens. You're up early."

"As are you. I'm getting ready for Mass. I see you're reading the Good Book."

She smiled at the man who appeared to be in his mid-thirties. "This is one of my lifelines."

"We all need those here." He sat across from her. "How are you adjusting to the 8055th?"

Shelby closed her Bible. "I'm getting the lay of the land."

"The terrain can be very rugged here. You strike me as a wholesome girl who spent her Saturdays watching the local football team and attending Cary Grant movies."

Pots and pans clanged in the kitchen. The smells of coffee and bacon wafted in their direction.

"You have me pegged, Father." She laughed before growing reflective. "This place is like nothing else I've ever known, but then I'm a nurse, a Christian nurse. My job isn't to focus on myself or the suffering but to relieve it as much as possible. As long as I think that way, I'm not overwhelmed."

"A helpful strategy! You and the nurses do these boys a world of good, you know."

"Thank you."

"If ever you need spiritual counsel, I'm here for you." He paused. "I take it you're not Catholic."

"How could you tell?" She tilted her head to the side.

"You seem a tad awkward calling me 'Father.'"

"I'm from the German Reformed tradition."

"I know that denomination. Chaplain training introduced me to all the major Protestant expressions." He chuckled, leaning forward. "I confess, the Pentecostals make me a might uneasy with their exuberance." He rose. "Well, then, blessings on you this day."

"Thank you, Father, and on you as well."

He grinned at her. "How nice to be the one blessed! Thank you."

Shelby finished removing her underthings from the makeshift laundry line strung across part of their quarters. Vickie hovered nearby, scowling.

"I hope you're finished doing your wash."

She faced her sassy roommate. "Why? Do you need to use this?"

"I have better things to do. You just have a look in your eye."

"What look?"

"Determined. I see that book on your bunk." She pointed to *A Man Called Peter.*

"So what if I do my wash and read a book in my spare time? This is how I cope with the intensity."

"You read that book on the troopship. You need to go with me to the O Club and dance."

"Why would I want to dance with you?" Shelby's eyes twinkled.

"You are so trying, Miss Goody Two-Shoes! If you come to the O Club with the rest of us," she waved toward the off-duty nurses sprucing themselves up, "I'll buy you a drink, and you can hang out with some dishy doctors."

Nurse Evelyn entered the conversation. "I don't think Shelby drinks."

"For your information, my people use wine for communion."

Vickie turned up her nose. "Yeah, but you don't drink hard stuff. Okay, so how about I buy you a glass of wine?"

Shelby tucked her folded stockings into her small end table. "I accept your offer."

"Yippee! I'll be ready in just a minute!"

For the most part, the jukebox featured an elderly assortment of records left over from the last war. The songs reminded Shelby of her early teens when she'd skated under Mom and Pop Long's watchful eyes at Bushkill Park. Now she was jitterbugging with a lieutenant from Amarillo and a doctor who'd acted as anesthesiologist while she'd assisted Dr. Danielson this morning. After she sat out a few dances, he wandered over.

"Hello, Nurse Kichline. May I join you?"

"Yes, Doctor."

He folded his sleek frame into the neighboring chair. "Call me Danny, everyone does. We're pretty informal around here, especially after hours."

She smiled. "Okay, Danny. I'm Shelby."

"I like that name."

"Thank you. My parents gave it to me."

He laughed, placing his glass on the table. "How are you doing here so far?"

"Pretty well. A lot of what I've experienced is a blur, so much so fast."

He sipped his drink. "How have you processed it?"

"I write in my journal, pray ..." She paused, lowering her voice. "Some of what I see I don't want to think about too much."

"Most of us feel the same way. Within an hour after my arrival, I got thrown immediately into surgeries that lasted the entire day. When I couldn't stand any longer, someone took me to my tent where my duffle bag and footlocker sat on a bed. I pushed them aside and slept for twelve hours. When I finally woke up, I unpacked."

Shelby moved her head forward. "How long have you been here?" Someone's cigarette smoke reached her twitching nostrils, and she suppressed a sneeze.

"Six months and three days."

"Ah, but who's counting? Where did you come from?" Vickie moved into her line of sight from the dance floor. She looked at Shelby, then Danny, then back to Shelby, and raised her eyebrows. *That Vickie!*

"I'd just finished my residency at Johns Hopkins. Before that, Cornell."

"Impressive. Are you from New York or maybe Baltimore?"

"Baltimore."

She imagined this handsome doctor on the arm of an Elizabeth Arden debutante.

"And what of your background?"

"I'm from Easton, Pennsylvania."

"Home of Lafayette College."

Shelby perked up. "You know Lafayette?"

"Of course. Cornell often played their teams."

"What sport did you play?" She waved her hands, closing her eyes. "No, no! Let me guess. You were the quarterback and captain of the football team."

Danny did a double-take. "How did you know?"

"Oh, I'm pretty good at reading people." She grinned.

"I'll say, and where did you go to school?"

"Easton High, then Temple School of Nursing."

"Is your family deeply imbedded in Easton?"

Shelby laughed. "That's a funny way to put it, but yes, the Kichlines were among the first settlers there—in the 1750s."

"Tell me about your family." He assumed a relaxed, listening position.

"I'm the oldest of three brothers and a sister ... and a cocker spaniel. My father teaches history at Easton High, and my mom keeps busy looking after all of us and running a bunch of church and town committees."

Danny gazed at her. "And is there a special someone waiting for you there?"

She looked up at the ceiling, then back at him. "There was a while back."

"May I ask what happened?"

"We dated for two years in high school. When I told him I wanted to be a nurse, he gave me a choice between him and nursing."

His jaw dropped. "He didn't say that!"

"Oh, yes, he did."

"And you sent him packing I hope."

"Lock, stock, and class ring."

"Good for you." He lifted his glass, taking a drink. "What made you want to be a nurse?"

"I think God gives people certain abilities, and this is mine. I'm here because my ancestors have fought in every American conflict since the French and Indian War. Korea is my war." His smile filled her heart. "Okay, now it's your turn. Tell me about your family."

"I've lived in Baltimore my entire life, except for being at Cornell. I have a younger brother and an older sister, both married. I'm uncle to a nephew and a niece. My dad is a surgeon, and my mom runs the local DAR chapter. Is your mother a member?"

"She is. So, is there someone waiting for you at home?" She asked as if there was nothing to lose, because there wasn't.

"I figured there would be time for that after med school and residency."

The mood in the O Club became more subdued when "At Last" started playing. Danny held out his hand, which Shelby accepted with a smile. The last time she'd danced to this song was at the senior prom with Michael. Being held by a man struck her as a decidedly different, and by no means less pleasant, experience. Vickie swooped past, nudging Shelby's arm and winking.

"Man alive, Shelby, you scored big tonight!" Vickie climbed into her cot and turned on her side as if they were at a slumber party. "I mean, Dr. Danielson! He's the biggest catch on the medical staff."

"Keep your voice down." Shelby shushed her.

She lowered it a decibel. "If I were you, I'd be leaping and dancing and praising God."

She laughed. "Now, how did you happen to reference a Bible verse?"

"I'm not a heathen, you know." She scooched closer. "What's he like?"

"He's nice. Kind heart, excellent dancer."

"Did your heart go thumpity-thump?"

Shelby tossed her pillow at Vickie. "Only when we jitterbugged."

CHAPTER SIX

"I don't think he heard what I said."

"No, I don't believe he did. Parker, oh, Parker, come in, please."

He emerged through a clouded glaze to behold the MASH 8063rd surgeons he'd followed into the mess tent. "I do apologize for falling asleep while you were talking to me."

The artificial lights, food-scented atmosphere, and multitude of conversations brought him to further awareness after twenty straight hours in the OR.

"Don Currenton is the only surgeon in South Korea who puts patients to sleep without anesthesia." Bill Hyde grinned at his colleague before biting into a stale dinner roll.

"Ha ha, you got me that time." Currenton turned to Parker. "Hey, don't worry about nodding off. If it's sleep you want, I recommend ditching the food and heading back to the bunkhouse."

Parker pulled a long drink of coffee, then ran his hands over his eyes. "I am not used to such conditions—or the intensity of surgery."

"That's right." Bill leaned his head to the right. "You're not a surgeon."

"I had only the basics in medical school and only ever dealt with stitches in my practice."

"You could've fooled me." Don spoke with his mouth full. "You did an amazing job in there."

"One must rise to the occasion when necessity requires."

Don turned to Bill. "I like this guy. How long will you be with us, Parker?"

"My colonel in Seoul seemed to think this assignment would be a matter of days, perhaps a few weeks at most while you are short-handed."

"Who knows how long that will be?" Bill closed his eyes. "I guess you weren't told what happened to Mike Baroni, one of our surgeons?'

"No, I was not."

"He was on his way back here from a battalion aid station and stumbled into North Korean territory. They took him as prisoner." Bill stared at the table.

"I am truly sorry to hear that." Parker processed the information, mournful about the doctor's difficult situation. Given the circumstances, he might be in this MASH unit longer than he expected. He hadn't realized before coming here how good the conditions were at the Army hospital in Seoul. He wondered how being here might affect his search for his maternal grandfather. Then again, he'd made no headway at all there.

"Are you from Korea?" Bill asked.

"I was born in Seoul." He took a bite of meat, wondering just what animal he was eating.

"You speak pretty darn good English," Don said.

Parker closed his eyes and smiled. "I learned the language as a boy. I was educated in the States at Princeton, then medical school at the University of Pennsylvania."

Bill's eyes widened. "Those are some decent credentials. How'd you get mixed up in this man's army?"

He gave details about his journey toward American citizenship, his mother's health, and his grandfather's disappearance.

"How's she doing?" Bill asked.

"She is so improved I had to urge her not to overextend herself. Now that she is feeling a little better, she desires to be all in."

The two surgeons laughed at his expression. Then they sobered, Don inquiring after Parker's grandfather.

"I do not know yet where or how he is." He rubbed his fingers. "Many prayers are being said on his behalf, and I believe they will be answered."

Bill smiled. "So, you're a praying man, are you?"

"I am a Christian. And you?"

"In my better moments, yes." He sighed. "At times here, I feel a million miles away from God. But there are moments when it seems he's right beside me."

"And so, he is right beside you," Parker said. "And what of your faith, Don?"

He sniffed. "My parents took me to Mass, and I was a dutiful altar boy, but it never took. I'm not hostile or anything. Religion just isn't for me."

Parker felt the presence of someone entering their space and jumped when he saw the familiar figure. "Pastor Frank!"

"Parker Tate! Is that really you?" He opened and closed his eyes again.

They shook hands, grinning.

Bill waved his fork at one, then the other. "Do you two know each other?"

"Yes!" Frank exclaimed. "And, oh, have my prayers been answered. I've been inquiring about you, where I might find you, and here you are right in my own unit!"

"You were looking for me?" Parker's heart thumped.

"Let's go someplace quiet to talk."

Andrew Frank's tent was smaller than the quarters Parker shared with Bill and Don, and much neater. A wooden cross above the chaplain's writing desk imparted a touch of peace, a fire burned in a portable stove. Frank motioned to a chair then sat across from Parker at his desk.

"Would you like a cup of coffee? Mine's better than the mess tent's."

"Yes, thank you."

The chaplain filled two mugs and handing one to Parker asked, "When and how did you happen to get here?"

He explained the circumstances concluding, "I think I have been here three days. I have had little time to process my arrival, so much has happened very quickly."

"Things can get chaotic in a MASH unit. I'm sorry I wasn't here to greet you, but I was at a chaplains' gathering in Seoul. Imagine my surprise when I saw you in the mess tent!" His ruddy face hadn't stopped beaming.

"I am happy to see you as well."

"How is your mother?"

"She is well, thank you." He spoke of her diagnosis and recovery.

"This is wonderful news." He rubbed his hands together and shivered. "I suppose you're used to Korean winters."

"I have lived away for so long I am needing to readapt." His senses on the alert, he wondered what the chaplain had on his mind.

Frank leaned forward, as if brushing away the last of their chitchat. "I have important news for you, which is why I wanted to find you."

His hand trembled around the coffee mug. "What has happened?"

"During the Christmas truce, I was allowed to visit our imprisoned surgeon. Let me tell you, that camp's a rugged, dismal place. While I was there, I learned your grandfather is among the prisoners."

Parker stood, gaping. "You saw my grandfather?"

"Yes, and I had an opportunity to speak with him briefly."

Wonder enveloped him as he retook his seat. "How is he?"

"Alert and speaking of his faith but weak from exposure and malnourishment. He needs medical attention."

Parker cracked his knuckles. "How did he get there?"

"He was leading refugees from Pyongyang to Seoul and making decent progress when a Korean People's Army unit overtook them. Everyone managed to escape except him. From reading between the lines, he wanted to ensure the safety of his charges more than his own. That was sometime last fall." He spread his hands. "He's a brave and godly man, Parker."

"Yes, he has always been those things."

"I believe there may be something we can do to help him."

He perked up. "Oh, please, what can be done?"

"One of the guards, name of Ko, took me aside just before I left. He said he was one of your grandfather's students before the war broke out, and he's a Christian who was impressed into the North Korean PKA army. He's been looking after your grandfather, sneaking him extra food, such as it is, providing blankets and socks. Of course, it's not enough, and he wants nothing more than to escape, along with your grandfather and our Dr. Baroni."

Despite the fire's heat, Parker shivered. "How can this happen?"

"Ko has devised a plan, but it'll take great effort and not a little danger. All the way back here, I thought and prayed about how it might be carried out, but there was one major piece missing." He met Parker's gaze. "I think God may have sent you here for just such a time as this, as an instrument of their deliverance."

Parker's scalp prickled while Frank explained the scheme. This Ko fellow seemed to have covered every contingency.

When the chaplain finished, he asked, "Well, what do you think?"

"His plan might just work."

"We'll go see Colonel Pruitt tomorrow. Without his permission, we can do nothing."

"Why not today?"

"You need to be on your knees about this, Parker, to be absolutely certain God wants you to do this. I'll pray with you, beginning right now."

Colonel Chase Pruitt paced with his hands behind his back, muttering to himself while Parker and the chaplain waited quietly. After some minutes, Pruitt took a seat and started tapping his fingers on the desk.

"This is a hare-brained scheme if I ever heard one, Chaplain, but I sure would like to get Baroni back. As for you, Tate, a man like your grandfather deserves to be rescued. I've never been in the espionage business, but my company clerk is a wheeler-dealer who can get just about anything." He paused. "What do you think the chances of success are, Frank?"

"I don't know. The best I can do is commit this scheme to God and trust him for the outcome."

"What about you, Tate? Are you up for this?"

"Yes, sir."

"You'd be putting yourself in a boatload of danger."

"I see my coming to this MASH, when and how I did, as God's leading. How can I live with myself if I do not try to do the right thing?"

Pruitt raised an eyebrow. "You're a better man than I, Gunga Din."

Parker smiled at the film reference, pleased he'd made time while at school to see some American movies. "I believe, sir, if you were in my place, you would do the same thing."

The colonel turned to Frank. "I think we'd better keep this thing as tightly under wraps as possible, just you, me, Tate, and Mike Howden. I'll tell folks you were needed elsewhere, that we need an actual surgeon here. Once Howden rustles up a PKA uniform and officer's credentials, we'll send you on your way." He frowned. "How will you get up there, Tate?"

"With your permission," Frank said, "I'll take supplies to the orphanage in that area, hiding Captain Tate in the truck. Once we're close enough, I'll drop him off with coordinates to the prison camp. He would only need to walk about three miles to get there."

Pruitt grimaced. "And if he's spotted?"

"He can say he got lost. Parker's story will be that General Kim Mu-Chong requested he bring his grandfather, Ko, and Baroni to his headquarters so he can personally interrogate them. Parker will require a fake letter from the general along with falsified identification."

Parker added to the conversation. “Once I am in place, I will lead them out of the camp as quickly as possible before all of this is discovered.”

The colonel raised his hands palms up. “What could possibly go wrong?”

“So, where’s the Army taking you this time?” Bill asked.

Parker shoved a pair of socks into his duffel bag, bristling at the first of his subterfuges. He’d been raised to be strictly honest in his dealings and hoped an underground rescue operation wouldn’t count as a lie. He tried out his response like a child transitioning from training wheels to a bike.

“I have been instructed to report for duty today, and then I will know more.”

Bill held out his hand. “I’ve enjoyed getting to work with and know you, Parker.”

“I too have enjoyed my time with the two of you.”

Don smiled at him. “You’d make a good surgeon. If you ever want to end up doing this, don’t hesitate. Some people have it, and some don’t. You’re among those who do.”

At a secluded spot three miles from the MASH, Corporal Howden stopped the Jeep when they caught sight of Chaplain Frank in an Army truck. Parker hopped down to the ground and approached the minister.

“I hope we did not keep you waiting in this cold.”

“I got here not five minutes ago. Everything is ready. How about you—are you ready? There’s still time to back out.”

“I have no doubts. There is no turning back.”

The chaplain clapped him on the back, Howden transferred Parker’s belongings. “I’ll keep your things in my tent until after your mission." He rubbed his gloved hands together. "Your new uniform is ready, including fake ID papers. Too bad you need to do this in such bitter conditions—at least I have some padding to protect me." He motioned to his stomach.

Parker steeled himself against the gnawing cold. Standing between the two vehicles, he quickly removed his American clothes right down to and including his skivvies. They couldn't permit any carelessness about details, including the wearing of American army-issue socks or underwear. Frozen as a Yeti, his teeth chattered and limbs shook so violently his friends had to assist him.

When he finished dressing, he said, "There is one thing I insist upon having."

"What's that?"

"My Bible."

Frank whistled. "That could cause a lot of trouble."

"I will be discreet, and the Bible is small."

"Just don't let anyone see it."

Parker grinned. "Perhaps God will make it invisible to unfriendly eyes."

"I wish you wouldn't, but I understand. So, are you ready?"

"Yes, Pastor Frank."

The chaplain put his hand on Parker's shoulder and prayed for a hedge of protection and a successful mission. Then they all shook hands, and Parker thanked the two men for their help.

"I wish you the best, Captain Tate, or should I say, Major Moon Soo Yi?" Howden said. "I hope you find your grandfather and our surgeon, and you all get back safely."

CHAPTER SEVEN

Vickie's breath poured over Shelby's shoulder. "Just how many Christmas cards did you get?"

"I don't know, I haven't counted them all. Maybe a hundred?" The bounty puzzled her.

She rubbed her brow. "I don't know that many people, and I'm from New York."

Shelby gazed into the largest of six boxes of holiday cheer, aware none of the other nurses had received close to as much. Fortunately, two of her packages were from church members who asked her to share the contents with MASH personnel.

"Most of these cards are from people I don't even know."

At the top of one container she found a letter attached to the inside.

> Dear Lieutenant Kichline,
>
> These Christmas cards are from your many friends back home. In late October, The Easton Express ran an article about your service to our country and invited readers to send Christmas greetings. The response overwhelmed us. We hope you will enjoy these expressions of friendship and support.

> You'll find several addressed 'Dear Nurse,' 'Dear Doctor,' and 'Dear Patient.' Please distribute these as you see fit.
> Thank you for serving our great nation.
> Sincerely yours,
> Edward O. Nowack, Editor-in-Chief.

She showed the message to Vickie.

She laughed and raised her hands. "I guess that's what happens when you come from a small town."

In her family's box, one tin bulged with Christmas cookies. "Oh, you're a doll, Mom!"

"What are you babbling about, Shelb?"

She breathed deeply of the treasured scent. "My mom sent my favorite Toll House cookies. No one makes them like her."

"I'll bet mine does." Vickie put her hands on her hips.

"You may have the first one." Shelby moved the container toward her.

Biting into the cookie, Vickie's eyes lit. "By golly, you're right." She stretched across her bunk and retrieved a box lined with wax paper. "Here, try one of my mom's."

"Mm. Very nice, plenty chewy." She swallowed. "I still like my mom's best. But if you prefer this texture, your mom's wins our little contest."

Vickie laughed. "Maybe you should be a diplomat instead of a nurse!"

The door swung open, admitting a frigid blast. Major Nancy McKaig entered, rubbing her hands against her arms, the duty roster banging against her coat. She stood for a long moment observing her staff and sniffing. "What is that smell?"

Evelyn Hoyle called out, "Evening in Paris. I just opened the bottle."

"Well, don't fumigate the rest of us or the patients." McKaig fanned her face. "I'm happy that your gifts arrived before Christmas. Last year, they didn't get here until Groundhog Day."

Vickie held out her cookie box. "My mom's Toll House. Would you like one?"

McKaig accepted the gift. "Thank you. I'll save it to have with my coffee."

"Here's a napkin," Vickie said. "Have another. One cookie does not a coffee break make."

The head nurse squirreled them in a pocket. "Well, ladies, I have tomorrow's duty roster, so pay attention." She rattled off the assignments and frowned as she reached the end. "Lieutenant Kichline, I see you're paired up with Dr. Danielson again."

Shelby knew an insinuation when she heard one.

"You seem to be assisting him more than the other surgeons. You might want to give another nurse a chance."

She flinched. "I'd be happy to work with a different doctor, Major McKaig."

"Then why don't you?"

She didn't want to sell the fellow down the river and chose her words carefully. "Dr. Danielson has been requesting my assistance."

McKaig stared at Shelby then moved closer and lowered her voice. "Is the captain doing anything to make you feel uncomfortable?"

"Oh, no, not at all." She realized saying more would just muddy the waters.

"That's good to know." She pushed a pencil behind her right ear. "Nevertheless, I think I'll have a talk with him."

Evelyn stopped by Shelby and Vickie's table at the evening meal bearing two bedpans.

Vickie waved her hands. "Ew! Why are you bringing those into the mess tent?"

The diminutive nurse blushed. "Sorry, Vick, I couldn't find baskets. Trust me, these are spic and span."

"Why are you toting bedpans around?" Shelby asked.

She brightened. "Because everyone is supposed to pick two names, one from each. This one," she slanted her head to the left, "has the names of everyone in the unit. The other one has the names of local children and orphans who'll be coming on Christmas Eve. I want to make sure everyone gets a present. Some folks haven't had any word from home yet."

Shelby beckoned Evelyn, and closing her eyes, drew her two names.

"My turn," Vickie said, reaching into the receptacles.

"Thanks! You don't have to give a lot, you know; simple things are best. Be sure to put your name on the child's gift, but not on the staff members'. We're hoping the little ones will better connect with us so they'll know we're their friends."

Shelby had enjoyed meeting folks from the neighboring village while assisting with a medical clinic. She wondered if the child whose name she'd chosen, Woo Sung, was a girl or a boy. *Father Stephens might know*.

"Simple things are the best what?" Danny sidled up to Evelyn with his dinner tray.

"Oh, hi, Danny!" Evelyn glanced at her fellow nurses. "He already knows about the gift exchange."

The surgeon set his tray on the end of the table and selected names from the bedpans. "When is the party again?"

She batted his arm. "You know—Christmas Eve, here in the mess tent. Father Stephens will bring the orphans by at six o'clock, and Colonel Sheppard told the local families to come then too. If everyone brings their presents here by noon on Christmas Eve, Nurse Arlene and I will collect and organize them."

"If you need help, let me know," Shelby said.

"What are we supposed to use for wrapping paper?" Vickie asked.

"Anything, I guess. How about leftover gift wrap from your family's presents or newspapers?"

"Will there still be midnight mass, after the party?" Vickie asked.

Shelby jerked her head back and gave her friend a long look. Since when had Vickie been interested in mass, midnight or otherwise?

"Of course. The children won't be here that long. Well, I have miles to go. Thanks so much!" Evelyn proceeded to the next table.

Danny turned to Shelby. "Do you mind if I sit with you?"

"Not at all." She felt Vickie's smirk.

He settled onto the bench and organized his utensils according to every good housewife's etiquette before he forked a mouthful of meatloaf. Shelby noted he hadn't said grace, realizing she'd never seen him pray or attend any of Father Stephens's services. Her forehead wrinkled. Come to think of it, whenever she'd mentioned her church or faith, he'd been detached, although once he'd mentioned being raised Episcopalian. His lack of devotion niggled, but she reminded herself they weren't dating or anything.

"So, how are you, Vickie?" he asked.

"Fine, and you?"

"Last night was my first eight hours of sleep in more than a month. I'm on top of the world today." He turned to

Shelby. "I'm happy to see you. I haven't had the pleasure of working with you in the OR the past couple of days."

She decided between responding defensively, furtively, or humorously and settled on the latter. "I happen to be in great demand. Major McKaig wants me to share my considerable talents with the rest of the surgeons."

He grimaced. "So, she told me."

"Uh, I think I'll go back to our quarters." Vickie rose with her tray. "I need to figure out what to do about these gifts. Toodle-oo!"

He seemed not to notice her departure. "We have some crackerjack nurses here, but you're the best."

"Thank you, Danny. That means a lot to me."

"Does it?"

The clamor and conversation of the mess tent receded. Her stomach fluttered. "Well, yes, as I'm fresh out of nursing school and basic training." She recognized being on the threshold of babbling and doused the impulse with a sip of coffee gone cold.

He gazed at her, and she looked away, forcing herself to appear casual. Was Dr. Robert Danielson, darling of the surgeons, flirting with her?

"That isn't exactly what I meant," he said with a small smile.

Yup, he's sweet on me.

Shelby went through the gifts from home designated for others, selecting appropriate ones for the Christmas party. Her adult staff gift was for Arlene, and she chose a store-bought wool scarf in an Orr's of Easton box. She imagined the store front just off the Circle, graced by an old-fashioned clock against snow-covered Northampton

Street. She remembered spending an entire morning with her Grandmother Kichline combing the burgeoning aisles the week before Christmas. When they finished shopping, they'd put all their pocket change in the Salvation Army kettle outside the store and ventured across the street to Woolworths for a hotdog. On this damp, chilly day, the memories eased her sudden homesickness.

She focused instead on what to give her child, whom Father Stephens told her was one of the orphan boys. Someone from her church had sent an afghan made of soft crimson lambswool, and she knew the little boy would benefit from its warmth. She carefully rewrapped the gift with the same paper it had come in. On the top, she attached three barley sugar lollipops from the Carmelcorn Shop. Then she chose one in the shape of a drum for herself. The sweet, satiny texture took her straight back to Centre Square and the heady aroma of popping corn, chocolate, and nuts.

While she was choosing gifts, she thought a present for Vickie might be in order. The colonel had discouraged staff from giving to the officers to avoid awkwardness, but surely, exceptions could be made for friends. She grinned at the copy of *A Man Called Peter* a lady from church had sent, along with two crossword puzzle paperbacks. Vickie might just benefit from the biography of Peter Marshall, which Shelby had already read three times.

When she finished wrapping gifts, she sat on the edge of her bunk with her chin resting on her hand. Should she give something to Danny, cookies maybe, or a Christmas card? Did she, in fact, need to give Danny anything at all? She'd spent a good deal of time with him dancing at the O Club, and he was becoming rather exclusive with her.

Whenever she took a walk, he seemed to be there. When they had staff meetings, he sat next to her. Given what he'd said to her in the mess tent, she thought they might be heading in such a direction, but she wasn't entirely sure. She didn't want to do anything inappropriate, especially under her supervisor's keen watchfulness. Shelby decided not to give him anything.

The mess tent didn't look like itself, and a gentle dusting of snow had transformed the dismal compound. A Christmas tree boasted paper chain garlands, while underneath lay a charming assortment of oddly-wrapped packages for the staff. "Santa Claus is Comin' to Town" played in the background. Shelby breathed in the aroma of hot apple cider and freshly-showered Army personnel who'd put their new bars of soap and bottles of shampoo to good use.

The staff arrived fifteen minutes ahead of the children, and just before six o'clock, Shelby heard trucks braking outside. Children entered the tent, their faces alight with barely-contained excitement. She savored their joy as she helped Nurse Evelyn invite them to come inside and fill their plates. MASH personnel followed their guests in the food line. Shelby found a seat next to Father Stephens, who was with Eileen Fish, the English doctor who ran the orphanage. Vickie was across the room sitting with a Korean family, but Shelby didn't see Danny. The other surgeons were all there, but not him.

As the children took a liking to her, Shelby used her English to Korean dictionary to communicate with them. She accompanied three of them to the dessert tables and pointed out what she considered the best of the offerings—Toll House, sugar, and molasses cookies, gingerbread, and chocolate cake. Each of them, their eyes aglow, also received a candy cane from Major McKaig, who greeted them at the end of the table.

Some twenty minutes later a commotion broke out near the tree, and Shelby turned to see what was happening. A rather large figure in a red suit was lowering himself through an opening in the tent roof, shouting "Ho ho ho!" This Santa Claus was considerably taller and leaner than the ones on whose laps she'd sat in Pomeroy's Department Store as a child. The children shrank back at first then coaxed by the MASH personnel, quickly encircled him. His helper, Nurse Arlene, explained in Korean he had gifts for each of them, and they must wait their turn. One-by-one, he called out their names and gave them a present. By the third child, Shelby had figured out why she hadn't seen Danny all evening. She smiled as she watched him interacting with the boys and girls. He really was a terrific guy.

After several presents were distributed, Santa Danny called out, "And here is a gift for Woo Sung from Nurse Shelby." An orphan about the age of four walked toward him and accepted the package, bowing. Shelby went over to him and pointed at herself. "I am Nurse Shelby." When the boy frowned, she pointed to the present and said, "This is for you." She gestured to Woo Sung, then to herself. "From me."

The child's eyes brightened, and he reached out for Shelby's hand, the little fellow melting her heart. Woo Sung's eyes filled with something like wonder when he unwrapped the afghan, and Shelby draped it around his slender shoulders. Then she handed him the barley sugar lollipop and pretended to lick it.

When the time came for the children to leave, Shelby approached the director.

"May I come to the orphanage with Father Stephens to visit Woo Sung?"

Dr. Fish put a hand on Shelby's shoulder. "We'll all be disappointed if you don't. Woo Sung certainly took a shining to you."

Between their guests leaving at nine o'clock and midnight Mass, the staff continued to party in the mess tent. Santa also distributed their gifts, Shelby receiving a linen handkerchief from Major McKaig. She smiled when Arlene opened her present of the wool scarf and exclaimed over how badly she needed it. She wanted to collect her thoughts before the Christmas Mass and rose to leave when Santa approached her, minus his hat and whiskers.

"You did a wonderful job tonight, Danny," she said.

"Are you leaving?"

She explained her desire for some solo time.

"Oh, okay. I guess we'll have to dance another time, then."

"I guess so."

"Before you go, Santa has a present for you."

"I already received one."

"Not from Santa."

Her right eyelid twitched. "Why, this is unexpected," she said, reaching out to accept the flat package.

"I saw this in Tokyo and thought of you."

She let this sink in.

"Olive drab probably gets to you sometimes. Pretty women like pretty things."

Her breath caught when she pulled out an exquisite silk shawl with a delicate floral pattern against a fuchsia background.

"This is beautiful! Thank you." She kissed his cheek, sticky from the fake beard. "I, uh, I'm afraid I didn't give anything to Santa."

He grinned. "Oh, but you just did."

CHAPTER EIGHT

If he considered the MASH primitive, the North Korean POW camp was Neanderthal. The stench overpowered him when he rolled into camp in a GAZ-67 he'd flagged down after Chaplain Frank had left him in God's hands.

He assumed a brusque manner. "Where is your commanding officer?"

A weedy soldier jerked his thumb toward a building. "Over there, sir!"

"And just who is this fellow?" Parker wanted to be sure of the man's name. "They change command so frequently."

"Yes, sir. Colonel Chai just came here three weeks ago."

I am glad I risked asking for his name.

"That will be all."

The young man stood at attention as Parker walked toward what had probably been a village schoolhouse. Inside, the most basic office furniture and accoutrements comprised the one-room quarters. A wood-burning stove provided the only heat in this place of shadows, reminiscent of Dante's Inferno. Not even the CO had it good here. The gaunt commanding officer appeared to be in his mid-thirties with a face that could have cut paper. He looked up from his desk.

"Yes, and who might you be?"

Parker saluted. "Colonel Chai, I am Major Moon Soo Yi on business from General Kim Mu-Chong." He produced his fake credentials and letter.

Chai's bravado dissipated. "The general has sent you here?"

"Yes, sir." Parker willed himself not to tremble.

Chai examined the letter then dropped it on the desk before returning Parker's credentials. Just in case the officer had kept the paperwork, Corporal Howden had made two copies for Parker.

"I do not understand why he would want to examine these prisoners, but that is not for me to know." He barked out someone's name, and like a spider, an assistant emerged from a dark corner. "I want you to bring Dr. Oh and the American surgeon Baroni at once."

One of Parker's chief concerns was what might happen if his grandfather recognized him. Although he and his co-conspirators had tried to consider every angle of the mission, there were some aspects only God could control. Parker worked his anxiety into in a stern expression of near-impatience.

At last, a guard brought the two inmates, who shuffled into the room in slippers meant for a mild climate. Their ragged clothes drooped from emaciated frames. A thrill spread through Parker upon seeing his grandfather alive, but he let anger over the man's condition fuel him. Fortunately, their heads were bowed.

"You call these prisoners? They look like mangy dogs! I cannot imagine what the General wants with the likes of them or why he should involve me. They must be of some use to him, however, especially the American."

Colonel Chai sneered. "You can have them!"

"I will require a driver." Parker tapped his cheek with a finger. "You have, I believe, a guard named Ko."

"Kang-Pil Ko."

"Yes, he is the one."

Chai barked orders to his subordinate, and moments later Ko stood before them at attention. Only once did the guard's gaze meet Parker's, who returned it as if to say, "I am here. Let us do this thing."

Parker struggled with an impulse to have Ko pull to the side of the rutted road and reveal himself to his grandfather. Mercifully, the liberated prisoners appeared to be asleep, his relative's head resting against the doctor's chest.

Ko gave him a long look. "I am sorry there is nothing hot to drink or blankets for our friends. I did not wish to raise suspicions."

"Would you like to know who I am, Ko?"

The youthful soldier glanced sideways. "You are sent by the chaplain Frank, yes?"

"I am. I know him from the States."

Ko's eyebrows rose. "You are from the US?"

"I am from Seoul. I was educated in the States and practice medicine there."

"You are a doctor!"

"Yes. I encountered Chaplain Frank at a MASH unit. He told me about your plan to defect and to free my grandfather and Dr. Baroni."

Ko's voice cracked as if he were twelve-years-old. "He is your grandfather?"

"That is why I have come."

"What is your real name?" Ko asked.

"My Korean name is Tae-ho Park, but I go by Parker Tate." He paused. "I am grateful to you for undertaking such a dangerous mission."

"You must understand, I want very much to be free and to free these good men. When I was at the seminary, your grandfather was my teacher. I still want to become a minister like him, but as you can see, the PKA had other plans for me. When Dr. Oh and the chaplain were brought to the prison camp, I knew I must do everything in my power to free them, and myself if possible. I remembered Dr. Oh saying that with God, everything is possible."

Parker reflected on this extraordinary story. "Please tell me what is next."

"There is an American aid station to the east of our present location. Once we arrive, we will put your grandfather and Dr. Baroni in their care, and I will surrender." He looked Parker up and down. "I regret you will need to explain why you wear the North Korean uniform."

He took a deep breath, the frigid air stabbing his lungs. "I will do my best to disclose my identity." He motioned toward the back seat. "I would like to speak to them before we arrive."

"You will have an opportunity shortly."

Diffused sunlight cast itself on the travelers when Ko pulled to the side of a deserted road. The passengers awakened as Parker rose from the vehicle, reaching his arms to the sun and feeling his lower back pop. His grandfather's iced-caked eyes were a blow to Parker's gut. He could bear the charade not a moment longer.

He addressed the liberated prisoners. "Ko and I are taking you to the American aid station, to freedom."

"Glory be!" Baroni's tears immediately froze on his face. "I wondered if that might be what was happening. He and Chaplain Frank let me in on some of the plan." He pointed toward Parker. "Are you a North Korean?"

"I am from this country and a captain in the American army." He squeezed the old man's shoulder. "I am Parker Tate, and this is my beloved *harabeoji*." He held out his hand to the old man, who grasped it as if for dear life.

"Tae-ho!" Light filled the old man's eyes as they embraced for a long moment.

Then Parker looked to Ko. "When will we arrive at the American station?"

"I believe we are fifteen minutes away. When we get there, we will abandon the GAZ quickly, so don't leave anything behind. I know this area because my family used to live here." His brow creased when he asked the former prisoners, "Will you two be able to hurry?"

"Yes, yes, of course." Dr. Oh seemed to rise to a renewed strength.

Parker gazed at his grandfather. "I will carry him if I have to."

"We must all move as one," Ko said, "because when the Americans see us, they will be immediately on guard when they see these North Korean uniforms."

Baroni interrupted him. "Dr. Oh and I will tell them exactly who you are and what you have done."

"Thank you. I am counting on you."

Parker took a deep breath. *So am I.*

Just outside the aid compound, Parker knew with a few steps more they would all be safe. He hoped with all of them vouching for Ko, the Americans would find a place for him other than prison camp, perhaps in intelligence. Baroni was helping Dr. Oh alight from the vehicle when a sudden rumble of artillery erupted. Parker stood open-mouthed until a mortar shell aroused him from his confused state. He ran in the direction of his companions, who hustled through a copse of trees toward the aid station, until an earsplitting crash stopped him in his tracks. An American soldier lay under a fallen tree next to a burning Jeep and screaming for help.

Instinct drove him to the man's side, the American flinching at the sight of the enemy uniform. Adrenaline pumped through Parker as he worked to extricate the man from the blazing wreck.

A few yards away, a North Korean soldier shouted, "*Meonchuda!*"

Despite the command to stop, Parker continued the perilous rescue, wondering if he was about to enter Glory in a gas explosion or at the end of an SKS. Just as he freed the American, gunfire erupted, and Parker fell to his knees. When another bullet struck him, he writhed on the frozen ground, unable to cry out. He heard the American cuss the PKA soldier just before blacking out.

CHAPTER NINE

Seven layers thick—long johns, woolen socks, a shirt, sweater, coat, wool beanie, and leather gloves—and Shelby's shivering still vibrated the cot.

"I hate mid-January." Vickie thumped her upper body cross-wise with her arms.

Shelby had always loved snow days and sledding on Lafayette's campus, then trudging home for a mug of hot Ovaltine. In the nurses' quarters, only a stove shielded them against weather out to possess a person's mind, body, and soul. She vowed not to complain, though, when doing so helped no one. Besides, Vickie whined enough for everyone else.

She laboriously turned a page of her book with a leather-gloved finger. "Your head looks cold. Would you like to use my shawl?"

Vickie stared her down. "Why aren't you using it?"

"It doesn't fit."

"How in the heck a shawl doesn't fit is beyond me. Sometimes *you* are beyond me."

Shelby retreated to her fictional dream.

Apparently abandoning the inquisition, Vickie shifted to a different topic. "I'm going to the O Club. With all those bodies jammed inside, it's got to be warmer there. Come with me?"

"No, thanks. I want to stay here and read."

Vickie grimaced. "You've been spending a lot of time with your head in a book."

She gave a laugh. "You sound like a suspicious mother who thinks her child needs to spend more time outdoors."

"You do need to get out more."

She closed the paperback, using her index finger to mark her place. "Look, Vickie, I like being alone, and privacy is hard to come by around here. Sometimes, I need to deal with what happens in the OR by myself, and other times I want to be around people. Tonight, I happen to prefer solitude." She waved in Vickie's direction. "Go. Blow off some steam."

Her roommate thumped back down. "Okay, but first I need to ask you something."

Shelby dialed back the volume of her sigh. "What is it?"

"Are you avoiding Danny?"

"Why do you ask?"

"You're not coming to the O Club much or dancing with him when you're there."

"I do too dance with him."

"Not like you used to, not exclusively. You two were becoming an item right around Christmas. What happened?"

Shelby started to say, "That's none of your business," but bit her tongue. "We're still friendly."

"I don't understand you, Shelb. Don't you realize who he is?" Just in case she didn't, Vickie expounded. "He's the darling of the 8055th, plus he's stinking rich. If you married him you'd be on Easy Street."

Shelby had spent time considering these things since Christmas when he'd given her the expensive shawl, lovelight in his eyes. Even so, when he kissed her, the experience had been a rote meeting of lips. She wanted a meeting of souls.

Vickie leaned closer, touching Shelby's elbow. "What's wrong?"

"I don't love him."

"Why not?"

"You might as well tell me why you prefer green to blue, or pizza to steak." She paused. "You once told me you couldn't love a man who disliked the New York Giants."

Vickie scowled. "What does that have to do with the price of eggs?"

"You love baseball. You can't wait for spring training, and you know the names of all the players. You're passionate about the Giants."

"O-kay."

"Stay with me here, Vickie. What am I most passionate about?"

"Your religion."

Shelby gazed at her. "There's nothing more important to me than my relationship with the Lord Jesus. The man I marry has to share this with me. Otherwise, we'd be unequally yoked. Why date someone who can't ever be that man?"

"What the heck does that mean?" She spread her hands.

"One of us would drag the other one down. Normally, the one who doesn't believe drags down the one who does."

Her voice softened. "Your faith is that important to you?"

"Yes."

"Danny's a Christian, right?"

"No, he isn't."

"How do you know?"

"Because every time I've mentioned my faith, his expression goes blank, as if I'm speaking Chinese. Every time I've asked him to go to services with me, he has an excuse. He once told me he's more of a Christmas and Easter person. Faith has some bearing on his morals but nothing more. We simply can't connect any deeper than we've gone." She looked up at the ceiling. "There can't be anything between us but friendship."

Vickie grew quiet, a rarity for her. Then she said, "Does he know how you feel?"

"I haven't sensed the timing is right, so ..."

"You're avoiding him in the meantime."

"I suppose so, but I meant what I said about treasuring these quiet moments."

Vickie slapped her palms against her thighs then stood. "On that note, I will hie myself to the O Club."

A voice began to speak over the unit's intercom. "Attention everyone. Wounded are on their way into the compound. Everyone on duty report!"

"Ugh! I happen to be on duty, and I've already worked a ten-hour day."

Shelby swung her legs over the side of the cot and set her book aside. "I'll go for you."

"You will?"

"I owe you one. You filled in for me when I had a sore throat."

"Are you sure?"

The ambulances rumbling into the receiving area shook the ground.

"Sure, I'm sure. Go to the O Club. Have a drink and a dance. If the casualties mount, they'll be calling on you anyway, so have some fun while you can."

Vickie hugged her. "You're the best!"

Shelby ran toward two soldiers on litters, Major McKaig shouting instructions that rose on puffs of steam.

"Can you handle them, Kichline?"

She'd done triage plenty of times before, but always under a senior nurse's supervision. She sensed the major's vote of confidence.

"Yes, major." Shelby crouched to the unforgiving ground, startling when she saw a North Korean lying next to an American. She'd never seen a PKA up close before, and this one was unconscious and bleeding from several directions, including his throat. The wounded American grabbed her arm.

"Take him first."

"You want me to treat the enemy ahead of you?"

"My leg and wrist can wait. If he doesn't get immediate help, he'll die."

Shelby wondered how he knew so much about the wounded Korean or why he was concerned. A shadow cast over her and she looked up. "We have a North Korean, Doctor Olsen."

He gestured with his gloved hand. "Take the American inside."

"Doc, I want you to take care of him first," the soldier said.

"I never take the enemy ahead of our boys."

Shelby glanced from the doctor to the soldier, then back down at the North Korean, who'd begun twitching. She touched his shoulder as if he might be armed with explosives. His eyelids flickered open and upon seeing her, he seemed to relax, and a smile crossed his lips. Then his head lolled back onto the pallet. A rush of adrenaline pumped through her. *What was that all about?*

She didn't have time to consider what had passed between them. Danny arrived against a background of braking ambulances, headlights, gurneys, and people yelling orders.

"What's going on here? We need to pick up the pace."

"Please operate on him first!" The American soldier directed his plaintive plea to the new guy. "This doc won't do it."

"You know I always take our own first," Olsen told his colleague.

"I know." Danny grimaced, seeming to make a quick assessment.

"The North Korean is badly wounded," Shelby said. "He's suffered multiple wounds, has lost significant blood, and he's in shock."

"See!" the American said.

"I need a surgeon here," Major McKaig bellowed.

"You go ahead, Neil," Danny said. "I'll take care of this."

Olsen didn't need to be told twice.

Danny looked down at the soldier. "Why are you so eager to help him?"

"That man saved my life. Take good care of him."

Danny made an initial examination of the Korean. "Corpsman! Take this man to pre-op. Shelby, prep him for surgery immediately."

Her initially quiet evening turned into a marathon OR session. She assisted Danny for nearly five hours to repair two gunshot wounds, one to the right shin, the other to the patient's abdomen. Shell fragments had to be removed and torn arteries carefully sewn back together. A piece of shrapnel had penetrated the North Korean's throat, resulting in severe blood loss and requiring Danny's most expert attention. When Shelby reported a precipitous drop of the patient's blood pressure, he suddenly went into cardiac arrest.

"He's in hypovolemic shock." Danny sprang into action to save the man's life.

When his condition finally stabilized, Shelby went temporarily weak-kneed.

"Are you okay?" the doctor asked.

"Yes."

"I can get a replacement," he said, his hands working the surgical instruments.

"Thank you, doctor. I'd like to see this through." She saw him smile beneath his mask.

By the time the North Korean was in post-op and the American's broken bones and lacerations had been dealt with, the neighborhood rooster was crowing. She wanted to stay with her recovering patients, but Danny insisted she rest. Without the energy to eat, she plodded back to her quarters where the other nurses were getting dressed.

"Shelby! You look exhausted."

"I am."

"Were you in surgery all night?"

"Yes." She fell onto her cot.

"Let me help you with your boots," Vickie said.

Before she could assist her friend, Shelby had fallen asleep. Her bunkmate pulled the covers over her and left for the morning meal.

She wasn't entirely refreshed when she awakened at eleven, but she dressed quickly in the frigid quarters. Outside, smoke rose from the various buildings, and she went to the mess tent for a quick cup of coffee and a leftover donut. At the post-op ward, she checked in at the duty nurse's desk to ask about the American and North Korean patients.

Evelyn Hoyle checked her notes. "The American is stable, had a good night. The other one ..." She frowned. "His blood pressure plummeted earlier, but he's holding his own now."

"I'm going to check on them if you don't mind."

"Be my guest."

Shelby walked past other recovering soldiers. The North Korean was sleeping, and she pulled back his blanket to check his throat, mid-section, and leg. Drainage appeared to be minimal and normal. She gazed at him for a long moment, intrigued by his placid expression, embarrassed to note how handsome a fellow he was. The American was sitting up, and he smiled as she approached.

"Hello, soldier." She briefly consulted his chart hanging from a rail at the end of the bed. *Private James Ward.*

"Good morning."

She stood between his bed and the Korean's. "How are you feeling?"

"Not too bad."

"How's the pain?"

"Nothing I can't handle."

She detected a southern accent. "Where are you from?"

"Tulsa, Oklahoma."

"Do you go by Jim?"

"Yes, ma'am. You were there when they brought me in last night."

"Yes, I was."

"And in the operating room."

"That's right, although Dr. Olsen was your surgeon. I assisted Dr. Danielson."

He jerked his thumb to the left. "How's he doing?"

"He had a rough go of it." She briefly looked upon the North Korean's face before sitting on a chair next to Jim Ward. "What happened that made you so insistent we treat him first?" She rested her hand on her chin.

"When my unit came under sudden attack, I started firing back at the enemy." He looked down at the bed, picking the covers with his right hand. "I don't remember how, but I got pinned under a burning Jeep."

"How awful that must've been!" Shelby touched her hand to her chest.

"I thought I was a goner. I kept trying to pull myself out of there, but with a broken leg and wrist, I couldn't. The next thing I knew, this North Korean comes running at me, and my heart pounded almost out of my chest. He started yelling something—I couldn't hear him because of the noise—but there was just something about the way he looked at me, I knew he wasn't going to shoot. Come to think of it, I don't think he even had a gun."

"You're speaking of him, right?" She pointed toward the other patient.

"None other. So, he starts pulling me under my arms, trying to drag me from the Jeep, and he almost gets me free when this other PKA officer shows up and starts screaming at him. I don't know their language, but I do know 'stop' when I hear it. My rescuer ignored him, and the other soldier starts shooting him. I don't know how I did it with a broken wrist but I grabbed my rifle and killed the guy. I, uh, I'm sorry if that upsets you."

Shelby shook her head. "You did what you had to do."

"Yes." He breathed out. "Then it was my turn to help my rescuer, who was by now unconscious. I was able to roll us both away from the burning wreck just before it exploded. You see stuff like that in movies, but it really happened to me, to us." He looked over at the North Korean. "The next thing I know, we're at this MASH unit." He paused. "I hope I didn't hurt him when I shoved him away from the Jeep."

Shelby grinned, delighted by the heroism these men had displayed. "You saved his life."

"He saved mine first."

"What an amazing story! I'll let you get some rest now, Private Ward."

She rose and consulted the Korean's chart, wondering why he'd risk his life for an enemy soldier. Father Stephens came into view, and she waved him over.

"Good morning, Shelby."

"Good morning, Father. I have a favor."

"Ask away."

She pointed to the medical chart. "We don't know this man's name. I wonder if you can check his effects and let me know what you find about him."

He took a deep breath. "My, my. I'm sure you won't be the only interested party."

"What do you mean?"

"The MPs will be here soon enough. They always come when we get a North Korean."

"What happens to them?"

"They go to a prison camp. Well, then, I'll go at once to find out who he is."

CHAPTER TEN

He was having the strangest dreams, a convergence of the improbable as well as the impossible. He and his grandfather were fishing at a pond on the Princeton University campus, Albert Einstein instructing them in German while playing his violin. Now, Parker's adult sister and brother were talking while their father preached, their mother shushing them. Then he was seeing a patient in Hopewell who turned into a North Korean and took his receptionist Mrs. Albano hostage. Parker desperately tried to summon police help on a phone in which the numbers were mixed up, like random Scrabble tiles. The dreams took him on a wild ride over boisterous rapids, and in each one was another presence, strengthening, encouraging. He wondered if this might not be the Lord himself. He could face anything with the Lord nearby. And there was someone else with nearly purple eyes drawing him away from the chaotic dreamscape toward light, voices, and the smell of disinfectant.

Parker squinted against dagger-like light, using his hand as a shield and trailing IV lines. Pain ripped through his middle. He smelled blood. Voices mingled like an orchestra warming up, at first dissonant, then harmonizing. His chest tightened—was he in a North Korean hospital? What had happened to his grandfather, to the surgeon, and Ko? Were they here too? But wait. These were American voices. He turned his throbbing head toward them.

"Danny! The Korean's waking up!"

This had to be an American medical unit, perhaps a battalion aid or MASH—Danny obviously wasn't a Korean name. He opened his mouth, his lips weighing about five pounds, and discovered not only was his throat searing with pain, but he couldn't speak. What had happened to him? Why did his leg ache and his stomach feel ripped open and stitched back up? He broke out in a cold sweat.

A nurse bent over him, speaking slowly. "You are at a MASH. You are safe."

He wanted to tell her he spoke English, that he wasn't a North Korean officer, but there were no words. He didn't know what had happened to them. He began to hyperventilate, until he gazed upon her astonishingly blue eyes flecked with gold around the edges, pools of liquid peace. When she looked back at him all else faded, including his panic. He began to say something, his hand going to his throat, his body aching as if he'd bench pressed a thousand pounds.

Her hands slid into his. "You have had a hard time, but you are going to be all right." She shook her head, muttering, "I hope he understands English."

Parker squeezed her hand, hoping she'd know he meant to communicate, "I do understand!" He desired her to keep talking, so he could hear her voice, carrying on the breeze of a distant memory.

She angled her head to the right. "Wait. Do you understand English?"

He looked straight into those eyes, managing a feeble nod.

"Oh, good!"

He dozed off falling into her smile.

Danny walked over to them, peering down at the wounded soldier. "You said our patient was awake?"

"He was a minute ago. He's unable to talk, but he understands English. Oh, wait! He's coming to again."

The surgeon leaned into Parker, examining the wounds from top to bottom, focusing on the abdomen. Parker gritted his teeth against the pain.

"His fever indicates infection, although the wounds are clean. We'll have to keep an eye on that belly. It's also going to be a while before he's talking again."

Parker choked on an avalanche of fear, smothered by his muteness. What if he could never talk again? What if he couldn't practice medicine? What if he died? His blood pressure spiked.

"Is he okay, Doc?" A voice drifted from the next bed, Parker following the sound.

"He's stable. Shelby, increase the dose and timing of the antibiotics for the next two days and if his pain intensifies, give him additional morphine."

"Yes, Doctor."

Parker slipped back into edgy sleep.

When the fog of fever and medication subsided, every movement proved tortuous. At the sight of an American MP talking to a doctor while looking in Parker's direction, another fear assailed him. What if they took him to a prison camp? They appeared to be arguing. He had to let them know who he was, that he had only been posing as a North Korean to rescue his grandfather and Dr. Baroni. Not knowing what had become of them struck him as hard as the physical pain. He couldn't speak, but he could pray. *Please, Lord, help my grandfather, Ko, and the doctor. Watch over them wherever they may be. And help me to trust in you even here, especially here. Help me find a way to let them know I am one of them.*

He was unable to keep track of the amount of time he spent awake or the days he'd been here while nature took its healing course. Now he awakened around the sounds and smells of lunch being served to the other patients, and for the first time his stomach rumbled. He always used to tell his patients when they started to feel hungry, they were turning a corner. Might he be turning such a corner? Pain shot familiar darts into his stomach and throat, but his leg was no longer on fire. A thrill of hope enlivened his spirit.

As he watched the scene unfolding, suddenly she came into view, the nurse with the dazzling eyes. He watched her writing something on a chart and she paused, looking up as if she'd been interrupted. When her gaze reached Parker, her smile soothed him. She hung the clipboard on the other patient's bed and came to his side, a winsome, heaven-sent beauty.

"Well, look at you! You're awake."

She lifted his hand as if to check his pulse, his emotions experiencing a different kind of tenderness. She seemed to search his face, and in some unexplainable way, he felt drawn to her.

"Your pulse is almost normal," she said while popping a thermometer under his tongue. "Are you hungry?"

He smiled around the glass tube, noticing the endearing way she'd slipped her blonde hair behind her right ear.

"That's good. You're not up to solid food yet, but you're definitely heading in that direction." She removed the thermometer, looking up to read the number. "Ninety-nine. The antibiotics are doing their job. What's your pain level? Use your fingers to tell me—one is almost no pain, ten is the worst."

He raised eight fingers.

"That's still pretty high."

Parker managed to point his right index finger toward her.

She frowned, then brightened. "If you're asking what my name is, I'm Nurse Shelby. I'm hoping to find out your name as well."

Parker. Parker Tate. He closed his eyes, smiling. *Shelby. How unusual and pretty!* When he opened them, she was speaking to a man in a clerical collar, probably the unit's chaplain. *Might he know Andrew Frank?* He looked at the nurse, then toward the priest. After they'd conferred with each other they neared his bed, one on either side.

"Well, hello, Major Yi. I am Father Stephens, the chaplain here."

Determined to let them know he wasn't Yi, Parker moved his head back and forth, eyes closed. If only he could tell them!

"Oh." Stephens glanced at Shelby, now wide-eyed. He addressed Parker again. "Son, your name is Major Moon Soo Yi, is it not?"

He managed a guttural growl that cost him dearly. Shelby sat next to him on a chair and took his hand, Parker grasping her fingers as if for life itself.

"But we found that name among your identification," Stephens said.

"Excuse me, Father." Private Ward reached across to him from his bed.

"Yes, my son."

"I think he's trying to tell you he's not who you think he is." He pursed his lips. "I've had a strong feeling there's more to him than we know."

"Why do you say that?"

Shelby spoke. "Private Ward, this might be a good time to tell the Father your story."

Parker tried to shift his body to see who was talking, but pain tore through his middle. He vaguely recalled pushing someone away from an explosion, but maybe that was just another of his fever dreams.

Private Ward sat up. "He's the reason why I'm here and not in the morgue waiting to be shipped back to my folks in a box."

Stephens sat on the chair between the patients' beds, Parker catching a whiff of Old Spice. His brother John wore Old Spice. He wished he could tell the priest to sit further back so he could see the soldier's face. When Shelby spoke up, he marveled how she seemed to have anticipated his needs.

"Father Stephens, I wonder if you could move slightly so our patient can get a better view of Private Ward."

"Oh, yes, of course." He shifted. "Is this all right?"

Parker nodded his "yes."

"Hey, buddy," Ward said to Parker. "I'm happy to see you're awake."

Parker smiled toward him, wondering who he was.

"Well, Father, my unit came under sudden fire from the North Koreans. Everything had been pretty quiet until then. I remember seeing an old man and another guy in rags, and they were with a PKA heading toward our side. I was curious and immediately on guard, but before I knew it, I was underneath a burning Jeep with a broken leg." He knocked on the cast, making a hollow sound. "I saw him," he pointed toward Parker, "coming at me, and I figured I was a dead man. He started telling me in English to relax, and he would get me out of there. The fire was spreading, and I knew that vehicle was going to explode any minute. Just as he was freeing my leg, this North Korean comes over and starts yelling at him." He gestured toward Parker again. "He paid no attention and wouldn't stop helping me."

The scene replayed in Parker's mind. *I remember now. I am so happy he is alive.*

"Well, the PKA starts shooting up this guy, and I figured after what he'd done for me, I couldn't let that creep finish him off, so I nailed him. Next thing I knew, the Jeep had blown, and I was here, rather than kingdom come." He pointed toward Dr. Olsen. "That doc didn't want to operate on him first even though his wounds were ten times worse than mine, but I insisted."

Thank you. You are a kind man.

Father Stephens tapped an index finger against his chin. "What an extraordinary story! I wonder why you," and he looked at Parker, "would risk your life for your enemy."

Parker squeezed his lips together and closed his eyes, his heart pounding.

"I think you're upsetting him," Shelby said.

"I certainly don't mean to, but we have a mystery on our hands." He looked at Parker. "You say you are not Major Yi."

Parker moved his head on the pillow.

"Then who are you?" He sighed. "How soon before he can talk again, Nurse Shelby?"

"We don't know." She looked toward Parker. "Do you think you're strong enough to write? Oh, too bad. He's fallen asleep. Father, we'll have to try again later."

"In the meantime," Private Ward said, "try to keep those MPs away from him. He doesn't belong in a prison camp."

Shelby tucked the American soldier back under his covers. "You've both been through an ordeal. Get some sleep, and don't you worry about them."

He hated the dream, the agony of trying to reach his grandfather on the telephone only to be thwarted by those Scrabble-like numbers again. Instead, Parker hopped into his 1948 Chrysler Town and Country sedan and decided to drive to Korea, wondering how he'd get across the oceans. Did he have enough money for the trip? He drove the car onto a bridge, but halfway across the span ended, and the car hurtled toward the water. Parker awakened in a cold sweat just before impact. He took in the sight of two doctors and a handful of nurses checking other patients, writing on charts, administering medication. Where was Shelby? He craved her consoling, beautiful presence. He also wanted his Bible. His eyes fell upon the soldier he had rescued.

"Hey, my friend," Ward said. "I'm glad you're awake. You slept all morning, right through your sponge bath."

As he briefly considered this, he saw her. Had she bathed him? His face went crimson at the thought.

The soldier grinned. "She sure is pretty, isn't she?"

Parker flinched at the man's admiring gaze, but at least he had the good sense to notice.

Moments later, Shelby came over, wearing her signature smile. "Hello, men. How are we?" She consulted Ward's chart. "How's your leg? Is there any throbbing?"

"A little, but I'm not in pain."

"Good." She turned to Parker, removing his chart from the foot of the bed. "And how about you?"

If only he could communicate not just regarding the unremitting physical pain but his anxiety for his family and the urgency of letting these people know who he was. His eyes searched hers.

"Can I do something for you?" She sat next to him, placing his chart on her lap.

He gestured toward the clipboard.

"Yes, this is about you."

Parker pointed to the pen.

"Do you want me to write something?"

How frustrating this was, like those dreams with the telephone. He pointed back to himself.

"Do you want to write something?"

He reached for the pen.

When her hand touched his, he sighed with contentment. How kind and lovely she was, and she wore a gold cross. Might she be a Christian? *Focus, Parker. You only have so much strength.*

She flipped to the back of the pages to an empty spot and leaning close, held the clipboard steady. With every ounce of determination he possessed, Parker made a hash out of scribbling a few letters. When she examined his scrawl, she narrowed her eyes. "Let me see. 'I' something." She looked at him. "I. Is that right?"

Parker smiled.

"Okay. I, uh, 'am'... no, maybe it's 'mar'."

His temples throbbed. Three minutes later, her eyes opened wide as she repeated, "'I am American.'"

CHAPTER ELEVEN

Shelby tapped a pencil against her cheek, wondering who she might talk to about their intriguing Korean patient. Earlier in the day she'd wanted to show what he'd scrawled to the lurking MP, but some instinct held her back. He didn't seem like a tough guy, but his job was to guard North Korean patients and turn them into POWs as soon as they were well enough to leave. Then a convoy of wounded soldiers had demanded her attention. She guessed the most logical person to speak to would be Father Stephens, a repository of good will and given to unraveling knotted threads.

"Hey, you."

Shelby felt someone's breath on the top of her head and looked up from the nurses' desk to see Danny, his face and torso flecked with casting plaster. She grinned. "Did any of that get on the patient?"

Other doctors and nurses began their shift change, sliding past each other in the narrow main aisle.

"A little." He brushed at his scrubs. "I'm about to hit the showers, but I came to remind you of two things."

"Yes?"

"First, you need to clock out."

She couldn't resist a sassy comeback. "How does a swanky guy from Baltimore know about the working-class practice of clocking out?"

He snorted. "I must've failed to mention the summers during college when I worked construction."

"Good for you!"

"Yes, it was good for me."

"What's the second thing you want to tell me?" She set her pencil aside.

"You owe me a dance. I'll see you at the O Club after dinner."

Her mind was a hundred miles away from entertainment, but she managed an "Okay."

Danny smiled, and she waited for him to leave the ward before doing one more thing. She went over to the Korean, Private Ward looking up from a book and waving.

"I thought you'd left for the day. You sure do keep long hours."

"How are you feeling?"

"Good. How long am I going to be in this thing?" He knocked on the cast.

"Doctor Danielson thinks six weeks."

Ward groaned. "That's what I thought. Am I going to be here that long?"

"Once patients stabilize, we send them to Seoul or Tokyo to complete their recovery."

"I guess that's not too bad." His voice lowered. "Do you think they'll send me back to the front?"

"That depends on how well you heal." She gazed at him. "Do you want to go back?" She knew some wounded soldiers would sacrifice their eye teeth to avoid future battles.

"Honestly, I'd rather go home." He jerked a thumb toward the Korean. "What about him?"

She looked at the sleeping figure, as peaceful as a child, and she silently thanked God for the patient's reprieve from gnawing, constant pain. "I'm not sure. If you'll excuse me, I'm going to check on him before I leave."

"The new shift nurse just did."

She adjusted her Daisy Mae hat. "Well, I want to see for myself on my way out."

Shelby went to the other side of the Korean's bed and gazed at his placid, handsome features. He seemed to be smiling which brought out dimples she hadn't noticed before. *Dimples.* Her skinned pricked with a sense of déjà vu. The patient's eyes fluttered open and when they rested on her gaze, her breath hitched. *Could this be the man I met on the troopship?* Her heart thundered in her ears as she clawed through a tangle of thoughts.

She put on her best professional voice to cover her emotions. "You seem to be resting nicely. Are you in much pain? Use your fingers to tell me, one for not too much, two for yes, three for ... well, you get the idea."

He lifted his left hand and held up three fingers.

She reached for his chart. "Much better! I see Nurse Evelyn gave you pain medication a couple of hours ago. I, uh, am about to go off my shift. Well, I, uh, guess I'll see you tomorrow."

Before she knew what was happening, the Korean reached up and touched the cross she was wearing.

She took a step back. "D-do you like my cross?"

He nodded his head.

"My grandparents gave it to me." *Why is he so interested in my cross?* "It symbolizes my faith."

When he lightly pressed his finger back at himself twice, she gasped. "Are you trying to say you're also a Christian?"

His smile, and the dimples, reappeared.

"Nurse Shelby, your shift is over." Major McKaig peered down at her.

"Yes, ma'am." She jumped up, her heart pounding.

Danny was a good dancer, and unlike some of the other MASH personnel, tended to be temperate with alcohol. She allowed herself to let go of the day's stress when they jitterbugged and enjoyed his closeness as they slow danced. The coziness she felt, however, was like dancing with her dad or an uncle. "Long Ago and Far Away" filled the O Club, and she wondered, if Danny were a Christian, would she love him then? He checked all the rest of the boxes for her ideal man. Then again, if she really loved him, wouldn't she do so whether he believed or not? Couldn't she help bring him to faith in Christ? Maybe she wasn't giving him enough of a chance.

Past the other couples, Shelby noticed a lone figure who'd just entered the club, seeming to have blown in with a gust of wind. He quickly shut the door and stood peering into the crowd as if he were looking for someone. When she circled back around in mid-dance, she noticed the man was Father Stephens. He was waving toward her, using his eyes to communicate, "I need to speak with you." She lifted her right index finger, wondering what the priest had on his mind. She'd been wanting to talk to him, too, ever since the Korean patient had told her in so many words he was an American and a Christian.

She broke away from Danny's embrace. "Father Stephens just came in and needs to talk to me. Will you excuse me?"

The physician frowned. "Well, okay, but don't be too long."

She balked at his possessiveness and moved through the crowd, meeting the priest near the door. Frigid air inflicted itself on her as she pulled her parka around herself. "Hello, Father."

"I'm sorry to interrupt your evening out." He looked in Danny's direction where the doctor had sat next to Neil Olsen at a table.

"That's all right."

"I wouldn't have done so if I didn't have something important to tell you. How about if we go to the office? Corporal Unger is out tonight, so we'll have some privacy."

The chaplain sat in the company clerk's chair, and Shelby took the other seat in the office dominated by olive drab filing cabinets and telecommunications equipment. On Unger's neatly-made bunk lay a copy of a Batman comic.

Stephens adjusted his wire-rimmed glasses. "This is about Major Yi, or maybe I should just call him our Korean friend."

Shelby's heart thumped. "I also have something to tell you about him."

"You do?"

"Yes, Father, but you go first."

"I thought you should know I discovered some mighty interesting things while going through his belongings. First, he only had two items on him. Most soldiers who come through here have far more things like wallets, photos, and letters from back home."

"What did you find?"

He pulled a small leather book from inside his coat and pushed it toward Shelby.

Her eyes widened. "The Holy Bible?"

"Not only is that the first Bible I've ever seen on a North Korean, but it's in English."

She leafed through the pocket-sized edition searching for further clues. The Bible wasn't new, the edges were worn, and the tissue-like paper bore finger smudges. She frowned. "There's no title page. Don't Bibles always have a place to write your name?"

He reached for the book and pointed inside. "Look at this."

She leaned closer, following the tracing of his finger against one of the first pages. "It's as if he deliberately removed his name."

"Exactly. Now for the other thing." Father Stephens produced the Korean's identification papers. "I've seen any number of PKA documents, and there's something amiss about this one. The signature is on the right. All the others I've seen are in the middle."

"What does this mean to you, Father?"

"If I'm not mistaken, his identification was forged. I don't think he is this Major Yi."

The information swirled then settled around and between them. Shelby started bouncing her right foot in place. Her instincts were being proven right.

"Now then, you said you have something to tell me."

"I do, Father. Two rather curious things happened today. First, our Korean friend wrote on his chart with great effort that he's an American."

Father Stephens shot up from his seat and stood there, suspended in seeming disbelief.

"That's all I was able to get out of him because the effort cost him dearly. Right before I went off my shift, he reached for my cross and managed to 'tell' me he is also a Christian."

The chaplain resumed his seat. "Glory be. That certainly would explain why he has a Bible." He paused. "It also speaks of great courage."

Shelby was tingling. "The kind that would rescue a soldier from a burning Jeep while being shot at?"

"Precisely. If he is a believer, and for some reason was posing as a North Korean, he took a great risk in carrying a Bible." He lowered his voice. "Could he be a spy?"

She blew out a breath, staring past ice crystals lacing the windows. "If he's not Major Yi, if he is an American, just who is he?"

The priest clapped his right fingers into his left palm. "We have to find out before he gets dragged off to a prison camp."

CHAPTER TWELVE

Parker had always maintained an even emotional keel, and truly, life hadn't knocked him around much. He'd enjoyed mostly good health with barely-worth-mentioning colds and childhood scraped knees. He'd never had surgery, not even a cavity. Nothing had prepared him for this abject helplessness and constant pain. One minute he'd been in the fullness of health, the next, bullets and shrapnel had rendered him mute, hamstrung, and with a gaping belly wound. Initially, he'd been too out of it to fathom the severity of his condition. Now the pain meds were gradually being reduced, and he was managing to move more without continual suffering.

He also was beginning to take greater notice of his surroundings, a dull but clean MASH unit with a dozen or so patients and their khaki and white-clad medical team. At times, the sound of music from someone's radio drifted into the ward from outside. The place bore a striking resemblance to the 8063rd he'd been assigned to just days ago. Or had the time been longer? Parker chafed at not knowing such a basic thing as what day it was.

Was the almost constant presence of an MP roughly the size of King Kong about himself, or might there be another

North Korean prisoner-patient? When their eyes had met on one occasion, Parker had shrunk inwardly at the soldier's frostiness. Even if there was a true PKA prisoner here, Parker was clearly in this MP's sites.

Everyone else treated him kindly except for one surgeon who openly expressed his lack of time for commies depriving American and South Korean soldiers of beds. Parker wondered whether Nurse Shelby had believed his scribbled message about being an American and his feeble attempt to let her know he was a Christian. The way she had reached for his hand and smiled had been a good sign. He let his mind rest there rather than drift on the edge of dread about his fate as a perceived PKA soldier.

When that specter wasn't rearing its ugly head, he wrestled with the suffocation of not being able to speak. How much damage had his vocal chords sustained? If he could speak doctor-to-doctor with the elegant physician who treated Parker as well as any other patient, he might be able to perform his own diagnosis. If he were left without a voice, how could he as a mute physician compensate? There was no end to worries assaulting him, especially not knowing the status of his grandfather, Dr. Baroni, and Ko. Were they safe in the arms of the UN forces, or had they been recaptured, or worse?

When the enemy of his thoughts came in like a flood, he was learning to depend on God to raise up a standard against the foe. He yearned for his Bible, but minus its physical presence, he reached into his memory for verses to minister to his spirit. His favorite was the twenty-third Psalm. He repeated the words so frequently he was absorbing its assurance of the Shepherd's constant presence in this valley of shadows. Other promises came to mind, including the verse from Philippians, "I can do all things through Christ who strengthens me."

Additional balm came in the form of Nurse Shelby. He couldn't quite explain why he felt this way, but there was something of recognition between them whenever their eyes met. Did she experience the same thing, or was she just as kind to all her other patients?

The scent of eggs, toast, and coffee drifted from his neighbor's tray. Parker tried not to stare at Jim Ward, who wolfed down his food in a few hungry bites, not wanting to appear as woeful as he felt. He had drifted back to sleep wondering how much weight he'd dropped since being here, being sustained by intravenous nourishment. He'd have to spring for some new clothes once this ordeal was over, if he didn't end up wearing prison attire.

An hour or so later, his eyes flickered open, and he took in the welcome figures of Nurse Shelby and Father Stephens.

"Well, look at that smile. I'm happy to see you in a good frame of mind," the priest said.

I am whenever I see her.

"How are you feeling?" Shelby asked.

When she lifted his wrist to check his pulse, her touch created tenderness in his chest. Was it any coincidence he heard the song "Unforgettable" playing in the background? This woman most certainly was.

"Now let's see about your temperature." She placed the familiar glass tube under his tongue and chattered about the weather while waiting for the reading.

"I never liked the cold," Father Stephens said, "especially in January. Winter without Christmas has none of the holiday's charms."

"Where are you from, Father?" she asked.

"Ohio, near Dayton. What about yourself?"

Parker's ears perked, hungry for details about her life.

"I'm from a small city—Easton, Pennsylvania. It's on the Delaware River an hour north of Philadelphia."

I know where that is! It is also an hour north of Princeton.

"So, your winters are about like ours," the priest said.

"I suppose so." She smiled at Parker. "I always liked winter. My family and I would go sledding and ice skating. Once in a while, we'd go skiing, but with four children and my father a teacher, that was not an everyday thing."

He caressed this information about her. She was a Christian. She came from a place not far from Hopewell. Her father was a teacher, and she had four siblings.

Shelby extracted the thermometer and grinned. "Ninety-eight point six. You're normal!"

"Oh, what good news!" Father Stephens clapped his hands. "Now, then, my son, I have some things to show you." He sat next to Parker's bunk while Shelby took the chair on the other side.

The chaplain took a black leather Bible from inside his coat and presented it to him. Parker's eyes widened and misted as he clutched the Bible to his heart, unaware of the look passing between the nurse and minister.

"I'm happy to have been able to return this to you," Stephens said. "How curious it's in English, like an American would have."

Parker smiled and nodded, hoping his identity was becoming clearer to them.

"There's something else."

When he saw the identification paper, Parker shook his head and grunted what he hoped sounded like "no."

Shelby touched his arm, her voice soothing. "Doctor Danielson doesn't want you straining your throat. We'll do the talking for you. We think you're trying to tell us the person on this paper isn't you. But was it ever someone you portrayed?" She cocked her head to the side.

He managed a sigh.

She drew a breath then released it. "Oh, I wish you could tell us."

"Perhaps he can."

"How Father?"

"I have a notion to make up an alphabet and have him point to letters to form words. It might be less difficult for him than writing. Might that work for you?"

Parker smiled his agreement. With his limited strength, however, he'd have to choose what he said carefully, beginning with who he was. Then he could go on to more details, like the whereabouts of those he'd tried to rescue.

"Very well. I'll be back after lunch. Don't worry, my son. Count on Nurse Shelby and me to sort this out." He made the sign of the cross over Parker and left.

Shelby smiled, revealing straight white teeth and the scent of something like peppermint. "I don't have to go just yet. Would you like me to read from your Bible?"

He closed his eyes and smiled, resting against the pillow.

"What shall I read?" She looked up at the ceiling, then back at him. "Since I don't know your favorite books or passages, I'll start with some Psalms. I know they're my favorites, especially whenever I'm going through a hard thing."

He wondered, besides the daily stresses of being a surgical nurse in a war zone, what difficulties she might have faced in her young life. She seemed so innocent and unspoiled. A desire rose in him to protect her from all harm.

She leafed toward the middle, handling the delicate pages like the sacred writings they were. "Here we are. I love Psalm 34. 'I will bless the Lord at all times: his praise shall continually be in my mouth. My soul shall make her boast in the Lord: the humble shall hear thereof, and be glad. O magnify the Lord with me, and let us exalt his name together. I sought the Lord, and he heard me, and delivered me from all my fears. They looked unto him, and were lightened: and their faces were not ashamed. This poor man cried, and the Lord heard him, and saved him out of all his troubles. The angel of the Lord encampeth around about them that fear him, and delivereth them. O taste and see that the Lord is good: blessed is the man that trusteth in him.'"

Parker had just settled into a pocket of peace when a shadow passed over them.

"You're wasting your time on this one, Nurse Shelby." Dr. Olsen was sneering.

"Oh, I don't think so."

Parker watched the exchange.

"He probably can't understand a word. You're just throwing pearls after swine."

"If you will excuse me, Captain, I'm going to continue casting these pearls."

He sniffed and walked away, Parker's eyes glistening with the first mirth he'd experienced in many weeks. When Shelby winked at him, he would have laughed out loud if he could have. She certainly had spunk.

"Just ignore him," she said. "I often do."

This wasn't difficult when he had her to focus on. She continued reading, for how long he wasn't sure because he fell asleep listening to her lilting voice conveying the Word of the Lord. By the time she prayed for him, he was back in dreamland.

"Now then, I know this doesn't look like much, but I hope it works." Father Stephens sat on Parker's right with Shelby on the other side.

Parker noticed she was wearing woolen gloves with the fingers cut out, and a matching scarf encircled her neck. He knew from the expressions and exclamations of the doctors, nurses, and other staff how bitter the temperature was outside. Shelby had made sure Parker had two extra blankets, and she always kept two pairs of socks on his feet. Was she warm enough? How were her living conditions? His milieu was doctor to patient, not this other way around. He fought a rising sense of helplessness, willing his mind and emotions toward the present task.

Father Stephens produced a piece of cardboard fashioned from a box of medical supplies. "I'm afraid the letters aren't as dark as I would have liked, but I did the best I could with crayons. I like to share them with the orphans, you know."

Shelby leaned closer to the board. "I can see the letters quite well." She turned her eyes on Parker. "Can you?"

"Here you go, son."

The priest handed the board to Parker, who took it with his left hand. He could see everything clearly.

"I have an idea," Shelby said. "I'll hold the board for him. That way, he can point with either hand."

"Good idea!"

Father Stephens handed a pencil to Parker. "Now then, I suggest since you have limited physical energy, we start with your name."

He lifted the pencil and pointed to the "P."

"P?" Shelby asked.

He gave a terse nod.

Next, he gestured toward "A," and after repeating the letter, the priest wrote it down.

By the time they got to the last "R," Parker needed to rest.

"Are you finished?" she asked. "I mean for now?"

He closed his eyes, and Father Stephens read aloud, "Parker. Your name is Parker. I wonder what your first name is."

He frowned.

"Parker isn't your last name?"

He formed "no" with his lips.

"Let's give him a moment," Stephens said.

They waited in silence until Parker nodded toward the board Shelby held ready for him. He proceeded to point to the four letters of his last name.

"Tate," the priest said. "Your last name is Tate?"

"Is your name Parker Tate?" Shelby asked.

Although his head throbbed, he smiled at the golden sound of his name on her lips.

"Well, then, perhaps we should call it a day," the priest said. "This gives us a lot to go by, and you need your rest."

Parker's eyelids drooped, but there was one more name he needed to convey. He pointed to the board.

"I think he needs to tell us something else," Shelby said.

"All right, my son, if you feel you must."

With his last bit of strength, he began spelling the letters F-R-A-N-K.

Shelby looked up from the board. "Frank? I wonder who or what this means."

"We won't being finding out just now," the chaplain said. "Parker Tate has just fallen asleep."

CHAPTER THIRTEEN

Shelby lingered in the mess tent, sipping coffee by the wood burning stove while the KP crew clattered pots, pans, and food trays. *Parker Tate. That's not a Korean name, although Park is. I wonder if his current name is his birth name, or if he Americanized it at some point.*

Several Korean nationals who worked at the 8055th had taken American-style names to simplify the complexity of their culture's naming and pronunciation.

He said he's an American. I remember distinctly the man I encountered on the troopship had an accent. How strange it would be if he's the same guy, but then what was he doing in a PKA uniform? If it is him, is he some kind of spy?

Shelby looked up at the canvas ceiling twitching in the wind. Danny had told her just today Parker might regain his voice in a few weeks. The throat wound was healing as well as could be expected. If the scarring remained in check, the surgeon also predicted within a week Parker might be able to eat pureed foods and liquids.

Her imagination ran wild. *If he were acting as a spy, that would explain why he endangered himself to save an American soldier.*

She glanced about, grateful no one could read such juvenile thoughts. Was she becoming her brother Neil with his penchant for Hardy Boys novels? Still, there was something about this Parker Tate, so unlike any other soldier she'd nursed. No matter his story, she'd felt inexplicably drawn to him from the get-go.

Her roommate's voice caused her to jump.

"Man, you're skittish! I thought you'd have left by now."

"I'm still here."

Vickie rubbed her gloved hands near the fire. "In reality, you're a million miles away."

Before she could check herself, she blurted, "I'm thinking about that Korean patient."

She huffed, looking upward. "You're always thinking about him."

Her comment was a wasp sting, and she stopped short of saying, "I do not." In her heart, however, Shelby knew Vickie was right. She had considered telling her what had happened today, but not now.

"I'm headed to the O Club. Wanna come and think about something else for a change?"

The door swung open and Father Stephens blew in with the wind, his eyes brightening. "There you are! I've been looking for you. Oh, hello, Vickie."

"Hello, Father. We were just about to go to the O Club."

"You were about to go," Shelby said.

Stephens looked from Vickie to Shelby. "Well, I do have something to tell you, but it shouldn't take long. That is, if you have time."

Flush with excitement, she urged the nurse out the door. "Sure, Father. Go ahead, Vickie. I'll catch up with you later."

"I know when I'm being dismissed."

After she left, Father Stephens sat down. "Vickie seems put out by my interruption."

"Don't worry about her. She's just that way." She leaned forward. "You're all lit up as my mother used to say when I was little and excited about something."

"Funny, my mother used to say the same thing. Well, yes, I am rather excited. I think I know what Parker Tate was trying to tell us before he fell asleep."

Her senses heightened. "You do?"

"I kept racking my brain before suddenly remembering there's a chaplain named Frank in another MASH."

"First name or last?"

"Last. I'm afraid I can't recall his first name."

"Do you know him at all?"

"I've met him a couple of times. Nice chap."

She tented her hands. "Why would Parker be trying to tell us about a minister?"

"I find this very curious indeed, Shelby, but I think this may be yet another indication he isn't North Korean."

She breathed deeply before diving into the deep end. "Father, I'm pretty sure I've seen Parker Tate before."

His voice rose a pitch. "When? Where?"

She waited for some nurses who were laughing outside the thin mess tent wall to pass before disclosing her experience on the *Beaudoin*.

"How extraordinary! What makes you think Parker was the same man?"

"I know this is going to sound silly, but he has the same smile. When he smiles, he gets these dimples ..." Her voice trailed, her cheeks pinking.

The priest's eyebrows rose, along with his chin. "I see. Well, when I talk to him again, I'll not only ask if he was referring to Chaplain Frank, I'll also find out if he was on that troopship."

She peered into his eyes. "When will you see him?"

He laughed. "Now seems like a good time."

"I can go with you."

He smiled. "You've already put in a full shift. I can come and go more freely."

She appreciated his unspoken discretion. "Will you let me know as soon as you can?"

"I will do just that."

An hour after Shelby's conversation with the priest, he found her in the O club nursing a Coke. While Vickie and some other nurses were talking a mile a minute and tapping their feet to Benny Goodman, Shelby was staring into the distance. When she saw him, she perked up.

"Do you have news?"

"Yes, and Colonel Sheppard has asked to see us both in his office."

"Colonel Sheppard?" She'd expected him to say something about Parker, not the CO.

She grabbed her coat and bade a hasty good-bye to her fellow nurses, ignoring Vickie's glare. As she followed Father Stephens across the frozen compound, she wondered why he was being so quiet. Had something gone wrong? Was she in trouble? When they reached the colonel's office, Shelby swallowed hard when she saw Major McKaig positioned at the commander's left. She felt about six years old and having just been sent to the principal's office.

"Father, Nurse Shelby, have a seat." Sheppard motioned with his right hand to a pair of chairs across from his desk.

Despite his avuncular demeanor, Shelby trembled.

"The good father tells me we have a mystery on our hands, and you both have uncovered what may be a significant clue."

"Y-yes, sir," she said.

"You believe our Korean patient isn't PKA but was for some reason unbeknown to either of you posing as one."

"Yes, sir."

"He told me the reasons why you both consider him an American." Sheppard rose from his desk, absently touching a photo of his wife and children. "Naturally, I don't want to hand one of ours over to the MPs, but I need to make darn sure we're not being taken. It's no small matter to harbor the enemy."

Shelby wanted to spring to Parker's defense but held her tongue. This felt like knowing the answer to a question, but the teacher hasn't called on you.

"This may be providential, as you would say, Padre," Sheppard continued. "Not an hour ago I got a call from the 8063rd asking if we could spare any penicillin. They're only operating on a day's supply and replacements can't get to them for three days. Seems they have a new company clerk, and there's been a snafu with a requisition form."

Shelby tingled, leaping to his conclusion.

"I've asked the good father if he'd take medicine over there and maybe bring you along so you can talk to Chaplain Frank."

Ah! Parker must've told Father Stephens he had been referring to the MASH chaplain.

"Major McKaig also has given her consent."

Shelby restrained herself from throwing her arms around the woman. She settled for an earnest, "Thank you, ma'am."

"This may be a wild goose chase, you know," McKaig said, "but I find myself hoping you won't be disappointed. The Korean patient is a nice man. With all the pain he's been in, he's never been unpleasant. Nurse Shelby, while you're there, you may be called upon to help out, and I expect you to conduct yourself with decorum. You are representing the 8055th."

"Yes, Major, I will." Her heart pounded.

"I'm having Neil prepare the supplies and Jeep now," Sheppard said. "You can leave as soon as you get yourselves in order. Better dress especially warmly. I don't want either of you getting frostbite or suffering from exposure. You could, of course, wait until morning."

Father Stephens looked at Shelby, who smiled. "Thank you, sir. We prefer to leave as soon as possible. We're both grateful for the trust you're placing in our intuition."

"I just hope you're proven correct."

Shelby piled on an additional sweater and two pairs of socks plus her Army-issue hat with fur ear flaps. She jotted a hasty note to Vickie about where she was going, slipping the envelope under the nurse's pillow. If she had a moment to spare she'd slip over to tell Parker where she was going. When the company clerk knocked on the door, she realized there wasn't going to be time.

"Father Stephens is waiting in the Jeep," Neil Unger said. "Can I carry anything for you?"

"Thank you. I'm ready."

The 8063rd compound was almost devoid of personnel, Shelby guessing they were all hunkered down inside various buildings. She hugged herself, bouncing up and down on her feet to keep warm while Father Stephens uncovered the stash of boxes and picked one up.

"Let's take this to the CO and let him know we're here. Then we can ask him where to find the chaplain."

"Okay, Father." Her breath suspended in a crystalline haze.

When a gust blew them into the main office, the company clerk jumped up to shield the papers on his desk.

"Oh, please forgive me, son," Stephens said. "The wind truly is wicked."

The young man, who looked about the age of Shelby's oldest brother Keith, looked up. Seeing the priest's collar, he grinned as he resettled his paperwork. "That's okay, Father. You couldn't help it." He glanced at Shelby.

"I'm Father Stephens and this is Lieutenant Kichline from the 8055th. Colonel Sheppard sent us with a supply of penicillin."

"I'm Mike Howden. You guys are life savers. I'll go tell Colonel Borsch." He jerked his thumb toward an inner door. "He's just inside."

Shelby watched the door swung open and saw cigar smoke drifting from the room. Moments later, a heavyset man with steel gray hair emerged, a stogie clamped in his teeth.

"Well, hello, Father Stephens!" He thrust his hand toward the priest. "How good of you to pay us a visit, especially on such a bitter cold night!"

"We are well aware emergencies are no respecter of the weather. Besides, you've assisted us when we've had our own shortages. Colonel Borsch, may I introduce Nurse Kichline?"

"Hello, Lieutenant."

She did the only thing she could think of in the presence of this bulldog commanding officer—she saluted.

"At ease, my dear. At ease."

"We have several boxes of penicillin in the Jeep just outside," Father Stephens said.

"Howden, go bring them in. Grab one of the motor pool fellows if you need help." He turned to his guests. "Would you care for a drink?"

"Perhaps a cup of coffee," Stephens said.

"I'll direct you to the mess tent."

"Um, first sir, we have also come on an errand to see your chaplain."

"Frank? I'm afraid you just missed him." Borsch scratched his ram-like head. "The da-uh-darndest thing, he just went to Seoul to pick up penicillin from the Army hospital. Our supply was that low, and we didn't imagine you'd get here so quickly."

Shelby's jaw dropped, Father Stephens rubbed the back of his neck. She couldn't believe their bad timing.

"When do you expect him back?"

"Oh, probably tomorrow morning."

"It is imperative we see him. Might we make ourselves useful to you while we wait? That is, if we may wait?"

"Certainly, Father, but you might want to get some shuteye first. We can put you up in the VIP tent and Lieutenant Kichline with the other nurses." His dark eyes narrowed. "I'm curious why you have to see Frank."

"It's about one of our patients, a rather complicated situation."

"I see." The colonel leaned against a bookshelf, which creaked. "Might I assist you?"

Father Stephens looked toward Shelby, who shrugged as if to say, "Might as well."

Shelby caught the sound of doctors and nurses at work in the neighboring post-op ward.

"Now then, tell me about this patient of yours." He cradled his hands behind his head.

"He came to us about a week ago," Father Stephens began. "He'd been shot several times and sustained a throat injury, which has rendered him temporarily speechless."

Borsch regarded him with a look Shelby thought bordered on impatience.

"He came in with another wounded soldier and immediately caused a stir because he was in a North Korean uniform. The wounded American said the PKA saved his life." Father Stephens unrolled the rest of the story.

"Interesting, Father." Borsch blew smoke from his cigar.

"Nurse Shelby has been taking care of the Korean, who scribbled that he's an American. I was intrigued and went through his personal inventory where I found a small Bible. This astonished me because how many North Korean officers carry Bibles?"

Borsch's eyes narrowed, and Shelby wondered if he was growing more interested or more impatient. She wanted to jump in, to mention how she had read the Bible to Parker and prayed with him, but she didn't want to interrupt Father Stephens. Nor was she sure the colonel would be interested in Parker's religious faith.

"We just learned a few other important things. First, he wanted us to contact Chaplain Frank. Second, his name isn't Major Yi, it's Parker Tate."

Shelby's chair shook when Colonel Borsch blasted off from his seat, his cigar tumbling out of his mouth. She gaped at Father Stephens, who returned the same look.

"Tate? Did you say Parker Tate?"

CHAPTER FOURTEEN

He was asleep more than not, often left to wonder if he was awakening to a new or the same day. The smell of eggs and toast, the winter sun leaking through the post-op's frozen glass, told him this was morning. He saw the back of a nurse nearby and his senses heightened, then faded into disappointment. She wasn't Shelby. Her shoulders were broader, her hair dark. When she turned and smiled, he greeted her with a polite upturn of his lips and looked past her. He didn't know how, but the woman seemed to have read his mind.

"Good morning. I'm Nurse Evelyn, and I've taken care of you before. I'm guessing you're looking for Shelby. She and Father Stephens had to go to the 8063rd, but I expect they'll be back this afternoon."

His pulse quickened. Had they gone to see Chaplain Frank? Were they chasing down the scant clues he'd been able to provide about his identity? If so, the ever-present threat of prison camp, and the ever-lurking MP, would vanish. He might even find out sooner rather than later what had become of Ko, Baroni, and his grandfather. Might they be able to get word to his family of his whereabouts and condition? He hated how worry about him might be setting his mother's health back. Even so, hope surged through his veins. He tried to clear phlegm from his throat desiring he could talk to the kind nurse.

"I wish I could offer you breakfast, but you don't have orders yet for clear liquids." She patted his hand, staring at him. "You seem a bit thick in your throat. I'll have the doctor take a look."

Private Ward's voice drifted to him from the adjoining bunk. "I can't imagine going without food as long as he has. I wish I could give him some of mine."

"You have a good heart, Ward," the nurse said, "especially since he's a North Korean."

The private hitched himself onto his elbow. "I think you may have the wrong end of that stick, Nurse Evelyn."

"I did hear he saved your life."

"That's right, and as far as I'm concerned, he's my friend, not the enemy."

Taking his tray from an orderly, she arranged it on Ward's lap.

The soldier reached for the mug of coffee. "So, when will he be able to eat?"

Parker listened closely to her response, his stomach growling. Even powdered eggs from an Army mess tent made his mouth water.

"I don't know, but soon I hope."

Moments after she left, his doctor joined them. "Hey there, Yi. I understand your throat is giving you some trouble."

Parker grunted.

"Okay, let's have a look." Danny bent down, his white coat draping over Parker's right side.

He opened his mouth, allowing the tongue depressor to probe until he started gagging. The doctor straightened.

"Sorry to cause such distress. These exams can't be easy for you.

"You do seem to have some new thickness. Are you having any difficulty breathing?"

Parker considered the question. Yes, come to think of it, he was a bit breathless. He raised a hand, bringing his forefinger and thumb almost together.

"I think there may be a scar forming from your shrapnel wound, but don't worry. I'm going to keep an eye on it, and you let us know if the discomfort gets worse." He chuffed. "I know you can't talk, but you can always wave us down or throw something at us."

He knew a vague medical answer when he heard one.

The doctor looked to the nightstand. "I see you're reading the Bible."

Parker pointed to Danny as if to ask, "Do you?"

"What? Do I read it? I used to. My mom took me to Sunday School, and I got stickers for memorizing verses." His gaze was far away, perhaps back in those innocent childhood days. "I don't have a Bible here, but if I'm an American I believe in God, right? It's in the water."

Parker knew Danny's type, a casual believer who acknowledged a Creator without any personal connection to him. He glanced at the alphabet board, wishing he could talk to the doctor at length, wanting also to tell Danny he was a doctor. There was so much he wanted to say but couldn't with a thimble's worth of energy and no voice.

"All right, then. Let me see what I can do to help you."

Parker watched Danny speak with Olsen, the obnoxious surgeon, and Nurse Evelyn. If only he could consult one-on-one with them, he could get a more comprehensive view of his injuries and prognosis for recovery. He needed Shelby and the priest to clear up the confusion about who he really was. For now, he strained to hear above the clanging of food trays, managing scraps of conversation—"needs more than we can give here," "an obstruction," "he's okay," and "he's got you snookered. You can't trust those PKAs."

Bristling, he wondered how much Shelby might have told Danny. He had watched them work closely together, knowing they'd made plans at least one time to meet at the officer's club. He'd never seen her look at him with anything but friendly interest, but maybe he was just indulging in wishful thinking. Danny was a decent enough fellow, but there was no way he was right for a woman with Shelby's deep faith. Parker hoped she would agree.

In the far corner, the MP caught Parker's eye and sniggered.

Parker struggled past an even bigger lump in his throat when Jim Ward reached out to shake his hand in farewell. The soldier started to say something, stopped, and looked down at his feet.

"I'll never forget you, my friend. I hope you'll always remember Jim Ward from Tulsa, Oklahoma, who's going to manage the family shoe store when he gets home."

Despite his tight control, Parker tasted a salted tear. He and Ward were bound to each other for life, even if they never saw each other again.

"Okay, you two." Evelyn got behind Ward's wheelchair to take him away.

Parker motioned with his hand, hoping his friend could understand the unspoken question, "Where are you going?"

"I'm going to the Army hospital in Seoul. Depending on how my leg heals, I'll either be back at the front or going home. I'll find a way to let you know."

"Thank you," Parker formed with his lips.

"You bet."

Colonel Sheppard came into view, reaching out to shake Ward's hand. "I just came by to see you off, son. You've been a model patient, and I wish you the best of luck. Those doctors in Seoul will get you back on your feet before you know it."

"Thank you, sir." He inclined his head toward Parker. "Please do me a favor—take good care of my friend. He's a good man."

"Will do," Sheppard said.

Ward shot Parker a final smile, and Nurse Evelyn rolled the soldier to a waiting ambulance. The colonel unexpectedly sat in the chair between his and Parker's beds.

"I just want you to know my chaplain and one of my best nurses are even now trying to find out exactly who you are. I have a couple questions about you, but I know Father Stephens well enough to give him the benefit of any number of doubts."

Parker gulped, nearly choking on his saliva.

"I promise we'll get to the bottom of your identity, and nothing will happen to you that shouldn't—if you get my meaning." The colonel's glance took in the MP's presence.

Parker gazed into the man's eyes, taken aback when Colonel Sheppard guffawed. "I never saw a North Korean come in here with a Bible before." He patted Parker's good leg and left.

The lack of Jim Ward's presence, along with Shelby and Father Stephens's absence, left a void in Parker's spirit. Seeing his Bible on the chair to his left, he maneuvered himself with painful difficulty to reach the leather book. He was exhausted from the effort but laid back and opened to the Psalms where Shelby had left off. He began reading of the travails and trust of Israel's shepherd king until he fell asleep. Again.

Parker awakened with a start, his throat aflame. His ears rang, and the room seemed to close in on him. Colonel Sheppard was talking in the near distance with Danny and Olsen, the latter pointing in his direction.

"I think that commie has you both hoodwinked."

"Captain Olsen, if I didn't know any better, I would think you are calling me a bad judge of character."

"Of course not, sir." The doctor seemed to back pedal.

"I don't happen to agree with your assessment. What about you, Danny?"

"I'm trying to keep an open mind, Colonel. He's a decent fellow, and he did put himself in harm's way to save an American. Nurse Shelby and Father Stephens seem to think he's on our side."

"What a liar," Olsen muttered.

"What was that?" Sheppard asked.

"Uh, nothing, sir."

"You bet it was nothing. I think once the padre and Shelby get back, we'll be getting all the answers we need. In the meantime, what's with his condition?"

"Everything but the throat wound is healing normally," Danny said. "He has a recurring, residual fever, which is why he's sleeping so much. When I examined him earlier,

I noticed a growing obstruction in his throat. He had a lot of phlegm, and he was clearly uncomfortable. The best I can do is trach him if he stops breathing. None of us here is familiar with the procedure to repair his overall problem, and let's face it, our conditions aren't ideal."

Parker willed himself to stay awake enough to continue listening and breaking down their assessments, dire as they were.

"There are specialists in Seoul and at Tokyo General," the colonel said. "Danny, I'd like you to consult with them and report back to me. We'll make a decision once we get more direction about his treatment." He paused, shaking his head. "I'd prefer not to move him until Father Stephens can tell us one way or the other just whose side this Korean is on."

"I agree," Danny said. "If he is an American, we'd do him a grave injustice to treat him like the enemy."

Olsen looked down at his feet.

"In the meantime, I'm going to have a talk with that MP," Colonel Sheppard said. "I can't have him skulking around here anymore. He gives me the heebie jeebies."

Parker let out a weak breath, his emotions jackknifing between hope and utter despair.

Not an hour later, Parker awakened to shaking limbs and a sensation of choking. Although the effort cost him, he growled to draw Nurse Evelyn's attention. When she hurried over to him, he put his hand to his throat, his eyes bugging.

"Oh dear. You're not doing well at all, are you?"

Parker needed his Bible, his hands clutching at the bedding until he located the lifeline.

The nurse waved Danny over. “Doctor, please come quickly.”

By now Parker’s heart rate had skyrocketed. Was this the end, all he would get to experience of life? *Yea, though I walk through the valley of the shadow of death, I will fear no evil for thou art with me ...”*

Danny’s form blocked out everyone else. Darkness was falling over the earth.

“I’m going to perform a trach, but we need to evac him to Seoul as quickly as possible.”

“What about Tokyo?” Evelyn asked.

“He won’t make it to Tokyo. Prepare my instruments.” He turned toward Major McKaig, who had responded to the emergency. “Nancy, we have to send this patient to Seoul, stat. Inform Colonel Sheppard, and tell Unger we need a chopper.”

“Yes, doctor.” Major McKaig hurried toward the exit.

Parker gazed up at Danny, choking, his eyes pleading.

“I’m going to help you breathe, then we’re sending you to Seoul for surgery. You’re going to be all right.”

Nurse Evelyn brought a tray of instruments. *If only Shelby were here*. If the doctor was wrong, if these were his last moments, he wanted her face to be the last one he saw. *The Lord is my shepherd ...*

CHAPTER FIFTEEN

Father Stephens rocked on his heels. "Why, Colonel Borsch, do you know Parker Tate?"

"He served in this MASH a short time ago. I've been wondering what the devil happened to him."

The priest and Shelby echoed, "Served?"

Stephens edged closer to the desk. "In what capacity?"

"He's a doctor."

Shelby's hand flew to her lips. "He's a doctor?" Although Father Stephens hadn't found out for sure yet, Shelby was almost certain Parker Tate was the man she'd encountered on the troopship.

"That's what I said, Lieutenant. How did he end up at the 8055th? Is he all right?"

"He was severely wounded saving another soldier's life," Stephens said. "But please, tell us more about him being here. Nurse Shelby and I need to put all of this in context."

The CO thudded onto his chair. "He was at the Army hospital in Seoul and was sent here when we were down a surgeon. Our Dr. Baroni had gone to a battalion aid to assist and lost his way coming back. Unfortunately, he ended up in a POW camp."

"So, he was here?" Shelby's cheeks flushed. She regretted the dumb question.

The colonel gave her the fish eye. "At Christmas, Pastor Frank took advantage of an opportunity to visit Mike Baroni in the prison camp, you know, take some personal items, assure him of our support. Baroni was in pretty bad shape—malnourished, awful living conditions. Those North Koreans are a vicious lot." His cigar smoke wafted across the desk, making Shelby's eyes water. A knock interrupted them.

"Enter!"

Corporal Howden stuck his head inside. "We unloaded the Jeep, sir. Can I get you anything else?"

"Good. Bring us some coffee."

"Yes, sir." The clerk disappeared, the door clicking shut behind him.

"Where was I?"

Father Stephens made a circling motion with his right hand. "Chaplain Frank saw Dr. Baroni at the prison camp."

Shelby hung on every word, wondering how this related to Parker Tate, *Dr. Parker Tate*.

"So, Frank encounters this PKA guard—I forget his name—but he's none too pleased with his situation. He wasn't simpatico, if you get my meaning. Frank can tell you more about him when he gets back."

Oh, good! He might just let us stay until then. She didn't think she could leave without knowing the full story.

"Anyway, the guard has this idea about helping Dr. Baroni break out and escaping himself, and he asks for Frank's help."

Father Stephens scratched his temple. "A most extraordinary story, but sir, how does Parker, uh, Dr. Tate fit into all of this?"

"I'm getting to that, Father. There are lots of pieces to this puzzle." He leaned back in his chair. "Like I said,

Chaplain Frank knows all the ins and outs of this, but Dr. Tate's grandfather was in the same POW camp as Mike Baroni. Somehow the guard had known Dr. Tate's grandfather before the war. This North Korean knew if he didn't get the old man out of there soon, he'd die. So, the guard and Pastor Frank concocted a scheme which involved Tate posing as a North Korean officer with fake orders to escort his grandfather and Dr. Baroni to a different camp. He was also supposed to bring the guard."

Shelby clapped her hands. "So, that's why he came to us in a North Korean uniform!" She and Father Stephens gazed at each other.

Borsch pointed his cigar at her. "And you've been thinking all this time he's PKA."

She wasn't about to correct his mistaken impression. "Colonel Borsch, what happened with the escape plan?"

"Again, Chaplain Frank was involved, so he can tell you more. I do know Baroni made it to safety, and I'm pretty sure the grandfather did too. Baroni's at the Army hospital in Seoul. We expect to get him back in a few weeks."

"And what about the guard?" Stephens asked.

"Maybe Frank knows." He sighed. "Dr. Tate's a good man. What kind of shape is he in? You said something about severe wounds."

Shelby appreciated the colonel's concern about her patient.

"Pretty bad," Stephens said. "The rescued American told us a North Korean officer ordered Dr. Tate to stop trying to free him from a burning Jeep, and when he wouldn't, the PKA shot Tate several times. With his little strength, the American managed to kill the North Korean. Unfortunately, Dr. Tate took shrapnel to his throat, and he's been unable to talk. We've been communicating with an alphabet board, and he's been able to write a few words. One of them was 'Frank,' and I learned he meant your chaplain. He's so weak we haven't been able to get much beyond that little information."

Shelby asked, "Is he an American, Colonel Borsch?"

"Korean-born but lives in the US."

So, he was born here. I wonder when he went to America.

"There's an MP hovering around the unit just waiting to get his hands on Dr. Tate," Stephens said. "Is there something you can do about that?"

"I'll contact Colonel Sheppard right away."

An announcement over the loudspeaker suspended their conversation. "Attention all personnel. Choppers are on their way with casualties. Everyone, report for duty."

"I'm afraid that call will have to wait."

The priest spoke up. "Can we offer our services?"

"You can fill in for Chaplain Frank. Nurse Kichline, how about helping in the OR?"

"Yes, of course, sir."

For the life of her, she couldn't remember the name of the head nurse or the surgeon she was assisting. She focused on the wounded, knowing she'd have to process what she'd learned about Parker Tate afterward. Since the CO hadn't asked her how long she'd been doing MASH nursing, she didn't tell him. He could tell at a glance how young she was, which was perhaps why he kept looking over at her during surgery. His eyes telegraphed a silent "are you okay" when one soldier lost three toes to frostbite. She'd never participated in an amputation before, but knowing the surgery would save the soldier's foot helped her bear the gruesome procedure. On the second patient—or maybe he was the third—the doctor she assisted moved beyond requesting instruments to friendly banter. Shelby realized how tightly wound she'd been when she found her shoulders relaxing.

"You're pretty good, nurse. How long have you been at this?"

"Just a few months."

"You're from the 8055th, right?"

"Yes, doctor."

"You work like a veteran."

"Thank you, sir."

"What's your name again?"

"Shelby, sir. Lt. Shelby Kichline."

"Nice to meet you." He continued working on a nicked colon, a whiff of bowel reaching her nose. "Where are you from?"

"A small town in eastern Pennsylvania, an hour north of Philadelphia."

"I'm Don Currenton from Nebraska. So, what brought you here today?"

"I came with Father Stephens to see your chaplain. We're waiting for him to return."

"Too bad the colonel didn't give you some magazines and tell you to wait in the lobby."

"I'd rather be useful."

He looked into her eyes, and she blushed. "They make them nice in Pennsylvania."

"Thank you, sir." She watched how skillfully he resected the bowel, admiring his work.

"So, what's the draw with our chaplain? He doesn't get many visitors."

She jumped at the chance to discuss Parker. "He has important information about one of our patients."

"Since when has Chaplain Frank been in the doctoring business?"

"Oh, he isn't, Dr. Currenton. We have a severely wounded patient who couldn't tell us who he was. He was wearing a North Korean uniform and had saved one of our soldiers."

"The plot thickens." He tossed a bloody cotton wad to the floor.

"He speaks English, and he was able to write a little and point to letters on an alphabet board. He told Father Stephens and me he's an American and he, uh, mentioned Chaplain Frank. Our colonel sent us here to interview him."

"Does this fellow have a name?"

She drew in her breath. "Parker Tate."

Currenton stopped in mid-procedure, staring at her. "Did you say Parker Tate?"

"Yes, Doctor." Her pulse echoed in her ears.

"He's a physician, and he was here not long ago, a top-notch kind of guy. How the hell did he end up in a MASH in a North Korean uniform?"

"That's what we came to figure out. Colonel Borsch was telling us his story when we got called to surgery."

"Well, that's one I'd like to hear."

A long moment passed, Shelby wondering if the doctor was angry or just puzzled. "He really isn't North Korean."

"I'm relieved to hear it. Otherwise, I'd begin to doubt myself as a judge of character."

At the risk of making herself vulnerable she asked, "What did you think of him?"

"Truly nice guy, eager to be of service, soft-spoken, polite like many Koreans." He gave a laugh. "Religious fellow. Seemed to take it pretty seriously."

Hearing this was like daffodils waving a golden welcome on a spring morning.

"He told us something about going to school in the US—one of the Ivies, I think—and how he volunteered to come here. He'd been stationed in Seoul, and when one of our surgeons got captured, the Army sent Tate to us." He paused. "And just like that, he was gone. I wondered what had happened to him. Maybe when the padre comes back, you'll invite me to your conversation."

"Of course, doctor."

"For now, let's get this kid closed up and save the next young life."

Shelby had gone into the day expecting a rigorous trip to the 8063rd and a visit with the minister followed by another rugged trek back to the 8055th. Instead, she'd assisted with six surgeries while fretting she and Father Stephens might have to leave before Chaplain Frank returned. She ate a late-afternoon meal in a slouch her mother would have had something to say about. She was too weary to straighten up and figured her mother was, after all, seven thousand miles away. Judging from the slumping forms around her, no one would hold her accountable for her lapse in etiquette.

"There you are! Look who I found!" Father Stephens's grin lit up his face. "Shelby, I'd like to introduce Chaplain Frank."

She straightened her spine, newly energized. "Am I ever happy to meet you!"

"Likewise." He shook her hand. "I'm sorry I wasn't here to greet you. It seems we were both on similar missions. Thanks for bringing penicillin. Now we'll have plenty for a good while. I understand you've also been asking about Dr. Tate."

"Yes, we have."

"Do you want to talk here or in the chapel?"

"Here is fine," she said, unwilling to lose a precious minute.

"Ah, there's the good pastor." Dr. Currenton wandered over. "Nurse Shelby and I were talking about you in the OR. Mind if I join you?"

"Not at all."

The mess tent's sounds and smells receded. Shelby's stomach fluttered.

"We're all eager to get to the bottom of this." Father Stephens rubbed his hands together.

"How do you folks know Parker Tate? I'm as anxious for news about him as you are."

Shelby communicated, "You tell him" to the priest, who unfolded their story.

When Stephens finished, Frank whistled. "Tell me, how's he doing now?"

"He's had a rather rough go, but I think the worst may be over. Did you meet Dr. Tate here?"

Frank leaned back. "I met him in the States, in Princeton, before he joined the Army. I do some teaching at the seminary, and he and his family are good friends with one of the other professors, Dr. Cullen. Dr. Tate and his brother have a medical practice in a neighboring town."

Shelby absorbed this bit of news. "Did he go to Princeton, then?"

"Yes, for his undergrad degree. I believe he went to Penn for medical school. His brother recently finished his residency."

He went to Princeton and Penn. He lives an hour from Easton! He has a brother who's also a doctor.

"The family's still in Seoul, and like most Koreans, suffered during the siege. His father is a minister, and the grandfather was a professor at the seminary in Pyongyang. Parker's mother became seriously ill, and no one could figure out what was wrong. His grandmother had fled to Seoul as the war was breaking out, but the grandfather wanted to rescue as many Christians as he could. Unfortunately, he went missing. The father sent an urgent plea to Dr. Tate to come to Korea to examine his wife and see what Parker could about the grandfather." Frank moved his shoulders side to side as if to get out some kinks. "He went to Dr. Cullen to ask for advice, and Cullen called me in since I was in the reserves as a chaplain. I told Parker he couldn't likely get to Korea any other way than joining the Army. I thought he might have some leeway in terms of his service, rather than waiting to be drafted."

"Chaplain Frank," Shelby said, "do you happen to know when he arrived in Korea?"

He looked up, then back at her. "I seem to think it was last November."

A chill ran up her left calf. "Might he have come here on the *Lt. Raymond O. Beaudoin*?"

"Could be. Why?"

"I was on that troopship," she said, telling them how they had run into each other.

Frank gave a low whistle. "What an amazing thing." He paused, sipping his coffee. Shelby spoke up again. "How is his mother?"

"When he was here at the 8063rd, she was coming along. She'd been suffering from acute anemia, and he had her on the road to health. I believe Colonel Borsch told you what Parker got involved with after coming here."

They traded stories about what each of them knew, and after exhausting their knowledge, Father Stephens looked to Shelby. "Well, I think we'd best be getting back. Colonel Sheppard will be growing concerned."

They rose and shook hands with Dr. Currenton and the chaplain.

"I'm relieved to finally know what happened to Parker," Frank said. "I'll make sure Colonel Borsch places that call to your CO to vouch for him. Please tell Parker I'll come out to see him tomorrow or the next day."

She needed to be snug and to sleep after the grueling day. Even more than desiring her bed, however, Shelby longed to see Parker, to assure him everything was going to be all right.

"Good night, Father." She climbed out of the Jeep wanting to rub her cold, sore behind, but there were some things you just didn't do in front of a priest. "Thanks for everything."

"You are quite welcome. What a day! You go get a good night's sleep."

"I will, after I pay Dr. Tate a brief visit."

She went into the dimly-lit post-op ward, stepping lightly so she didn't awaken any of the patients. Various decibels of soldierly snoring provided a soundtrack for her movements. Evelyn was on call, sitting at the desk, her head down over paperwork, and Shelby didn't bother to disturb her. She wandered toward the end of the unit, but when she looked down into Parker's bed, she stumbled backward. Who was this husky blonde? Maybe they'd moved Parker. She looked over her shoulder and saw Evelyn beckoning her with a crooked finger.

"Where is Parker Tate?" Shelby asked. "Did he get moved?"

"Yes, Shelby. He got moved. To Seoul."

CHAPTER SIXTEEN

Voices tunneled into Parker's consciousness. Blinking, he tried bringing his fuzzy vision into focus, but his eyes cowered at the onslaught of light. Two women were tugging at him, their conversation a word salad. He slipped back into sleep. When he awakened, he took note of the antiseptic-scented room and two nurses, realizing he wasn't at the MASH where he'd been for who knew how long. There was something familiar about this place. Apparently, he'd had another surgery. He remembered choking, the medical team springing into action, and being whisked away on a helicopter, but that's where the memory train left the tracks.

He tried raising his right hand to his throat, which burned as if someone had set a match to it, but his arm lay at the mercy of an IV. He needed water to put out the fire. *Where am I? Does Shelby know where I am? Will I ever see her again?*

When he attempted to clear his inflamed throat, a twisted sound emitted from him.

"He's waking up. Hello there. Just relax. I'm going to check your blood pressure."

A brunette put the cuff on his left arm and began pumping. "Your pressure is a bit elevated, which isn't unusual after what you've been through."

He pointed to his throat with his left hand.

"You had extensive surgery to clear the scar tissue in your throat and repair damage caused by the wound. Those MASH doctors did a wonderful job, but you needed a lot more than they could give you."

The other nurse reached behind him and plumped his pillow. "Are you in much pain?"

He responded with a grimace. He also waved his hand as best he could toward them and the room, hoping they understood he wanted to know his whereabouts.

The women regarded each other, then the brunette said, "You're at the Army hospital in Seoul. I'm Nurse Garrett, and this is Nurse Nason."

His heart gave a small leap. Although he didn't recognize either of them, surely there would be someone with whom he'd worked here. He wondered whether the colonel back at the MASH unit had believed Shelby and Father Stephens's story about his identity, especially when they were just sorting out the facts themselves.

He motioned toward his mouth, pretending he was tipping a glass to his parched lips. He was dying for a sip of water.

Nurse Garrett caressed his left shoulder. "I know. You're in terrible need of a drink. We're giving you intravenous hydration, but that doesn't do your throat any good."

When she smiled, he noticed her two front teeth slightly overlapped, giving her the appearance of a young girl.

"I'll ask Dr. Brumbaugh if you can have some ice chips."

His eyes brightened, and he grunted again, heartened by even that much sound coming from his throat. Maybe he was on the road to recovering his voice. Maybe he was going to be okay after all. *The Lord is my shepherd ...*

"He shouldn't be in this room. We don't know for sure who or what he is."

"I don't think we should be discussing this here."

Parker awakened to the sound of two doctors talking at the edge of his room. Clearing sleep webs from his brain, he glanced toward one of two windows, seeing it was still daytime.

"Look, Rick, as far as I know, this is Parker Tate, who came to us from a MASH. We were told two things that don't match up—one, he's an American, and two, he was brought to the MASH in a North Korean officer's uniform."

"He might be a commie sympathizer."

"Or he might have been doing something underground for our side."

He wondered who would score the next point in the verbal ping pong match.

"Unfortunately, there isn't much to go by, no dog tags, no paperwork. The CO at the MASH said his PKA ID showed every sign of forgery."

"Aha! There's your answer, Clarence."

The doctor leaned back from the waist. "I say we give him the benefit of the doubt. I realize I could be wrong, but my gut tells me this is a good man, maybe even a heroic one."

Parker exhaled slowly. When would he be able to tell his own story? And when would these doctors stop yammering and give him a few lousy ice chips?

Nurse Garrett raised him up in the bed and gave him a paper cup filled with slivers of ice, which he savored as if they were a medium rare steak.

"I'll bet that feels good." She smiled down at him.

He pushed a "yesh" through his lips.

"Take it easy, soldier. Doctor doesn't want you trying to speak just yet, but I'm thrilled you can make sounds! That's progress."

He shrugged his shoulders as if to ask, "When?"

"I wish I knew. Maybe a few days. Don't worry, though. You're healing beautifully, and I think you'll be talking again before you know it."

He wondered whether she was the kind of nurse who shot straight or said what she thought the patient wanted to hear. Either way, he would hang on to the hope she offered.

She turned to face the door. "I think you have a visitor."

A man with cropped auburn hair limped into the room on a cane, a standard issue bathrobe over his GI slacks. He had the look of someone who'd been sick but was on his way back, and Parker thought there was something familiar about him. The friendlier of his doctors guided the man toward the bed, and Nurse Garrett made introductions.

"This is one of your doctors, Clarence Brumbaugh, and this is Dr. Mike Baroni."

"Is this the man you were telling us about?" Brumbaugh asked the other physician.

Parker's limbs tingled. *This is the man I brought out of the prison camp! I wonder if he knows what happened to my grandfather.*

Baroni limped closer, and smiling at Parker, shook his left hand since the right one was hooked up to an IV.

"He sure is." He looked back at Parker. "The last time I saw you, I thought you were a goner. How are you doing?"

Parker nodded his head, then he pointed toward Baroni. "They had me pretty far down at the prison camp, but you and Ko got me out just in time."

"You're absolutely sure Parker Tate is the North Korean officer who helped you escape?" Brumbaugh asked.

"As sure as I'm alive, and he's not North Korean." Baroni beamed at Parker. "He took a great risk to spring me and his grandfather."

"His grandfather?" the doctor and nurse echoed.

At last! Word of Grandfather! How is he? Where is he?

"Yep. The PKA guard who concocted the scheme had been a divinity student of Parker Tate's grandfather in Pyongyang. He was conscripted by the North Koreans. He hated the way they treated us prisoners, even shared part of his food ration with Dr. Oh, Tate's grandfather, who would then share with me. When Ko was ordered to interrogate us, he went easy, sometimes even pretending to beat us, and we played along."

He explained the plot Ko had devised when Chaplain Frank came during the Christmas truce. "We just needed someone to pose as a PKA officer with fake orders to transfer us to a different facility." He inclined his head toward Parker. "That's where our friend here comes in."

Parker's heart stampeded. Happy his good name was being cleared, he yearned for news about his grandfather's condition. He bored a look into Baroni's eyes, and mouthed, "How is my grandfather?" He started coughing, and Nurse Garrett handed him the cup of ice chips.

"How's his throat, Brumbagh?" Baroni asked.

"When you folks came under fire, he took shrapnel to it. The MASH docs did a good initial job, but we needed to finish it here. I think he'll be talking again in a few days." He paused. "What happened when you were attacked?"

Parker squirmed, but no matter how impatient he became, his agitation wouldn't help Baroni tell the story any faster.

"We were nearly into American-held territory when the shooting started. Ko shielded me and Dr. Oh. And when I asked Ko where Tate was, Ko told me not to worry, just keep moving toward the American line. Then I saw Tate trying to free an American from a burning Jeep." His voice softened. "Did you get him out?"

Brumbaugh spoke up. "According to the MASH CO, that's when Tate was wounded. A North Korean ordered him to stop and when he refused, the PKA started shooting. The rescued American finished off the guy."

Baroni whistled. "So, he gets taken to a MASH unit in a North Korean uniform."

Parker could barely contain himself. With his left hand, he grasped Baroni's wrist and mouthed, "Grandfather?"

"An American unit picked us up and brought the three of us here. Dr. Oh was a lot further down than I was, but I do believe he's going to recover, Tate. It's just going to take some time. I told the Army to go easy on Ko for what he did, and I have every hope they will."

Grandfather is in this very hospital. I will see him again!

"How in the world did Dr. Oh end up in a prison camp?" Nurse Garrett asked.

"He was helping some people from his church escape to the south, and he got caught."

Brumbaugh scratched his chin. "Courageous family."

"Take my advice," Baroni said jerking his thumb, "and ditch that MP. This is a true-blue American—and a hero."

The doctor sucked in his breath. "I'll see what I can do. Your story is strong evidence, but the brass is going to want proof, and our friend here hasn't any dog tags or Army ID."

When Nurse Garrett finished checking his vital signs and recording them before going off her shift, Parker motioned to her and mimicked writing on her clipboard.

"Hmm. I think you want me to write something for you?"

He pointed to himself, then the chart.

"Oh! You want to write something."

He smiled.

"Okay, let me get some blank paper. I'll be right back." She returned shortly and handed him the clipboard and a pen.

He scrawled, "Family in Seoul."

She scrunched her eyebrows. "Your family is in Seoul?"

He wrote, "Yes."

"I'm guessing they haven't heard from you in a while, and you want them to know you're here."

"Yesh," leaked through his lips.

She started to take the paper away, but he tapped the pen harder. "I worked here," he wrote and handed her the clip board.

Her voice rose a pitch. "You worked here? At this hospital?"

He wrote, "I am a doctor."

"Wow! Well, I'll be. This situation just gets curiouser and curiouser."

CHAPTER SEVENTEEN

Shelby clutched Evelyn's arm. "W-what happened?"

The nurse guided her friend onto one of two chairs at their station.

"While you were away, about midmorning, he started choking. Scar tissue was obstructing his airway, and Danny trached him, but it wasn't enough to fix the problem."

Shelby sat forward, almost in Evelyn's personal space.

"Major McKaig said the best doctor for the job was in Tokyo. Danny and Colonel Sheppard didn't think the patient would survive the trip, though, so they helicoptered him to Seoul."

She closed her eyes. *If only I'd been here with him! He must've been so scared.* "Have you heard anything since then?"

"I'm afraid not."

"Maybe Colonel Sheppard has." She rose, but Evelyn grabbed her hand.

"Shelby, it's almost midnight. He's asleep by now, and you should be too. I didn't expect you to be gone so long. How did that go anyway?"

She flicked her hand. "I can tell you more about that later. I simply have to know if Parker Tate is, is ..."

"Honey," she lowered her voice, "You're too emotionally involved with this patient. You know what Major McKaig always says about keeping a professional distance."

Shelby looked into her friend's light brown eyes, knowing she was way past keeping any kind of distance from Parker Tate.

She didn't even try to sleep but spent the restless night in prayer. A few times, she drifted into slumber only to awaken to the reality of Parker's absence and not knowing if he was alive. Oh yes, she was emotionally involved and no two ways about it. In their everyday encounters, in their Bible readings and prayers, she'd become closer to him in two weeks than she'd been in two years with Michael Hendry.

When her alarm clock's glowing hands stretched to the five and the six, she sprang from her bunk. Dressing quickly, she splashed her face with cold water then went to the chapel for Mass. Not only would the service substitute for her private devotions today, but she could also discuss Parker's situation with the priest directly afterward. Ten other MASH personnel were at prayer, and not wanting to disrupt, she smiled at the chaplain before kneeling.

The rite bolstered her spirits, although she couldn't fully participate in the Eucharistic part because she wasn't Catholic. She would have liked to receive Communion, but she would need to wait for Sunday's Protestant service. She lingered while the other attendees shook the priest's hand, then she walked over to him and told him what had happened to Parker Tate.

"Oh, dear. I'm sorry to hear that. I was so looking forward to telling him about our trip to the 8063rd and how we learned he is indeed one of us."

"Father, we have to find out how he is. Will you come with me to see Colonel Sheppard? We can tell him what we discovered yesterday and ask him to put a call in to the Army hospital." She didn't realize she was bouncing from foot to foot.

"Yes, of course, Shelby, we'll do it right after breakfast."

Her eyes implored him.

"Make that before breakfast."

The CO rubbed the back of his neck. "Colonel Borsch called me yesterday with the news. Not only is Tate on our side, he's a bona fide hero."

"Is? You said 'is?' Does that mean he's still alive?" Shelby felt like her heart leaped in her chest.

"Let's hope so." Sheppard called out, "Neil, come in here, will you?"

The company clerk pushed through the door. "Sir? Oh, good morning, Father, Shelby."

"Get me on the horn to the head honcho at the Army Hospital in Seoul. I need to check on a patient."

"Would that be the North Korean we had here?"

Sheppard's face reddened. "That would be the Korean *American*, Corporal Unger."

"Yes, sir. I'll get on it right away."

Shelby watched Unger disappear next door, reeling in her impatience. All night, she had concocted possible scenarios in which she'd be able to visit Parker, but she didn't think anything would get her past her CO's, or her major's, gate. *What would I tell them—that I simply have to see Parker because I have strong feelings for him?*

Unger poked his head in the door five minutes later, pointing to Sheppard's desk phone. "The Army Hospital's on the line, sir. A Doctor Brumbaugh."

He picked up the phone. "Colonel Sheppard here, MASH 8055th. I'm trying to get information about one of our patients who was evac'd by helicopter yesterday for emergency throat surgery. Right. That's him. Oh, you're the operating surgeon?"

Shelby clutched the cross around her neck. *Please, Lord, let him be alive.*

"That is good news. Ah, I see. A long recovery. Yes, yes ... I'll look into it. Thank you, Doctor. No, that's it for now. Goodbye." He hung up and gave a small laugh. "Just look at you two, hovering over my desk like my grandkids on Christmas morning."

"Sorry, sir." Father Stephens leaned back. "How is Dr. Tate?"

"He got to Seoul in the nick of time. The poor soul might have choked to death otherwise." He unwrapped a cigar. "He's making a good recovery so far. This doctor says Tate's able to make some sounds and hopes he'll be able to talk before too long."

"How wonderful!" Shelby clapped her hands.

Sheppard eyed her. "He asked us to send any of Tate's personal belongings."

"His Bible is here," she said.

"The only clothes he had were that PKA uniform, and he won't be needing that."

"I suppose not, Father. I wonder where his American uniform, dog tags, and personal effects got to."

"I'll bet Chaplain Frank knows. He was in on the rescue mission."

"Will you check and see?"

"Of course, sir."

Shelby's thoughts raced, and she blurted, "Sir, I would be happy to deliver Dr. Tate's belongings to him."

His eyes narrowed. "And why would you want to do that?"

He's not making this easy.

"It might do him good to see someone from our MASH unit, might aid in his recovery. I mean, to be yanked away like that and face a life-threatening situation ..."

Realizing how ridiculous she must be sounding to this battle-seasoned CO, she looked down at the scuffed floorboards.

"He's getting excellent care in Seoul. Thanks for all the footwork you and the padre did to clear him. It would've been downright criminal to have sent him to a POW camp."

"You're welcome, sir." As she turned to leave, her legs felt like cooked macaroni.

She didn't see Father Stephens following her movement as she left or hear him say, "May I have a personal word with you, sir?"

She moved through her shift in a mental fog. The trip to the 8063rd and the painstaking toil in the OR, added to the shock of Parker Tate's absence and emergency surgery, enervated her. She got through the day on strong coffee and her trust in the one who made all things work together for good to those who love him. The second night after her return, she slept straight through to reveille.

She ate a piece of toast in the mess tent before reporting for duty, second-guessing herself for allowing the close connection with the Korean doctor. Just as quickly her thoughts shifted. *This is no crush. This is a spiritual bond, and I think he felt the same way. Besides, was it just a coincidence we bumped into each other that night on the troopship, or that he ended up in this MASH? I can't just let him go.* She lifted her eyes to the leaden sky. *Lord, help me know what to do now that he's gone. Above all, please continue to heal him and give him your peace. If you want us to see each other again, please take care of that too. Amen.*

There were no new casualties, but the post-op was populated with those who'd come through in the previous two days. Having shifted her burden to the Lord, Shelby concentrated on raising the spirits of the wounded and received her own boost when a private said he was from Bethlehem, Pennsylvania.

"Is that so? I'm from Easton!"

"I'll be darned. Imagine running into someone from Easton in Korea."

She noticed freckles across the bridge of his nose. "Where did you go to high school?"

"Liberty. Did you go to Easton?" He pushed himself up on his right elbow.

"I did."

"I really like Easton. My mom is crazy about some candy store in the Circle."

She grinned. "The Carmelcorn Shop." She leaned forward and said in a conspiratorial voice, "I still have some barley sugar candy left over from Christmas, and I'm willing to share."

"That would be great!" He poked his tongue through his lips and closed his eyes.

"You'll have it as soon as I get a break."

"Thank you!"

She moved on to the next patient whose dressing needed to be changed. Just as she completed her task, she felt someone's presence and looked up.

"Nurse Kichline, Colonel Sheppard would like to see you in his office."

"Yes, Major McKaig." She patted the soldier's freshly-bandaged arm and forced a smile. "I'll see you later, Private Crawford."

"I can't wait!"

Shelby swallowed hard when Neil Unger greeted her in the outer office.

"He's waiting for you."

She knocked on the door with a trembling hand.

"Enter!"

"Hello, sir. Major McKaig said you wanted to see me."

"I do indeed. Have a seat. Lieutenant, how long have you been here now?"

"Um ... about six months I, uh, think." For the life of her, she couldn't remember, like the time she'd forgotten her youngest brother's name while introducing him to a friend.

"And in that time, you have worked your ... uh, well, you've worked very hard. I've been nothing but satisfied." He ran a finger across his upper lip.

She picked her thumbnail, wondering where this was heading.

He poked a file lying on his desk. "I see in all that time you haven't had any leave."

"Uh, no, sir, I haven't."

"Everyone needs R and R, especially overworked nurses. I've spoken to Major McKaig, and she agrees you need a three-day pass."

Her voice rose an octave. “Thank you!”

“Unger filled out the paperwork for you to go to Seoul where there’s a nice hotel near the Army hospital. A driver will be here in an hour. Will that give you enough time to pack?”

“Oh, yes sir!” She wanted to spring out of the chair and holler.

He reached into his drawer and pulled out a Bible—*Parker’s Bible*. “I thought while you were in Seoul, you might just have an opportunity to return this to its rightful owner.”

“Thank you so much, sir.”

“You’re welcome. Now get going.” He offered a half-smile, followed by a wink.

CHAPTER EIGHTEEN

Parker wouldn't have given chicken broth a second thought a month ago, but today he delighted in every soothing sip. How much he'd taken for granted—everyday pleasures of eating and drinking, of being fully mobile and pain-free. If he survived this trial, and he was beginning to think he would, he resolved to cherish each day as a gift.

He lay back contented, his head sinking into a chubby pillow and thoughts drifting westward to his brother. He wondered how John was managing the practice and their apartment on his own. Parker guessed John didn't have any idea what was going on thousands of miles away in Korea. And what about their family? Did they realize Parker had been wounded? He guessed not, since he'd shown up at the MASH in the guise of a North Korean officer bearing no contact information.

He gazed out the frosty window. *Does Chaplain Frank still have my personal effects? Will I be able to talk again soon? How much time will pass before I can resume my former life?* He found himself twisting his sheet until a still, small voice spoke to his spirit. *All in time. Yes, all in good time.*

His post-breakfast slumber had been light, and he began stirring at the sound of women talking near the doorway. *Probably the nurses.*

"Here he is."

"Thank you for showing me the way and for the update."

Hope rose in him, but he cautioned himself. *I must be dreaming, just as I have so many other times.* Blinking to open his eyes, he gasped. "Shel-by!"

The hospital nurse clapped her hands. "He speaks!"

Shelby cast her shimmering smile over him and took hold of his hands. "Parker."

He couldn't help himself when tears skittered down his cheeks. He wouldn't have minded if only she had witnessed them, but the nurse couldn't possibly understand.

"I'll leave you two alone," she said and slipped out of the charged room.

Shelby was crying now. She let go of his hand and reached up with a handkerchief to blot his tears, then clasped his hands again. They smiled at each other for several minutes, silently speaking a great deal. In this one breathtaking moment, Parker knew he had found the pearl of great price.

"I was afraid I'd never see you again," Shelby said. "Father Stephens and I went to the 8063rd to deliver penicillin and speak with Chaplain Frank about you. We wanted to make sure we got your story straight so Colonel Sheppard would know who you really are."

He continued holding her hand, hungry for its tenderness.

"I had no idea you were such a heroic person."

Parker closed his eyes, his ears growing red.

"I knew in my heart you weren't a North Korean soldier, but I had nothing but intuition to go on. Have you ever felt as if God were impressing upon you something you just knew had to be true?"

He pushed a shaky "yes" through his lips.

"Am I ever happy to hear you speak! I've never heard your voice before this." *Or had she on the troopship?* She tilted her head, and the ceiling lights glimmered against her dark-blonde hair. "Father Stephens and I were so excited to get back to the 8055th and tell the colonel, but when I went over to the post-op, my heart nearly stopped when you weren't there." Her voice caught. "Nurse Evelyn told me what had happened. I was afraid you might not be ..."

He reached up to stroke her hair. Shelby met his eyes, her lips trembling.

"How?" he asked.

"How? Oh, how did I get here? Colonel Sheppard gave me a three-day pass."

Apparently, his affection for Shelby hadn't gone unnoticed. *I must thank him one day.* He mouthed "How long?"

"Three days."

His eyes crinkled at the thought of having her to himself.

The door opened, and Nurse Garrett entered behind Dr. Brumbaugh, who offered a breezy greeting. He stared at Shelby.

"I was told you had a visitor, Dr. Tate. I had no idea it would be such a pretty one." He walked over to the bed as Shelby jumped up and saluted. "At ease, Nurse. We don't go by a lot of Army protocol here. I'm Dr. Brumbaugh, and you are?"

"Lt. Shelby Kichline, sir, from the MASH 8055th."

He chuckled. "You're the first MASH nurse I've ever known who makes house calls."

Parker enjoyed the mirth in the physician's eyes, the knowing. He wondered how Shelby would respond.

"Well, you see, he left something important behind, and Colonel Sheppard thought it should be returned in person."

"And just what did he leave behind?" Brumbaugh crossed his arms.

Shelby reached into her bag. "This!"

The doctor guffawed. "A Bible?"

"Yes, sir."

Parker accepted the volume from her hands and fingered the familiar leather.

The physician winked. "If you ask me, he left something a lot bigger than that behind."

Brumbaugh performed a brief examination, followed by an assessment.

"I believe the surgery has enabled you to turn a corner, Tate. I removed the extraneous scar tissue, and now we just have to wait for the healing process to run its course."

"How long?" Parker whispered.

"Although I'm delighted to hear your voice, don't strain it for at least a day or two." He glanced at Shelby. "That might prove difficult, but do your best. You'll most likely need to stay here several days, so I can keep a close eye on you. I don't want to discharge you before you're ready."

Shelby's brows furrowed. "He won't be able to serve after this, will he?"

Brumbaugh huffed. "Not likely. He'll need some rehabilitation in Army facilities, though, which could take a while. Then he'll go home."

Home! Back to New Jersey, to John and my practice! His thoughts immediately turned to Shelby. *How long is her tour of duty? I know she lives not far from Hopewell, but I can't remember where.* He sighed to himself. *I feel I know her deeply, but there are many details I do not know.* He realized Brumbaugh was still talking.

"... slowly, gradually, so don't force it. I'm convinced you'll regain your voice. Everything that could be repaired has been repaired. I'm told you lost a lot of blood and had a cardiac event at the MASH. Your other wounds are healing nicely, and there are no signs of infection. I will say, though, that gut's going to be tender for a long time. They really did a great job at the 8055th. We just need to let Mother Nature do the rest."

Parker winced. *That would be God.*

"As far as eating goes, let's continue working through the liquid phase. Gradually we'll introduce some purees." He looked into Parker's eyes. "Do you agree so far, Doctor?"

"Yes." Parker enjoyed the sound of his own voice.

"While your, uh, nurse is here, you can get out of bed for short walks, as you're able." Brumbaugh clapped his hands. "Well, then, do you have any questions, Doctor?" When Parker shook his head, Brumbaugh glanced at Shelby. "Nurse?"

"Not that I can think of just now."

He gave a comical bow and excused himself, Nurse Garrett following.

Garrett smiled as she removed a tray from the dining cart and handed it to Shelby.

"How kind of you! I didn't expect this."

"Don't worry, this was something I wanted to do." She leaned closer to Shelby. "You need to make the most of your time with him."

"Thank you so much."

"Okay, you two, enjoy your lunch." She waved on her way out the door.

"Do you pray before meals?" he whispered.

"Always." Her grin widened. "I think you'd better let me say this one."

He closed his eyes as she held his hand and thanked the Lord for their food.

"And dear Lord, thank you for allowing Parker to take nourishment again. We pray you continue healing him completely, according to your perfect will. And, uh, Lord, thank you for this time together. Amen."

When he opened his eyes, he caught the staining of her cheeks. He lifted the spoon to his mouth and swallowed the salty liquid. "Tell me—about you." He coughed, knowing he'd used too many words all at once.

"Are you all right?"

He touched the bandage covering his throat. "Uh-huh."

She laid her sandwich on the plate. "I'll be happy to do most of the talking for now. Let's see, I think you know I'm from northeastern Pennsylvania. I understand you went to Princeton then Penn for medical school. I went to Temple Nursing School. Where do you live now?"

He mouthed, "Hopewell, New Jersey."

Her eyes glowed. "Imagine that!"

He did, imagine seeing her again when this was all over. How good God was!

"Okay, let's see now. I have three brothers and a sister. I'm the oldest. I heard you have a brother."

Parker raised two fingers and whispered, "Brother, Hopewell. Sister, here." With his throat drying, he swallowed more broth.

"How nice! Wow, I just can't believe how close we live to each other back home."

He grinned then sipped more broth while she continued her story.

"My father teaches history at Easton High School. What does your father do?"

"Pastor."

"How about that. My grandfather is a minister. Well, he's retired now."

Parker abandoned his meal, the mention of their families stirring a different kind of need in him. He wondered if she might be able to fill this one too.

"You look tired," she said. "This has been a big day for you. Are you finished?"

"Yes."

She rose to remove his tray. "I'll sit with you while you sleep."

"I need ..."

She leaned so close he smelled the freshness of her hair.

"My parents to know ... I'm here."

Her lips parted. "They don't know you're in the hospital?"

"No."

"Oh my. I'll be happy to get word to them. Where do they live?"

"Seoul."

"Oh!"

His eyelids dragged. "Will ... you ... tell ... them?"

"Of course. I'll just need their address." She rummaged through her bag, producing a pad of paper and a pencil.

He focused on writing the information, then fell back exhausted.

"You just get some rest, and I'll go to your family."

CHAPTER NINETEEN

She waited until he fell asleep before leaving, suppressing an urge to kiss his forehead. *Not yet.* Shelby stepped quietly into the hall where she found Dr. Brumbaugh and an MP.

"Nurse Kichline, you're just who I wanted to see."

"Oh?"

The intercom blared a request for one of the physicians to report to post-op. When the announcement ended, he guided her to a waiting room.

"There's a bit of a rumpus about Dr. Tate's paperwork and I'm wondering, since you are, well, close to him, if you might be of assistance," Brumbaugh said.

She tingled over the recognition of their attachment. "Certainly. What's the problem?"

"Hospital records show Dr. Tate served here when he came to Korea last fall. Then he went to a MASH unit. We don't have additional information, no proof of citizenship or dog tags, no ID, just a record of him being brought to the 8055th wearing a North Korean officer's uniform."

"I guess you don't know his story, then."

"I've heard what he did. In fact, the doctor he rescued is recovering here. There are plenty of people to corroborate

Dr. Tate's identity, and a call between your CO and mine would go far. However, until there's official paperwork ..." He jerked a thumb at the guard.

"I understand. The last I heard, the soldier he saved was also brought here. He could tell your CO what happened. I know it's not paperwork, but might it help?"

"Couldn't hurt. What's his name?"

"Private James Ward from Oklahoma."

"I'll look into that," Brumbaugh said. "All the stories I've been hearing about Tate add up." He scrutinized her outerwear. "You seem to be heading out."

"Dr. Tate's parents don't know he's here or what happened to him."

"That's gotta be rough on them. Where do they live?"

She showed him the paper with their address, her skin prickling at the thought of meeting his family. She knew little of Korean customs and worried she might totally mess up.

"This isn't far from the hospital but on the edge of too far to walk, especially in those shoes." He pointed to her regulation pumps. "Do you know how to get around Seoul?"

"No, sir, but I went to nursing school in North Philadelphia."

Brumbaugh snorted. "Wait here. I'll get a driver for you."

"That's terribly kind of you."

"Seoul is crawling with soldiers, and an unaccompanied American woman will definitely attract more attention than I think you'll want. Wait right here."

She sat alone, collecting herself. She'd been planning to freshen up at the hotel before meeting his parents, but she knew she'd be half-crazy with worry if her father or one of her brothers hadn't been heard from in weeks in a war zone. The sooner they knew, the better. Did they even speak English? She guessed they did. "Lord," she whispered, "would you supply anything that may be lacking in me? Help me communicate with them. Help me be a blessing."

Her Army driver, Private Mark Post, pulled the car up next to an apartment building in an area still recovering from the 1950 siege. "This is the place."

Shelby laughed through a case of serious jitters. "You really didn't have far to bring me."

"That's true, ma'am, but you saw all those uniforms." His southern accent complimented his gentlemanly concern for her safety. "I'll wait here for you."

When she slid across the seat, he popped out of the vehicle and opened her door.

"Why, thank you, Private Post."

"You're welcome, ma'am."

She smiled into his earnest face, noting his prematurely receding hairline. "I'm not sure how long I'll be."

"Take as long as you need. Doctor's orders."

"Well, then, we can't argue with the doctor, can we?"

Moments later, Shelby stood at the apartment door and lifted her shaking hand to knock twice. She startled when a young woman looking for all the world like a female version of Parker answered. Her dark brown eyes widened at the sight of an American in uniform.

"*An-nyeong-ha-se-yo.*"

The woman bowed. "*An-nyeong-ha-se-yo*. You are American?"

"Yes, do you speak English?" Shelby asked.

"Yes."

"I am here about Dr. Parker Tate."

"Oh, my!" She touched her lips.

"I have news of him."

"Is he—is he ...? We have been so afraid."

She rushed to the chase. "He is alive."

The young woman swung the door open wide and began calling out in Korean. A middle-aged couple, the man in a western-style suit, the woman in the kind of wool skirt and sweater Shelby's mom wore around the house, appeared at the entry. The woman gasped as the younger family member spoke in rapid Korean and the man waved Shelby inside. Upon hearing her son's name spoken by an American Army woman, his mother's face drained of color.

"Come, come!" she said, and Shelby went further inside their home.

All her life, when she entered someone else's house, she'd felt like she was opening a kind of portal to a different world. Now she truly was. The aroma of unfamiliar spices and delicate artwork featuring Korean words in columns were downright exotic to Shelby. An old woman was sitting on a couch, and hovering in the background, a little girl and a woman watched the unfolding scene. On a black piano were family photographs, and Shelby's heart caught when she moved close enough to detect Parker in them. Despite their stern expressions, he wore the hint of a smile. In a faded photo from the last century, an unsmiling couple sat next to each other in traditional Korean clothing.

"Please tell us who you are," his father said.

Uncertain of their proficiency with English, she spoke slowly and clearly. "I am Lieutenant Shelby Kichline, a United States Army Nurse stationed with the 8055th Mobile Army Surgical Hospital."

"I am the Reverend Park, Sung-Doh, and this is my wife, Yung Sook."

"I am pleased to meet you." Shelby guessed Parker's first name reflected his family name.

"This is my wife's mother, Jeongsook Oh."

Shelby greeted her in Korean with a bow, and the woman's eyes shone approval.

"And this is our daughter, Yuna, who goes by Anna." He gestured toward the figures in the background. "These are refugees who are staying with us."

"I am very pleased to meet all of you." Shelby's knees knocked under her skirt, and she pressed her hands against them. Judging by the tension on their faces, everyone in the room had butterflies.

"Anna says you have brought us word of Tae-ho."

Shelby frowned. "I am sorry. I don't understand."

"You have word of our son."

Anna spoke up. "Tae-ho is his Korean name."

"Ah yes, of course." *Tae-ho.*

"My brother changed his name when he went to Princeton."

"How is my son?" The pastor gazed into Shelby's eyes.

"He is in the Army Hospital here in Seoul. He was brought there two days ago after being at the MASH unit where I serve."

"Please forgive our lack of manners for not offering tea, but we are most eager to hear news. We have been quite worried."

"Please, do not worry about refreshments. I understand. The information I have is from another MASH's chaplain, Captain Andrew Frank. When your son served at the 8063rd, Chaplain Frank told him he had seen ..." She hesitated, unsure how to describe Parker's grandfather with the right word. She settled on, "Mrs. Oh's husband. He was located in a Korean prison camp Pastor Frank visited at Christmas."

She filled them in on the story about Parker being asked to pose as a PKA to help the guard smuggle Dr. Oh and Dr. Baroni to safety.

Mrs. Oh spoke so quietly Shelby strained to hear.

"I have seen my husband in hospital. He told us of Tae-ho's deed, but he did not know what became of him after my husband's rescue."

So, the family knows some of the story. How amazing that Parker's grandfather is in the same hospital! "How is your husband?"

"He is weak but improving."

Anna clasped her hands together. "What happened next?"

Shelby shared the rest of the account, how Parker and the American he'd saved were brought in together, how she had been their main nurse. She concluded, "The other day, while I was away, Parker, uh, Tae-ho, began to choke. He was brought to the Army Hospital here in a helicopter, and I was able to get away today to see him, to return his Bible."

Mrs. Park's hand rested on her chest. "What happened?"

She explained his condition and concluded, "He is healing well and is even able to talk a little. I must ask, are you feeling all right? I do not mean to upset you."

Parker's mother rattled off something to her husband. Then she spoke to Anna, who rose with a frown on her face, seemingly to carry out an order. The young woman went to the phone and started speaking in her native language. When Anna hung up, Mrs. Park addressed Shelby. "Tae-ho's fiancée will be here directly. Then we must go to him at once."

His fiancée? Pastor Park was saying something but she was imprisoned by the crushing realization Parker belonged to someone else.

Shelby found herself in the Army car's back seat between a Korean woman in a smart yellow suit and Mrs. Park. The pastor rode in the front with Private Post, and Anna had stayed behind with Mrs. Oh. Shelby drew back, trying to make herself smaller, feeling like a giantess from Greek mythology next to the petite Soonja. She closed her eyes, forcing her emotions to toe the line. How could he be engaged and yet so linked to her? Parker was no cad. Something else had to be going on.

When they arrived at the hospital, she started to say goodbye. She wanted nothing more than to go straight to her hotel where she could weep and gnash her teeth. There was, however, no balm in Gilead.

"I am sure Parker, uh, Tae-ho, will be happy to see all of you. I enjoyed meeting you."

"Oh, but you must take us to him," Mrs. Park said.

"I am sure someone else can help you." Seeing the woman's trembling lips, she changed her tune. "Yes, of course, I will take you."

One foot in front of the other, Shelby. As soon as you deliver them, make your excuses, tell them you're certain they'd value some privacy. Don't let them know you're anything to him but an attentive nurse. They probably won't even know you're gone.

She entertained another thought as their heels clicked along the corridor. She wanted to see the look on Parker's face when he saw Soonja. He wore his emotions on the surface.

"Here we are," she said, when they got off the elevator and walked to the second door on the right. The MP stood a few feet away, and she wondered if they realized the soldier was guarding their son. When the family hung back, she knocked on the door and opened it. Parker was sitting up reading his Bible, his eyes lighting up when they met hers.

"Shelby," he whispered.

"I brought some people to see you." She stepped aside and allowed them to pass.

Parker broke into a smile at the sight of his parents, who tearfully greeted him with careful touches and tender Korean words. She heard Mrs. Park say something ending with "Soonja," and the young woman minced her way toward Parker's bed. Shelby held her breath, watching as he turned pale, as if he'd seen a ghost. Just before she left them, he caught her eye. She'd never seen such a helpless look on his face, not even when he couldn't speak. She was crushed, but not in despair.

CHAPTER TWENTY

"*Eomeoni*," he whispered. "Are you ..." he paused, swallowing, "... following my orders?"

"She is sometimes troublesome, but I see to her behaving. How happy we were to get word of your whereabouts and what has happened." His father's eyes misted. "You have done well, my son."

"Grandfather?"

"We have visited him in this hospital," his mother said.

He looked toward the door, wishing Shelby hadn't gone. His muscles tensed at the sight of Soonja at his bed smiling at him. *What is she doing here? Didn't Father tell Mother as I asked him to?* He scolded himself for not speaking to her himself. He was sure the young woman's presence was his mother's doing. A knife twisted in his gut at what his mother might have told Shelby about Soonja. *I must see Shelby alone as soon as possible. What if she leaves, and I never get a chance to tell her the truth?*

To his vast relief, she didn't go away. Some fifteen minutes later, she reappeared pushing an old Korean man in a wheelchair—*Grandfather!* Parker reached for the bony hands, the two of them having literally survived the same battle. A quick visual examination told Parker his grandfather was healing but had a way to go to regain weight and stamina. As for his spirit, the man could have been ten feet tall.

"You saved my life," he said. He looked at the others. "My grandson saved my life."

Fifteen minutes later, his parents were speaking to the doctor, who'd entered the room, Shelby hovering near the doorway. Brumbaugh was nodding his head, and then, he spoke.

"I am sorry to have to break this up, but I can see Dr. Tate is tiring. Perhaps you can wait in the lounge while he rests or come back tomorrow." He gestured toward Nurse Garrett. "Will you take Dr. Oh back to his room?"

"Yes, Doctor."

Parker smiled at his grandfather as they clasped each other's hands again.

After they left, Dr. Brumbaugh escorted the parents and Soonja from the room. Parker waved toward Shelby, who had cast a plaintive look in his direction. She looked to the doctor, as if for permission, and when he grunted, she went to Parker's side.

"Thank you," he whispered.

"It was my pleasure. They are lovely people."

He frowned, his throat sore. "Why Soonja?"

She pinched her lips together for a moment. "Your mother invited her. She, um, introduced her to me as your fiancée."

He noticed her lips were trembling, and he touched them with his finger, fairly melting. "No."

Shelby jerked her head back. "What?"

His breaths came harder, weariness overtaking him. “My mother ... for years ... I was never ... interested.”

She gripped his hand and closed her eyes. “Let’s talk more after you rest.”

“Don’t ... go.”

“I’ll stay right here, but you must promise to rest.”

He reached for her hand and closed his eyes.

He stirred when the night shift nurse entered the darkened room and spoke to Shelby.

“You should leave. It’s eight-thirty, and I understand you’ve had some kind of big day.”

He couldn’t imagine where the time had gone. He watched as she rose from the chair, gathering her coat and bag. Then she touched his shoulder.

“I’m going to the hotel, Parker.”

He muttered, “Tomorrow?”

“First thing. Good night, and God bless you.”

Except for being awakened every few hours for blood pressure and temperature readings or the administration of medication, Parker slept through the night. He awakened to a crisp winter morning wondering what day this was. Nurse Garrett appeared carrying a tray.

“Ah, you’re awake, Dr. Tate. Good morning!”

He hitched himself up, finding his belly wound less sensitive.

“I thought you might like to get cleaned up before your, uh, friend returns.”

He submitted to the humiliating ritual, grateful the woman chattered the entire time as if to distract him.

"I'm so happy your family visited yesterday, and you got to see your grandfather. He's a delightful man, so dear. He's always asking how everyone else is doing." She tilted her head. "You know, I think you look a little like him. It's your smile. You have the same dimples."

She finished her task, setting aside the basin while he buttoned his pajamas. "Are you hungry? Doctor Brumbaugh says you can try some Jello today."

He'd never had much use for the wiggly dessert Americans seemed so fond of, but this morning, it would be a special treat. "Good. Can I ... get out ... of bed?"

"Maybe later today you can try a few steps. Remember, don't talk too much."

When he'd finished eating, Shelby appeared in the doorway, the sunlight framing her. His heart skipped, grateful she hadn't come during the sponge bath, but when he considered just how many she must have given him at the MASH, heat stained his cheeks.

"Good morning, Parker." Her eyes sparkled. "Nurse Garrett said you had Jello!"

He smiled at her as she drew closer. "Did you ... sleep well?"

"I hardly remember closing my eyes before nodding off. Your voice sounds stronger."

"Yes."

"Wonderful!" She reached into her bag. "I thought I could read to you this morning."

"Your Bible?"

"Yes."

"Did you ... eat?" He was enjoying the sound of his own voice, despite some hoarseness.

"I grabbed a cup of coffee and a Danish on the way here." She settled into the chair. "I love the book of Luke. Would it be okay if I started there today?"

"Luke ... the physician."

When she smiled at him, the fog from Soonja's visit seemed to clear.

Dr. Brumbaugh made his rounds an hour later, checking Parker from stem to stern. He grinned as he draped the stethoscope over his neck. "As sick as you were when you came here, Dr. Tate, you're making amazing progress." He half-whispered as he looked toward Shelby, "I think this one is the best medicine going."

"She is." He smiled at the way she blushed.

"Are you feeling up to a couple more visitors?"

"Yes." He wondered if his parents had returned this early in the day, dreading they might bring Soonja. *I must speak with my mother at the first opportunity.*

He and Shelby waited less than two minutes before Dr. Mike Baroni and Private Jim Ward hobbled into the room on their canes.

Shelby stood and brought her hands together. "Private Ward! Just look at you!"

"Nurse Shelby!" He broke into a huge grin. "I didn't expect to see you here."

"I, uh, am making a house call."

Ward winked at Parker. "So I see."

"Mike Baroni," the doctor said, reaching out his hand. "I'm the fellow Dr. Tate sprang from the POW camp."

"I'm so happy to meet you!"

"Tate." Baroni moved closer to the bed and gently shook Parker's hand. "How are you, my friend? You've really been through it."

"I am ... much better." Happiness flowed through him. "How are you?"

Baroni said, "I'm probably going to break out of here in a week. I never thought I'd say this, but I can't wait to get back to the 8063rd."

"What about you, Private Ward?" Shelby asked.

"Just 'Jim.' They tell me I'll be going home in a couple of days, home as in Oklahoma." His face glowed. "What about you, Doc?"

"Not sure."

Brumbaugh reentered the room, crossing his arms. "That remains to be seen."

"Dr. Brumbaugh, are you aware of what this man did?" Baroni asked.

"I've heard some of the story. We weren't sure what to make of Dr. Tate when he got here, only what the MASH CO had wired ahead. Without dog tags or ID, we had only hearsay to go by." He gazed at Parker. "Where are your dog tags and ID anyway?"

He reached back into his recent, addled memory. "Chaplain Frank, 8063rd."

"I'll put in a call to him. We're going to need proof of citizenship before this show is over, although these eyewitness testimonies have me convinced you had nothing to do with the PKA." He addressed Baroni and Ward. "Will you two come with me? I'd like you to tell your story to the hospital CO. Nurse Shelby, might you have anything to add?"

"I could tell him the only personal possession Dr. Tate had on him besides forged North Korean papers was his Bible. That's what tipped me off."

Baroni reached for Parker's hand before they left on their mission. "We'll clear you," he said. "You have my word."

CHAPTER TWENTY-ONE

"You seem antsy." Shelby laughed at his raised brows. "You know, restless."

"I would like to ... get out of bed to ..." His face colored.

His smoky voice, reminiscent of her grandfather's pipe tobacco, thrilled her. She also caught his meaning. She'd helped multitudes of wounded soldiers use the facilities or assisted them with unwieldy bedpans without batting any eye. She had done so for Parker when he first came to the MASH, but not now. The personal lines they were crossing could not be withdrawn.

"I'll ask Dr. Brumbaugh." She left the sunlit room and searched the hallway, finding the physician emerging from another patient's room.

"Why, good morning, Nurse Shelby. I don't need to ask what you're doing here today." He attached his pen to a lab coat pocket. "What can I do for you?"

"Dr. Tate is eager to try out his legs to, uh, use the bathroom. What are your thoughts?"

"He's been making remarkable progress with you here."

She blushed and looked at her feet.

Brumbaugh spoke over the blaring intercom. "I have a minute. Let's talk to him."

They wandered into Parker's room and saw Nurse Garrett was removing a food tray.

"Oh, hello! I was just coming to find you, Doctor. Dr. Tate has a request."

"So, I hear." He smiled at Parker. "I don't think there's any reason why you shouldn't get out of bed to relieve yourself." He glanced at Shelby, then at the other nurse. "Garrett, will you help me get him up?"

Shelby stood close to the door where she'd be out of their way and not embarrass Parker.

"How's that bum leg?" Brumbaugh asked.

"I feel no pain, just stiffness."

"As you get out of bed more, the kinks should work out and any limping resolve. Here, hold on to me."

Parker draped his right arm around the doctor's shoulder and gave a small hop onto his bare feet.

"Nurse Shelby, can you see if there are any slippers around?"

She flew into action, finding them under the bed gathering a light dusting. "Here they are!" She helped him into first the left one, then the right. When she raised herself, she took note of Parker's height, which she guessed to be around five feet nine. As for his current weight, she refused to consider how close it might be to her own.

Shelby noted the set of his jaw as he put one foot before the other on his way to the rest room. She held her breath, knowing if he did begin to fall, Brumbaugh would catch him. When they reached the privy, Nurse Garrett swung open the door, allowing the doctor to accompany Parker inside. Closing it, she gave Shelby a sheepish grin.

"He's doing so well. You've been great medicine for him."

When he'd finished this first expedition, Parker slumped into the recliner and closed his eyes.

"Before I go," the doctor said, "I want to tell you I spoke with your MASH chaplain."

Shelby's eyebrows furrowed. "Where he served, or my unit, where he was brought?"

"Where he served, fellow named Frank." He turned back to Parker. "He said he has your personal effects, enlistment papers, and dog tags."

"This is good news." Parker accepted a glass of water from Nurse Garrett and sipped.

"He's either going to bring them here himself or have them sent today or tomorrow. My CO is quite pleased. He's heard about your heroism and wants to make sure there are no complications or misunderstandings when you leave. As soon as he sees the paperwork, we ditch that fellow." He inclined his head toward the door and the ever-present MP.

"How long will ... I stay here?"

"I'd like to see you eating solid food and walking around first. Rehab can be done in Tokyo, then you'll go to a Stateside Army hospital to finish recovery before being discharged."

Parker shot a lingering look in Shelby's direction, which she answered with a forced smile. *Tokyo. Then the States. I may not get to see him again after tomorrow, at least on this side of the world.* She focused on the conversation rather than her surging emotions.

"One more thing, Tate. Where's your passport? There's been some confusion about your name. In some instances, it's Tae-ho Park, but mostly Parker Tate."

"My passport is ... with ... family here. It shows my American ... and Korean names." He coughed into his right hand and took a drink of water.

"Easy on the throat," Brumbaugh said. "It's great you can speak more, but don't strain those vocal chords. So, then, do your parents have a telephone?"

"Yes."

"Get that number, Nurse Garrett, and ask them to bring the passport here. Once we have that, the Army record, and dog tags, Colonel Kitterman can clear Dr. Tate."

"Yes, sir." She handed Parker her clip board, and he wrote the phone number. "I'll go make that call if there's nothing more, Doctor."

"Go ahead." He went toward the door and smiled at Parker. "Keep up the good work."

Shelby pulled up a chair next to him and took his hand, stirring at the physical contact. "There's something I've been meaning to mention to you. I, uh, believe we both came to Korea on the same troopship, the *Lt. Raymond O. Beaudoin.*"

His eyes widened. "Was that you ... on the deck ... that windy night?"

She tingled all over. "Yes, that was me."

"I have felt somehow ... as if ... I knew you before—" He waved a hand. "—all of this."

They observed a moment of awed silence. He gazed at her then and asked, "How old are you, and when is your birthday?"

She grinned, welcoming the opportunity to speak of mundane things, to get to know details about this man whose soul she already knew. "I'll be twenty-two on May twenty-ninth. How about you?"

"My birthday is ... August the third ... I am twenty-nine."

"You seem much younger."

"I have what Americans call ... a baby face."

She peered into his brown eyes. “I love your face.” *Did I really use that word?* Her heart thudded, her message hanging between them.

Parker lifted her hand and touched his lips to her fingers.

Shelby had finished reading a chapter to Parker from her current favorite book, which she’d read three times so far, *A Man Called Peter*. At first, she wondered if she should share a story which had become so personal to her faith. Then, she knew without a doubt she was safe with Parker. Quickly, he became absorbed in the winsome biography about a Scottish immigrant who became Chaplain of the US Senate.

“I suppose,” Shelby said, “in Christ there really is no east or west.”

When he smiled at her, she knew Parker didn’t regard her being an American as a detriment. She knew this to be true when he said, “All are one in Christ.”

When he looked toward the door, her gaze followed along.

“Look who’s come to see you,” Nurse Garrett said.

Anna and his grandmother greeted Parker with grins and yips of joy. He broke into a dimpled smile, holding open his arms first to Mrs. Oh, the old woman speaking Korean but whose meaning Shelby clearly understood. Once they’d exchanged their earnest greetings, Anna and Mrs. Oh turned to Shelby with more restrained bows, a gesture she returned.

“I am very happy to see you again,” she said. “Nurse Garrett, this is Dr. Tate’s grandmother, Mrs. Oh, and his sister, Anna Park.”

"I've already met Mrs. Oh, but not Miss Park. I did meet your other sister yesterday."

Anna frowned. "I am afraid I do not have a sister. Tae-ho, uh Parker, is my oldest sibling, and our brother John is in America."

Garrett looked to Shelby. "Who was that woman with Mr. and Mrs. Tate, uh, Park?"

The words escaped Shelby's lips before she realized what she was saying. "Oh, that was Soonja, his fiancée."

There was gawking and dead silence, Shelby looking wide-eyed toward Parker. What followed was the first time she'd ever heard him laugh.

Parker wanted to see his grandfather.

Nurse Garrett volunteered to show Shelby the way to Dr. Oh's room while Parker visited with his family.

"I don't know if you could find it on your own," she said as they entered the hallway. "This hospital's corridors are a maze."

As they passed an array of hospital workers, the nurse asked about Soonja.

"Parker's mother wants them to get married, but he's never wanted or agreed to it. He regrets not having been firmer with his mother, but when he first came to Seoul, she was quite ill."

She whistled through her teeth. "In Korea, the parents have a tremendous amount of authority over their children."

"Even grown children?"

"Even them. They take 'honor your father and mother' to new heights." They paused before an elevator and Garrett pushed a button. "Well, the bridge has been crossed now."

"What do you mean?"

"They're not stupid, Shelby. Anyone can see he has strong feelings for you."

The only mark against her happiness was the possible tension between Parker and his mother and the possibility of his caving to her wishes. She refused to consider either. Not now.

When they arrived at Dr. Oh's room, the sun illuminated the small man who sat dozing in a chair. Shelby smiled at the halo effect over his full head of gray hair. He wore a contented smile, hands folded across his lap in a peaceful repose.

Nurse Garrett made the initial move. "Dr. Oh. Dr. Oh, I've brought a visitor."

His eyelids fluttered, and he straightened, looking first at Garrett, then Shelby. He bequeathed a welcoming smile. "Hello."

She bowed in the Korean custom.

"This is Nurse Shelby Kichline. She took care of your grandson at a mobile surgical hospital."

The faded brown eyes sparkled. "I am most grateful to you. May I go to him?"

"Do you feel up to it, Dr. Oh?" Garrett asked.

"Oh, yes, yes I do."

Shelby bathed herself in the fondness this dear family expressed for each other. They sat in chairs encircling Parker, Shelby having chosen the one farthest away, not wishing to impose. Fortunately for her, they spoke English.

Dr. Oh clasped his grandson's hand. "I am so very glad you are well. When you came for me, I was shocked when I saw you in that North Korean uniform."

"I longed to ... speak to you. I had to get you ... out of there ... without detection."

Shelby noticed the similarities in their features, especially around their mouths and how their voices carried the same smoky tones.

"You are very brave, my son. I am so grateful to you." Dr. Oh turned to Shelby. "Tell me once again, what is your name?"

"Shelby Kichline. I'm with the 8055th MASH where Parker, uh Tae-ho, was brought after being wounded."

"Kichline." He raised his face upward as if reaching for a memory. "I knew a Jacob Kichline at the seminary in Pyongyang a very long time ago."

Shelby gasped. "Jacob Kichline is my grandfather."

All eyes turned to the two of them.

"Your grandfather was in Korea?" Anna asked.

"Yes, he was. After he graduated from Princeton Seminary, he came here with the Presbyterian Mission Board."

Dr. Oh wore a huge smile. "I counted him among my dearest friends. I always wondered what happened to him as we lost touch after the second world war."

Shelby trembled, dazed by her and Parker's family's tie. "After returning to America, he served several churches."

"And does he still live?"

"Oh, yes. I can't wait to tell him about you, about all of this."

Dr. Oh sighed. "Perhaps I may have the pleasure of hearing from him once again."

"I am sure you will." She smiled at Mrs. Oh's nod of approval.

The grandfather gazed at her. "And you, my dear, do you also follow our Christ?"

"Yes, sir, since I was a little girl hearing my grandfather preach."

"This is good. Our Tae-ho has also followed Jesus since his youth. Many stray when they leave the family home, but you have not."

A benediction of silence rested upon them.

After Parker fell asleep, Shelby wheeled Dr. Oh back to his room, and Anna took their grandmother home.

"Would you like to sit in your chair or go to bed?" Shelby asked the elderly minister.

"I desire the bed just now."

She assisted him, then covered him with the sheet and blanket.

He reached for her hand, his own conveying a vital force. "Shelby Kichline, granddaughter of my friend Jacob."

She beamed at him.

"You have his blue eyes, a color I have not seen in anyone else." Dr. Oh settled his head against the pillow. "Tell me, are you in love with my grandson?"

Shelby's jaw unhinged.

He chuffed a laugh. "I sometimes forget. Americans are far subtler than Koreans, especially old Korean men. Do not worry, my dear, you are safe expressing yourself to me. I could feel and see how the two of you were together, even with others present."

Her voice cracked. "I have to leave tomorrow."

"Tao-ho also will leave here, and like you, return to America." His eyes shone.

CHAPTER TWENTY-TWO

Almost as quickly as he experienced renewed strength, the surge would ebb. Fortunately, Shelby seemed to understand. After the enlivening visit with his grandparents and sister, he asked Shelby to help him back to bed.

He reached for her hand after she tucked him in. "Please, stay."

"I'll be glad to, but you need to sleep."

"Yes, Nurse."

She laughed, and he grinned at her.

"There is one thing."

"Yes?"

When she leaned closer, he caught his breath at her nearness. He whispered, "How much longer ... is your tour ... in Korea?"

"I'm to be discharged in July or August."

He calculated the months.

"You'll already be in Hopewell."

He gazed into those remarkable eyes, astonished at seeing himself reflected in them. "When you leave ... tomorrow, I may not ..."

She squeezed his hand. "I know. I very much doubt I can get away for another visit."

"You will write?"

"Of course. Will you write to me?"

"Yes."

He watched her pull out paper and a pencil from her bag and begin writing.

"I'm leaving my address at the MASH, along with my home address and phone number." When she finished, she asked him where she should put them for safekeeping.

Parker opened his Bible, and she slipped the note inside. Then he wrote his Hopewell address and phone number.

"Do not be sad." He touched her soft cheek. "If God brought our grandfathers together ... fifty years ago ... he can make ..." His eyes shuttered.

"Please, rest your voice. I know what you're trying to say. What we share is deeper than distance."

Parker awakened to the sight of the winter sun leaking rays through the windows.

He looked toward the wall clock and saw a nurse with her back turned away from him.

"Shelby?"

Nurse Garrett wheeled around. "I wish I looked like her, but thanks for the compliment."

Parker realized by the clock he'd slept for ten hours. "No one woke me."

"I gave strict orders to the night staff to leave you alone."

"Thank you."

"How are you this morning?"

My last one with Shelby, at least for now. "I am quite thirsty."

Garrett poured a fresh glass from a pitcher and handed it to him. "I know you'd probably like to gulp this, but take it slow."

He held himself back from doing the very thing he wanted. How had she known he wanted to guzzle the cool drink?

"Do you need to use the restroom?"

"Yes."

Garrett helped him out of bed. "How does a shower sound?"

"Wonderful."

"Do you want to try having one?"

"I would."

Some twenty minutes later, he lay back in bed.

"I'll get your breakfast. Just sip that water nice and slow," Garrett said, leaving the room.

He picked up his Bible and turned to Psalm 125. "Those who put their trust in the Lord are like Mount Zion, which cannot be shaken but stands fast forever. As the mountains surround Jerusalem, so the Lord surrounds his people both now and forevermore."

"Good morning!"

He looked up from his reading, feeling suddenly weightless. "Shelby. I hoped you would come early." He soaked up the sight of her graceful steps as she neared the bed. Had she any idea of her loveliness?

"Your voice sounds much stronger!"

He tried on more words for size, pleased at the result. "I believe you are right."

"I want to spend as much time as I can with you before I have to leave." When he laid the Bible aside, she took his hand, and they smiled at each other. "Wait. Your hair seems damp. Did you have a shower?"

"Yes, and I slept for ten hours." He grinned, enormously pleased with himself.

"That's great. No wonder you look especially handsome."

He grinned. "Did you sleep well? Your stay here has not been much fun for you."

"I'm fine, and my time here is exactly what I've wanted." She looked into his eyes. "There's no place I'd rather be."

His ears pricked up when he heard "Unforgettable" drifting in from a patient's room across the hall. "I very much like this song."

"'Unforgettable?' Oh, I do too. Nat King Cole is one of my favorite singers, and this song, well, reminds me of someone." She dipped her chin.

"Who might that be?'

"Who do you think?" She winked at him.

They enjoyed the quiet of each other's company until Dr. Brumbaugh came on his rounds. At the end of his examination, he smiled at his patient. "You're doing great. I think you can start using your voice more, but rest if you get fatigued. Nurse Kichline, I understand you're due back at the MASH today."

"I have to leave right after lunch."

"Dr. Tate, you're not going to reverse course after she leaves, are you?"

"No. I have much to live for."

"I'd say so." He glanced at his watch. "I understand you're going to have visitors today."

He raised an eyebrow. "Visitors?"

He popped his hand against his mouth. "Well, the cat's out of the bag now. I haven't been told much. Ah well, I'm off to the rest of the races." He waved his hand and left the room.

"What did he mean?"

She shrugged her shoulders. "I don't know. I guess we'll find out together."

He took her hands and fixed his eyes on hers. "Are you all right about leaving today?"

Her lips quivered. "I wish I didn't have to go."

"Our time will come again."

She closed her eyes and bowed her head as Parker slipped into a spontaneous prayer.

"Lord, thank you for bringing us together. We trust you to keep us in your care. Help us honor you as we wait to be together again."

"Amen."

A stirring at the door ended the sacred moment. They released each other's hands when Mrs. Park entered the room with Anna and Soonja. Parker knew forced smiles and stiff bows when he saw them.

"Good morning, *Eomeoni*," he said. "Hello, Anna. Soonja."

"You are looking and sounding well today." Mrs. Park gave Shelby a terse nod as she brushed past her.

"So are you." He spoke through gritted teeth.

"You have made me well again." She clapped her hands. "Today is a special day."

He narrowed his eyes. "How?"

Anna spoke up. "We got a call from the hospital to be here at ten o'clock. Father and Grandmother are bringing Grandfather here."

He loved his family dearly but regretted every minute they leached from him and Shelby. He also resolved to make this nonsense with Soonja stop before going any further.

He looked first at Anna then Shelby. "Would you please excuse us? I must speak with my mother and Soonja."

His sister gaped at him before she and Shelby wordlessly left. His mother's face lit up, and he steeled himself to do this thing.

"You said my family was asked to come. Soonja is not a family member."

His mother's mouth opened, closed, then reopened. "But she is your intended."

He held up his hand when she looked like she was about to argue. "When I arrived in Seoul, I wanted to end your matchmaking, but you were ill." He looked at Soonja, his heart wrenching at her sudden draining of color. "I thought if I didn't encourage you, the matter would resolve itself. I ask your forgiveness." The many words strained his throat, but he knew they had to be spoken.

Soonja continued staring at him.

"You have always been to me as a sister." He emphasized the last word.

His mother's eyes flashed. "Soonja is right for you, Tae-ho. She knows you. She is Korean. She will make a fine wife."

"She will make a fine wife," he said, "but not mine."

"I must go." Soonja turned quickly toward the door, but Mrs. Park grabbed her hand.

"You must stay. I will leave you alone to talk."

She turned to Parker and bowed. "Goodbye, Tae-ho."

"Goodbye, Soonja."

His mother stared after her before glaring at Parker. "I do not understand you."

"*Eomeoni,* you must let this go."

"I suppose you have feelings for this other one." She pointed toward the door.

"For Shelby, yes."

"You hardly know her. Your father and I do not know her. She is American."

"I know her."

A commotion broke the awkwardness. The door burst open, and people poured into the room, Dr. Brumbaugh leading the procession. Parker's father pushed Dr. Oh's wheelchair and by his side, Mrs. Oh came smiling into the room followed by Anna, Nurse Garrett, Shelby, Dr. Baroni, and Jim Ward. He gaped at the sight of Chaplain Frank and Colonel Kitterman, who seemed very much aware of his own importance.

Brumbaugh waved his arms. "If everyone will please come in!"

Parker's family drew near the head of his bed, and he locked eyes with Shelby, hoping she would come closer. She telegraphed her need to stay within her rank. He exchanged visual greetings with all the others who had come for whatever purpose had brought them here.

"This is an important day for Dr. Parker Tate, formerly Tae-ho Park," Brumbaugh said. "I would like to present Colonel Hugh Kitterman, CO of this hospital."

Kitterman shook Parker's hand. "We may have had some doubts about you when you arrived, but thanks to your friends, we know exactly who you are and what you did under fire."

Parker's head tingled.

"Chaplain Frank has returned your personal belongings, which prove you are a soldier in the United States Army. You are also a very brave man. Captain Tate, I am proud to present you one of the military's highest honors, the Purple Heart." He continued his speech while he pinned the medal on Parker's robe. When he finished, Parker saluted the colonel.

"I also want to tell you, Captain, the Army is aware of your application to become a United States citizen. Until now, Koreans have not been admitted to citizenship, but I have it on good authority this is about to change. I promise you'll be among the very first of your people to attain American citizenship." He posed for several pictures with the honoree and his family, Parker wondering if he wasn't dreaming this.

Afterward, people began trickling out of the room. He noticed his mother beginning to droop and motioned for his sister. "I think *Eomeoni* needs to rest."

She leaned closer. "Did you speak to her about Soonja?"

"Yes."

"I wondered why she wasn't here." Anna hugged him. "I am very proud of you, Parker."

"You are a good sister."

She drew close and whispered, "I also support you in, well, the other thing."

He closed his eyes, smiling.

Before leaving, Chaplain Frank gave Parker a large envelope containing his dog tags, identification papers, and other personal effects.

"Thank you. I am happy to have them back."

"It was my pleasure. I'm honored to know you." He scratched the side of his nose. "I almost forgot, Colonel Sheppard and Father Stephens send their congratulations." The chaplain turned to Shelby. "The colonel also told me to accompany you as far as the 8063rd, then a driver will take you back to your unit. We'll be leaving the hospital right after we get a bite to eat in about ..." He lifted his watch. "I'd say a half hour or so. Would you care to join us for lunch?"

Her voice dropped. "Oh. No, thank you. I'll stay here until you're ready."

Frank looked from her to Parker. "Okay. I'll be back in a bit."

When everyone had gone, Parker reached for her hands, recording the look and feel of her on the tablet of his heart. He could tell by her stiffened shoulders she was holding back a dam's worth of emotion. Although his fatigue reached all the way to his feet, he strained with his remaining energy to say what needed to be said. "How can I thank you for what you have done for me, what you have meant ... what you mean to me?"

She looked down, slowly shaking her head.

He caressed her cheek, and she raised her eyes to his. "This is not the end. If God brought us together on the troopship and at the MASH, if he ..." He cleared his aching throat before continuing. "If he brought our grandfathers together ... we will see each other again."

She brushed away tears with a handkerchief and blew gently into it. "Yes."

"Sit next to me."

She climbed onto the side of the bed and they held each other's hands. Although he fought sleep so he wouldn't miss a single precious minute with her, Parker was so drained he nodded off. Forty minutes later, Shelby hopped to the floor and smoothed her skirt when Chaplain Frank arrived.

"Are you ready?" the pastor asked.

"I'll be with you in a minute."

"I, uh, I'll wait in the hall."

"Parker, Chaplain Frank is here. I have to go now."

He stirred and searching her face, reached again for her hands. "May God be with you."

"And also with you." She pressed her lips to his forehead and when she reached the door, turned to him one last time.

CHAPTER TWENTY-THREE

As Shelby bounced back to the 8063rd, her emotions mimicked the World War II-era truck's unsteady shocks. The malfunctioning heater alternately gushed sauna-like heat followed by an arctic blast, its cabin reeking of smoke. She only spoke when spoken to, thanking the Lord that Chaplain Frank and Colonel Borsch kept up their own steady stream of chatter.

She closed her eyes to the sun's strobe-like flickering through bare trees and relived the awkward moments after Parker had dismissed her and his sister. Judging from Soonja's ashen face, he'd set the matter straight. Shelby recalled how Anna had reached out to the woman.

"I am so sorry my mother misled you. She did not mean to."

"Did you know he did not love me?" Soonja spoke in a monotone.

"Until Parker came back to Korea, I had no reason to disbelieve my mother."

Soonja shot a look at Shelby. "How could you take him from me?"

In that moment, Shelby remembered her eighth-grade crush on Johnny Theodoris at summer camp. Throughout

August, she'd crossed out the days on her calendar and told her best friend Louise this was her "Countdown to Johnny." She didn't know Louise had written to him about it. On the first day of school, he'd confronted her in front of God and everybody saying he wasn't her boyfriend while Louise smirked in the background. There was no way she was going to humiliate Soonja, who seemed in every way a lovely person.

Fortunately, Anna had responded for Shelby. "Soonja, he was never yours."

The petite beauty had turned toward Shelby again. "You can never know him as I do. You are not Korean." She'd lifted a handkerchief to her eyes and hastened down the hall.

Anna had touched Shelby's arm. "I am sorry she said that to you. She is hurt."

"I'd be just as upset if I were in her shoes."

"I like you, Shelby. Although my brother is recovering from severe wounds, I have never seen him happier. You are good for him."

"Although I'm not Korean?" She'd lifted her hands, palms up.

"The Bible says in Christ we are all one family. Perhaps you do not know our culture, but you and Tae-ho share a deep faith."

Shelby had teared up. "Thank you, Anna. How will your mother take this?"

"She has had her heart set on Soonja and loves her dearly. She will be hurt and perhaps ashamed. Please do not despise her. My mother has made a mistake."

"I will show her grace," Shelby said, wondering where those words had come from. She'd expected to say, "I'll be nice to her" or "It's okay." But yes, she would pray for

God's grace to be upon Mrs. Park and to show the woman kindness.

A vast pothole catapulted the Army vehicle, and Shelby narrowly avoided biting her tongue when she thudded back onto the torn cushion.

"Are you okay back there?" the colonel asked.

"Yes, sir. I'm fine, thanks."

"This rust bucket is about ready for the junk yard. These roads are killers."

She rearranged her hat and crossed her arms against the cold. Although there hadn't been much time with the Park family after Soonja left, she would never forget her last interaction with his mother. Before leaving her son's room she'd said, "Thank you for taking care of Tae-ho and bringing us news of him."

Shelby suspected the gesture may have taken Parker's mother enormous effort and had wanted to hug her, American-style. Instead she had bowed and said, "You are most welcome, Mrs. Park."

Now she stared out at the passing, war-pocked scenery. *I think Anna could become a friend. She's a wise young woman, and I liked her right away. And Dr. Oh is such a dear man. I think he understands my relationship with Parker and seems to approve. I'm not as sure about Mrs. Oh. She's so quiet, but she's also been kind to me. What a nice family! I can't wait to write Poppa about all that's happened. He'll be the first person I tell. He won't believe what I have to tell him. I can hardly believe it myself. This situation is the Lord's doing. I wonder, though, what exactly it is he's doing.*

Shelby was back at the 8055th by suppertime. The Jeep she'd ridden in for the final leg of the journey came to a juddering halt, inflicting one last insult to her backside. She thanked the driver then schlepped her bag to her quarters where the old Korean woman who did their laundry was placing clean bundles on the beds.

"*An yeong haseo.*" Shelby bowed to the lady, who returned the greeting.

She gestured toward Shelby's bag.

"I do have some laundry for you, Mrs. Kwang. Just give me a minute." She raised her index finger before putting her dirty clothes on the end of her bed. She checked her watch and realized if she wanted to eat, there wouldn't be time to change into her everyday uniform.

Inside the mess tent, she got behind the dwindling line. The server was plopping meatloaf, peas, and mashed potatoes onto trays, hardly the gracious dining she'd enjoyed in the hotel's restaurant. Nevertheless, she was suddenly ravenous, having skipped lunch to spend every remaining minute with Parker. She decanted a cup of coffee and found a spot with Evelyn and Vickie, who whooped and hollered at the sight of her.

"Well, well, if it isn't Shelby Kichline returned from the big city."

"Don't you look spiffy."

"How was your leave?"

"Do tell all."

Their faces were almost in her plate as they clamored for information.

"It's good to be back." She wondered why she'd said such a thing when she wanted to be nowhere else but at Parker's side. She swallowed a sob and faked a smile.

Evelyn touched her arm. "You look tired, Shelby."

"It's been a long day, and getting back here wasn't like traveling in my dad's Buick."

She moved closer. "How's Dr. Tate? We've heard bits and pieces about his improvement and his name being cleared and something about a medal, but we need details."

"He's doing quite well." She sipped her coffee, noting their empty trays. They'd eaten and were ready to talk, but she was hungry and irritable and wanted to be left alone. *Lord, help me not to bite their heads off. They're just being nice.*

"That's all you have to say?" Vickie was in full sass mode.

"I haven't eaten since this morning."

"Oh, okay." She exchanged glances with Evelyn.

"Eat your dinner, and we'll talk later," Vickie said. "Just let us know you're okay."

Shelby thawed. "I'm fine, more than fine. I just need time to process everything."

Just then Captain Olsen stopped by. "Well, if it isn't Nurse Shelby."

She sighed. "Hello, Captain."

He sniggered. "So, how's your little gook?"

Her nostrils flared, but before she could answer his insult, someone else broke in.

"That was uncalled for, Neil."

Danny.

"Oh, she knows I'm just teasing her."

Shelby vented her roiling emotions. "No, I don't know, Doctor Olsen. I don't call any insulting language funny."

"Well excuse me for trying to lighten things up around here."

Danny took his colleague by the shoulder and led him away. Before exiting the mess tent, he turned around and mouthed "sorry" to Shelby.

"Good for you." Evelyn clapped her hands. "I'm glad you gave him what-for."

Shelby's ire dissipated when the nurses expressed enough outrage for all of them. By the time she reached for her fruit cocktail, Colonel Sheppard was at her side.

"Welcome back to the 8055th, Nurse Kichline."

"Thank you, sir."

"I'd like to talk to you. If you're too tired tonight, how about tomorrow morning right before breakfast? I think Major McKaig is giving you the second shift."

All she wanted was to return to her cot and write to her grandfather. Then she reminded herself this man had made her trip to Seoul possible.

She unveiled her story to Colonel Sheppard and Father Stephens in the CO's office while wind rattled the windows. Sheppard puffed a cigar, the priest nodding his head as she spoke.

"I'm mighty glad Tate's on the mend. He went through a tough time, then to be mistaken for a North Korean. When Colonel Kitterman called about the Purple Heart, I was mighty glad."

"Was Dr. Tate's family able to be there?" the priest asked.

"They were. I especially enjoyed meeting his grandfather who Parker, uh Dr. Tate, rescued from the prison camp, and Dr. Baroni." She squirmed under Colonel Sheppard's scrutiny. "Actually," she said, "the most astonishing thing happened. Dr. Tate's grandfather was good friends with my grandfather many years ago when mine was a missionary in Korea."

"You don't say." Father Stephens slapped the desk with the flat of his hands. "If I didn't know you, Shelby, I'd say you were pulling my leg."

"I can't wait to tell my grandfather."

"Well, you've had quite a day, quite a few days," Sheppard said. "Go get some shuteye."

"I will, sir, and thank you again for the three-day pass."

"You're welcome."

Just as Shelby rose, Major McKaig knocked on the door and entered.

"I heard Shelby was back."

"Hello, Major," she said.

"How was your leave?"

She searched for an adjective appropriate to the occasion. "Fulfilling, ma'am."

"I see." She peered at Shelby then turned to the commander. "Sir, I'd like to have a word alone with my nurse if you don't mind."

"Why yes, yes of course." He rose. "C'mon Padre, I'll buy you a cup of coffee."

Shelby stood facing her superior.

"How is our Parker Tate?"

"He's doing very well after the emergency surgery."

"I'm glad to hear it. I also heard about the Purple Heart." She paused, staring at Shelby. "I gave you permission to leave because I thought you needed some time to work through this. So, did you get him out of your system?"

She wondered what the major expected her to say. Gulping, Shelby decided on the truth. "No, ma'am, I didn't."

She folded her arms. "I cannot allow you to let this interfere with your work."

"I assure you, Major, it won't."

Her eyes suddenly smiled. "Where does he go from here?"

Relaxing, Shelby said, "When he's strong enough, he'll go to Tokyo, and when he can stand the trip to the States, he'll go there for the final recovery phase. Then he'll be discharged."

"That sounds about right. Where does he live?"

"New Jersey, about an hour from my family."

McKaig lifted her chin. "Isn't that interesting? So, would I be correct in assuming this is not the end of the road?"

"That would be correct, ma'am."

"Just so you're aware, I can't give you another pass before he leaves."

"I had no intention of asking, Major. You've already been so generous."

"Good girl." Her expression softened. "You aren't the first nurse who's fallen in love with a soldier, or in this case, a doctor. None of them forgot what they were here to do."

Shelby hadn't used those words herself yet, but there was no denying her feelings. "Neither will I."

McKaig squeezed her shoulder. "I know you won't. For whatever it's worth, I was quite impressed with Dr. Tate. Character shows through in tough times. You've chosen well."

CHAPTER TWENTY-FOUR

"You look especially tired, Dr. Tate." Nurse Garrett helped him back into bed after he used the rest room. "You've had quite a day."

He sighed with a blend of contentment and no small amount of longing. Shelby was gone, and with her, the light seemed to have withdrawn from the room. When would he see her again? How would he get along without her?

"I hope you don't mind my asking, and if you do, please say so." The nurse stepped back, crossing her arms. "Is everything okay? I mean, I picked up some tension with your mother and that other girl. I, uh, I hope I'm being more concerned for you than nosy."

He offered a small smile. "You speak like a Korean who is always direct. I cleared up the matter between us." He lowered his voice. "It was not easy."

"I think most of our mothers mean well. Sometimes they overstep, at least in America they do. I know mine does."

"Here too." He laughed. "Especially here."

Garrett smiled. "Again, I'm sorry if I said too much. I've grown to care about you and Shel ..." She cleared her throat. "Would you like me to turn off the lights?"

"No, thank you." *I need the light.*

She shuffled out of the room, closing the door no longer guarded by a rock-jawed MP. Somewhere down the hall, a radio played what sounded like a Perry Como song. He liked Como and Sinatra, although his tastes ran to the classics, especially Mozart and Dvorak. He sank into the pillow's comfort wondering what kind of music Shelby favored. He could imagine her on a dance floor jitterbugging to a swing band. He would write and ask her this and many other questions about herself, things they hadn't had time to find out about each other. Perhaps in this way they could continue to forge their bond even while they were apart.

He prayed silently as he drifted into sleep. *Dear Lord, thank you for this day you have made. You have showered abundant blessings upon me for which I am deeply grateful. You brought my family, Private Ward, Dr. Baroni, Chaplain Frank, and Shelby. Thank you for allowing her to be with me here and for bringing her into my life. Bless her and keep her in her difficult work as a nurse. Give her joy and peace. And Lord, thank you for giving me courage to speak to Mother. I know she meant well, and I hope I honored her and let Soonja down gently. Please forgive me for allowing the situation to go on far too long. Will you ...* He wafted into slumber. *Will you comfort ... restore ... them? Thank you, Lord. I praise ... your ... name.*

He slept the entire rest of the afternoon and awakened with a sense of purpose. First, he asked Nurse Garrett if she would contact his sister. He wanted Anna to bring a photo of himself for Shelby, so she would not feel as if he were so far away. He would ask her to send one of herself as well, preferably in color so he could gaze upon her incredible eyes. He also would ask Anna to write to their brother about all that had happened. No doubt the family had told him when Parker had gone missing as well as when he'd turned up in the Army hospital. Now he wanted John to be updated and at peace.

"What kind of photo should I ask her for?" Garrett brought him out of his thoughts.

"I sent a few to the family not long ago from New Jersey."

"Is there anything else you need?"

"Do you have writing paper and a pen?"

"I can get those items for you." She smiled at him before leaving the room.

That is one insightful woman. My heart seems to be an open book to her.

Within a half hour, Parker was poised to begin writing to Shelby. Nurse Garrett had spoken to Anna, who said she would bring a photo after her morning classes.

> Dear Shelby,
> I pray your journey back to the MASH went smoothly for you, and you are settling into your routine. How you blessed me by coming to see me here, using a precious three-day pass when you could have been out enjoying yourself. I do not take the sacrifice of your time lightly. You have only been gone for a few hours, but already I miss your dear presence. I try not to think about how much time must pass before we see each other again. In the meantime, we must make letters suffice. Perhaps this will be a good time to get to know each other better. I feel I know you from a deep place in my soul, but there are details I wish very much to know, such as your family's story. Where do they come from? What are your parents and siblings like? Who are your friends at home? What is your home like? What was your favorite subject in

school? What kind of music do you like? What is your favorite color? You see, I have many questions.

My favorite color is the remarkable blue of your eyes. As for music, I am especially fond of Dvorak and Mozart. Classical music is what I mostly enjoy, but I also like American popular singers, including your Perry Como. Do you dance? I imagine you do. I was busy studying in my youth and never learned, but I am willing once my leg heals. Perhaps you will teach me?

I hope to include a photo of myself. I have asked my sister to find a recent one, so you may keep me close in this way. Will you also send one of yourself? In color, if possible.

May the Lord bless and keep you.

He wondered if he should sign the letter "love." He knew he would be declaring himself, his heart open to getting hurt. If she'd harbored any doubts after the Soonja affair when there had been no time to speak about that situation, he wanted Shelby to know his feelings for her. He signed his letter ...

Love, Parker

Nurse Garrett beamed at him when she removed his empty dinner tray. "How did you like the mashed potatoes and strained peas?"

"Very much."

"Did you have any discomfort while eating?"

"None."

"These are good signs. Oh, here's someone to see you." She smiled at the young man in a bathrobe.

"May I see Dr. Tate?"

Parker leaned to his left so he could see who the man was, joy filling him at the sight of Jim Ward. "Come in!"

"You heard the doctor." Garrett left with the tray.

Ward shuffled his feet. "I thought I'd come to see you since I'll be leaving first thing tomorrow morning."

Someone else was leaving. He rallied to express joy for the young private's good news. "I am happy for you. Please sit down."

Ward did as he was told. "I'm really happy you can talk."

"I am as well."

According to Dr. Brumbaugh, Parker had come from pretty far down. He was young and strong, however, and could anticipate a full recovery from his leg and stomach wounds. Once his throat had healed, there might be a permanent hoarseness. He could live with such a small infirmity after what he'd been through.

"I can't wait to tell my family back home about you. I wouldn't be sitting here without you. I'm glad you got that Purple Heart. You deserved it."

Parker was at a momentary loss for words. Then he said, "I praise God you came through that battle. You are a true hero, my friend."

Ward cocked his head. "You're pretty religious, aren't you, Doctor Tate?"

"Please call me Parker. I have a personal relationship with Jesus Christ, if that is what you mean."

"I guess so." He shrugged his shoulders. "I have some religion but it's mostly going to church and knowing right from wrong. Being here, well, I've had a lot of time to think about my life. Sometimes I feel sort of empty, like I know stuff about God, but I don't know Jesus, not the way you talk. How can you know someone who isn't even there?"

"You tell him you are sorry for your sins and ask him to live in your heart. Then his Holy Spirit lives in you and is very real. This relationship changes everything."

"I would like to know him like that. Can you help me?"

He grinned. "I am a minister's son. Yes, I can help you. Let's pray. Just repeat after me."

They bowed their heads. "Dear Jesus, I come to you as I am, a sinful man in need of your grace and mercy."

Jim Ward spoke the words.

"By your death and resurrection, I accept your gift of salvation. Now I give my life to you to do with as you please, for your glory and for my good. Amen."

When Ward looked up, his face shone. "You've just led me to safety, a second time."

Dr. Brumbaugh stopped by before leaving for the night, humming a song Parker thought sounded something like "Mairzy Doats."

"Well, good evening, Dr. Tate. How's our Purple Heart recipient?"

"I am well, thank you. And yourself?"

He stood next to the bed and laughed. "I'm usually the one asking that question. I'm happy to be seeing you doing as well as you are. Your vital signs have been good, and your wounds are healing without any signs of infection. You're a lucky man, let me tell you." He consulted his chart. "You've been able to eat gradually more solid foods. I know it's little more than baby food, but tomorrow I want to try a step up. How do eggs and toast sound?"

Parker's eyes gleamed. "Delicious. A good American breakfast."

"Hmm, might you prefer something more Korean, like rice and a protein?"

"I have lived in the States a long time and enjoy both cuisines. Perhaps at lunch I might have rice."

"I can arrange that. If you tolerate those foods and can walk down the hall and back with Nurse Garrett tomorrow, I'll release you to Tokyo General the following day."

"I will do my best. How will I travel there?"

"You'll fly in a MEDEVAC transport plane. My guess is you'll be there a few weeks, maybe a month at the most. Then, you can go to an Army hospital in the States for the final lap of your recovery."

"I very much look forward to being home and becoming an American citizen."

"You already make a great one." He squeezed Parker's foot. "Are there any questions?"

He dreaded what he might hear, but he needed to know. "When I finish my recovery, will I be well enough to work?"

"That's the goal. Your body has been invaded by bullets and undergone two grueling surgeries, so you'll need to rebuild your stamina. Do you work in a practice?"

"Yes, with my younger brother."

"Terrific! He'll help you ease back into your routine. Well, then, have a good night."

"And you as well."

Exhaling his worst fears, he read the Bible where Shelby had left off, then prayed himself to sleep.

"Is this one okay?" Anna handed him a photo.

"This is perfect. Thank you."

"It's for Shelby, right?" Her dark eyes shone.

"Yes."

He and his sister glanced at their mother, who stood next to his chair. He'd had a shower, eaten eggs and toast, and taken a walk with the nurse. He felt ready to take on the world—in a few weeks.

"You look well," his mother said in Korean.

"I am well. Please sit by me."

Anna perched on the side of his unmade bed, and his mother sat next to him on a chair.

"How are you? Are you following my doctor's orders?"

Mrs. Park smiled. "You have made me well. You are a good doctor." She looked straight at him. "And a good son."

"And you are a good mother. I am sorry about Soonja. I should have told you earlier."

She looked at her hands. "I should not have planned your future."

Parker sucked in a breath, and his sister's hand went to her mouth. Their mother was apologizing! Was the world still turning? He realized how difficult such an admission must be for her, and his heart softened. He took her hand and brought his face close to hers. "We are all right now. We can go forward."

As if to dissipate the awkward moment, his mother presented him with a large tote bag and spoke as he rummaged through its contents.

"The items you came to Korea with are here, along with some Korean food."

He discovered packets of his favorite teas, rice noodles, kimchi, and brightly colored handkerchiefs. "Thank you, *Eomeoni*. I will surely enjoy all of these."

She nodded, wordless.

After Parker put the package to the side, Anna spoke. "Do you love Shelby?"

He caught his breath. *I might as well be honest.* "Yes, Anna. She is a beautiful Christian woman with a deep love for our people."

"Grandfather says he knew her grandfather when he was in Pyongyang, that he was a good man."

His mother looked into his eyes. "Perhaps this is God's work after all."

Another bombshell. He didn't know if he could take anymore. They fell into a pool of silent grace.

After some moments he spoke. "I will most likely be leaving for Tokyo tomorrow. Then I will return to the States."

His mother's eyes moistened.

"You must come to see me."

"After the war."

Anna started crying. "I wish you could live here, Tae-ho, or I could live ..."

He was glad she stopped short of saying what he thought would be "in the US." His mother didn't need such a heaviness just now. Years ago, when his parents had sent him to Princeton, they had known he might stay. Maybe one day, they would all live in America.

He walked with them to the door at the end of their hour-long visit, sharing gentle hugs.

"Until we meet again," he said.

CHAPTER TWENTY-FIVE

> Dear Parker,
>
> The hour is late, but I have to write two letters before I can hope to fall asleep—the first is to you, the second, to my dear grandfather. What was the rest of your day like after I left? I'm still rejoicing over your Purple Heart and the promise of American citizenship. I'm thrilled you've been proven to be exactly who you are.

She frowned when Dr. Olsen's rude slur came to mind but quickly brushed it aside.

> I promise to write more, hopefully tomorrow, but I wanted to let you know I arrived safely at the 8055th. Thank God you were evac'd to Seoul via helicopter and not on the frightful roads between here and there. Colonel Sheppard, Father Stephens, and Major McKaig were eager to hear news of your wellbeing. The other nurses are bursting to know what happened during my trip, but I'm holding those memories close to my heart. Until tomorrow ...

She hovered the pen over the page, lamplight spilling onto the vellum, wondering how to sign the letter. "Love" seemed either too presumptuous or too glib. As a woman, she wanted him to use the word first. "Sincerely" was much too business-like. She considered "yours" and "fondly."

All at once, she knew.

God bless you, Shelby.

She smiled while folding the paper into thirds and slipping it into an envelope, which she addressed to Parker in care of the Army hospital. Then she lifted another sheet from the box of stationery her sister had sent her for Christmas, grateful the other nurses were working, asleep, or at the O Club.

> February 29, 1952
>
> Dear Poppa,
> I'm writing to you from my MASH unit after a most astonishing experience. You may be wondering why I'm not also including Grandma, but these thoughts are for you first. When you believe the time is right, I invite you to share what I've written with her, and with Mom and Dad. I think they'll understand.

A piece of kindling fell to the bottom of the warming heater casting sparks upward.

> A little less than a month ago, we had among our wounded soldiers an American private named Jim Ward and a North Korean officer. From time-to-time we treat enemy soldiers before they get sent to POW camps. I felt drawn to the Korean, a gentle man whose only possessions were identification papers and an English language Bible. Naturally, this raised my curiosity. Private Ward told me the North Korean had saved his life despite another PKA officer ordering him to stand down.

Shelby filled in the rest of the details.

Private Ward asked me to take very good care of the wounded Korean, Major Moon Soo Yi. Major Yi couldn't speak because of a shrapnel wound to his throat, yet his nonverbal communication was filled with kindness. I looked forward to my shifts and especially enjoyed the times when he "asked" me to read his Bible to him. He managed to let me know he was a Christian, which is unbelievable for a North Korean officer.

Normally, I don't get close to my patients. They're in and out in a few days, and there are so many of them. A certain emotional distancing is necessary for work like this. (That doesn't mean I don't care about them.) This time, however, I became fascinated with Major Yi along with a growing conviction he wasn't who his uniform and papers said he was. He had no other identification or possessions, which was also unusual.

When he was strong enough, he wrote "Parker Tate" on my clipboard, then pointed to himself. Using an alphabet board our chaplain made, my patient revealed he was a doctor from America. He mentioned the name of another MASH's chaplain, Captain Frank. What an irresistible mystery this was! (Naturally, I owe this to the Nancy Drew books you and Grandma fed me as a girl.)

Shelby looked up, stretching her neck side-to-side before resuming the letter.

A few days ago, our chaplain Father Stephens and I dropped off a supply of medicine at Captain Frank's MASH. He was delighted to know what had happened to Dr. Tate, then unfolded an amazing story about him.

She continued unrolling the account.

I couldn't wait to return to tell my CO. When I arrived back at the 8055th, however, Parker Tate wasn't there. He'd had a medical emergency while I was away, and they evac'd him to the Army hospital in Seoul. I was terribly worried. Colonel Sheppard and the head nurse kindly offered me a three-day pass to see how he was doing, and I've just returned.

There's so much to say about what happened there, but I'll just write the highlights for now. Parker got through his surgery well and can talk again. His face lit up when he saw me. I spent nearly all my time with him, except when he asked me to go to his family in Seoul with news of his whereabouts. While they knew he had helped rescue his grandfather, the story ended there. Incidentally, his Korean name is Tae-ho Park.

His father is a Presbyterian minister in Seoul, and Parker's younger sister is a student at the university there. He and his younger brother John have a family medical practice in Hopewell, New Jersey. He studied at Princeton and earned his MD from Penn.

As if all of this hasn't been incredible enough, there's yet another dumbfounding aspect to all of this. His grandfather, who is recovering at the same hospital, is Dr. Oh, and he brightened when I told him my last name. He asked if I were related to Jacob Kichline and said you were very good friends in Pyongyang many years ago! I was beside myself. Isn't God amazing how he weaves the tapestry of our lives? Dr. Oh asked me to convey his very best wishes. Please, Poppa, tell me your memories of him.

Parker will be going to Tokyo General shortly for further rehabilitation, then back to the States. Before I left him today in Seoul, he was awarded a Purple Heart and assured of becoming a full US Citizen. I'm so proud of him and grateful how the Lord helped Father Stephens and me vindicate him.

Finally, dear Poppa, I want you to know Parker and I have developed strong feelings for each other. While there haven't been any declarations, there's something

> precious between us. I've never felt so linked with someone in this way and see how God brought us together under extraordinary circumstances. (Actually, there's a little more to my story about that, but the hour is too late.) I pray the Lord will continue to work in and through us as Parker and I write to each other across many miles. I won't be able to see him again until I'm discharged in the summer.
>
> Thank you for listening to me, dearest of grandfathers. I will eagerly await your response. This letter comes with a boatload of love and hugs.
>
> Shelby

"Oh, good, you're still awake." Vickie plopped down on her cot making the springs squeak. Her face radiated expectation.

Shelby's heart sank. She was hoping to be under her covers with the light out by the time Vickie returned.

"I was just writing some letters, and now I'm ready for bed." She yawned for emphasis.

"Not before you tell me what happened in Seoul." Vickie peered at Shelby.

"I'll tell you when I'm ready."

"I thought we were friends." She appeared close to pouting. "Close friends tell each other's secrets you know."

"Vickie, haven't you ever had something happen you needed to think through before you could discuss it?"

"Nope."

I don't doubt it.

"Well, I'm that way about deep things."

"So, what happened in Seoul is a deep thing?" She was as eager as a dog sniffing a treat.

"I will say that much."

"A good deep thing."

Shelby laughed. "Yes, it was a good deep thing."

Vickie began unbuttoning her jacket. "Well, I guess I'll just have to wait then."

The second shift was low key, and while tending the patients, she kept looking toward the corner where Parker had been. A redheaded corporal from Arkansas now lay in the bed.

When Evelyn came in to relieve her, Shelby updated her about the patients' statuses. Then Danny wandered over, placing his hand over a yawn.

"I'll walk you back to the tent or to the O Club, your choice."

"Actually, I could use a drink—a soft one—before I turn in," Shelby said. Maybe this would give her an opportunity to set him straight about a few things.

She shivered against the icy night, and when Danny put an arm around her shoulders, she sensed he wasn't just trying to keep her warm. The O Club was nearly full, and they took a seat near the juke box, which was playing "Rag Mop." A few soldiers stood by holding beers and tapping their feet. Fortunately, Vickie wasn't among the patrons, nor was Dr. Olsen, who'd replaced Danny on the night shift.

"What'll you have?" he asked.

"Ginger ale."

"I'll be right back."

He returned moments later with an iceless glass of fizzing soda and a beer. "I'm glad you're back from Seoul." He sipped his drink and paused. "I hear our patient is making progress."

She almost laughed at his choice of words. "Yes, he is. I'm happy the Army found out who he really is and awarded him for his heroism."

"Did you see a lot of him?" He looked up at the ceiling, seeming like he was trying to appear casual.

She traced a line through the condensation on her glass. "I did."

He placed his hands behind his head. "Is there something between the two of you?"

"Yes, there is."

"You know, Shelby, emotions run high in a war zone. Sometimes people make rash decisions and live to regret them."

"You're right. That's why I'm glad we can take time to get to know each other."

"You hope to see him again, then?"

"He lives an hour from my family, and we plan to get together when I'm discharged."

Danny's eyebrows raised, then he grinned. "Well, then, I still have a few months to try to change your mind."

CHAPTER TWENTY-SIX

"I'll be happy to mail your letter, but this other thing you're asking, Dr. Tate ..." She clucked her tongue. "I don't want you to fall, especially not this close to being discharged."

He smiled at her. "I understand, Nurse Garrett, but I would very much like to see my grandfather before I leave. Doing so under my own strength would please me very much."

She put her hands on her hips. "Normally, doctors make poor patients, but you've been so cooperative all along."

"Being unwell is difficult for me."

"I know. Let me see what Dr. Brumbaugh has to say."

Parker waited in his easy chair. Shelby had promised to write when she returned to the 8055th, but would her letter reach Seoul before he left tomorrow? He considered this unlikely. When Nurse Garrett returned, he shot her an expectant look.

"So, Doctor Brumbaugh says you may walk to the elevator using a cane, then to you grandfather's room. On the way back, however, you have to use a wheelchair."

"Thank you. I promise to be careful."

"Are you ready now?"

"Yes, if you have time to take me."

"I sure do, but a nurse from the second floor will have to bring you back." She handed him a cane. "By the way, I sent your letter."

"Thank you."

"The mailbox is near the nurse's station, and we always keep a supply of stamps there. Shelby should receive your letter in a couple of days."

He leaned on her arm as he rose. "I have been wondering what will happen to anything she sends here."

"We'll forward everything to Tokyo. Believe me, this happens all the time."

Parker limped toward the door.

"I can send word to her about your leaving tomorrow."

"You are very kind. Yes, please do so." He paused at the door. "I want also to write to my brother, who has not heard from me since I was wounded."

"Good idea."

He shambled down the hall as if he were three times his age but sensed a coming return to strength. By the time they got to his grandfather's sunlit room, Parker was ready to sit.

"Tae-ho! You have come to see me, and you are walking!" The old minister grinned.

"Yes, *Harabeoji.*"

"I'll leave you two to visit. Enjoy yourselves."

Parker spoke over his left shoulder. "Thank you, Nurse Garrett."

"How are you feeling?"

"Much better. And yourself?"

"I am ready to go home, but the doctor says I must stay another week."

His grandfather's fingernails had grown long, and Parker glanced at his own. His grooming wasn't exactly up to par either. He sighed to think of how Shelby had seen him at his absolute worst.

"For two active men such as ourselves, inactivity is difficult. Your prison ordeal must have been very hard on you."

Dr. Oh looked away. "Unredeemed man is capable of great cruelty."

Parker took his hand, hardly knowing how to respond to such pain.

"My former student Ko was good to me. If not for him and your courage, I would probably be in Heaven by now. I thank you for all you did."

He gently squeezed the wrinkled hand. "Do you know what happened to Ko?"

"If my testimony has had any effect, he will find a use with the Americans." He paused. "You are looking much better, Tae-ho."

"I will be discharged tomorrow to the Army's hospital in Tokyo."

"This is good news, but you will be greatly missed. I do not know when we will see each other again this side of eternity."

"That is the one negative aspect of living in America," Parker said.

Dr. Oh's eyes glimmered. "You will return to the lovely Shelby Kichline, though."

He smiled, warming to the subject. "Yes, *Harabeoji*. I was astonished to find her family lives near Hopewell, and you knew her grandfather."

"Our God's ways are unsearchable."

He turned the cane around slowly. "You are in favor of her though she is not Korean?"

"She is a fine Christian woman." He emphasized the word *Christian*. "How has your mother taken this?"

Parker explained what had happened with Soonja.

"My heart is glad you were able to resolve this. You may count on me to help your mother further understand."

"I am grateful. Please tell me more about your relationship with Shelby's grandfather."

Dr. Oh folded his hands on his lap. "We met a long time ago in Pyongyang just before the 1907 great revival. Koreans were rushing to know the Lord Jesus as if their lives depended on it, for surely, they did. Christianity was still young in our country. Missionaries had set up schools in which Koreans helped train leaders to spread the gospel. I had recently completed my studies to become a minister and was pursuing a further degree, so I could teach other men to become pastors. A young Princeton Theological Seminary graduate came to help with English translation, Mr. Jacob Kichline." He smiled at Parker. "I recall his amazing blue eyes, just like your Shelby."

Parker's arms tingled.

"Although Jacob had been seminary-educated, his heart was far from God."

"Oh?" His voice rose.

"He was a proud man, proud of his education, proud of his family, proud of being American. He scoffed at the revival, saying emotionalism was not Christianity. For him, faith was a matter of reason. Miracles and God's actions in human affairs were not possible because they defied such reason. We had many friendly debates in those days. I invited him to the services, but he always made an excuse. Then one day I said, 'Jacob Kichline, you spend all your time criticizing something you have not experienced first-hand. If you do not come with me tonight to see how God is moving, I will not speak to you of it any further."

Parker imagined the two men facing each other. "What did he say?"

He raised his hands. "He accepted my invitation. In the initial moments of that night's service, he was stiff necked. Then something happened. A young Korean minister gave his testimony, confessing how he had believed he was doing God a favor by becoming a Christian. Then the Lord broke into his spirit and convicted him of his sinfulness. He said none of us can stand before a holy God with anything but a bowed head. Something inside Jacob seemed to break, and he began to weep. After some time, he went to the altar to pray and didn't stop until early the next morning."

Parker's jaw had dropped.

"The Holy Spirit transformed him. Jacob's countenance changed—from an arrogant to a humble, gentle, man. We became close friends, truly brothers in Christ. He stayed in Korea for a while, I forget exactly how long, before he returned to the States. We stayed in touch until the second world war. Although we have not written to each other in several years, I often think of him and pray for him. I like to think he does the same for me."

Parker whispered, "And now, all these years later ..."

"His granddaughter has come to you." Dr. Oh's eyes glistened. "As surely as I sit here, Tae-ho, I know God is in this. You must treasure and nurture this relationship. Some will oppose this because you are from different parts of the world, but God's word tells us in the third chapter of Galatians all believers are one in Christ. There is no Jew, no Greek." He smiled. "No American, no Korean."

March 1, 1952, Seoul

My Dear Brother John,
Greetings in Christ Jesus our Lord! I pray this letter finds you well and thriving back in Hopewell. By this time, our parents and sister have shared my journey with you. I want to reassure you by my own hand of my ongoing recovery. Tomorrow, I will begin rehabilitation in Tokyo. Once I am strong enough, I will go to the Army hospital in Washington, DC, for the last phase of my recuperation. I am hoping to return to you by the end of April. My doctor in Seoul believes I will be able to get back to work soon after coming home while regaining my former stamina. I assure you I feel quite well. My wounds are healing without infection, and one complication with my throat has been addressed.

He took a deep breath before continuing.

I have met a dear Christian woman, a nurse in the MASH unit where I was taken. Quite to my amazement, I had bumped into her on the troopship to Korea months ago. Added to this, her grandfather was a missionary in Pyongyang at the time of the revival and was friends with our grandfather. I have developed deep feelings for her, John. After I was taken to Seoul for emergency surgery, she visited me on her leave and met our family. Mother was at first unhappy because I finally gathered courage to tell her I would not marry Soonja. Grandfather has given me his earnest blessing to pursue this relationship, however. My American friend's name is Shelby Kichline. She lives not far from us in eastern Pennsylvania, and we plan to see each other after she completes her tour here, sometime this summer. I think—I hope—you will like her.

Please forgive how much this letter is about me. I long to hear your news and that of our patients, church, and home. I think of you often. If you write to me, your letter might not reach me until I have left Tokyo, unless I am there longer than two weeks. I very much look forward to seeing you again. Take good care of yourself. Please greet Mrs. Albano for me. I imagine she is doing her best to keep you in line. May the Lord bless and keep you.

Your affectionate brother,
Parker

The flight in the Army transport had been bumpy but mercifully brief followed by a seamless ambulance ride to the hospital. Although he wasn't surrounded by other wounded soldiers as he'd been at the MASH, nor did he enjoy the privacy he'd known at Seoul. Parker was taken to a room shared by another patient.

"Here we are," a nurse named Angela Hale announced as she wheeled him inside.

A dark-haired American looked up from a game of solitaire at the room's one table.

"Bill Reed, I'd like you to meet Dr. Parker Tate, your new roommate."

Parker reached out his hand, and the husky fellow offered a trifling shake. "I am happy to meet you."

"Doctor, eh?"

His chest tightened at the underlying hostility in the man's expression.

"He's not only a doctor but a war hero."

Parker winced at the nurse's callow enthusiasm.

"Dr. Tate was just awarded a Purple Heart. He can tell you all about it."

Reed's eyebrows rose. "Is that right?"

When Parker reached his designated bed, he rose unsteadily from the wheelchair.

"Would you like to sit up or lie down?" Nurse Hale asked.

"I prefer to lie down. This has been a demanding day."

She helped him into the bed. "I'll bring fresh pajamas and hang up your uniform. Dr. Rakowski will come by in a little while to meet you."

"Thank you."

She promised to return shortly, and Parker rested in the simple comfort of a firm mattress and crisp sheets. There were many things he was learning to appreciate, like taking time to notice people and things instead of constantly rushing to accomplish something. He didn't regret his years of intense educational training, but from now on, he would take time to linger over God's blessings and share his faith with others. His new roommate interrupted his thoughts.

"So, are you Korean?" Bill Reed gazed at him after placing a ten of clubs on a Jack.

"I was born and raised in Seoul, but I live in the United States. Where are you from?"

"Kansas City, Missouri. Where do you live in the States?"

"Near Princeton, New Jersey, where I went to school."

He huffed. "Princeton, eh? Welcome to Tokyo."

"Thank you. If you do not mind, I must rest."

"Suit yourself. I'm not outta here for another few days."

He wasn't sure this was a good thing given the fellow's gruff exterior. As he slipped into slumber, Parker remembered the importance of thanking God in all things.

CHAPTER TWENTY-SEVEN

She sat on the edge of her cot trembling—Parker had used the word "Love." *Now that his feelings are out in the open, I'm free to respond.* The wonder of learning to love someone she'd known for a little over a month covered her like a cozy eiderdown. She smiled at the ways of God, so sublime they made her head tingle.

"Aha! I know that look!" Vickie burst into her thoughts. "You can't fool me, Shelby Kichline. You're in love with our Korean, aren't you?"

She was struck by the way Vickie used the word "our," which softened her defenses against her plain-spoken roommate. Shelby turned coy. "What makes you say that?"

"Love is written all over your face, missy, L-O-V-E."

Evelyn entered the nurse's quarters and took to the banter like a child to a lollipop. "Who's in love?" She plunked down next to Vickie without removing her Army-issue parka.

Shelby laughed. "You two are too much!"

"It's true, then, isn't it?" Vickie asked.

Evelyn's eyes glimmered. "Are you finally going to tell us what happened in Seoul?"

She saw no use in further resisting them. Besides, she didn't have to tell them everything.

"I had a wonderful time, not the wining and dining kind, but getting to know someone on a very deep level."

Vickie sniggered. "I'll bet you spent your time reading the Bible and praying."

How could she make sacred things seem so banal? *I need to do a better job of leading her to Jesus.* In the meantime, Shelby couldn't expect her to understand.

Evelyn elbowed Vickie. "So, what if they did. That would be a whole lot better than getting drunk with a man in the O Club."

She reached over and squeezed Evelyn's chilly hand. "Thank you."

"What's his name again? That part still confuses me," Vickie said.

"His American name is Parker Tate, Dr. Parker Tate. His Korean name is Tae-ho Park."

"And you call him, what?"

"Parker." She savored his name on her lips.

"What else happened in Seoul?" Vickie asked.

She grinned. "He received a Purple Heart for being wounded while rescuing three men, and his citizenship papers will be approved when he returns to the States."

Evelyn's hand went to her chest. "What an impressive guy! No wonder you like him."

Vickie nodded. "He's done good. What else?"

She considered how much she wanted to say. "Well, I met his parents, sister, and grandparents. I also discovered his grandfather and my grandfather were close friends when mine was a missionary in Korea nearly fifty years ago. Can you imagine?"

"That is some kind of unbelievable!" Evelyn said. "It's like God arranged all this."

"I think he did. He's full of surprises." She also told them about the night she first saw him on the troopship, which they found incredible.

After letting that bit of news sink in Vickie asked, "So, how's Doc Parker doing? He left here in bad shape."

"He's coming along very well, talking, eating, and starting to walk. He was going to Tokyo General. In fact, he's probably there by now."

"Then what?" Evelyn asked.

"As far as I know, he'll finish rehabbing at an Army hospital Stateside—I heard Walter Reed mentioned—then go home to New Jersey. He doesn't live far from my hometown."

"Wonderful!" Evelyn clapped her hands together. "You'll get to see each other again."

She was at peace about having uncovered part of her precious treasures. "So, did I tell you everything you want to know?"

Vickie leaned forward. "Is he a good kisser? I never kissed an Oriental. I wonder what it would be like."

Evelyn's eyes widened. "Vickie, isn't that a bit personal?"

If she had a dollar for every time Vickie had made her bristle, she'd be driving a Cadillac. She relived the feel of him when she'd kissed his forehead, shivering at the thought of what his lips would taste like. She'd only ever kissed Michael before, unless she counted the boy from down the street. He'd chased her after school one day in the first grade and when he caught her, planted one on her lips. She'd run home and washed them with soap and water three times.

"Shelby? Hello!"

She decided to respond with a hint of slyness. “How do you know I kissed him?”

“People in love have been known to kiss each other.”

“And this is the part, Vickie, when I tell you it’s none of your business.”

The camp’s loudspeaker crackled. “Attention, all personnel, heavy casualties are on the way. Everyone, report for duty.”

Vickie groaned. “I thought I was getting a break but no, it’s back to the salt mines.”

Shelby cradled Parker’s letter in her Bible next to the dear photo he’d sent. Reaching for her coat, she knew how she would be signing her next letter to him.

She’d lost count of the patients they’d operated on, but she thought she must have accumulated every blood type on her apron. She admired how Danny stood up to the pressure, keeping things light, telling stories, making jokes. Colonel Sheppard, Father Stephens, and Major McKaig kept the processes moving along with a combination of military crispness and compassion. Even Dr. Olsen rose to the occasion with professionalism.

The unit was well into the small hours of the next day when the marathon session finally ended. Shelby scrubbed up and removed her grubby surgical garb.

Evelyn sagged against a wall. “I’m heading to the O Club for a drink before I go to bed. Wanna come?”

“I will,” Vickie said. “I can never get right to sleep after a shift like that one.”

She knew the feeling. The times Shelby had gone straight to bed, the OR had barged into her dreams forcing her to revisit the surgeries. Sometimes, she’d unwind with the banter and music of the O Club, but other times she preferred to be alone.

"I might join you later, but I want to take a walk first. I'm stiff from all the standing and repetitive movement."

Vickie stretched her arms. "I'm going to remedy my condition by bending my elbow."

Shelby decided to walk full circle around the interior of the camp, knowing wandering outside the compound in the dark would be pure foolishness. She'd gone half-way when familiar voices speaking in low tones alerted her to Danny and Neil Olsen's presence. She slipped into the shadows.

"I wouldn't worry too much, Danny. You're here, and that gook is long gone."

She fisted her hands, gritting her teeth.

"Neil, you have to stop using that word. He's a human being."

Good for you, Danny!

"If you say so."

"I do say so. I don't want to hear that word again."

"Okay, okay! I just think after she hasn't seen him for a while, she may get over her little crush. You know how nurses fall for patients, especially the pathetic ones."

She strained to hear them as they walked further away.

"Play your cards right and you could still win her, Danny. He may seem exotic to her now, but she'll come to her senses and realize she's better off with one of her own."

She didn't hear Danny's response, if he had one. Suddenly chilled, she huddled inside her coat. She wanted to vacuum her spirit of the corrupting words, how Neil had made her relationship with Parker seem so common. No way this was a schoolgirl crush. Or was it?

She hadn't slept well, her dreams active and troubled. Before she awakened, Parker had come to see her but faded away before she could touch him. Frustration enveloped her when she woke up to another freezing morning. When would spring ever come to Korea? By this time in Easton, crocuses would be pushing through the winter-hardened ground, along with the first sightings of robins. She opened her Bible for her daily reading, nestling under the covers, listening to Vickie snoring. When Shelby had gone to bed, Vickie and Evelyn were still at the O Club. She had gone for a short time, scrupulously avoiding Danny.

Lord, please calm my spirit. I believe you brought Parker and me together under amazing circumstances. I've never felt so attached to another person as I am to him. This isn't just a war-zone romance. This is different, isn't it? Still, what Neil said last night about getting over Parker sticks like a burr. Will you continue to heal Parker and watch between us while we're apart? If this is of you, I know what we feel for each other will not only last but grow.

She dressed and headed to the mess tent where the server offered creamed chipped beef, hashed browns, and coffee. She opted for the potatoes remembering an unfortunate run-in with the gravy during her first week at the 8055th. She hankered for a fresh orange or banana, but at least there were canned peaches. She poured a cup of coffee and sat with two other nurses who weren't particularly chatty. Shelby didn't feel much like talking anyway.

Major McKaig approached with her tray and sat next to her.

"Good morning, Shelby. I was hoping to find you here."

"Good morning, Major."

She arranged her napkin on her lap and reached for the salt. After she had eaten a few bites, the head nurse said, "I'm going to Tokyo General later today for a nurse's conference."

Shelby splashed her coffee onto the table. "Tokyo?"

McKaig laughed. "Yes, Tokyo. Might there be anything you'd like to send with me to give Dr. Tate?"

She fought an impulse to giggle. "Oh, yes, ma'am. That's so kind of you. Thank you."

"I don't have much room, so it has to be small, and I need it by two o'clock."

"Thank you again." Shelby jumped up, realizing she'd made a mess, and quickly cleaned the spill with a napkin. Her meal forgotten, she hurried back to her quarters as if she'd received a shot of adrenaline. She would definitely send a photo and letter, which she'd write now, then something else, but what? Suddenly she knew.

> My Dear Parker,
> Your letter and photo brought me such joy. I'm pleased you're feeling stronger and happy about the things you shared about yourself. I want you to know I return your affection in full measure.

"There. I declared myself," she muttered under her breath. She was writing in the chapel, resting the stationery on one of the benches.

> Major McKaig kindly offered to bring this letter to you during her trip to Tokyo for a nurses' conference. As you can see, I'm enclosing a photo of myself and one of my family, and the copy of *A Man Called Peter* which I started reading to you. Perhaps you will "hear" my voice as you read this book. I'm an avid reader, and I believe we may share this in common. I like biographies, C.S. Lewis, and classical literature for children best. I've

read *Little Women* at least ten times and all the works of Charles Dickens and Jane Austen. Who are your favorite authors? I also like T.S. Eliot, although I'm not generally fond of much poetry.

And now, to answer your questions. My family is a typical middle-class American family. My parents' roots go far back in American history, including ancestors who fought in the Revolution. My parents are involved in our church and community. One of my ancestors, Colonel Peter Kichline, helped to build the church we attend—the German Reformed Church. The building just underwent a major renovation project my father was part of, and I look forward to seeing what they did when I get home.

My sister is a sweet, boy-crazy teenager, and my brothers love sports, especially American football and basketball. My middle brother Neil always has his head in a book. He does sports, I suspect, to keep pace with the others, but he's more brains than brawn. We live near several aunts and uncles and my grandparents on both sides. I grew up in the house we live in, which has two-stories and a large front porch. My mom is known for her flower gardens. We live a few blocks from Lafayette College where my father went to school.

As for music, I especially like Bing Crosby and Nat King Cole, whose song "Unforgettable" I first heard when you came to the 8055th. It will always remind me of you. Like you, I enjoy the classics, especially Bach, but I think Mozart is wonderful too. You're right about me and dancing—I would be happy to teach you! Do you like hymns? I'm not sure if Koreans know American hymns. (There's so much I hope to learn about Korean customs and traditions. I told Father Stephens I want to help him at the orphanage. I can get to know more there while helping with the children.) My favorite hymn is called "Faith of Our Fathers."

She looked up at the cross on the altar, wondering if she should disclose her deeper thoughts. She decided to take the plunge. This was, after all, Parker. If anyone could understand her feelings, he could.

> Yesterday, we had a difficult session with so many casualties I lost count. I always hurt when we lose a patient, and we lost two. I try to focus on the ones we save and believe in my heart those who died did so according to God's timing for their lives. As long as I consider the good we do here and not all the suffering and loss, I'm able to cope. The long hours do take a toll, though, and sometimes I feel especially vulnerable. Last night, or rather early this morning, as I took a walk before going to bed, I overhead two doctors talking about me. One of them predicted I would forget you after we've been apart for several months. I don't think they're right, but the words hurt.
>
> Perhaps you can send a letter back through Major McKaig. I pray the Lord is blessing your recovery and surrounding you with kind and capable people. Do you have a roommate there? If so, what is he like?
>
> I keep your photo in my Bible and the memory of you in my heart.
>
> Love,
> Shelby

CHAPTER TWENTY-EIGHT

He'd just returned from physical therapy when a familiar woman in a dress uniform entered the room. Bill Reed sat up straighter in his bed and put down his men's magazine.

"Good day, Dr. Tate. I hope I'm not disturbing you."

"Not at all."

"I'm the head nurse at the MASH 8055th."

"Yes, how nice to see you again, Major." He glanced at her name badge—*McKaig*.

She stepped forward. "I'm glad you remember me."

His palms turned sweaty. Was this about Shelby? Was she all right? He remembered his manners. "Please, have a seat."

She took the chair next to his.

"Allow me to present my roommate, Mr. Bill Reed. Mr. Reed, this is Major McKaig."

"Nice to meet you, doll face."

She turned her back to him and sniffed. "I wish I could say the same."

Parker scowled at the man. "I am truly sorry. You deserve respect."

"Believe me, Doctor Tate, guys like that are everywhere, and I've met most of them." She smoothed her skirt. "You're probably wondering why I'm here."

"I am concerned you may have unpleasant news."

She waved her hand. "There's nothing unhappy about my presence."

His jaw relaxed.

"I'm here for a conference, and Nurse Kichline sent you some things."

He was a boy again, and this was his birthday. His eyes followed her movements as she pulled a small package from her bag and handed him a wrapped gift.

"I'll be here for two days and will come to see you before I leave. There might just be something you'd like me to take back to her."

"You are so very kind, Major. I am deeply grateful."

She rose, looping her purse strap over her right shoulder, and he stood out of politeness. "It was my pleasure. I'm happy to see you looking so strong. You were in rough shape when you came to us, as well as when you left."

"God has been very gracious to me."

"He has a way of doing that." She shook his hand. "Well, then, I'll see you in two days. Good day, Dr. Tate."

"Good day, Major McKaig." He was unsurprised when she ignored his roommate.

The only thing he could wish for in the next moments was privacy, but none was to be had. He couldn't wait to see what was in the package, yet he would not open the gift in Reed's presence. Suddenly inspired, he used the call bell. When Nurse Cindy O'Lone arrived a few minutes later, he asked if she might walk with him to the chapel down the hall.

"Sure, Dr. Tate." She cast a look in Reed's direction. "How about you? A trip to the chapel would do you some good."

"Bah! I have no use for such drivel."

Parker walked slowly using his cane, Nurse Cindy commiserating with him. "I sure am sorry someone as nice as you got stuck with Bill Reed. Want me to try to switch roommates?"

"You are kind to offer. Perhaps the Lord has a purpose for this."

"Good luck with that." She laughed.

"Worse sinners have come to the faith."

"Bill Reed's conversion is something I'd like to see."

By the time the red-headed nurse returned twenty minutes later, Parker had read Shelby's letter three times and delighted in the photos of her and her family. Her parents were a handsome, happy-looking couple, her brothers and sister, fun-loving and close judging from their expressions. He thought Shelby looked like her father except for her chin. He loved this picture, but his favorite was her nursing school portrait. He would write to her this very day to try to allay her fears about being apart. He would tell her how certain he was God had brought them together and since that was the case, no one could sunder their extraordinary relationship.

His muscles protested by the time he returned to his room. He sat heavily in his chair and set his treasures on the side table. "Thank you, Nurse Cindy."

"My pleasure, Doctor Tate. Let me know if you need anything else."

Bill Reed sat on the edge of his bed. "Did you hear from your girlfriend?"

"Yes, I did."

"What's she like?" He made eyes.

He thought better of saying too much. "She is lovely."

"Do you have a picture?" He was on his feet now, walking toward Parker.

He laid his hand on her gifts.

"Oh, c'mon. I'd like to see what she looks like."

"Maybe another time. I am very tired." He closed his eyes, ending the conversation.

When Parker awakened, he breathed a sigh of relief to find Reed wasn't there. He didn't know the nature of the man's wounds, only that he would be leaving soon. Parker reached for the book Shelby had sent and removed her picture, his heart skipping at her Mona Lisa smile. He remembered Nat King Cole had a song by that title. He wanted to send something back to her and briefly considered this hospital might have a gift shop. Somehow, though, a mass-produced trinket didn't seem right. He got up and pulled out the lower drawer of his nightstand. He decided to send Shelby some NoK-cha, his favorite tea, and a copy of a light-hearted C.S. Lewis novel, *The Lion, The Witch, and the Wardrobe* he'd brought with him from the States. He would wrap them in one of the colorful silk handkerchiefs his mother had given to him.

His roommate entered on the arm of another nurse, with whom he openly flirted. "If you'll just put me to bed and tuck me in, I'll be good as new."

"This is where I leave," she said, raising her eyebrows.

"You don't know what you're missing," he called after her. He laughed as he hopped up onto his bed. "So, Doc, are you still mooning over your girl?"

He remained silent.

"You promised to show me her picture."

"I did no such thing."

He taunted like an eight-year-old boy on a playground. "Maybe she's not as good-looking as you say."

Without speaking, Parker raised her portrait, and Reed leaned in.

"Wowee! She's a looker all right. A nurse, right?"

"Yes, in a MASH."

"So, how does an American girl fall for a guy like you?"

His lips tightened.

Reed didn't get the hint. "I mean, it's against the natural order of things. We should be with our own kind." He smirked. "Did you try some Oriental technique with her that drove her crazy, something I could pick up from you?"

Parker spun around so quickly he almost lost his balance. His eyes and nostrils flared. "I forbid you ever to speak to me about her. You are far from God, and I fear for your soul."

Reed lifted his hands and started to say something.

Parker interrupted him, aflame. "Do you understand?"

"Yeah, sure, Doc." He laid down and pulled the covers over his head.

Although Bill Reed had gone out to play poker, his dirty words had sullied their room. Parker ambled slowly to the chapel on his own and sat in the back to compose his response to Shelby's letter in a sacred space. He found a hymn book to write on and made himself as comfortable as the stiff pew allowed.

> March 5, 1952, Tokyo
>
> Dear Shelby,
> You can imagine my surprise when I received a visit from Major McKaig earlier today. What a joy to be with

> someone who is close to you! When she handed me your letter, photographs, and the gift you had so lovingly prepared, my heart sang for joy. I am sitting in the back pew of the hospital chapel where I feel not only closer to God, but to you.
>
> Your photos are treasures which I will keep in my Bible. Your family appears so joyful, and your portrait reminds me how beautiful you are every time I look at it, which is every few minutes.
>
> I also relish knowing more about your likes and dislikes, especially your favorite authors and books. Like you, I enjoy Dickens, especially *A Christmas Carol*. I grew up reading many English titles, and a missionary long ago introduced me to America's Hardy Boys. I spent many pleasurable hours imagining what life would be like in the US, solving mysteries instead of being in Japanese-occupied Korea.
>
> When I went to Princeton, I learned about C.S. Lewis through a friend of my family, Dr. Cullen. He had taught at our seminary in Pyongyang and is now at Princeton Theological Seminary. Lewis's writings have enabled me to grow in my faith, and I read them whenever I can. I am pleased you also admire his books, and because you still enjoy classic children's literature, I am sending you his recent work, *The Lion, the Witch, and the Wardrobe*. He weaves the story of our Lord's work of redemption into a fantastic world of magical beasts and winsome scenes. I do hope you enjoy it as much as I am picking up where we left off with *A Man Called Peter*. You are correct that I "hear" your voice as I read the words about this godly man.

He lifted his head to the lighted cross above a plain altar, receiving their benediction. Except for a patient who knelt at a front pew, he was alone. Parker had grown up in a densely populated city where privacy was at a premium. Since living in America, he had developed a taste for solitude, especially now when sharing a room with a reprobate.

> Your prayers mean so very much to me, dearest Shelby, and I believe God is answering them. Each day I become stronger. My throat feels much improved, and I am starting to tolerate tender meats cut into very small pieces. I am enjoying the simple pleasures of meals as never before. Do you enjoy cooking? If so, what foods are you most adept at making? I like American food very much, including what I call "fun foods" like pizza and hamburgers. I am not so good of a chef. My brother John and I muddle along, often eating out. I am pleased to know you hope to learn more of Korean customs, and I know you will bring great joy to the orphans. I will tell you of one such practice.

Before he did so, Parker rolled his shoulders and flexed his hand.

> When we give someone a present, we wrap the gift as a reflection of the value we assign to the recipient. I could not help but notice how your letters and book were encased in American gift paper, which must be hard to find. Thank you for the sweet gesture. Along with my letter and book, I am sending you two traditional Korean presents. The first is a packet of tea called NoK-cha. My mother sent me to Tokyo with many items which she thought I would enjoy including this, one of my favorite teas. I do hope you can brew loose tea—I realize most Americans use tea bags. (Do you like tea or coffee best? I prefer tea, but I learned to drink coffee in medical school.) The second thing I am sending is a Korean handkerchief, which I am using to wrap your package. I noticed while living in Princeton, my classmates carried white handkerchiefs, which greatly puzzled me. White is the color of death in Korea, so we use colors and patterns in our handkerchiefs. I do hope you like this.

You are correct that I spent most of my youth engaging in studies, also a Korean trait. I recall attending a few parties at Princeton, but I felt awkward not knowing how to dance and not given to strong drink. I also found the women who attended more willing than they should have been. I instead focused on becoming a doctor.

He took a deep breath before beginning the next section.

And now, dear Shelby, I will address your concern. You touched my heart by trusting your feelings with me, and I promise to treat them gently. There are people who say things that should never be uttered, which help no one and only cause pain and confusion.

He grimaced, thinking of Bill Reed's contemptable comments, which he would never sully Shelby with. He didn't even want to answer her question about a roommate.

Distance can be an obstacle when people care about each other and long to be together. However, I have known many fine people whose relationships weathered such seasons well and came out stronger for them. I do not want you to fear these months but to seek God's blessings in this time He has ordained for His purposes. You need not worry about my affections, which are secure, as I am also secure in yours. That God would bring you to me and choose you to care for me causes me no amount of wonder and gratitude.

Before I close, I will tell you my favorite hymn is "This is My Father's World." I feel cheerful whenever I sing this song. I know many western hymns, ones I learned as a boy in Korea as well as from the church I attend in Princeton. I do like your favorite as it speaks of the role of faith in America's history.

I think I will be in Tokyo perhaps ten more days, and then I am told they will send me to Walter Reed Army Medical Center to complete my recovery. After that time, I will return to my home and my practice, which my brother has faithfully tended to in my absence. I am happy to think about seeing my patients again and in a few short months, you. Until then, may God watch between us and keep us.

Love,
Parker

"Well, hello, I thought I might find you here."

He looked up to see one of the hospital's chaplains. Pastor Monroe, a cheerful Methodist, had introduced himself on Parker's first day.

"Hello, Pastor."

"I see you were writing a letter."

"Yes." He grinned.

"Oh, that kind of letter. Where does she live?"

"Pennsylvania, although she is currently a MASH nurse."

The man's thick eyebrows rose. "I guess you met her while you were a patient."

"Yes. She is a beautiful Christian woman."

"The best kind. I'm married to one of those." He paused. "I thought you might like some help getting back to your room."

"Yes, thank you. I am often unsteady."

As they left the chapel, Monroe asked, "How are you getting along with your roommate?"

Parker wondered what had prompted the question. "He is, well ..."

"He's one of the most profane men I've ever met."

He gave a laugh. "Yes, that is one way to describe him."

"To be with such a man must be a trial to someone like yourself."

"Perhaps God has a purpose beyond my comfort."

"Do you think he'll listen to you—Reed, I mean, not God?"

"I pray he will."

"Then I will too."

CHAPTER TWENTY-NINE

Shelby had planned to write daily to Parker, but by the time she had a moment to spare, a week had passed. When she hadn't been in the OR ankle-deep in bloody gauze, she was helping patients cope with pain and infection during a shortage of morphine and penicillin. Twice during rushed meals, she'd broken out her writing pad only to be interrupted by Vickie, Evelyn, or one of the other nurses.

Then came the bugout.

When the fighting drew dangerously near, I Corps ordered Colonel Sheppard to relocate, disrupting the 8055th for days. Shelby stole a half-hour to write to Parker inside their canvas chapel. She smiled at the photo of him, taking pleasure in his kind eyes and endearing dimples.

> My Dear Parker,
> This is now my third attempt at writing to you after a period of mayhem at the 8055th. Since I would much rather speak of pleasant things, I'll just briefly mention how, after endless hours of surgery and post-op duty, we bugged out four days ago. We haven't received mail in over a week. Back home in Easton whenever I needed to talk to someone far away, I could just pick up the telephone. Wouldn't it be nice if we could do the same

here? How I would love to hear your voice. If I sound discouraged, I suppose I am but just a little. I do believe I'm more tired than dejected. You served at the 8063rd and understand how MASH conditions can take a toll. How is your recovery progressing? I rejoice to hear you're on solid food and have been taking walks. I also wonder how your dear grandfather is. I know how much he was looking forward to going home after his ordeal.

I want to thank you so very much for the letter and presents you sent back with Major McKaig. The book is completely delightful, offering me a fictional dream escape into a fantastic world. My parents and church raised me on the assurance of God's victory over sin and death, and I love how C.S. Lewis combines this biblical truth with such charming story-telling. The Pevensee children remind me so much of my brothers and sister. I also have enjoyed the tea you sent, and like you, I prefer tea to coffee. The kind you shared with me is the most unusual and best I've ever tasted. I asked our cook if he had a small strainer I could use to brew the tea, and he kindly lent me one. As we get more settled here, I'm looking forward to longer sessions with a hot cup and the book.

The handkerchief's bright color delights my senses, and the silk is beautiful to touch. I didn't know about white being the color of death in the Korean culture, and I will be careful about making any faux pas in that regard. I have the handkerchief with me all the time as a way of keeping you close. I hope that doesn't sound foolish.

I want to thank you for what you said about the possibility of growing apart in these months of separation. You greatly reassured me, and I'm much more at peace. I also believe the Lord can use this season for his purposes.

Before I close, you asked whether I enjoy cooking. Indeed I do. When I was very small, I used to watch my mother and grandmothers in the kitchen, fascinated by measuring spoons and recipes. They seemed to harbor great mysteries that materialized in the form of mouth-watering main dishes and baked goods. I don't pretend to be as good as they are, but I'm told by the severest critics of all—my siblings—that I'm fair. To be honest, I enjoy baking more than cooking, especially cakes and breads. My last name is Swiss and in German means "little cake." My family speculates our ancestors were bakers, so I come by my interest and any skill honestly. As for my favorite foods, I like anything with potatoes (like a good Swiss-German girl). My favorite meal would have to be the traditional American Thanksgiving feast. I've eaten very little Korean food, but I do like kimchi. I hope you'll teach me all I need to know about your favorite dishes. Maybe I can learn to make them. In Easton, I know of two Chinese restaurants, but that is as far as this German-oriented place stretches in terms of Oriental cuisine.

I can't wait until your letters arrive in our long-overdue mail, to hear your news, to see your dear handwriting. For a physician, your penmanship is quite easy to understand!

Until we meet again, I am ever—
Yours,
Shelby

Colonel Sheppard had given her permission to find out whether Dr. Parker Tate was still at Tokyo General. She hung around while the company clerk put through the laborious call, marveling at the tangle of wires constituting their communications system.

"Tokyo General? Corporal Unger from the MASH 8055th calling on behalf of Colonel Sheppard. We're trying to find out if a former patient is still there, a Dr. Parker Tate."

Shelby's pulse quickened.

"Tate. T-A-T-E." He cupped his hand around the receiver. "They're checking." Someone on the other end reclaimed his attention. "You do? I'm not sure I understand. Oh, okay. Yes, I got it. Thanks." He hung up, Shelby, shifting her weight from one foot to the other. "He's there but is scheduled to leave tomorrow."

She felt like hugging him. "Oh, thank you!"

He leaned back against the desk. "He's a real nice man. I'm glad you two are an item."

"We're an item, are we?" Her cheeks pinked.

"Uh, yes, I mean, I think so. Right?"

"You are rarely wrong, Neil Unger."

Two weeks after the last postal delivery, "Mail call" sounded over the camp's loudspeaker. Between rainstorms and the bugout, Uncle Sam had taken longer than usual to deliver coveted letters and packages to the 8055th. Shelby was on duty in post-op when the announcement crackled and nearly dropped a blood pressure cuff. A general hum broke out, and everyone who could high tailed to the delivery area outside the colonel's office.

"You folks are like us soldiers on the front lines." Shelby's nineteen-year-old patient from Flint, Michigan, sported a boyish grin. "We live for mail call."

"I'll bet you do." She completed the reading and recorded his BP on the chart.

"It's a wonder the delivery guy doesn't get stampeded. I'm sure doctors and nurses are more civilized."

Shelby laughed. "Don't count on it." She jerked her head to the right. "Just look at us."

The soldier grinned while the personnel flowed like lava to their mail. "I suppose you'll want to be going out there."

Despite her longing heart she said, "I'll wait a few minutes rather than risk being trampled."

Evelyn hurried over to her, breathless. "C'mon, Shelby. Let's get our mail! Everything's quiet in here, and Colonel Sheppard told Major McKaig we could take a break."

Shelby grinned at her patient. "So much for waiting."

She hefted a cardboard box weighing at least twenty pounds along with ten letters from Parker. Sitting on her cot, she arranged them in chronological order, noting they'd all been sent from Tokyo. She decided to open the last one first, then savor each of the others one at a time, like a box of good chocolates.

In the twilight's glow, Shelby sipped a cup of NoK-cha, grateful for the rare quiet in the nurses' quarters. Each of them busied herself with her own cards and letters, allowing Shelby to retreat into her own space. Parker said he was to leave the following day for Walter Reed Army Medical Center in Washington and hoped he'd be there less than a month. He was going to travel by hospital ship, a roughly two-week journey, and would continue writing and mailing letters as he was able.

> Now that I am leaving Tokyo, I will tell you I did have a roommate, someone I did not enjoy being around. I believe, however, the Lord had a purpose in putting me with such a person, and I have prayed often for his soul.
>
> As I face the journey across the Pacific, I think of being on that troopship to Korea when our story began. Wherever I may be, I will carry your love in my heart and pray for you.

She sighed, hugging the letter. Then she read the others, reveling in his declarations of affection written in a charming, blocky handwriting. She learned he enjoyed Italian food, taking long walks, and going to the movies. His favorite film was *Casablanca*, and he especially admired Spencer Tracy and Olivia de Haviland.

When she finished all the letters, she tucked them in a shoe box she kept in her footlocker. Then she opened the carton from her family, finding an assortment of homemade cookies, candy from the Carmelcorn Shop, a box of stationery, underwear, and socks. Each of her siblings had written to her. In addition to five Peanuts comic books he'd sent, Neil told her about his church confirmation and how he thought he might become a minister like their grandfather. Paul shared his passion for collecting bugs, and Diane had literally sealed her letter with a kiss, the imprint of her bow-like lips in bright pink lipstick.

> Oh, Shelby, I've heard Mom and Dad whispering something about your having a new boyfriend. I am soooo excited! You'll tell me if this is true, won't you? If you do have a new boyfriend, what's he like? He must be terribly handsome. Is he one of the doctors you work with? Do tell all! Not much happening here. I'm making B's and have started helping Mrs. Sheldon with her second-grade Sunday School class. I like being an assistant teacher.

She took a moment to treasure her little sister's innocent delights before opening letters from her parents and grandfather. Her mom and dad expressed a certain reserve about the news Jacob Kichline had shared with them. Her mother wrote:

> Your grandfather tells us of your relationship with a man and that you will share details when you are ready. Just

> be careful with your heart in a war zone where nothing is ever quite normal. We await further word from you and pray for God's wisdom.

She could live with that. Her hands trembled as she unfolded her grandfather's letter, written on ruled tablet paper.

> Dear Granddaughter,
> That you chose to tell me your heartfelt story continues to bring me a full measure of joy and happiness. We've always been close, and I want you to know I fully understood what you shared with me about your experience with Dr. Tate. Sometimes our Lord takes us by great surprise, as in this case for you and for me. The close friend of my youth is alive and getting well again, and you have entered a relationship with his grandson. I'm not surprised to know Parker Tate is as brave and faithful a Christian man as his grandfather.
>
> Going back many decades now, Soon-hee Oh saved my life in a manner of speaking. I went to Korea with the mission board as an arrogant young American so full of myself there was little room for Jesus Christ. But the Lord was patient with me and introduced me to young Pastor Oh, whose deep faith put mine to shame. I can still see his earnest face with a smile that could light up a room. I imagine he has many wrinkles now, but I'll bet his smile is just the same. Through his friendship, I was brought to repentance and came into a saving knowledge of Christ during a revival I had initially scoffed at.
>
> I rejoice with you Shelby that when you return this summer from serving in Korea, you will get to see Dr. Tate again. I have no doubt he's a fine young man because he comes from a strong Christian family and because you have the gift of discernment. However, I would like to see him for myself, just to make sure. Ha ha. Should you encounter any difficulties from others because of your

> differing cultural backgrounds, let me know so I may stand in the gap for you. The Word of God says in Christ such differences are unimportant—we are all one in him. If you happen to see Dr. Oh again, greet him affectionately from his old friend, your loving Poppa,
>
> Jacob Kichline

There was that verse again, the same one Dr. Oh had quoted to her in the Seoul hospital. Shivers ran through Shelby—the very Lord had spoken.

CHAPTER THIRTY

Dr. Rakowski concluded his morning exam with a grin. "Not only are you fit enough to leave, we just received a call from the MEDEVAC folks. It seems today's four-thirty run is minus two patients who weren't quite ready to be discharged. I can get you on that flight, or you can take a hospital ship back to the States, your choice."

"I should be grateful for a shorter journey," Parker said.

"I'll let them know to expect you."

"Will the people at Walter Reed be ready for me so soon?"

"I'll alert them as well."

"Thank you, Doctor. At this point, how long do you think I might be there?"

"Oh, maybe a couple or three weeks. You might be released by the end of April."

"Will I be able to return to my practice then?" He was counting on this plan and braced himself, hoping to not be disappointed. His rehab at Tokyo General had gone well, his recovery faster than he'd imagined, so the path ahead seemed clear enough.

"I think so. Maybe start at a quarter time the first week, half-time the second if you feel up to it, and full-time within a month. You'll be the best judge." He frowned. "Then again, we doctors aren't always the best at this sort of thing."

Parker gave a laugh. "You are correct about this, but I assure you, I will be prudent. I do not wish to have a setback."

Rakowski reached out to shake his hand. "All the best, Dr. Tate. I've enjoyed knowing you."

"Thank you."

When he walked toward the door, Bill Reed spoke up. "When do I get to blow?"

"Not soon enough."

Reed huffed. "How do you like that? I get stuck here, and you get to go stateside."

Parker didn't know what he could possibly say, so he said nothing.

"Don't get me wrong, I'm happy for you. Do you have family in the States?"

Surprised by the man's civil tongue, he said, "Yes, my brother is there. The rest of my family is in Korea."

"Well, anyway, good luck to you. I, uh, I'm sorry I gave you a hard time before when, uh, I said some things ..."

Parker breathed out. "I do hope you will find the peace of Jesus in your life."

"Are you sure you're not a preacher instead of a doctor?"

"I am a doctor of broken bodies which often house broken souls."

Nurse O'Lone swept through the door bearing a clipboard.

"Well, then, Dr. Tate, I have the usual discharge paperwork for you to fill out. Don't look so dismayed. I know my way around this paper jungle." She sat next to him. "Are you ready to get out of here?"

"Yes, of course, but I am grateful for all you have done."

Cindy O'Lone eyed Bill Reed. "Now, why can't you be more like Dr. Tate?"

Reed grumbled. "You sound just like my mother."

"Yeah, well, maybe you should've listened to her."

"There! We're finished." Nurse O'Lone passed the back of her right hand over her forehead. "There were more forms than usual because you're a Korean applying for American citizenship, but I've dotted every 'i.'" She rose. "I'll get your items from storage and help you pack."

"I wonder if I might call my parents in Seoul with my news."

"I'll ask Dr. Rakowski, and he may need to get authorization. I'll do what I can."

"Thank you, Nurse O'Lone."

She winked at him. "Is there anyone else you might like to call?"

His stomach fluttered. "There is, but this may not be possible."

"Why not?" She shifted her weight.

"She is a nurse in a MASH unit."

"She sounds like someone who should be kept in the know."

After a corned beef hash lunch and a few antacids, Parker saw the nurse carrying a box.

"Here are your personal effects, Dr. Tate."

He experienced a wellspring of joy at the sight of his clothes, books, and photos.

"As for the phone calls ... Yes to your parents, no to your girlfriend. I'm sorry. I tried."

He smiled to hear Shelby referred to as his "girlfriend."

"I'll come back in ten minutes. One of the operators will put you through to your family."

"Tae-ho!" His mother was the first on the line. "You are calling from where?"

"Tokyo General. I will be discharged in a couple of hours, and they permitted me to talk to you for a few minutes. I am going to a hospital in Washington, DC, for the rest of my recovery, then home to New Jersey."

"You are well again?"

"Yes, *Eomeoni*, I am growing strong. Are you feeling well?"

"Yes, yes. I am well. You are a good doctor and a good son." She said something to someone nearby. "Your father is not here, but your grandfather, grandmother, and Anna would like to speak to you."

"Grandfather is home! Yes, please let me talk to him."

"Tae-ho! Is that you?"

"Yes, Grandfather. How are you?"

"Very well, but these women are fussing over me."

He laughed. "You must listen to them. They are very wise."

"How are you, my son?"

"I am going to America in a few hours."

"Have a safe trip and write to us when you get there."

"I will."

"Take care of your Shelby."

He grinned. "I will, *Harabeoji*."

He spoke briefly to his grandmother and Anna, then said good-bye to his weepy mother.

"I will see you again. You must come to me next time."

"Yes," she said, "I will come to you."

He would have preferred to leave on his own two legs, but hospital protocol mandated a wheelchair. His roommate hopped off the side of his bed.

"Good luck to you, Doc."

He reached out his hand. "And God bless you, Bill Reed."

"You know your girl?" He looked down at his feet as he spoke.

His shoulders stiffened. "Yes."

"She's a lucky woman to have you. A lot of guys are jerks, like me."

"I see something better inside of you."

If he wasn't mistaken, the hard-bitten soldier seemed to have a tear in one eye.

Most of the passengers sneezed and sniffled throughout the protracted, frequently turbulent flight to the States. Parker occupied himself with his Bible and Shelby's letters. When he caught the unsuspecting eye of a soldier who elbowed his buddy, Parker returned the sneer with a smile. The fellows abruptly turned away. He wondered what Shelby was doing—perhaps she was in surgery or the post-op, at a meal, or chapel. Maybe she'd gone with Father Stephens to the orphanage where he was sure she was winning those forsaken children's hearts. A darker thought broke through—she might be at the O Club being flirted with by Danny or one of the other MASH personnel.

He shifted in his lumpy seat, closing his eyes. He would not take her affection for granted, but he would not obsess about the urbane doctor either.

By the time the transport reached its stopover in San Francisco, all the soldiers were ill, including Parker. In his feverish state, he barely remembered transferring planes.

When they reached Washington, Parker couldn't stand on his own two feet. Two orderlies half carried him to the ambulance, placing him at a window seat near the front. The mild spring air would have felt downright balmy after a harsh Korean winter, but he shivered with cold. The last thing he remembered, before a nurse helped him into Army-issue pajamas and he fell asleep, was thanking God for a safe journey and asking his blessings on Shelby.

CHAPTER THIRTY-ONE

She squinted to tell the time in the mustering dawn, a Bible verse running through her mind. "Now on the first day of the week Mary Magdalene came to the tomb early while it was still dark ..." *It's Easter morning! He is risen!* At home everyone would be shouting the ancient greeting followed by, "He is risen indeed!" The kids would sneak jelly beans on the way to church where the opening strains of "Christ the Lord is Risen Today" always made her hair stand on end. But she wouldn't be there, and now Parker was on the other side of the world. She was running his handkerchief across her cheek when a sudden moan caught her attention.

"Vickie. What's wrong?"

"I feel terrible, like someone's stabbing me."

She sprang to her feet. "When did this start?"

"It's been off and on for a few days. Figured the food was giving me indigestion. When the USO troop came and that comedian told his stupid jokes, every time I laughed I hurt." She groaned. "This is the worst pain I've ever had."

"I'll get Major McKaig."

"Better make it Danny."

She dressed quickly and ventured into the nippy morning, streaks of dawn slicing the sky. When no one answered her knock on the doctors' door, she rapped again then stepped inside.

"Danny!" He was sound asleep, his mouth open and hair askew. She touched his shoulder. "Danny, wake up."

The other doctors stirred.

"Huh? What?" He opened his eyes half-way. "Shelby? What's going on?"

"I'm sorry to wake you, but Vickie's in a lot of pain."

"Oh, okay. Is she in the nurses' tent?"

"Yes."

"I'll be right there."

She rushed back to Vickie. "Danny's on his way."

"He'd better hurry."

She rubbed her roommate's shoulder. "Would you like me to pray for you?"

"If you have to, but can you do it silently?"

Stung, Shelby managed a gentle response. "Of course." *Lord, you know Vickie's condition, both physically and spiritually. As I pray for her healing, please touch her spirit so she may have the joy of knowing you. Help me know how to help her. Thank you, Lord. Amen.*

She clutched her middle and winced. "Did you pray?"

"Yes."

"Good. I need all the help I can get."

Shelby smiled to herself.

"I think this might be a hot appendix."

Danny arrived and after examining Vickie, reached the same conclusion. "Get Major McKaig, will you Shelby? Tell her to prep for surgery. I'll carry Vickie to the OR."

Shelby ran to get the head nurse, explaining the situation and offering her services.

"No, thanks. I'll take care of this." She shoved her feet into her boots.

"I'd love to help."

"You can—pray!"

Vickie was in surgery by the time the sunrise service started. After the last "amen," Shelby scurried to the OR where she hovered outside the door.

"Have you had any word about her?" Father Stephens asked after joining her.

"Not yet. I know I could go inside, but I just can't." She picked at a cuticle.

"When someone we care about is in there, it's different than tending to a wounded soldier we've never seen before." He lowered his head. "Shelby, I have a feeling something more than Vickie's emergency is on your mind. You've seemed a bit low lately."

She knew she could trust him. "I-I've always managed to maintain an even keel here, but lately ..." She lifted her hands. "I feel like I belly-flopped off a high dive."

He gave a laugh. "You do have a way of putting things. I've felt exactly as you describe. I haven't met anyone here yet who hasn't, no matter how strong they are. Think of the madness we're subjected to every single day. Why do you think the O Club is so popular?" He gazed into her eyes. "Forgive me, but might this have something to do with missing Parker Tate?"

She swallowed a sob.

"The two of you became extraordinarily close in the short time you had together."

"Sometimes, I feel like I made him up, and he won't be there when I get home."

"I was there, Shelby. I assure you he's quite real, and you two have something truly special, something I believe has come straight from the hand of God."

"Why do I doubt like this when I know what you're saying is true?"

The chaplain's voice was firm. "You'll get past this mood. I assure you with the utmost confidence, it was God who brought you together. In fact, yours is one of the most inspiring relationships I've ever had the privilege to witness."

"Thank you," she whispered, dabbing a tear.

"I assume you're writing to each other?"

"Yes, a lot."

"Where is he? I've sort of lost track."

"He's probably at Walter Reed by now."

"And when are you due to go home?"

"Sometime in July."

"We're midway through April, then there'll be just two more months before July."

"I didn't mean to complain, Father."

"I know, and you're not. Remember, God has given us the firmest of foundations to rest upon. He is risen!"

Her eyes shining with tears, Shelby answered, "He is risen indeed!"

After the words found their mark, Father Stephens said he knew what might cheer her.

"The orphans have been asking for you. I told them you've been too busy taking care of wounded soldiers to come the last two times and promised you'd be back soon."

"I've missed them. When can we go again?"

"Dr. Fish will be bringing the children here tomorrow for a medical clinic, and I just happen to need some volunteers."

"Count me in, Father."

"Terrific. I also heard some scuttlebutt about our MASH unit getting up a softball game with a Marine outfit."

"How wonderful."

"See, you feel better already, don't you?"

"I do."

He squeezed her shoulder. "Just know it's okay when you don't."

Shelby pounced on Danny when he emerged from the OR, pulling off his mask. "Is she okay?"

"She's fine. Another few hours and the story could have been quite different."

Before she thought twice, she threw her arms around him, a sisterly gesture Danny seemed to interpret differently. He pulled her closer, causing an internal alarm to sound, and she broke away.

"I'm so thankful she's going to be all right." She scampered outside to distance herself from the awkward situation.

The cooks at the 8055th had done their best to present a holiday-worthy table, even breaking out white tablecloths. That the ham had the texture of boot leather and the mashed potatoes were made with powdered milk and oleo didn't matter. The men had done their best with what little they'd been given. Even the canned fruit cocktail tasted better than usual.

Shelby went up to the head cook on her way out. "Thank you for the Easter dinner."

His shoulders slumped. "I'm sorry it wasn't fancier."

"Who needs fancy when a meal is made with love?"

"Thanks, Nurse Shelby." His face brightened.

She wandered over to the post-op wishing she had some flowers for Vickie, who lay on the far side of the unit. There she had a measure of privacy from the male patients.

"Well, hello there."

Vickie tendered a weak smile. "Shelby."

She sat in the chair next to the bed. "How are you feeling? Are you in much pain?"

"The morphine's helping, but it makes me pretty wacky."

"That's not the morphine." Shelby winked at her.

Vickie batted her friend's arm, causing the IV line to swing.

"You need your sleep."

"How was Easter dinner?" Her eyelids drooped.

"The cooks did their best."

"Let me guess—they stuck spam with cloves."

Shelby laughed. "We had real ham but no cloves."

"I miss my mom's creamed peas."

"Maybe she saved you some."

"Would you write to them?" Her voice slurred. "Address book in footlocker."

"I'll be happy to." When her roommate yawned, Shelby rose. "Have a good night, and I'll see you in the morning."

"Shelby."

"Yes?"

"Thanks—for praying."

"You're very welcome."

CHAPTER THIRTY-TWO

Through his window, Parker watched as dawn began breaking over Washington. He didn't know exactly how long he'd been here, having been feverish and miserable upon his arrival. Now every time he swallowed, pain seared his throat, and he had to fend off worry and self-pity. Instead, he started to consider just how many men shared his quarters at Walter Reed's Forest Glen Annex barracks. Judging by the symphonic snoring and coughing, they were legion. He found his Bible on a nightstand and snatched Shelby's photos when they slid onto the bedcovers. A shadow cast itself over him, and he lifted his face in the half light.

"Good morning, Dr. Tate." A nurse, who appeared to be all of twelve years old, bore a metal tray with the implements of her trade.

"Good morning." His voice came out raspy.

She bent closer, smiling. "Is this your girlfriend?"

He detected a southern accent. "Yes."

"She's beautiful! Where's she from?"

Some of his roommates moaned as if trying to ward off the little noise they were making.

Talking through his blazing throat hurt but speaking of Shelby was worth the effort. "Pennsylvania. She is a MASH nurse in Korea."

"I wanted to be a MASH nurse, but my parents wouldn't let me. Is that where you met?"

"Yes."

"Will you see her again?"

"Yes."

"Well, then, let's get you all better to hasten that day." She shook down a thermometer. "I hope your fever will be lower than one-o-two. I don't like that number. One good thing, you're a lot more with it this morning than your first three days here."

Three days! Just what he needed when the end of his road to recovery was so close.

The nurse, whose name tag read "Lt. Betty Hughes," slid the thermometer under his tongue then swept her hand toward the other men. "You fellows brought some nasty germs with you on that medical transport. I heard even the pilots got sick."

He raised his eyebrows, hoping for more information.

"We think it's a respiratory flu. Fortunately, it's not long-lasting, but with men who've already had injuries and surgeries, healing naturally takes a little longer." She waited another minute, then held the thermometer to the light. "Ninety-nine-five. That's progress."

The reading cheered him. "May I have water?"

"I'll bring a fresh pitcher, and you can take your pills."

"Thank you."

He lay back, listening to the soft shuffling of her feet as she ran her errand, and the sounds of the ward coming to life. One of his roommates hacked like a cat struggling to dislodge a furball. He closed his eyes. *Hear my prayer, O*

Lord. I thought this hospital stay would be brief, that I would come here for a couple of weeks, then go home, but now I am discouraged. The other men here probably have similar feelings. Help me accept this illness as coming from you in your wisdom. Please extend your healing to these men and the pilots who brought us here. May we not be laid low for long in mind or in body. And Lord, please strengthen, protect, and encourage Shelby. Watch over our families, including my recovering grandfather and mother, and grant us your peace. Thank you, Lord. Amen.

Nurse Betty returned with a clean glass and a metal pitcher glistening with droplets. "You can take those pills on your tray. Breakfast will be here soon."

He relished the cold against his throat.

"My, you're thirsty!" She took and refilled the emptied glass. "Is there anything else I can get you before I check on the others?"

"I need to write a letter to—her."

"I'm sure she's eager to hear from you. I'll come back after my rounds to lend a hand."

"Thank you."

"Nurse!" a voice called from the other side of the room. "I need water."

"Coming!" She looked at Parker and grinned. "Just call me 'Molly Pitcher!'"

His physical therapy took two hours a day leaving the rest of the time to relieve boredom by reading and writing letters to Shelby. His roommates mostly hung around the lounges smoking and playing cards or listening to the radio. The beefy Protestant chaplain led Sunday and Wednesday services in Memorial Chapel, which Parker always attended, and they had visited a few times. Whenever he could, Parker used his burgeoning strength to go outside and sit in the sun where he reread Shelby's letters until the paper wore thin. He hadn't heard from her since his arrival at Walter Reed and craved a word from her, hoping she was all right.

He watched a robin procure a fat worm then return to its nest in the crook of a maple tree where tiny beaks vied for dibs. A mild breeze riffled his hair, and he realized his need of a barber, unable to remember when he'd last seen one. *I must be looking like John the Baptist by now.* He would ask the nurse if he might be able to get a haircut. The sun lulled him to sleep, and he awakened half an hour later to the sound of Nurse Betty's drawl.

"I thought I'd find you here," she said. "I know how much you enjoy being outside. You're getting quite a tan."

He pointed to the envelope in her hand. "You have brought me something?"

"I think this is from your girl. I wanted you to have it right away."

He accepted the envelope, smiling to see the slanting handwriting he adored. "You are most kind. Thank you."

"You're welcome. I need to get back inside. Those other patients will have my head if they don't get their mail."

The letter was dated April 15, a little less than two weeks earlier. His heart raced as he read her news.

> Dear Parker,
> I pray this finds you steadily improving. Your sister kindly wrote to tell me you were leaving for Walter Reed. Hopefully, the trip wasn't too hard on you, and you continue to make progress toward the day when you can return to Hopewell. I imagine your brother is especially eager to have you home. You've probably

> written to tell me about your journey and what WRAMC is like. As the mails are slow, I must allay any anxiety I have for you with the sure and certain hope that you are in God's loving hands.
>
> We've had some intense OR sessions, as well as in post-op. One day we had a Turkish soldier and a Greek soldier whose mutual animosity led to the reopening of their stitches. Fortunately, Danny and Neil were able to break them apart and afterward kept them separated. One of my roommates, Nurse Vickie, caused no small amount of alarm when she needed emergency surgery for acute appendicitis. She's doing well now, thanks be to God, and will be able to resume her duties in a few days. The experience seems to have softened her, if just a little. She's rather rough around the edges and frequently gets my goat—do you know that American expression—but I try not to respond harshly or with sarcasm. My mother could never stand sarcasm. Besides, Vickie has endeared herself to me by being a true friend.
>
> As you know from living in the US, Americans get excited this time of year for the start of baseball season. I think you should know this about me—I'm an ardent Philadelphia Phillies fan. Since Easton is halfway between New York and Philadelphia, our population is also half Phillies and half fans of the New York teams, the Yankees, Giants, and Brooklyn Dodgers. One of my aunts is a huge Jackie Robinson fan, and she puts down the Phillies at every possible opportunity. If you don't know or enjoy baseball, I can help introduce you to America's pastime. Not liking or knowing about baseball would be far better than if you were a Dodgers, Yankees, or Giants fan, but even that could be forgiven because of my affection for you.

Parker smiled, relishing her humor. The truth was, he knew little about the game, his only knowledge acquired from overheard conversations. He was certainly willing to learn and become like Shelby, a Phillies fan. He resumed reading.

> A week ago, our MASH unit engaged in a baseball game with some Marines who chided us endlessly about our "softness." They said we couldn't beat a little league team (small children who play baseball) let alone hard-core warriors like them. Colonel Sheppard did his best to get us in shape, and all of us were given an opportunity to play if we wanted. Although Vickie was on a high school softball team, of course she couldn't participate. Major McKaig is something of a tomboy (there's another American expression. It means a young girl who likes to play with boy's toys and climb trees and do sports, that sort of thing) and she became our first baseman. We had a fair number of corpsmen and members of the motor pool to make the doctors and nurses a little more competitive. I can swing a bat for singles, but to be honest, I'm afraid of the ball. It screeches across the field so fast if you don't catch it, or get out of its way, you can end up with a concussion. Colonel Sheppard put me in the outfield where I did little good and no real harm. Naturally, the Marines defeated us soundly, twenty-to-four, but we all had a good time and ended up sharing insults in the O Club.

He wished he could have seen her playing baseball against those tough Marines. Maybe she had pulled up her hair in one of those American ponytails. His heart rejoiced knowing she'd had a joyful respite from the suffering she so regularly witnessed.

> Father Stephens and I have been visiting the orphanage weekly, and I must tell you, those little ones have stolen my heart. They are so dear, and Dr. Fish, the director, does wonders with them. She came here after World War II as a medical missionary and has stayed on, a resilient, frugal woman whose all-out devotion to Jesus and these

children inspires me. One little fellow, Woo Sung, clings to me, and I try to soothe and mother him with the little time and attention I can offer. He's four years old and lost both parents in the opening months of the war. He's so very dear, and I hope to comfort and love on him while I'm here.

Speaking of which—I do hope to be discharged in mid-July, at least that's when Major McKaig thinks Vickie and I will be able to go home. We don't have final approval yet, but I'm counting the days until I can be with my family and friends again, close to you in Hopewell. I often dream of the day we'll see each other again, wondering what our reunion will be like. Will we be the same as we were in Korea? You'll be well, and we will be in more normal circumstances. Sometimes, I find myself worrying our feelings won't be the same. Do you ever think of this? Mind you, I can't imagine not feeling as I do now. I hope I'm making sense. Sometimes I don't even understand myself. In the meantime, I'm striving to do God's will here while looking forward to a bright future. I hold you close in my heart and pray for you continually.

Love,
Shelby

He sighed, lifting his eyes to the surrounding gardens. She was right about things being different when they got back together away from a hospital in a war zone where he was the patient and she, his caregiver. He hated to think she might have only responded to him out of compassion while he was far down physically. Then again, she had treated hundreds of other wounded soldiers without developing deep feelings for them. No, she was much more than his nurse. They were much more. In America, they both would be on more level ground. Sort of. He wasn't yet a citizen, and her family had been there since before the Revolution.

Would they and her friends accept her choice of a Korean man? Parker had known his share of those who embraced him as an equal before God while others treated him as an inferior.

He stared without really seeing birds and squirrels rollicking in the mild spring day. Yes, things would change with the circumstances. Their way of relating to each other would shift, but he was certain their deep love and the love of God would be the foundation to build all the rest upon. He prayed against a spirit of fear.

His roommates kept mostly to themselves, a group whose highest rank was corporal. Although he wasn't standoffish, they seemed wary of his status as a physician and officer, let alone a Korean. He was pleasant toward them but without pushing his way into their company. The largest of the men had hands the size of hub caps and no discernable neck. At times he overheard the fellow telling off-color jokes, resulting in guffaws and slapped knees.

Toward the end of what Parker hoped would be his last week at the Army hospital, he awakened in the middle of the night to a soft commotion on the other side of the room. His instincts spurred him to action as he hastened out of bed and found the big man silent as a tomb. One of their bunkies hovered over him, slapping his face. He looked up at Parker, shouting and awakening everyone in the room. Someone snapped on the lights.

"Something's wrong, Doc! I rang for the nurse, but no one's coming."

Parker pushed his way to the inert giant. "What happened?"

"A little while ago, one of the nurses came in and gave Hank some medicine. The next thing I knew, he stopped talking."

He found a weak pulse. "When was she here?"

"Just a few minutes ago."

The heart rate was tortuously slow, the skin clammy. Hank's mouth was a gate on open hinges.

"I think he is in shock, perhaps an adverse reaction to the medication. Get a nurse or doctor. Tell them to bring adrenaline. Hurry!"

The few passing minutes dragged until the night shift nurse and doctor arrived.

"Anaphylactic shock," the physician said. He administered adrenaline while the nurse monitored Hank's pulse.

"It's getting stronger," she said. "I think he's coming around."

A few minutes later, Hank blinked his eyes open and looked around. "What gives?"

The doctor pointed to Parker. "This man just saved your life."

In silence, he thanked God for allowing him, at last, to feel useful again.

CHAPTER THIRTY-THREE

"Shelby, would you mind going to the orphanage with me today? Dr. Fish is running low on penicillin and aspirin. Colonel Sheppard has given permission."

In the background a handful of orderlies shot hoops. She couldn't think of a better way to spend her birthday than to see those smiling faces. At least they would help her feel special on a day no one else had remembered. She expected her family to send cards and a gift, and Parker might recall she was born on May twenty-ninth, but the mail system was no respecter of personal holidays.

"Of course, Father. When do you plan to leave?"

"Since things are slow here, as soon as I gather the boxes and check out a Jeep we can go. I'll meet you back here in thirty minutes."

When they pulled up to the building, Woo Sung appeared with a face-splitting smile and hurled himself at Shelby. Other children waved and grinned at the Americans.

"Oof! You're getting to be quite the little man." She hugged him, laughing, then held him at arm's length. "I've only been gone two weeks, and you've grown at least an inch."

He jabbered something in Korean, and she listened with rapt focus despite not understanding a word. A sudden thought heated her face and ears. *If Parker and I do, uh, well, if he's the one, what would our children look like? Would they have dark hair and delicate eyes, or my light features, or a combination of both?*

"Shelby, would you mind helping me unload the Jeep?"

The sound of Father Stephens's voice made her face burn red, as if he'd read her mind.

"Sure, Father. Okay, you little scamp," she told Woo Sung, "I need my arms back."

Dr. Fish pealed the little boy off Shelby. After taking the boxes into the tiny clinic, they trooped into the main room, which served as a cafeteria, chapel, and school. The children kept giggling and staring at her, saying things behind hands held up to their mouths. She wondered if she might have left a button undone or hadn't wiped away the ketchup she'd poured over her powdered eggs. Finding nothing out of place, she shrugged her shoulders.

The director gathered the children together with Woo Sung standing in the front. "Nurse Shelby, would you sit right here facing the children?"

"Sure." She hopped up onto the table, wondering what was going on.

On Father Stephens's hand signal, they began singing in ragged English, "Happy birthday to you, happy birthday to you, happy birthday Nurse Shelby, happy birthday to you!"

Her breath caught. "Oh, my."

"We've been working on this for a week," Dr. Fish said, "as soon as we learned today is your birthday. Many happy returns."

"What a surprise!" She gazed at the children's beaming faces, knowing she'd always cherish this particular birthday celebration. "*Gam sa ham ni da*."

Woo Sung broke away from the others and pulled out his hand from behind his back. With a smile as big as Korea, he handed her a Hershey Bar. Her lips parted as she accepted the gift. "Wherever did he get this, Dr. Fish?"

"A GI gave the children candy a few days ago. Woo Sung saved his so he could give you a present."

Tears trickled down her face as she encircled the little fellow in a tight hug. She wanted him to have the chocolate, knowing how little access he had to treats, but she didn't want to hurt his feelings. She kept the Hershey Bar.

Shelby pushed her meatloaf around the tin plate, replaying the touching scene at the orphanage. Woo Sung's precious gift would lift her spirits for a month of Sundays, maybe for the rest of her life.

"Not hungry?" Evelyn sipped her coffee, elbows on the table.

"Actually, I'm quite full." She didn't want to call attention to her birthday.

"Too bad, because we're having dessert tonight."

"Funny, I didn't see anything in the chow line." She looked over her shoulder. People seemed to be smiling at her. Just then, Major McKaig appeared bearing a lopsided cake with four burning candles. The company began singing "Happy Birthday."

"Make a wish!" the head nurse said.

Shelby was quick to think. *I'll say a prayer instead. Please continue to heal Parker and bring us together soon, Lord.*

"Well, did you?" Vickie asked.

"Yes!"

"Then what are you waiting for? Blow out the candles!"

This required almost no effort, but everyone still applauded. Major McKaig set the cake on the table, and one of the cooks brought plates, forks, and a large knife for Shelby to begin cutting slices. Several people laid wrapped gifts next to her, and Evelyn produced a pile of mail, neatly tied with what appeared to be a pink hair ribbon.

"We hope you don't mind, but when the mail came yesterday, we held yours back so you'd have lots of nice greetings on your birthday."

"I wondered what happened to my mail." She laughed as she continued cutting the cake. Vickie passed out plates to those lining up.

"Too bad I can't open it until tomorrow. I have the night shift."

"That's where you're wrong," Vickie said. "We're covering for you tonight."

Shelby batted her arm. "You guys are too much!"

The first card she snatched bore Parker's handwriting from Washington, DC, followed by letters from him with slightly later postmarks. The basic greeting was discount store quality, and she guessed he'd found it in the hospital gift shop. His remembering her special day at all thrilled her more than all the fancy Hallmark cards in America. On the left side of the printed sentiment he'd written:

My Dear Shelby,

Hopefully, this reaches you in time for your birthday. This is not the card I would most have liked to send

> you, but there was not much of a selection here at the hospital. Know I send my love with it and look forward to celebrating your birthday next year under much different circumstances. Then you will have a card and a gift worthy of you.

Her heart soared at the thought of being with him a year from now. She continued reading, greedy for the rest of what he had to say.

> You will find a letter from me directly after I send this. I just wanted to make sure you had a birthday greeting from me. I am very thankful to God for the gift of your life and how he brought us together.
> Love,
> Parker

"It must be good." Vickie stood over her shoulder, grinning.

"Good isn't the right word for this card."

"Doesn't look like much to me, but then I can guess who sent it." She grabbed a sweater. "Don't let me interrupt. I'm just on my way to post-op but needed some extra warmth. As nice as these days have been, nights are still chilly."

"Thanks again for covering for me, Vickie."

She waved. "Enjoy your mail. Ta ta!"

Shelby reached for the box of popcorn Evelyn had made for her with just the right amount of salt and margarine. She had no idea how her friend had managed to find this treat. After being in Korea, she didn't know if she'd ever take for granted simple, everyday pleasures.

Her siblings had made cards for her out of construction paper and library paste, Paul having drawn a picture of her in her nurse's uniform. She grinned over his stick figure rendition with its enormous head and tilted cap, wishing she could wrap her arms around her little brother and muss up his curly hair. There were cards from her grandparents and friends from church. Her parents had sent a cardigan, stockings, socks, two books, and a few personal items. Nearly at the bottom of the pile of cards she found one she'd almost missed, in her mother's swirling hand. Something inside told her this would be especially meaningful as she slid her finger along the top of the envelope.

> My Dear Daughter,
> Along with your card, I want to write my own birthday greeting. This day always brings such lovely memories of when I held you in my arms for the first time at Easton Hospital. You were so tiny with a halo of blonde hair and the sweetest fingers and toes. Now you are a beautiful young woman serving her country, relieving the suffering of our wounded soldiers. I'm so thankful to God for you and cannot wait to see you again and look into your lovely face. That day will be here before you know it yet cannot come soon enough.
>
> I've been thinking a lot about what your grandfather has shared with me.

Shelby's insides quivered—was her mother was going to approve, or disapprove? She read on, grateful to be alone.

> He sounds like a good and brave man, a man of faith and substance. Since I first heard about him and his being severely wounded, I've been keeping him in my prayers. I do hope he is getting well and will soon be home and practicing medicine again. As most mothers do, I'm happy you're interested in a doctor, ha ha! As you're a nurse, you can understand each other's work. I can also imagine he must be quite handsome to have caught your eye. Grandfather told us Dr. Tate lives in Hopewell, New Jersey, so you'll be able to see each other when you both come home. All of us look forward to meeting him.

My dear daughter, while being in love is one of God's finest gifts, please take your time with this relationship. You have known each other in the midst of war, under unusual circumstances. Soon you'll be together in a far more normal place without such pressures. As he has lived in America for several years, he knows our customs, our way of life, but his background is still very different from yours. This could be a blessing—or a detriment. I know you have a good head on your shoulders, and your heart is usually in the right place. Just allow our Lord to guide you and your Parker Tate in His paths. I will be here to listen to your hopes and dreams all along the way.

Love and God bless,
Mom

"Thanks, Mom," she whispered. "You always did have an uncanny knack for knowing what I'm thinking. I love you back." After a long moment she put the letter aside and reached for Parker's next one.

May 15, 1952

Dear Shelby,
Did you have a nice birthday? I know the day isn't until May twenty-ninth, but this letter will take about two weeks to arrive. Hopefully, my card gets there in time. I do hope your friends remembered and were able to make the day special for you.

Rest assured, I am doing well. They have me doing a rigorous physical therapy program, and my leg is strong. My stomach has stopped hurting, and my throat is also nearly normal—the bandage came off a week ago. How thankful I am to God to be getting whole again. This period has taught me to understand my patients better as I had enjoyed only good health until a few months ago. My brother was able to get away for a brief visit this week, and what a happy reunion we had.

I hope to continue my recovery on pace to leave for home sometime in the next two weeks. As you probably are, I am counting the days until I see you again.

Have you been visiting the orphans? How is your little friend, Woo Sung? I must say, he has very good taste to be so attracted to you, but you must let him know you are already taken.

I pray you are at peace and will come home soon.

Love,
Parker

"Thanks for coming to see me, ladies. Have a seat." Colonel Sheppard pointed across his desk to two chairs.

Shelby and Vickie glanced at each other while their CO rested his cigar on a cock-eyed ashtray his grandson had made. The outside window was opened to the sound of vehicles moving through the compound and the smell of exhaust fumes.

He swiveled in his chair. "I've heard from I Corps about your discharges."

Shelby held her breath. Was this to be good news? She didn't know how she would handle the disappointment of a delayed release.

"You've both been approved to leave here in less than a month, on July 15."

Relieved, she grinned at Vickie.

He gestured toward paperwork. "The Army wants to make a counteroffer."

"A counteroffer, sir?" Vickie raised her eyebrows.

"If you sign up for another six months, you'll be promoted to first lieutenant status with an increase in pay." He peered at them. "Mind you, I'm not pressuring you. This must be your decision. I certainly know what I would do," he muttered.

"Let me think about it," Vickie said. "I mean, the offer is worth considering."

Shelby felt their eyes on her.

"Well, Kichline, what about you? Do you need time to think about it?"

She straightened up. "No, sir, I don't. I'm going home."

CHAPTER THIRTY-FOUR

June 1, 1952
Hopewell, NJ

My Dear Shelby,
As you can see from this heading and the post mark, I am home again in New Jersey. I made the trip from Washington just yesterday. My brother picked me up at Princeton Junction and we are enjoying a second happy reunion. John has handled the practice capably in my absence, even to the point of adding new patients. I also found the apartment in far better shape than I had anticipated. We were never good housekeepers, and I could just imagine what our home would look like with only him to keep it tidy. Fortunately, he took our receptionist's advice and hired her aunt to clean and cook twice a week. John has added a few pounds to his lean frame as a result, and Mrs. Shaw vows she will "put meat on my bones" as well. I am grateful for such a caring and amiable brother, and our house help.

Please forgive me for taking most of this letter to speak just of myself. Are you coping well in your work? Are you able to find relaxation and refresh your spirit? (Just not with Dr. Danielson.) Does Woo Sung understand you will be leaving Korea soon? I pray for him and the other orphans, who have a loving Heavenly Father.

> Be assured of my ceaseless prayers for you. I want to rush the days until you are back, and we can see each other once more.
>
> I remain your devoted, Parker.

He searched for stamps in the desk he shared with John but came up short. He would walk over to the post office tomorrow to send Shelby's letter. He sniffed at the fragrance of beef and tomatoes and wandered into the kitchen. John was at work with dinner preparations, and he'd tuned the radio to popular music. All around the clean apartment an array of floral and fruit gifts lent the appearance of a hospital gift shop.

"Have you also become an excellent cook in my absence?" he asked.

His brother grinned. "When Mrs. Albano, Mrs. Shaw, and our pastor heard you'd be home today, an army of women descended upon me with casseroles, roasts, and desserts. I'm reheating a beef dish—you look like you could use some red meat."

His mouth watered. "How very kind of them."

"There's so much to talk about, Parker. We didn't have much time at the hospital, and I want to hear from you how you got hurt. I've only heard bits and pieces, mostly from Anna."

"Oh, I must let our family know I have returned."

"Not to worry. I sent a telegram this morning." He moved toward the cabinet and pulled out two dinner plates.

"Thank you. Thank you for all you have done in my absence."

John closed his eyes and nodded his head.

"I want to hear all your news. You must have a good bit to tell me."

"I do, but I'm more interested just now in your stories. There'll be plenty of time for mine." He moved toward the refrigerator and opened the door. "We need more butter. Ah, here we go. Mrs. Stein brought homemade challah bread and didn't forget the butter."

Parker laughed. "How is Mrs. Stein?"

"She's her usual feisty self."

"I look forward to seeing her."

"Oh, I mustn't forget—Dr. and Mrs. Cullen have invited us to dinner this Sunday, if you feel up to it."

"Yes, I very much want to see them."

He inhaled sharply when the opening notes of "Unforgettable" started playing. He reached over to the radio and turned up the volume.

John raised an eyebrow. "Why the interest in that song?"

Parker dipped his chin and smiled.

They pushed back from the table, the meager remains of their evening meal attesting to their healthy appetites. John refilled his brother's glass of rice wine after hearing about Shelby.

"She sounds quite special, Parker."

"She is. I am convinced God brought us together."

"From what you told me, I'd have to agree." He sipped the wine, gazing at Parker. "You seem pretty serious about her."

"Yes, I am."

They fell into a congenial silence, a car passing by on the street outside the open windows. Parker closed his eyes for a moment, wondering if he might be dreaming this idyllic scene after so long away and under such circumstances.

Thank you, Lord, for my home, my brother, and my work. Please bring Shelby home soon, too, to her family and to me.

John was saying something, but Parker had missed the initial words. "I beg your pardon, but would you mind starting from the beginning?

His brother combed his fingers through his dark hair. "I'm glad to hear Mother has reconciled herself to your decision, which seems no less than miraculous than the way you met Shelby. Um, I'm just wondering if Soonja is okay with all that happened."

Parker searched his brother's expression. "Anna mentioned in a letter that Soonja is doing well. She seems to have gotten over me pretty quickly."

John's eyes widened. "That's good, I mean good she wasn't heartbroken or anything."

Parker cocked his head to the left. "Why are you interested in Soonja?"

His brother slid a finger inside his collar. "Might I tell you something no one else knows?"

"You may tell me anything."

"I hope you take this the right way." He looked up at the ceiling, drumming his fingers on the table. "I've always had feelings for Soonja but dared not let on since Mother clearly intended her for you."

Parker did a double take. "I had no idea."

"I hardly admitted the truth to myself. Before I came to Princeton, Soonja was around the house a lot. I found her so delightful, but I did my best to treat her like a sister. I doubt anyone suspected how I felt about her."

"And do you still feel this way?" He raised his eyebrows.

John tossed his napkin onto the table and met his brother's eye. "Yes. What do you think I should do?"

"Ask God to guide you. If he gives you peace, reach out to Soonja."

"What should I say to her?"

Parker smiled. "I believe your writing to her will in itself communicate a great deal."

June 10, 1952

Dear Shelby,

Are you numbering the days until you begin making the long journey home? When you receive this, you will likely be just two or so weeks away from leaving Korea. Since you will probably return to the United States on a troop ship, I must caution you against wandering in the dark on the deck lest you meet a mysterious man like you did the last time.

What have conditions been like at the 8055th? I have heard of truces and peace talks taking place, yet the fighting continues. Have you played anymore baseball games? I am eager to learn about this sport and have begun reading box scores in the paper. I like following the team captain, Granny Hamner. His name intrigues me.

Being home has been wonderful, everything is new and radiant. Being in my own apartment, shopping, reading the evening paper, and going to church make me almost giddy with joy. I rejoice to be practicing medicine again and now understand being on the other side of health. Just being well again exhilarates me. I believe I can take on the world. (Do not worry. I have been gradually resuming my duties and am now up to full strength. Besides, Mrs. Albano, my receptionist, would not let me overdo should I try.)

On my first Sunday at church, I found myself surrounded by hugging females (older women and little girls, of course), and bone-crushing handshakes. So many men slapped me on the back I thought I might require traction. One of the women's circles hosted a reception for me after the service, which was so very kind of them. A reporter from the local paper had come to interview me, but I did not wish to speak with him. He asked questions he had no business to ask and seemed to expect me to recount my "heroics" for the general public. I declined as politely as I could, but I did allow him to photograph me. I would rather have not but thought I owed him something for his trouble.

My dear friends Dr. and Mrs. Cullen had John and me over to dinner that night. Afterward, we retired to his study where I allowed myself to share more privately my experiences. Such intimacy is only meant for the closest of friends.

I have one more thing to tell you before closing. My brother confided to me he has long had feelings for Soonja, the woman my mother had intended for me. I was greatly surprised and urged him to pray for guidance. He did so, and within two days he had written to her. I do wonder if she might care for him. I would be happy if they found together even a small portion of what you and I share.

Dearest Shelby, when you are discharged, you will likely come through Fort Dix. I would be happy to meet you there and take you home to Easton. If you would rather your family met you, or you prefer to take the train from Trenton to Easton, I will be available to assist you. I do not want to impose myself, but I do so desire to see you.

The days will go quickly now, though at times they will appear to stand still. Take heart and know my heart is waiting for you.

Love,
Parker

"I must say, Mrs. Stein, you are the picture of health."

She peered at him. "You're looking good yourself, but you need to put on some weight. Are you all better now?"

"I feel wonderful. Your challah bread has made me strong again."

She laughed, a raspy sound courtesy of her two-pack-a-day habit. "Well, now that you're back in the human race, it's time to get you out there."

"What does this mean?"

"You need to start seeing girls, and I have just the one for you."

He swallowed a laugh.

"She's quite a looker, my sister's oldest. She's perfect for you. Can I arrange a date?"

"You are very kind, but you see, I already have a girlfriend."

Her eyes narrowed. "Since when?"

"I met her in Korea."

"Oh." She stretched the word into multiple syllables. "I'll bet she's a nice little Korean girl."

He was enjoying this far too much. "Oh, but she is not Korean. She is an American."

She frowned. "And what do your parents have to say about that?"

"They like her very much."

She suddenly brightened. "Well, there's always your brother."

He consulted the roster to see who was next—Mrs. Thomas with her five-year-old Marcia, complaining of a sore throat. Mrs. Albano interrupted him.

"Dr. Tate, I hate to bother you, but there's a phone call I think you should take."

He looked up from the clipboard. "Is anything wrong? Can it wait?"

"I don't think anything's wrong, but if I were you, I wouldn't wait." Her eyes twinkled.

For one wild moment he thought Shelby might be on the line. He hastened to his office where he picked up the receiver. "Hello, this is Dr. Tate."

"Hello, Dr. Tate," a woman said. "Please excuse me for calling you at your work, but I didn't know how else to reach you. I got your number from the operator."

"That is not a problem." He wondered who this could be.

"I'm Margaret Kichline, Shelby's mother."

Shelby's mother! His hand trembled. *Has something happened to her?*

"Oh, hello, Mrs. Kichline. Is Shelby all right?"

"Good gracious, I'm sorry for alarming you. She's just fine."

He blew out a breath. "Please do not apologize. I am happy to talk to you."

"Shelby has told us so much about you. We're delighted you've made it back home."

"Thank you. You are very kind to call me." His heart rate dropped from full-blown panic to merely heightened.

"I'm calling because we'd all love to meet you. Might you be able to join us for dinner this Saturday at our home in Easton?"

Was this *really* Shelby's mother, and was she asking him to meet the family?

"I would very much enjoy meeting all of you."

"Wonderful!" She gave him their address, directions, and their phone number. "Would you like to come at five o'clock?"

"Yes, ma'am. Thank you."

"I so look forward to meeting you. Goodbye, Dr. Tate."

"I will be happy to meet you as well. Goodbye." He hung up the phone and broke into a grin. He was going to meet Shelby's family.

CHAPTER THIRTY-FIVE

"Mind if I join you?"

Shelby looked up to see Danny standing before her with a cup of coffee. She laid aside her sister's letter and gestured toward the bench across the table. The kitchen crew was setting up for the evening meal while a small group of hospital orderlies huddled in a corner. Apparently, they were telling jokes, given their frequent outbursts.

"So, you're heading home in a few days. Do I ever envy you."

"Sometimes I have to pinch myself to see if this isn't just a dream." When Danny didn't respond, the mess tent seemed to shrink to pup tent size. She couldn't think of anything to say.

"I hear Vickie is staying on for an extended tour."

"She decided getting a promotion and additional pay would be worth the extra time."

"But you turned the opportunity down."

"That's right." *Is he criticizing me?*

"I guess you have a better offer waiting at home." His eyes searched hers.

"My family and friends are waiting there for me."

Danny sipped his coffee then put the cup on the table. "Will you continue nursing?"

"Yes." Frankly, she hadn't given much thought lately to a post-Korea career. She was more focused on building a certain relationship and re-entering a state of normalcy. "When I graduated from nursing school, my local hospital wanted to hire me, but I wanted to serve my country first."

"If you could do it all over again, would you make the same decision?"

She didn't hesitate. "I would."

Danny seemed to be trying to affect a casual air. "What about Dr. Tate? Will you be seeing him back in the States?"

Shelby met his gaze. "Yes. He's there now."

"Oh, I didn't realize he'd gone home. When was that?"

"Early last month."

"And he's well again?" He was chewing the edge of his lower lip.

"He is, thankfully. He's even resumed a normal workload."

"That's good."

They both retreated to their own thoughts.

"Well, I guess I lost that quest," Danny finally said with a small laugh.

She frowned. "What quest?"

"To win a certain lady fair."

Blushing, she ran a finger over a ragged thumb nail.

"Ah well, if I had to lose out, I'm glad you're going to be with a such a fine fellow."

She didn't want to tell him that even if Parker weren't in the picture, Danny wouldn't have been spiritually compatible. She didn't think letting him believe he'd had a chance would do any harm.

"I have a question for you," she said.

"Fire away."

"Last Christmas, you gave me a lovely shawl. I feel uncomfortable keeping it, you know, because we aren't, uh, dating or anything. I wonder if you might like to have it back."

"You may keep it as a memento of our friendship."

She knew she wouldn't be able to wear the shawl without remembering its giver, certainly not in Parker's company. Nor did she want to tell people back home who it had come from. She would figure out what to do with the expensive gift before she left.

Danny rose. "Well, then, when exactly do you leave?"

"On the fifteenth."

He ran a hand over his jaw. "Three days from now. I might not have another opportunity to say how much I've enjoyed working with you and getting to know you. I wish you all the best in the future."

Her voice caught. "Thank you, Danny. May God bless you as well."

She knew her last visit to the orphanage would be fraught with emotion, so she stuffed two handkerchiefs into a pocket before heading there with Father Stephens. She wasn't the only one in need of a hanky. Throughout her visit, tears adorned the little faces. Woo Sung was especially clingy, and Shelby vacillated between hugging him so tight she'd never let go and trying to stuff her searing grief.

The orphans presented her with handwritten cards and rice cakes, and she gave them every Peanuts comic book her brother Neil had sent her in various packages from home. She also shared the goodies she still had left from the last batch. While the children tucked into the treats with noisy chatter, Shelby handed the director a slim box.

"What is this?"

"Besides these incredible children, you don't have many pretty things around you, Dr. Fish. I'd like you to have this as a reminder that even in war, God's world contains great beauty."

The older woman opened the box and pulled out Danny's stunning shawl. "Oh, Shelby! This is glorious!" She wrapped the scarf around her slender shoulders, beaming.

"It suits you."

"How very kind you are." She hugged her benefactor.

"You are a treasure. You know, I'd like your advice about another gift. I'd like to leave my gold cross with Woo Sung, but I fear he may be too little for such a thing. I also don't want to make the other children resentful. What do you think?"

"That would be a lovely gesture, and I can understand why you'd like to leave a memento with him. I think you're right, though, about him being too young and the others feeling jealous. Honestly, Shelby, you've brought him and the others a lot of happiness today. Let the comic books and treats be enough."

She concealed her small disappointment with a smile. "I understand." She handed a piece of paper to the woman. "Here's my address, Dr. Fish. Please stay in touch, and if you need anything, I'll do my best to help. My church is generous, and they love lending a hand."

The two women embraced, sharing their bond of faith, and an abundance of tears.

July 12, 1952

Dear Mom and Dad,
How are you, and how is everyone back home? Are my brothers and sister enjoying their summer vacation? And how about you, Dad? Are you fishing as much as you'd like and tinkering with Poppa's old Model T? Soon, I'll be with you again, and although I missed July Fourth, there'll be plenty of time for other family picnics at Hackett Park.

And now for my news—I'll be shipping out in three days. I should be arriving in California roughly two weeks later, then taking a train to Fort Dix for my discharge. Although I could catch a ride to Trenton Station that would bring me directly to Easton, I have another plan. My friend Parker has told me he would very much like to pick me up at Fort Dix and drive me home. I hope you won't mind. I would so enjoy seeing you there, but since Parker lives a short distance from the base, it makes more sense for him to retrieve me. Maybe I'm worrying about this for nothing, but I want to be sensitive to your feelings. (I also can't wait for you to meet him.)

I'm going to close now. I want to make sure you get this letter so you can know when to expect my arrival. As soon as I get off the ship in California, I'll call.
Your loving daughter,
Shelby

She sealed and addressed the envelope, then rushed the letter to Corporal Unger's office.

"You're just in time, Shelby. The mail truck hasn't left the compound yet." He popped up from his chair. "Oh, and by the way, this package just came for you." He pushed the box into her arms on his way outside.

She examined what proved to be unfamiliar handwriting and a Seoul postmark. Puzzled, she took the package back to the nurse's quarters. The box contained a packet of letters, various teas, what appeared to be cookies and cakes, and two large jars of kimchi. She opened a letter from Anna Park.

> Dear Shelby,
> Tae-ho (Parker) told us you were about to leave Korea, and we hope this comes to you in time. If you would, please bring these letters and small gifts to him and our brother John in the United States. Be sure to help yourself as well. We enclose a letter written by our grandfather to your grandfather, along with his very good wishes and prayers. We all enjoyed getting to know you in Seoul and wish to thank you for your kindnesses to Tae-ho and our family while he was ill. I think you are very beautiful, and I am happy my brother loves you. May you have a safe journey home.
> Anna Park

Tenderness spread through her. Parker's family seemed to be accepting her, and wouldn't her grandfather be delighted to hear from his old friend.

Shortly afterward, Corporal Unger stopped by the nurse's barracks waving another letter.

"In my haste to get your mail out," he said, "I forgot to give this to you."

"Thanks, Neil." Her chest drummed when she saw Parker's handwriting. She didn't even notice when the company clerk left.

Leaning back on her bed, she tucked her legs underneath and opened the envelope.

> June 18, 1952
>
> My Dear Shelby,
> Hopefully, I am writing with enough advance before your departure from Korea. I imagine you are busy packing your belongings and saying goodbye to your friends.

I know you will be missed, especially by the orphans.
I remain so very happy to be back in Hopewell, and I know you will be happy, too, when you are home in Easton. Do expect to take some time to readjust. Now and then the hurriedness of American life and the abundance of material possessions overwhelm me. I go to the grocery store where there is such a large array of food and remember how the procurement of necessities in Korea is so difficult. Most people cannot understand what I have seen or been through, and this will also be true for you. I have found talking to my patients and church members who fought in other wars a kind of balm. We understand each other without needing to say much. I will be a source of support for you in your own transition.

I am still planning to meet you at Fort Dix and take you home, should you and your family agree to this. I cannot wait to see you and enfold you in my arms.
Before I close, I have rather astonishing news, which I have kept for last. Your mother called me a few days ago and invited me to have dinner at your house. I was surprised and delighted and very much look forward to meeting them this Saturday. I will tell you all about the visit when I see you. I admit to feeling a little fretful, wondering if they will like and approve of me. Then I remember how you met my family under difficult circumstances and did so very well.

May the Lord continue to watch over and bless you as you leave Korea and come home.

Love,
Parker

Shelby dropped the letter and laughed out loud. *Oh, Mom, you little devil, you.*

Before heading to the O Club for a farewell gathering, Shelby took leave of her closest friends knowing there'd be little time for meaningful goodbyes later. She called them over to her bunk, her heart swelling with affection for sweet-tempered Evelyn and feisty Vickie.

"I just wanted to say a few words before the party." Shelby toyed with her shirt buttons.

"I don't like goodbyes," Vickie said. "Couldn't we just avoid this?"

"Not before I tell you both what your friendship has meant to me. You've lent such beauty and life to this place. I don't think I could have made it without you."

Evelyn sniffed. Vickie looked away.

"I'd like you both to have one of my grandmother's lace-edged handkerchiefs."

"Oh, Shelby, how beautiful!" Evelyn said.

A tear slipped down Vickie's cheek. "Thanks."

"You will write to us?" asked Evelyn.

"Of course."

"I'll look forward to hearing from you. Being from Missouri, visiting won't be practical when I go home in a couple months."

"You never know. There's always the possibility."

"Listen, Shelb, I only have six more months," Vickie said, "then I'll be back in New York. You won't be living far from me in Hopewell, so we can see each other again."

She looked at her sideways. "I'm from Easton, not Hopewell."

Vickie grinned. "You will be."

The entire camp seemed to surround Shelby while Corporal Unger loaded her belongings into a Jeep.

Colonel Sheppard hugged her, his eyes glistening. “Shelby Kichline, it’s been a pleasure. Godspeed to you!”

Father Stephens made the sign of the cross over her. “May the Lord bless you and keep you, now and always.”

“Thank you, Father.”

“Goodbye, Shelby.” Danny gave her a quick hug.

“Bye, Danny.”

Even Neil Olsen wished her a safe trip.

All the nurses who weren’t on duty took turns hugging her. At the end of the line, Major McKaig smiled then embraced her.

“Shelby,” she whispered in her ear, “you’re one of the finest nurses I’ve ever worked with. Good luck in your future. I hope you’ll continue your career.”

“Thank you, Major, for everything. I’ll always remember your kindness.”

She climbed into the passenger seat and held onto her cap when the Jeep lurched to a start. As the vehicle left the compound, she turned back, waving and crying.

CHAPTER THIRTY-SIX

Mrs. Albano planted her feet astride and wrapped her arms across her bosom.

"You're as rangy as a cat, Dr. Tate."

Parker hadn't realized he was wearing a hole in the rug.

His receptionist squinted at him over the top of her readers. "Is anything the matter?"

Should he tell her? What lay on his mind did require feminine counsel, and he decided to take a chance.

"Please, have a seat." He could talk more easily if she weren't standing there like Brunhilda. He perched on the side of his desk and cleared his throat. "You see, I met a woman in Korea."

"I knew it! I just knew it. Mrs. Stein was trying to tell me you had a girl, but I didn't want to come right out and ask you. After all, your personal life is none of my business." She inched closer.

"Yes, well, I was going to tell you when I was ready."

"Are you ready?"

He grinned at her eagerness. "I suppose I am." He told her all about Shelby.

"And you say she's coming home next month, to Easton?"

"Yes."

"You must be over the moon to see her again."

"That I am."

"So, why are you pacing like a caged lion?" She tilted her head.

"Do you remember the woman who called here yesterday?"

"I sure do."

"That was Shelby's mother. She has invited me to have dinner with the family this Saturday, and I am wondering what to wear and what kind of gift to bring them."

She touched a finger to her lips. "When you say, 'the family,' just how big a gathering is this to be? I mean, is the whole extended family coming?"

His stomach roiled. "I, uh, did not ask."

Mrs. Albano gazed upward. "Somehow, I doubt they'd include the entire family, Dr. Tate. I'm guessing it's just her parents and siblings. She does have siblings, right?"

"Yes, a sister and three brothers."

"Here's my advice." She drew closer. "Wear your uniform. Take flowers. And for Pete's sake, get a haircut. Don't let the barber scalp you, just a nice trim."

"Yes, ma'am."

He scanned Hamilton Street's house numbers finding the Kichline's Craftsman-style residence on the hilly road's right side. Although this was a temperate June day, he began perspiring under his dress uniform when he pulled his Chrysler in front of the house. A border of multi-hued pansies flanked the cement walk, and four rocking chairs awaited guests on the front porch. Everything about the home communicated "Welcome," and he dared to believe he would find just such a greeting. The sound of children at play drifted across the yards. So far, he liked Easton. He could imagine Shelby growing up here, walking to school with her books and a lunch box tucked under her arm, laughing with friends.

He turned off the motor and pocketed the key, then reached across the front seat for the gifts he'd brought. *Please, Lord, help me overcome my nervousness. If they are also nervous about meeting me, please help them too.* Clutching the presents, he got out of the car and closed the door with his right foot, sniffing the scent of honeysuckle. At the front door, he rang the bell and waited for someone to answer. A dog began barking, and a glossy cocker spaniel appeared, lifting its face like a town crier.

A teenaged boy swung open the door, and looking back over his shoulder yelled, "Mom! He's here! Get back, Chester."

Two middle-aged people came to the door.

"You must be Dr., uh Captain Tate. I'm John Kichline. Please come in." He shook Parker's hand and waved him inside.

Just off the small entryway lay a living room with stuffed furniture centered around a fireplace and a Persian rug. White curtains fluttered above chintz-covered window seats. The dog sniffed Parker's ankles while four young people gathered around him. Everyone was grinning, except for Shelby's sister who couldn't seem to meet his eyes.

"Chester, get down!" The smallest of the mostly-blonde children pulled the dog away after the spaniel jumped up on Parker.

"Dr. Tate—or is it Captain?—welcome to our home. I'm Margaret Kichline."

With burnished brown hair and eyes to match, Shelby's mom didn't resemble her daughter, except for her winsome smile and the shape of her eyes. Her father's abundant hair and blue eyes mirrored his daughter to a "t." Of the children, only the middle son lacked their father's cloud of dark blonde hair. His heart tugged.

"I am very happy to meet you, Mrs. Kichline." He handed her a bouquet of yellow roses.

She received them with a gracious smile. "How kind of you. They're beautiful."

"And these are for everyone else." He presented a box of good chocolates Mrs. Albano had procured for him.

"Neat!" the youngest exclaimed.

"Is there anything else you can say?" Margaret Kichline nudged him.

"Oh, thank you, sir."

He bowed out of habit. "You are very welcome."

"You may open the box after dinner," his father said. "Come inside and have a seat. I'll introduce you to everyone."

Parker followed him to the living room and sat on the left side of the couch, the youngest boy crowding next to him. The others perched on wing chairs and a loveseat, openly staring.

John rubbed his hands together. "Well, then, this is Margaret. Oh, she already said she was Margaret." He gave a nervous sort of laugh.

"Hello again," Parker said, relieving some of the initial awkwardness.

She laughed like a schoolgirl. "Hello."

"Yes, well, I'll start with the oldest and work my way down the line. This is Diane."

"Hello, Diane."

Her face flushed, and she seemed almost unable to respond.

"Diane, would you please put these roses in my crystal vase? It's in the china cabinet."

"Uh, sure, Mom." She grabbed the flowers and followed her mother's instructions.

"I'd also like to present Keith, Neil, and Paul."

Chester wandered over and laid his head on Parker's lap.

"I think he likes you," Paul said.

"I do apologize, Dr. Tate. Chester does seem to have taken a shining to you," Margaret said.

"Please do not worry. I like him." Parker didn't know much about dogs as house pets, but he ran his hand along the top of the glistening head. The gesture calmed his sudden and rather embarrassing eye twitch.

"I play baseball. I'm a first-baseman. Do you like baseball?" Paul asked.

"I know little about the game, but I am learning. Shelby has introduced me to your Philadelphia Phillies."

The little boy's blue eyes widened. "How can you not know about baseball?"

"We did not play this game when I was growing up in Korea."

"You talk funny." He leaned his head to the right.

"Paul!" Keith looked up at the ceiling and blew out a sigh. "You shouldn't say stuff like that."

"I like the way you talk." The little boy inched even closer to Parker.

"Thank you."

"What sports did you play when you were growing up?"

"I was fairly good at Taekkyeon."

Paul's nose wrinkled. "What's teck-yoon?"

"It is a traditional Korean martial art." Upon seeing the blank expression, he gave a brief explanation. "This is a sport focusing on self-discipline and self-defense."

"Cool," Neil said. "Can you show us how it works?"

Margaret interrupted. "Boys, let our guest catch his breath."

"I would be happy to later." He grinned at the boy's enthusiasm.

"How was your trip here?" John Kichline asked.

"I enjoyed it very much, especially seeing the mountains before I came across the river."

"How long did it take you?"

"Just one hour."

Diane returned with the roses and set them in the middle of the coffee table between copies of Life magazine and the local newspaper.

"I made fresh lemonade," Margaret said. "Would like some?"

"Yes, please." His shoulders began to ease, along with the fluttering in his stomach.

Diane seemed to like being useful. "I'll get you a glass." She hurried toward the kitchen.

"Boy, you have a lot of medals." Wide-eyed Neil pointed at Parker's uniform. "Is that a Purple Heart?"

"Yes."

"Wow!" The boys all bent forward for a closer look, especially Paul.

Neil scolded his little brother. "Will you let the man breathe? So, how did you get hurt?"

His father shot him a stern look. "Paul, that is a very personal question to ask Dr. Tate."

"Please call me Parker." John Kichline was right—Parker didn't want to talk about how he got wounded because there was too much in the story that struck others as heroic. He could, however, speak about Shelby. "I can tell you that I was shot twice and sustained a shrapnel wound to my throat. I was taken to the MASH where Shelby is a nurse. She was terribly kind to me, and she helped me get better."

"Where did you get shot?" Paul's eyes roamed over Parker.

"That's enough, Paul," his father said. "So, uh, Parker, we understand you're from Korea but studied in the States."

Relieved at the change of subject he responded, "Yes, sir. I went to a Christian school in Korea, then to Princeton, and afterward, Penn for medical school."

"And you live in Hopewell?" Margaret asked.

"Yes, ma'am."

He accepted a glass of lemonade from Diane and took a refreshing sip. If he hadn't been in their company, he would have guzzled the entire contents in one swig. "This is delicious."

Margaret beamed. "Thank you. Diane, do you mind bringing glasses for all of us? One of the boys can help."

"I can manage." Once again she left the room.

"Do you have brothers and sisters?" Neil asked.

"I am the oldest, then my brother John and my sister Anna. Anna lives in Seoul where she goes to university. John and I practice medicine together in Hopewell."

"So, you'll be staying in America?"

He understood the meaning behind Margaret Kichline's unasked question. "Oh, yes. I am about to become naturalized."

She smiled at him. "I imagine you must miss your parents."

"Very much. We are a close family and hope to see each other at least every year, once the war is over, that is."

"How old are you?" Paul asked.

He laughed at the closed eyes and shaking heads of the boys' parents. This fellow was as direct as a Korean. "I am twenty-nine."

"You're a lot older than you look. Do you have television?"

"Not in Korea."

"What about here, do you have one here?"

"My brother recently bought a set."

"That's cool. We don't have one, but my friend Kenny does. Sometimes I go there to watch *Hopalong Cassidy*."

"How have your parents managed in the war?" John Kichline asked, leaning forward.

"The early going was difficult, as it was for all Koreans. My grandparents fled from Pyongyang to the south when the communists took charge, and my grandfather got caught by the Korean army and was imprisoned. Then, my mother became ill. I volunteered as a doctor and served in Seoul at first, where I could keep an eye on my mother, then at a MASH."

"Shelby's MASH?"

"No, Neil, it was a different one called the 8063rd."

"How is your mother now?" Margaret asked.

"She is well again, thank you."

"What about your grandfather?"

"He is well now, too, Mrs. Kichline."

Diane brought a large tray of glasses and began distributing them.

"We're having steak tonight," Paul said. "Do you like steak?"

"Steak is my favorite American food."

"Do you like hot dogs?" Neil asked.

"Yes, with plenty of ketchup and mustard."

Paul sipped his lemonade and put the sweating glass on the coffee table. His mother admonished him to use one of the coasters.

"What kind of food do Koreans eat?" Keith asked.

"We eat many vegetables and rice, beef, and pork. Most Americans find our food spicy."

"Someone told me Koreans eat dogs," Neil said.

"Oh, brother." Diane's eyes flared.

Parker put his hand over his mouth to keep from laughing.

"Is that true?" The boy was not to be put off.

"We do not keep pets like Americans. I am afraid some Koreans do use this kind of meat."

Neil hugged his dog more closely. "Do you?"

Parker leaned closer. "Never. Chester is quite safe with me."

"Is your family poor?" Paul asked.

His mother intervened. "I do apologize for these questions, uh, Parker. We don't mean to be quite so personal."

He chuckled, feeling at ease with these delightful people. "I am not bothered. You see, Koreans are a very forthright people. Paul, you remind me of a Korean."

"Really?" He puffed out his chest.

"My family is what you call middle class. My father is a minister, like my grandfather."

"And mine," Paul said. "My grandfather said he knows your grandfather."

"That is correct. They met many years ago in Pyongyang."

Margaret's eyes glistened. "I'm still amazed. How truly remarkable."

"It's like God brought our families together," Neil said.

Parker smiled at the earnest young man.

Margaret handed Parker a bulging brown bag. "Here's your potato salad, cake, and bread."

"You are very kind. Thank you. My brother will enjoy these as much as I did."

"Thanks for showing us your martial art," Keith said.

"And thank you for teaching me baseball."

"You're a natural," Neil said. "You'll be as good as Richie Ashburn before long."

John Kichline shook his hand. "Thank you for coming. We all enjoyed meeting you."

"I am grateful for your invitation and your hospitality."

The two men looked into each other's eyes, an unspoken understanding between them. Whatever test this might have been, Parker knew he had passed.

"Do Koreans hug?" Margaret asked.

"Oh, yes." He smiled when she put her arms around him.

Everyone called out "Goodbye" and waved as he got into the car and pulled away. His face was smudged and his hair, rumpled. He'd discarded his jacket and wadded up his tie in a pocket, rolled his sleeves to the elbows and opened his shirt at the collar to play with the boys. His socks drooped, and his left pant leg bore a palm-sized grass stain. He hadn't felt this alive since he'd been wounded. He'd never been happier in his life.

CHAPTER THIRTY-SEVEN

August 2, 1952

Dear Parker,

Warmest greetings from aboard the USS General William Mitchell where we're roughly a day out from the Port of San Francisco. I can't wait to hear about your visit with my family and hope they didn't scare you to death. My littlest brother never met a question he didn't like or didn't feel compelled to ask. How has it been to resume your medical practice? No doubt your patients are thrilled to have you back.

I've been lolling about reading, praying, playing the occasional card game with other nurses, eating, and sleeping. There's something tranquilizing about the sea, which I think is a good thing as I transition from being in a war zone. I'm happy to know you've been doing mostly well in this regard and that we can go through this reentry phase together. How are you feeling physically?

I'll mail this as soon as we reach California, so you have ample time to prepare for my arrival. I'm told the train ride will take three-to-four days and am counting on the US Postal Service to get this letter to you at least a day ahead of my arrival. Even if this doesn't get there before I do, I'll call you at my first opportunity once I'm off the train in New Jersey. No one seems to know how long the discharge process will take at Fort Dix, but there's a rumor it's hurry-up and wait. How I look forward to hearing your dear voice again and seeing your face, which is ever before the eyes of my heart. I regret every minute currently separating us while anticipating the hours, days, and months ahead.

Love,
Shelby

"Whoa, there! Watch your step, Nurse."

Shelby teetered on the gangplank, a man's grip preventing her from pitching headlong down the walkway. The joy of seeing the US again and the tugboats tooting their welcomes had distracted her from the far more mundane business of walking.

"Are you all right, Lieutenant?" Her rescuer was still grasping her arm.

She looked up at the face of a John Wayne look-alike minus the ten-gallon hat and leather vest. "Yes, quite. Thank you."

"You don't have your land legs yet, although yours are very nice indeed."

Since he'd prevented her from an inglorious arrival, she suppressed a sharp comeback. "You can let go now, I'm fine." Even if she did fall, the wall of soldiers would serve as a buffer.

He smiled. "I don't mind."

"I'm beginning to."

He removed his hand but stayed close enough she could smell cigarette smoke on his uniform. When she finally boarded the train, her champion followed close behind, although she'd tried to lose him in the crowd.

"Are you saving this seat for anyone?" His face gleamed.

She looked about to see if there were any nurses she'd bunked with on the ship and waved to a gal from Delaware. She caught Shelby's eye and pushed through the teaming aisle.

"Nurse Ennis will be riding with me to Fort Dix."

"Shucks." He snapped his fingers.

The vivacious brunette took the seat across from Shelby and seemed to size up the soldier. She jerked her thumb toward Shelby. "She's taken, but I'm not."

He twisted his mouth, then brightened. "In that case, I'll stay."

To bear the three-day journey, Shelby stopped looking at her watch every ten minutes and instead dwelled on how few hours now separated her from her loved ones. She watched the passing scenery, which she planned to describe in detail to her geography-minded brother Neil. She also had a front-row seat to a budding romance between Kim Ennis and the beefy soldier, whose name just happened to be Wayne Johnson. Mostly Shelby daydreamed about seeing Parker, who'd be picking her up at Fort Dix. Was he a fast driver or strictly law-abiding? Did he like having the radio on or off, the windows opened or closed? They'd been through the worst life can offer, now came the time to discover each other in the realm of the everyday.

Kim tapped her knee. "What are you grinning about? It's your doctor-captain, right?"

Shelby closed her eyes. "Yes."

"He must be something special."

"Oh, that he is. Would you like to see his picture?"

"You've already showed me five times, but what the heck—let's make it six."

"Hello, this is the office of Doctors Parker and John Tate. How may I help you?"

"Hello, this is Shelby Kichline calling for Dr. Parker. Is he avail—"

"Miss Kichline! Hold on just a moment." She seemed to turn away. "Dr. Tate, you're wanted on the phone." Then she whispered, "I think it's her."

"Shelby?"

She shivered at the sound of his voice speaking her name. "Yes, I've just arrived at Fort Dix."

"Welcome home."

"There's a line waiting to use the phone, so I just have a minute. I can't wait to see you."

"I cannot wait either. When should I be at the base?"

She was melting, and not just from East Coast humidity. "I wish I could say, but I have no idea. I don't want you to be kept waiting."

"I would wait all day and happily. The base is only twenty-five miles from Hopewell, so I can get there quickly. I will plan to leave in three hours, but if you get through sooner, call again, and I will come straightaway."

"Great. Oh, Parker, I have to go. The natives are getting restless. I'll see you soon."

If only I could take a shower and change into fresh clothes before seeing Parker again. I'm a mess and getting riper by the minute. She held her hand under her nose to block her fellow soldiers and nurses' pungency.

In the Army-drab quarters, a clerk handled stacks of paperwork while she stood in line sweating through her dress uniform. Her nylons were forming a second skin on her legs, and her feet swelled like her grandmother's. A revolving fan circulated across the room, blowing her hair upon each revolution. *Hurry up. I'm turning into a puddle.* She didn't want Parker waiting in this heat.

Six hours after her arrival at Fort Dix, the clerk pushed the last form across the table. She shifted from one foot to the next while he meticulously counted out her pay. Only then did he look up at her. "Do you need further transportation?"

She smiled at him. "Someone is picking me up."

"Well, there you go. Here's your discharge papers. Good luck to you. You can leave through that door over there."

Shelby followed his pointing finger and strode past the line of waiting soldiers. Outside the sun was setting, and she scanned a group of civilians, her pulse hammering in her ears. Maybe he'd gone home. If so, she would go back inside to call ... her lips parted. There he was, smiling in her direction. His eyes were crinkling, those alluring dimples deepening. Her knees went slack at the sight of him in a suit and tie straight from Brooks Brothers. She began walking toward him, everything else disappearing, unable to control her nonstop beaming but quelling an impulse to jump up and down. Then she stood before him, dropped her bag and gazed into his eyes, the connection they'd made many miles and months ago in the MASH unit rekindling.

"Shelby." He reached for her hand.

That voice.

"Parker."

He enfolded her in his arms, seeming oblivious to her bedraggled condition. She wondered if this might be the first time they would kiss and hoped he'd save the magical moment for a time when she wasn't sweaty and exhausted.

When at last they pulled away, he held her at arms' length. "You are as beautiful as ever." He placed a bouquet of red roses in her hands.

"Thank you. They're lovely." Before she could consider what she was saying, the words tumbled out of her mouth. "I almost didn't recognize you with clothes on."

His jaw dropped, and she popped her hand against her mouth, appalled. A moment later they burst into a fit of mutual laughter.

She slid next to him on the front seat of his Chrysler while he drove away from Fort Dix, squeezing her hand. "I am happier to see you than I have words to express."

"I feel the same." She wanted to nuzzle against him, to delight in his physical nearness, but hesitated in her scruffy condition.

"Do you care to hear the radio?"

"That would be nice. Just being in a car again with a radio is such a blessing."

"I felt similarly when I returned. So much I had taken for granted has become of special importance. Please put the windows any way that makes you comfortable. I prefer them wide open, but you may not."

"Wide open is good."

"Are you hungry? We could stop somewhere. Of course, you must be eager to see your family."

"They fed us at the base, steak if you can believe it."

Parker grinned. "Your family fed me steak."

She drew her head back. "No doubt made on the grill by my dad."

"Yes."

"How did the visit go, your meeting my family?" She eased into the way they were seeming to take up where they'd left off. Shelby didn't know about him, but she detected no awkwardness.

"I liked them very much. Your parents welcomed me with great kindness, your brothers taught me how to play baseball, and your sister showed me photographs of you when you were very small. They made me feel at home."

"Oh, I'm so glad, but then, I couldn't imagine they wouldn't."

"I understand even more about you by being with them."

The opening piano notes of "Unforgettable" began to play, and when Parker flashed a smile at her, Shelby's mood shifted. A tsunami of joy, relief, exhaustion, embarrassment over her Pigpen appearance, and that initial dumb comment broke. She started sobbing.

"Shelby, what is wrong?" Parker's eyes widened.

"I, I'm a mess!"

He pulled off the road and held her while she wept. She thought she heard him mutter, "Hysterics." Even in her addled state, she knew a shift was occurring. In Korea, she'd been the strong one, and now, he was taking care of her. She eased into his strength.

Several minutes passed before she could speak. "I'm so sorry. I don't know what just came over me."

"My dear Shelby, you have had many emotions on your long journey home. Now that you are here, and we are together again, you are feeling them all. The song was the catalyst."

"You mean I'm not falling apart?" Like a small child, she needed reassurance.

He cupped her face with his hand. "You are falling into place. Those are cleansing tears."

"I wish they would cleanse me in other ways. Oh, Parker, this isn't how I wanted to look when I saw you again. I wanted to be my prettiest for you, but I'm a mucky mess, and now my parents are going to see me like this too." Quiet tears started flowing.

"You could never be anything but beautiful to me." He paused. "I have an idea. My home is just fifteen minutes from here. Would you like to stop there to freshen up?"

She looked into his expectant eyes, the way he seemed pleased with himself for coming up with such a solution. She trembled at the thought of seeing where Parker lived, of being in his space. She lowered her voice. "Will your brother be there?"

He reached for her hand. "Yes, otherwise I would not have suggested this. Once you are feeling yourself again, we can go on to Easton. Is this agreeable to you?"

She touched his face. "You're a genius. A kind, sweet, genius."

He raised her right hand to his lips, then restarted the car.

Just before ten o'clock, when Parker crossed the toll bridge into Easton, Shelby began gesturing and laughing. "Oh, look, there's my church's steeple! I've dreamed of that steeple in Korea. And there's the dam at the forks of the rivers. The water's running low. And there's Lafayette's South College spire." She hugged herself. "Oh, dear, sweet home."

He grinned in her direction. "I am very happy for you."

A few minutes later, he pulled up next to the Kichline home where a hand-painted "Welcome Home Shelby" banner stretched across the front porch. Showered and wearing fresh clothes under her uniform, she broke into another huge smile. Just as Parker opened her door, her family stampeded out of the house and down the sidewalk. Chester announced her arrival to all the neighborhood dogs who began barking their own greetings. All along Hamilton Street, front porch lights snapped on.

Margaret Kichline reached Shelby first. "Oh, just look at you, my beautiful daughter."

She nestled into her mother's embrace, trembling with joy, the others crowding around her. Parker shook her dad's hand and stood off to the side, sporting a dimple-inducing smile.

CHAPTER THIRTY-EIGHT

The Kichline residence reverberated with joy, and Shelby flitted from one family member to the next, distributing hugs and gifts she'd brought from Korea. Parker contented himself with sitting on the periphery with the dog's head on his lap. Every few minutes, she looked in his direction and grinned. While he couldn't wait to be alone with her again, he thanked God she was home safe and had included him in this important moment. He remembered waking up in agony at the MASH, and when he saw her, he felt not only consoled, but inexplicably bound to her. If tonight was any indication, they were ready to commence a new journey, on this side of the world.

He watched as Shelby suddenly stood stock still and wondered what had stopped her in her tracks.

"What is it, dear?" her mother asked.

"Today's August third." She gazed at Parker. "This is your birthday!"

Her family echoed, "What?" "Really?" "No kidding."

"I can't believe I nearly forgot."

Parker grinned. "But you did not."

When John Kichline lifted his right hand, everyone began singing the American birthday song. Parker stood to receive their good wishes, shoving his hands into his pockets. When they finished, he thanked them with a bow.

"I would have baked a cake for you if I'd known," Margaret said.

Neil shook his hand. "Yeah, and I would have bought you a baseball glove."

He smiled at these loving people. "You are all so kind. I have opened many gifts today, but they are the kind one cannot wrap."

Shelby squeezed his arm and they gazed at each other, unaware of her family's nudges and sideways glances.

He hadn't gone to bed until two-thirty and was up at six to begin his day, but Parker rose with renewed vigor. While he percolated coffee, he thought about calling her but hoped she was sleeping in. He would phone her at lunchtime. He would also be seeing her on Saturday at a party the Kichlines were having to welcome both Shelby and him home from Korea.

"Oh, but you do not have to welcome me home," he'd said last night.

"We want to." Her mother's jaw had been set. "You deserve a welcome home."

"My church has already done so."

"That's nice. Now it's our turn."

He went to the window to watch the sun's ascent between tree branches. *They are the nicest people. We are blessed to have our families' approval.*

The door to John's room opened and tousle-haired, he padded into the kitchen, yawning. "You're up plenty early."

"Good morning."

"And you're certainly cheerful."

"How did you like her?"

"Big brother, you made out big time. She's fabulous."

He smiled ear-to-ear. "I think so too."

"Does she have any sisters?"

"One, but she is still in high school. Besides, I believe you are interested in someone else."

"You know I am." John popped his brother's arm.

John opened the refrigerator and pulled out a pitcher of orange juice, and Parker spoke of the coming weekend.

"Shelby's family will be hosting a welcome home party this Saturday afternoon, and they would like you to come."

"Me?" John pointed to himself.

"Yes, you."

"Wow, this is getting serious, Parker. How do you feel about that?"

He closed his eyes. "I feel very good indeed."

August 25, 1952

My Dear Mother and Father,

How are you faring? I am eager to know you are all well, that Mother and Grandfather continue healing, and Father's ministry is fruitful. How is Anna doing with her studies? Thank you very much for the gifts you sent with Shelby. She arrived home from Korea on my birthday, and I was able to pick her up at Fort Dix when she was discharged. I have rejoiced in having her near me again, and I am getting to know her family. You would like them. They are loving and fun Christians, always looking to the needs and feelings of others. Her grandfather is delightful, and upon seeing me for the first time, exclaimed how he felt he was looking into the face of a young Soon-hee Oh. I never realized I resembled Harabeoji quite so strongly, and I am honored this is

> the case. Mr. Kichline has told me stories of their days together in Pyongyang and sends his deepest regards and blessings to all of you. He plans to write soon.
>
> Less than a week after Shelby came home, her parents hosted a party to welcome us back from Korea, and they included John. The celebration was mostly outdoors with picnic foods and games of baseball. Shelby's brothers generously went together to buy me a leather glove and are teaching me to play. I also met other family members who live in and around Easton, finding them quite hospitable. I was not sure what to expect, being from a different culture, but they have made me feel very accepted.
>
> Shelby has decided not to work at the hospital for the time being, needing a season to rest from her war-time experiences. She is, however, volunteering at her church, and a few civic organizations have invited her to speak about being a nurse in Korea.
>
> I have had the opportunity to visit her beautiful church. Her ancestor funded its building during the Revolutionary War and since then, generations of Kichlines have worshiped there. The pastor has welcomed me most warmly, along with many in the congregation.

He gazed out the dining room window. He wouldn't tell his family there were a few who'd pointed and whispered behind their hands. He knew if he were taking Shelby to his church in Seoul, people would respond similarly.

> Shelby has also attended church with me in Hopewell, and Dr. and Mrs. Cullen had us over for lunch. We had a delightful time of Christian fellowship. You can imagine Shelby's delight upon learning that Jacob Kichline not only knew Harabeoji in Korea, but also Dr. Cullen. I continue to marvel at the ways of God in bringing people together across miles and generations. I would be remiss if I did not follow the Cullens' wish to be remembered

> to all of you, as well as the assurance of their faithful prayers for you and for Korea.
>
> I wish you blessings of health and spiritual prosperity. Please write me soon.
>
> Your loving,
> Parker (Tae-ho)

The festive tavern featured a Patti Page song playing in the background, the drone of conversations, and the smell of roasting meat.

The proprietor came over to them with outstretched arms. "Welcome home, Shelby. I wondered when you'd be coming in." After they hugged, he looked Parker up and down. "And who have we here?"

"I'm happy to see you, Mr. Seip. I've dreamed about being back here again. I would like you to meet Dr. Parker Tate."

His graying eyebrows rose. "Nice to meet you, Doctor."

Parker accepted a steely handshake. "The pleasure is mine."

"What, are you sick or something, Shelby?"

She bent toward him and whispered, "This is my boyfriend."

"Oh, I see. Did Shelby tell you this place was built by her ancestor?"

"Yes, she did." He took in the slightly musty colonial ambience. "You have a very nice inn."

"It's not what it used to be, but I try my best to keep it up." He turned to Shelby. "Be sure to show him the stream in the basement."

"Oh, I will. I know you're busy, but might you have a table for us?"

"For you, always. Follow me." He bypassed the hostess and escorted them to a table bathed in candlelight. "I'll have Stephanie bring menus."

"Thank you, Mr. Seip."

"Did he say there is a stream under the building?" he asked once they were seated.

"Yes. When my fourth great-grandfather Peter Kichline Junior built the Fountain House, he channeled the stream here into a masonry trough. For generations, the innkeepers have kept fresh trout there until ready for table use."

"And this is still used?"

"Yes, and I do recommend the trout. That's what I'm going to order."

"Then I will have this dish as well. I am honored to be in such a special place for you." He reached across the table and squeezed her hand.

Each course of the meal came served with special attention to their honored guest. Parker enjoyed their effortless conversation, the way their relationship was steadily deepening. But he detected a certain strain in her demeanor tonight and wondered what might be on her mind. After they'd finished dessert, she took him into her confidence.

"May I ask you something, Parker?"

"Anything."

"Do you ever have bad dreams about the war?"

His head tingled. "I have some, yes. Have you?"

She worked over her napkin. "This week I've dreamed twice about being at the 8055th and having to bug out. I end up getting left behind with North Koreans coming down the road."

He took her trembling hand. "This is normal, Shelby. You are processing what happened to you in a place where you were constantly dealing with casualties and often in danger."

She wiped a tear from her cheek. "I guess we must be patient with ourselves."

"Yes, and I will always listen when you need to talk about these things."

"Same here."

The waitress refilled their coffee cups, and Parker noticed Shelby's attention shift. Two young men at the bar were sniggering as they looked at her, then at him. Although she'd just disclosed something deeply vulnerable, her shoulders stiffened, and she raised her chin.

"Do you know those men?"

She grimaced. "The one on the left is Michael Hendry, the boy I dated in high school."

"The one who would not marry you because you wanted to become a nurse?"

Her eyes widened. "You remembered."

The guy with Michael said in a voice meant to be heard, "It looks as if Shelby Kichline has got herself a Jap."

Shelby abruptly stood, grabbing Parker's hand, and guiding him toward the men. His heart thudded.

"Good evening. I couldn't help but overhear you. I did not 'get me a Jap.' I got me a Korean-American who is a decorated United States Army war hero and a physician. I just thought you might like to know."

Parker suppressed an urge to burst out laughing but instead went through the motions of shaking the startled men's hands. Then he paid for his and Shelby's meal and swished behind her out the door to the chilly September night. When they got inside his car, they let loose, laughing until their sides ached.

"I guess I told them."

"I did not know what to expect when you approached them. I wondered if I might need to use some of my martial arts."

"I can't believe I used to date that guy." She became sullen. "His friend makes me sick, and mad. Why are people like that?"

He took her hand. "I am sorry this has hurt you."

"I don't care about myself. The thing that bothers me is how insulted you must feel."

"I am not insulted."

"You're not?" She fixed her eyes on him.

"People are intrigued by what is different from themselves. Sometimes those whose hearts are not pure feel superior."

"I just wish there wasn't such prejudice in America."

He touched her chin. "America did not invent prejudice, Shelby. Korea is an intensely homogenous society in which everyone from the outside is suspect. Only in the last few decades has this begun to change."

"Oh."

His heart galloped in anticipation of crossing a line. "Is the unkindness of others something you can live with?" He paused. "For the long-term?"

She squeezed his hand. "Nothing can separate us from the beautiful relationship God has given us."

Parker drew her to himself and tasted her lips for the first time.

He sat in the living room drinking coffee with John and Jacob Kichline. Shelby, her mother, and grandmother were at the kitchen table making favors for her cousin's upcoming wedding. Parker eased into the deep cushioned sofa and the men's amiable conversation, breaking into a smile when he caught Shelby gazing at him, her face glowing. He wasn't expecting what came next.

"So, Parker," the elder Kichline said, "you and our Shelby seem quite serious."

He nearly spluttered the sip of coffee he'd just swallowed.

"I didn't mean to startle you, son. Are you okay?"

"Yes, I am fine."

Jacob nudged his son, who spoke next. "I didn't realize my father was about to push us into this conversation."

Parker set the coffee cup onto a coaster. Could Shelby hear them? No, she appeared locked in a discussion with the women. "I will be happy to discuss my feelings about Shelby."

"Good." John cleared his throat and squared his shoulders. "So, Doctor Tate, just what are your intentions toward my daughter?"

The man's grin told Parker he had nothing to fear. Candor seemed like the best course of action. "Well, sir, I would very much like to marry her."

John tented his fingers. His father broke into a huge smile. "Have you spoken to her?"

"I would not until we have had this conversation."

"I like that." He leaned his elbows on his knees. "My wife and I are prepared to give our blessing, but how do your parents feel about this, especially since Shelby isn't Korean?"

Again, he chose honesty. "My mother had intended a Korean friend of the family for me, but when she saw how God had brought us together, she supported us."

"I see. And what about your father?"

"He is quite fond of Shelby, as are my mother and the rest of my family."

John rubbed his fingertips together. "You've told us you intend to stay here and not return to Korea, except to visit."

"Both my brother and I will continue to practice in Hopewell."

"Since John lives with you now, where would you live with Shelby?"

Goosebumps covered his arms at the thought of spending every day—and every night—with her. "We have a third-floor apartment which has recently become vacant. My brother could move up there if he wishes, and Shelby and I could remain above the practice until we can get a house."

"Are you in such a position to buy a house?"

Parker guessed John Kichline was asking indirectly about his financial situation. "I have enough put aside for a small down payment, but I prefer to, uh, begin marriage without indebtedness. I think after a year, I would feel more comfortable purchasing a house." He turned the tables. "Do you think Shelby, if she agreed to be my wife, would be all right with this?"

"You'd have to ask her. She likes nice things, but she's not materialistic. I don't foresee a problem." He rubbed the side of his nose. "There's something else, Parker. She once dated a fellow who was a lunkhead about her becoming a nurse. What if Shelby wants to continue?"

Parker had given this some thought. "Women should have opportunities to share their God-given gifts. I greatly benefited from Shelby's nursing skills and will encourage her to use them however God may direct."

Her father and grandfather smiled at each other, then at him.

He dove head-first into the deep end. "So, may I ask her?"

John Kichline reached across the sofa and shook his hand. “Any time you feel ready.”

CHAPTER THIRTY-NINE

"You're sure to turn heads driving this chariot, little lady." The used car salesman tapped the side of a 1950, bullet-nosed, two-toned Studebaker Champion Regal.

She'd just given the vehicle a test-drive through Palmer Township, thrilling at its speed and styling. She'd also noticed the way her father's right foot kept pressing an imaginary brake.

"What do you think, Dad?"

He pulled his chin. "A bit impractical, but very sharp."

The salesman butted in. "That straight-six engine isn't just powerful but gets good fuel mileage. This beauty also has an automatic transmission and self-adjusting brakes. There's a lot of space too—more than meets the eye. I'll open the trunk for you." He flew into action, and John Kichline took a closer look.

Shelby pictured herself cruising across Route Twenty-Two, then south onto Thirty-One in this red-and-white doozy. She and Parker had been discussing having her own vehicle since he couldn't easily get away from his practice to see her as much as they both wanted.

"How much are you asking for it?" Her father closed the trunk and slid his hands back and forth.

"Let's see, now." The salesman scratched his balding head. "This little number only has eight thousand miles on it. The owner kept it in a garage and traded it in for a convertible because he's moving to California. I think twelve hundred's a fair price."

Shelby's pulse quickened. She knew her dad was a cracker-jack wheeler and dealer and decided not to add her two cents.

"Those tires will have to be replaced before long, and the engine needs a tune-up. How about eleven hundred?"

The man kicked the driver's side tire. "I don't know what you mean. These have plenty of tread left. Tell you what, I'll throw in a tune-up and come down by fifty."

John moved closer to the fellow and said in a confidential tone, "My daughter is a United States Army veteran. She just got back from serving in Korea."

He did a double-take at Shelby. "In that case, I think eleven hundred is a fair price."

"With the tune-up?"

The salesman stared at him. "All right, with the tune-up. Do we have a deal?"

Shelby met her father's private wink. The number was well within her reach because except for some new clothes and books, she'd saved nearly all her Army pay.

She and her dad shook the salesman's hand before going inside to sign the papers. Every few minutes, her gaze returned to the gem she'd just bought with her own money.

She parked her new car in the lot connected to Parker's practice the next day. There were five other vehicles, including his Chrysler and John's Chevy. Shelby retrieved her purse and a bag of groceries, then walked to the glass door etched with "Parker Tate, M.D." and "John Tate, M.D." At four-forty-five, just an old man and a mother with a little girl were in the waiting room. The receptionist looked up.

"May I help ... Oh, you must be Shelby."

"Yes, and you're Mrs. Albano."

The bespectacled woman's grin took up half of her face. "I'm so pleased to meet you at last. My, but you're pretty."

Shelby's cheeks flushed. "Thank you."

"Dr. Tate told me to expect you. He and his brother are just seeing their last patients, and he asked me to take you upstairs. It's awfully nice of you to cook for them."

Shirley Albano opened a side door, and Shelby followed her through a well-lit hallway to the second-floor apartment. She'd been there a few times on weekends since her discharge, always when John was in residence. Now she got to putter around in the kitchen as if she belonged there. She set the bag on the kitchen table while the receptionist turned on some lights, then excused herself.

"Thank you, Mrs. Albano."

"Any time. I'm so happy to have met you at last. Dr. Parker talks about you all the time. Make yourself right at home."

She did feel at home. *What if things continue to go well? Might John move to the apartment on the third floor? I heard them mention it's now vacant.* Caution prevented her imagination from running away with her, but she did allow herself a little room to roam. Soaking in the tranquil atmosphere, she smiled at the photos of their Korean family members before pausing next to Parker's favorite chair. She touched the headrest, picturing him sitting there with a newspaper or book, the two of them enjoying each other's companionship after a long day. She turned on the radio, noticing there wasn't a speck of dust on it or the television set. Likewise, the windows gleamed in the mid-October twilight. Their house help was doing a good job.

She wandered to the edge of his room, soaking in details of what surrounded him when he slept and what he saw first-thing each morning. Her heart swelled at the sight of his leather Bible on the nightstand, the one she'd found among his possessions at the 8055th. His brown chenille bedspread seemed like an afterthought. *I would change that for a newer one, or maybe a down comforter with winter coming.* On the brink of intimate thoughts, she hastened to the kitchen's more neutral ground and began setting out ingredients for Steak Diane. Her mind drifted along with the voice of Rosemary Clooney to the conversation she'd had that morning with Easton Hospital's Director of Nursing.

"Well, Miss Kichline, are you going to join us now?"

"Not just yet. I'm still on sabbatical."

"Whenever you're ready, there will be a job for you here."

She knew in her heart what God was calling her to do. The only question was whether Parker was getting the same message.

October 20, 1952

Dear Evelyn and Vickie,

How happy I was to receive your recent letters, to know you're both in good health and spirits as your important work continues at the 8055th. I could just picture the two of you in surgery, post-op, the O Club, and mess tent, feeling as if I were right there with you. I'm so pleased to hear Father Stephens got the promotion he so richly deserves. Please congratulate him for me. And Evelyn,

> thank you for keeping up my work at the orphanage. Be sure to give Woo Sung a big hug for me, and ask Dr. Fish what supplies I can send. My church's Rebecca Circle really enjoyed making bed pillows for the children.
>
> Sometimes, I need to pinch myself that I'm really home. My sister and brothers are back at school, as well as Dad, who has my oldest brother in his history class. May God help them both. Mother is out of the house several days a week volunteering. I've assisted her on occasion and given some talks to civic groups about being a MASH nurse. The hospital has extended their earlier offer to me, but I'm not ready yet. I've needed this time to readjust to civilian life.

She tapped the top of the Bic pen against her teeth. She didn't want to tell them about the occasional nightmares or detachment she felt from old friends who couldn't begin to know what she'd experienced in Korea. Evelyn and Vickie would find out soon enough, and she would be there to help them. Fortunately, Parker understood, and they ministered to each other's unseen scars.

> Here's some especially happy news—a week ago I bought a new (well used) car. Parker was thrilled because now I don't have to wait for him to come see me on weekends. (You knew I'd get to talking about him sooner or later, didn't you?) I got a 1950 Studebaker Champion Regal, and I'm having so much fun with it. I feel so independent, not having to wait to borrow my parents' car, which is frightfully stodgy.
>
> As you can guess, my life is centered on God, my family, and Parker, and I've never been more content. With each passing week, Parker and I grow closer, and I count myself blessed. My family all love him, and he returns their affections. I didn't know if Parker and I would have the same attachment we had in Korea once we were back home, when he was no longer the patient

and I, the nurse, but I need not have worried. We're just discovering different aspects of each other's lives and personalities in this new context.

Vickie, you asked about his health. Except for a slight hoarseness, he's completely well. The gunshot wounds have left a couple of scars, but he feels no discomfort except when the weather gets damp and cold at the same time. He's even playing baseball with my brothers. Last week, we attended my oldest brother's football game, and although he enjoyed himself, Parker isn't interested in the rough and tumble of the sport. He's not averse to tossing a football back and forth in the yard, though, and has a good throwing arm.

This weekend, my family will gather for my cousin Louise's wedding at our church. I'm one of her bridesmaids. Although Parker won't be in the bridal party, he'll be my date at the ceremony and reception. Fortunately, the brother who will escort me has a girlfriend, so there won't be any awkwardness there. Parker has met some of my extended family, but there will be far more of them coming from outside the Lehigh Valley, and I'm excited to show him off.

In more good news, two weeks from now, he'll formally become a naturalized US citizen. I'm so looking forward to that happy day for which he has longed. My mom and grandfather will come with me to the courthouse in Trenton and after the ceremony, Parker's dear friends the Cullens will host a reception at their home.

Please give my very best wishes to Colonel Shepperd, Father Stephens, Major McKaig, the doctors, and nurses. Soon, you'll be home, too, Evelyn, then in no time, you will follow, Vickie. In the meantime, stay in touch and know I pray for you daily.

Love,
Shelby

She was the second bridesmaid to walk down the aisle of the German Reformed Church, on the groom's middle brother's arm. When Shelby stepped past the aisle where Parker sat with her family, she glanced at him, glowing at his obvious admiration. He was so dazzling in his dress Army uniform she barely heard the organ music. She smiled when she saw feminine heads turning in Parker's direction, knowing she had nothing to fear.

After the bride and groom shared the first dance, Shelby's cousin and her father took the floor, followed by the rest of the bridal party. Then Shelby beckoned to Parker with her eyes, her breath escaping as he took her in his arms for the next song.

"You are incredible, Shelby," he whispered into her ear.

She nuzzled his chin at the spot where her head reached, expecting to dissolve into a puddle when the combo began playing "Unforgettable."

Following the festive meal, toasts, and speeches, Shelby danced again with Parker, delighted at his skill. They sat down after swinging to Frank Sinatra's "East of the Sun."

"Who taught you to dance like that?"

He grinned. "Your sister, while you were having the wedding rehearsal."

"Remind me to thank her."

He reached for her hand. "Can we go someplace quieter?"

"There's a terrace, but it's cold outside."

"I will keep you warm." She followed him, grabbing the fur cape she'd borrowed from her mother.

Outside, stars glittered beside a waxing half-moon, and bare branches dipped as if to eavesdrop. Parker hugged her close, then lowered his head to meet her waiting lips. She knew she'd never be truly cold again.

Shelby, her mother, and grandfather arrived in Hopewell two hours before the naturalization ceremony in Trenton. While Parker and his brother completed their shortened work day, she introduced her family to Mrs. Albano, who never met a stranger. An examining room door opened, and Parker emerged with a middle-aged male patient. She caught his wink as he took leave of the man, then he hugged Margaret Kichline and shook Jacob's hand. He kissed Shelby's cheek before removing his lab coat revealing a dark suit underneath.

Mrs. Albano frowned. "I thought you were going to wear your uniform."

"I am going to change my clothes now." He turned to Shelby. "Would you come with me?"

She'd never been alone with him in his apartment, but when the others didn't bat an eye, she followed him upstairs. In the gray light of the mid-November day, Shelby looked toward him.

"Please have a seat." He gestured toward the couch with a sober face. "I will only be a moment."

I wonder why he's so serious? Maybe he has jitters about the ceremony. She started to make a playful comment, but something in his manner kept her mouth shut.

He went into his room and closed the door. Shelby crossed her legs, swinging the top one back and forth, examining her nails, her senses heightened. Not ten minutes later he reappeared, his handsomeness making her breath catch as he sat next to her and caressed her hands. He gazed at her with the tenderest expression she'd ever seen on the face she adored.

"What is it?" she whispered.

"I will never forget the first time I saw you, Shelby, on the troopship, and then there you were at the MASH when I was wounded. I did not know if I was going to die, but I did seem to know you from a deep place inside me and that the Lord had sent you." His smiled deepened the dimples she treasured. "I believe the three of us make a wonderful team."

Every sight and sound in the room intensified. "I agree."

"I have come to love you more than words can express, and I am hoping you feel as I do, that we should spend the rest of our lives together." He reached into a pocket.

She may have been sitting still, but inside she was doing somersaults.

"Shelby, will you marry me?"

She was so intent on his face, on his proposal, on the culmination of her future hopes she didn't notice the exquisite ring he produced. Instead, she wrapped her arms around his neck and answered his question with a lingering kiss. Only after she broke away did she look at the ring he'd slipped onto her left hand. Its radiant sparkle broke through her tear-filled eyes, a hexagonal center diamond framed by sapphires with two side diamonds in a platinum setting.

"Oh, Parker, this is stunning. How did you know my size?"

He grinned. "I am happy you like it. Your mother told me your size."

"She knew about this?"

"We spoke after she and your father gave their blessing. Do you like the sapphires?"

"Oh, yes. I couldn't have imagined a nicer ring."

"I knew this was meant for you, reminding me of your sparkling eyes, although no gemstone could ever match them."

"I'm so happy I could burst."

"I prefer you not to burst, but I could not be happier either." He took her hands, smiling down at the ring perched on her finger.

Before they went to tell the others, they sealed the sacred moment with a prayer.

Epilogue

THE EASTON EXPRESS—December 1, 1952

Miss Kichline Engaged to Dr. Parker Tate

Mr. and Mrs. John Kichline of College Hill, Easton announce the engagement of their daughter Shelby to Dr. Parker Tate, son of the Rev. and Mrs. Sung-Doh Park of Seoul, South Korea.

Miss Kichline, a Second Lieutenant in the US Army Nurse Corps in Korea, received her honorable discharge last August. Dr. Tate served as a Captain and physician in the US Army in Korea, where he received a Purple Heart. He practices family medicine in Hopewell, New Jersey. The wedding is planned for April 18, 1953.

Shelby sat in the coffee-scented kitchen with her mother the morning after the engagement party. Stacks of crusted pots, pans, party platters, and utensils cluttered the counters, and bits of napkin littered the floor. Chester was doing his best to sniff out every particle of dropped food and drink. The rest of the household still slept, not needing to get ready for church for another two hours.

Shelby's eyes were dreamy, but not from sleep. "Thanks for the great party, Mom."

"You are very welcome. I'm so happy Parker's brother, Dr. and Mrs. Cullen, Mr. and Mrs. Albano, and Mrs. Shaw could celebrate with us."

"They're all the family he has here." She flicked a flyaway hair and gazed at her engagement ring.

Margaret smiled. "And now he has us too."

"I love how our family and friends have embraced Parker. I was expecting more awkwardness."

Her mother's eyebrows raised. "Awkwardness? Was there any?"

"Oh, just something Donna said." She gave her right hand an uptick.

"What did Donna say?"

Shelby assumed her best high school pal's voice and mannerisms. "'Oh, Shelby, your doctor is a dreamboat. A Chinaman sure is different from the men around here.'"

Margaret laughed. "You sounded just like her."

Shelby reached down to pet Chester. "I've forgotten how many times I've told her Parker is Korean, but she doesn't hear me."

"Give her time. Be gracious as you are persistent." She sipped her coffee then said, "I love your plan, to take a few months to get established in your marriage, then start working with him and John as their nurse."

She quoted from Scripture. "'The lines have fallen in pleasant places.'"

"And when children come?"

"We'll work that out, Mom, but they'll always come before my job."

"How many would you like?"

She laughed out loud. “Don’t rush us, for Pete’s sake. Just for the record, we think two-to-four would be ideal, but we realize this is in God’s hands.”

“You are wise.”

Shelby changed the channel. “I’d like to discuss the wedding.”

“I would too.”

“We don’t want anything as elaborate as cousin Louise’s.”

Her mother leaned back and crossed her arms. “What was it about her wedding you disliked?”

Shelby caught a chill in the air but forged ahead. “There were so many fussy details—expensive printed name cards and imported chocolate favors, flowers at the end of every pew and strewn across the front of the sanctuary as if it were Easter morning. Then she had seven bridesmaids and groomsmen and a very expensive reception.” Her voice trailed. “Parker and I want something elegant but simple. We don’t want to distract from the meaning of our becoming man and wife in Christ.” She searched her mother’s face to see if she’d received the message. “Do you understand?”

Margaret sighed. “I confess, I’ve been imagining an all-out wedding, and you mustn’t concern yourself with the expense. Dad and I have money put away for this.” She gave a small laugh. “He’ll approve of your not having a bash like Louise’s. I’m just sorry Parker’s parents and sister won’t be here.”

“Me too. I appreciate their unselfishness in not asking us to wait to get married until the war ends and they could come.”

“They sound like lovely people.” She got up to refresh their cups of coffee, and they heard the ka-thump of the

Sunday paper landing on the front porch. “So, Shelby, let’s talk some more about this simple celebration you two want. Do you want a church wedding and bridesmaids?”

“Oh yes. I’ve been thinking of having three—Diane, of course, then Evelyn and Vickie, the nurses I was close to in Korea. They’ll be home by then.”

“How nice. What about Donna?” Margaret twisted her mouth.

“No, thank you, but maybe I can put her in charge of the guestbook.”

“Now there’s an idea. How about groomsmen?”

“Parker’s brother will be his best man, then Keith and Neil. Do you think Paul is too old to be the ring bearer?”

“Maybe we could make the role more age appropriate somehow. Are there any other friends from Easton, or any cousins you want in the wedding party?”

Shelby blew out a breath. “I’m just not close to those people anymore, Mom, and if I ask one cousin, then another one will be hurt.” While she was sharing harder ideas, she decided to put another one out there. “We’d love to have Poppa participate in the service to represent our two families. Do you think Pastor Creitz would mind sharing the ceremony with him?”

“I don’t see why, but you should talk to him as soon as possible—to both of them.”

A pair of cardinals dipped into one of the birdfeeders just outside the window.

“Now, what about flowers and a hall and a band?”

“As for flowers, maybe one quarter of what Louise had, and I prefer white roses. What about a simple reception at the church hall with finger foods and cake?” Shelby braced herself.

"No band? No sit-down meal?" She appeared as surprised as if Shelby had suggested wearing her chenille bathrobe to the wedding.

"Um, what do you have in mind?" She twirled her engagement ring, wondering if she was being too bare bones.

"I can't imagine not having a meal and dancing. What if we have the reception at the Fountain House or the Circlon and use a local band? We don't have to get a New York combo like Louise or serve lobster."

Shelby chewed lower lip, and her mother continued.

"And I would take care of all the details, so you can concentrate on getting the apartment ready for the two of you."

She found her mother's plaintiveness irresistible. "I think that would be all right. I'll ask Parker if he's okay with all of this. Mostly, he wants what I want for the wedding. Before I forget, I would like to serve traditional Korean noodles at the reception."

"If you can get a recipe and ingredients, somehow I'll make that happen." She clapped her hands together. "This is all good. Now, what about a wedding dress?"

She knew exactly what she wanted. "Satin, tea length, with a simple headpiece and veil."

"How beautiful you will be." Her mother's eyes were bright.

"I'd like Evelyn and Vickie to wear their uniforms."

"Oh. Okay. What about Diane?"

"She can wear a bridesmaid's dress."

"What will Parker wear?"

"Either a suit or his uniform. Do you have a preference?"

"He does cut a dashing figure in his uniform. Since you met in the Army and the bridesmaids will wear theirs,

I think that would be a nice touch." She rubbed the side of her nearly-empty coffee cup. "Have you discussed a honeymoon?"

"Dr. and Mrs. Cullen own a cottage at Lake Wallenpaupack, and they've offered its use to us as their wedding gift."

"How nice of them." She gazed at Shelby. "Are you at all nervous?"

She could almost read her mother's mind. "More excited than nervous about God bringing us to an even deeper part of our connection to him and each other."

A tear slipped down her mother's cheek. "What a beautiful thing to say."

"Wasn't that true for you and Dad?"

She gazed at her hands. "We didn't have your spiritual maturity back then. You and Parker have something truly special. I can't quite explain it." She smiled at her daughter. "I couldn't have wished for a better husband for you. He's such a strong man in every way."

Shelby winked. "Even if he is Chinese?"

Her mother chortled. Then she said, "I love Parker as if he were my fourth son."

Shelby choked up. "Thanks, Mom. Well, then, tomorrow let's make an appointment at Grollman's bridal salon."

March 20, 1953
Seoul, South Korea

Dear Shelby,
I am writing to welcome you into our family and to wish you and Tae-ho a joyous wedding. (I hope you do not mind my calling him by his Korean name.) I hope this reaches you before your happy wedding day. Although

we will not be with you in Easton, Pennsylvania, on April 18, we have resolved as a family here to spend the day in prayer to help lessen the many miles and oceans between us. The Bible speaks of the communion of the saints, and in some way, may this be true of our ties to you.

You will find enclosed a few gifts from our family to you and yours. Anna has explained to us the American tradition of the bride wearing white. In Korea, white is the color of death but in America, of purity and innocence. You will be lovely in your special dress. If you would, please, we would be honored if you and Tae-ho would carry Korean silk handkerchiefs, yours in red and his in blue as a gesture to his heritage. We are also enclosing some wooden ducks. In our country, historically the groom gifted the bride's mother a goose. This represented his commitment to always be as loyal to his wife as the geese who mate for life. More recently, this tradition has changed. Now the groom's family gives wooden ducks to the bride's family. I hope your mother and father will enjoy receiving them. When I see you again in person, I will give you a special gift I cannot entrust to the mail.

We all pray God's abundant blessings as you begin a new life together in Christ, in whom there is no east or west, north or south.

With love and affection,
Yung Sook Park

In the church's narthex, Shelby discreetly adjusted her slip, the organ playing the prelude in the background. Her grandparents had been seated, her mother had just walked down the aisle on John Tate's arm. Her brothers waited with Parker at the front of the historic sanctuary, including Paul who held the ring in a box.

"Shelby, you look more radiant than I've ever seen you." Evelyn's eyes glowed.

She squeezed her friend's hand. "I'm so happy you're here with me." Her lips parted when she noticed a tear in Vickie's right eye. "Why, Vickie."

"I know, I know." She dabbed at her eye with the red handkerchief Shelby had given to her. "Ever since I got here last night and saw you two together again, and now being in this incredible church, well, I'm an absolute mess. It's enough to ... to ..."

"Make a believer out of you?" Shelby tilted her face, grinning.

Vickie laughed, spreading her hands. "Who knows?"

Pastor Creitz's wife signaled the bridesmaids to line up, and Shelby listened for the "Wedding March."

"Are you ready?" her father asked.

"Absolutely. Are you?"

"What an unfair question." He kissed her cheek. "I love you, and I'm so happy for you."

"I love you too, Dad."

"Well, here we go."

The congregation rose when Shelby walked on his arm down the center aisle of her ancestral church. The venerable sanctuary glowed in soft candlelight, the pews filled with her family and friends. Parker's Hopewell contingent, including some church members and a few favorite patients, like Mrs. Stein, occupied three rows. He looked beyond handsome in his dress uniform and gazed at her with such love and intimacy she almost broke down. Then she stood before him as Pastor Creitz took up the words of the ages-old litany for Christian marriage.

"Dearly beloved, we are assembled here in the presence of God, to join this Man and this Woman in holy marriage, which is instituted by God, regulated by His commandments, blessed by our Lord Jesus Christ, and to be held in honor among all men."

The liturgy's lyrical poignancy went straight to her heart, especially the phrase, "to live as heirs together of the grace of life."

Then he asked, "Who gives this woman in holy matrimony?"

"I do." Her father kissed her cheek and placed her hand in Parker's outstretched one. She savored its warmth, its strength.

When Diane nudged her, Shelby passed her bouquet of red, white, and blue roses to her.

"Oh, God, whose presence is the happiness of every condition and whose favor hallows every relation," the minister prayed, "be present among us and truly join Shelby and Parker in holy marriage, sanctify them, and give them a new frame of heart fit for their new estate. May you enrich them with your grace and guide and protect them always. Amen."

The Reverend Jacob Kichline stepped forward and smiled. "Shelby and Parker, when I went to Korea nearly fifty years ago, I could never have foreseen the plans of our loving, sovereign God. I didn't know he would use your grandfather, Parker, to bring me into intimate fellowship with Jesus Christ. Nor could I have known that one day my granddaughter would also hear God's call to Korea and be instrumental in saving the life of my dear friend's grandson.

"Parker, your grandfather has wisely observed that according to Galatians 3:28, all who call upon the name of Jesus are one in him no matter their human condition. Marriage itself is a union of differences, of a man and a woman who covenant with God to be his image bearers in the world. The Reverend Jonathan Edwards once called this state a 'most excellent subject, treating of the love, union, and communion between Christ and His spouse, of which marriage and conjugal love was but a shadow.' This joining of a man and a woman was his idea at the beginning with Adam and Eve, and all history will culminate with a wedding between Christ and his bride, the Church.

"Shelby and Parker, as you look upon each other with gleams of adoration, so should all Christians desire that day when they see Jesus face-to-face. May you always know God's soul-satisfying, never-ending love."

Shelby gazed at her grandfather, detecting a mischievous look in his blue eyes.

"In my homily, I spoke from the Church's historical traditions and beliefs. However, I also want to bring to bear upon this solemn ceremony something more up-to-date." He looked first at Shelby, then at Parker. "You two are truly unforgettable."

AUTHOR'S NOTE

Korean War Honor Roll

To honor my readers' loved ones who served in the Korean War, I requested they send their family's loved ones' names, rank, and the branch of military in which they served. I was overwhelmed and grateful for the number of submissions received.*

- Joel R. Adams—PVT—US Army—POW
- Regulo Aguirre—PFC—US Army
- Bobby Akers—PFC—US Air Force
- Donald Aronhalt—SSGT—US Army
- William Bannister—CPL—US Army
- George Barnosky—CPL—US Army
- Lincoln S. Bauman—Gunner—The Queen's Own Rifles—Canadian Armed Forces
- Robert Bayless—HM2c—US Marine Corps
- Stanley Beardsworth—MSG—US Army
- Jack Bernaciak—A1C—US Air Force
- James Ulysses Bloodworth—PFC—US Army
- John Borgmann—SGT—US Army
- Seth Britt—PVT—US Marine Corps

- Robert Brown—CPL—US Army
- Joseph Capito—CPL—US Marine Corps
- Osborne Tommee Carlisle—CPT—US Air Force—MIA
- Gurdeon Emory Carpenter—SSG—US Army
- Bill Carnett—CPL—US Army—MIA
- Jack Cauley—MSG—US Army
- Donald Clark—MAJ—US Army
- Samuel Confer—CPL—US Army
- George E Cooper—SSG—US Army
- Lonnie Sherwood Cox—SFC—US Army
- Edward Eugene Cross—US Air Force
- Charles Damon—OSea—US Navy
- Joseph DePhillips—SGT—US Army
- Frankie Joe Ditmore—MSG—US Air Force
- Wayne Dotson—SGT—US Army
- Thomas J. Dunleavy—GySgt—US Navy
- Donald H. Eisenberg—CPL—US Army
- John Harrison Errington—TSGT—US Air Force—KIA
- Thomas S. Estabrook Jr.—QM3—US Navy
- Gale J. Eyer—PFC—US Marine Corps
- Thomas H. Fales—CPL—US Marine Corps
- Sam Fielder—SGT—US Marine Corps
- George L. Foote, Jr.—POW
- James Robert Fox—CPL—US Army
- William A. Fraser—PFC—US Army
- August J. "Gus" Furla, M.D.—CPT—US Army
- Glenn Galtere—PFC—US Marine Corps
- Charles Garrod—US Air Force
- William (Bill) Gartlan—SGT—US Army
- Eugene Germann—SGT—US Army
- Billy Gibson—A2C—US Air Force
- Barend Petrus Albertus Gildenhuys—Flight SGT—South African Air Force

- Al Gonzales—SGT—US Army
- Frank G. Grace—CPT—US Air Force
- R.N. Grauberger—HM2—US Navy
- Thomas B. Haines—PVT—US Army
- Raymond Hanaburgh—SSG—US Marine Corps
- John W. Hanback—MSG—US Army—US Air Force—POW
- William Henry Harbert—CPL—US Army—POW
- Ralph V. Harmon
- Homer E. Hartley—SGT—US Marine Corps
- Thomas Oliver Haymore—CPL—US Army—MIA
- Fred B. Hems—CPL—US Marine Corps
- Ellsworth C Hems—SGT—US Marine Corps
- Raymond Hernandez—SGT—US Army
- Peter S. Hildre—SGT—US Marine Corps
- Keith O. Hoard—US Army
- Leo Holden—LCpl—US Marine Corps
- Joe Houston—BM3—US Navy
- Zebulon Howard—PVT—US Army—(He died of wounds the same day)
- Guy Hupe—PFC -US Army
- William P. Hutchinson—KIA
- Marcus Jaquette—COL—US Army
- Raymond F. Johnson—PVT—Special Forces Service (Canada)
- Courtland Butler Jones—PFC—US Army
- Melvyn Royce Journey—CPL—US Army
- Dale D. Kachline—CPL—US Army
- Willie Frank Kee—SGT—US Army—KIA
- Robert Kloss—CPL—US Army
- Kenneth Arnold Knudson—PVT—US Army
- Paul Koch—CPL—US Army
- Raymond Krouch—US Army
- Henry. P. Kucinski

- Kassidy Keith Jones—CPL—US Army—MIA
- Anthony D Lawrenson—CPT—South African Air Force
- Leo H. Lesczynski—SGT—US Army
- Homer Litzenberg—COL—US Marines
- Thomas Logudice
- Edward J. Malhiot—Varied Ranks—US Navy then Army
- Joseph Mangione—SGT—US Army
- Gilberto M. Martinez—SGM—US Army
- John Martinko—PFC—US Army—KIA
- Robert L. Mattingly—CPL—US Army
- Martin Moak—SGT—US Marines
- Lewis Lavert Martin—AB—US Navy
- Pharis LaDon Martin—AB—US Navy
- Vance Rudolph Martin—AB—US Navy
- Raymond Lee McDonald—SGT—US Army
- Joseph James McGuire—PFC—US Army
- Charles Weston McLennan—SFC—US Army—CA—National Guard
- Russell Minett—CPL—US Marine Corps
- Ernest Vincent Mobilio—MSG—US Army
- Stanley Burdett Moomaw—US Army
- Antonio Munoz, Jr.—CPL—US Army
- Joseph J. Murphy—CPL—US Marine Corps
- Joseph D. Murri—CPL—US Army
- Arthur R. Nesbitt—PFC—US Army
- Richard Owen Nevard—US Navy
- Millard A. Oberlin—COL—US Army
- Richard Olenick—CPL—US Air Force
- Richard G. Owens—PFC—US Army
- Joseph A. Parone—PFC—US Army
- Mark. H. Peace—SFC—US Army
- Roman F. Percev—SSG—US Army
- Lewis Frank Perry, Jr—EM2—US Navy

- Tinley Bolin Perry—MSG—US Air Force
- Jack Petty—SGT—US Army
- Charles M. Phillips—PFC—US Army
- John Pierce—PFC—US Marine Corps
- Thomas Albert Piotrasch—US Army
- James O. Prewitt—HM—US Navy
- William K. Pund—CPL—US Army
- Jerome Ray—PFC—US Army
- Ronald John Remling—PVT—US Army
- Elmer Rogers—CPL—US Army
- Charles Ross—CSM—US Army—POW
- Thomas F. Rubas—SGT—US Army
- Robert Santucci, Sr.—US Air Force
- Myron Saline, MD—CPT—US Army
- William Schobelock—SSgt—US Airforce
- Adolph E. Shavlik—SGT—US Army
- Russell E. Smith—SGT—US Marines
- Stuart Smith—CPL—US Marines
- Charles F. Stanley—A2C—US Air Force/attached to Marines
- Thomas R. Stauber—SGT—US Air Force
- Harold Strawn—AB2—US Navy
- Daniel Arthur Stroup, Jr.—CPL—US Army
- Warren A. Sward—EN2—US Navy
- Charles L. Swearingen—PFC—US Army
- Donald R. Sweet—SSgt—US Marines Corps
- Fred Sweren—SGT—US Army
- Harold “Cye” Taylor—SGT—US Army
- Nicholas Elias Theodorou—COL—US Army—MIA
- Curtis Lonzy Thompson—CPL—US Army
- Enoch Thompson—TSgt—US Army
- Chris Tine
- Richard Trissel—AFC—US Air Force

- Richard Vadasy
- Vincent Angelo Vega—PVT—US Army—MIA
- Langley Wages—CPL—US Army
- James Walker—PFC—US Army—POW
- Robert J. Warner—SGT—US Army
- Hillary Lee Watson—CPL—US Marine Corps
- Fred Whitehead—SGT—US Army
- John B. Wilson, Jr.—EN2—US Coast Guard
- Joseph Francis Wolf, Sr.—SP4—US Army
- Marlin C. Wolf—SSGT—US Army
- Joseph Wong—SGT—US Marine Corps
- William Buren Workman—SGT—US Army
- Ronald Ziolecki—SGT—US Marine Corps

Served but not in Korea

- Elmer Rogers—CPL—US Army—Germany
- Hank Schyuler—CHAP—US Army—Japan
- Jay Bryan "JB" Munnerlyn Jr—SSGT—US Army—US

*Please accept my sincere apologies for any mistakes

ABOUT THE AUTHOR

Rebecca Price Janney is the multi-award-winning author of twenty-seven published books, including her beloved Easton Series. A historian and popular speaker, she lives with her husband, son, and Cavalier King Charles Spaniel in Pennsylvania's Lehigh Valley, where her ancestors settled nearly 300 years ago. Rebecca invites readers to contact her and sign up for her personal newsletter at www.rebeccapricejanney.com.

OTHER REBECCA PRICE JANNEY BOOKS

REBECCA PRICE JANNEY
Book Two in the Easton Series
Easton
in the VALLEY

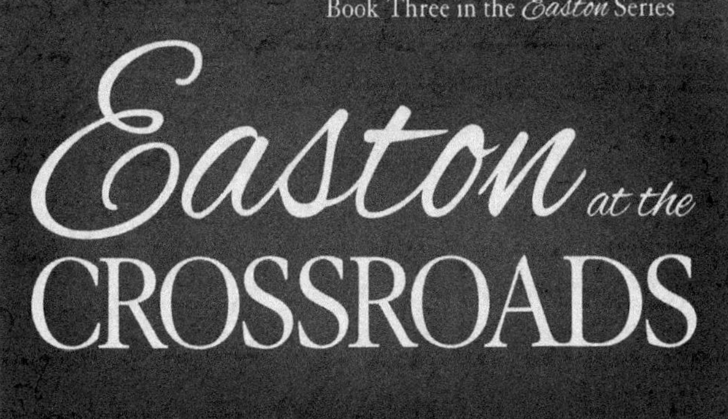
REBECCA PRICE JANNEY
Book Three in the Easton Series
Easton at the
CROSSROADS

2021
AWSA
Golden
Scroll
AWARD
REBECCA PRICE JANNEY
Book Four in the Easton Series
Easton
at the PASS

2022
Selah
AWARDS FINALIST
REBECCA PRICE JANNEY
Book Five in the Easton Series
Easton
at
CHRISTMASTIDE

REBECCA PRICE JANNEY
Book Six in the Easton Series
Easton
at
SUNSET

Morning
Glory
A Novel of the
First Great Awakening
Rebecca Price Janney

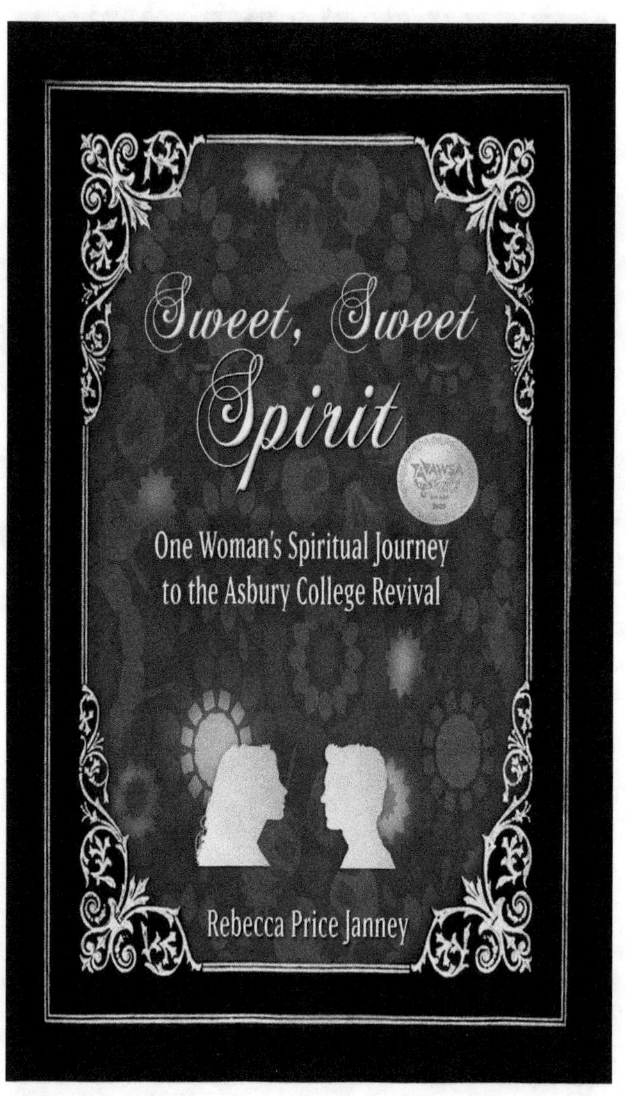
Sweet, Sweet
Spirit
One Woman's Spiritual Journey
to the Asbury College Revival
Rebecca Price Janney

www.ingramcontent.com/pod-product-compliance
Lightning Source LLC
LaVergne TN
LVHW010223110826
845148LV00022B/1331

* 9 7 9 8 8 9 1 3 4 3 2 9 0 *